Grief Species
aka: the demise of print media and bachelor parties

by Adam Doc Fox
Narrated by Pike, Logan

For my wife. (Also, thanks for letting me do that thing that time, wink, wink.)

Composed in "Speed Prose."
And to be enjoyed in similar fashion.

1.

"You want to get away from all the creative writing you've learned. I know your background, but news writing is nothing like that. It's just 'they said.' Not they pondered, thought, contemplated. Don't be too verbose. Just use your stylebook," editor Theresa said.

"What you have to understand is that the average person will only read the first two sentences of your story. We are partaking in a dying profession, Pike," said Winherst journalist Carly from across the cubicle on one side of the newsroom office floor.

What? That's stupid. Why kill the extra time it took English to invent all those extra "I said" words?

Carly proceeded to look up the statistics showing the steady decline of the printed word and state the "inevitability of its demise" so that everyone within 20 feet of her could hear.

Theresa: Isn't she a ball of joy? (She asked Pike via iChat.)

What am I doing this for? I'll never make this second week.

But on the third day of that second work week, being marked the 15th of March 2012 by the non-pagan calendar, that Pike, Logan, did in fact make it through, and he received a stack of business cards from the secretary.

There, it finally verified via printed word, that he was in fact a "writer."

A text was quickly sent to Pike's 13-year friend, T, in New Mexico: "I have a business card that says 'Pike, Logan, Writer.' Now it's official."

The response: "It was always official, Logan."

2.

"Think of it: perhaps the more insane a man is, the more powerful he could become." K. Kesey, *OFOTCN*.

Three weeks earlier, Pike was delivering furniture with the store owner's son, who in Pike's mind, looked like a cross between Elvis and Andy Garcia. And they both had been executing this profession for two years.

One of the less-admirable qualities of Pike, according to his father, was the way he could endure even the worst of jobs. Cope, adapt, rationalize, make it to the work break, medicate, go through the work week horror, repeat. For years. Without raise or possibility of advancement. But low responsibility. There was never a math problem or any real situation to solve.

It has been argued that there was severe arrested development in Pike from age 25 to 32.

Pike was living on the coast of Oregon, in the ocean-view town of Florence, when he received this call, at age 25, in January of 2006:

"Hello, Pike?"

"Mary, how's it going? I'm super tired after last night, but it was fun hanging out with you," Pike said stolidly.

"I have something to tell you," Mary said.

"What, you're pregnant?" Pike joked.

"Yes."

3.

"But what the prisoners figured was if every man from every gang brought just one little piece back with him, it'd be that much warmer in the barracks." A. Solzhenitsyn, *ADITLOID*.

With the news, Pike decided there was to be one last "free" night on the light-a-little-longer northwestern Pacific Coast.

The evening was a full-nostril coke escape, a drug Pike actually hated, but when it came to a drink-till-you-puke mentality, nothing beats many burning, baby formula-cut low-grade cocaine lines drawn off a chipped square piece of glass.

After lethargically but quickly descending the low hand-railed steps of the two-story apartment complex known to the locals as "The Warzone" of all beach community locations in Florence, this call was made from Florence to Portland.

"Ya, guy?" Pike's brother Dale answered. It was 8 a.m.

"Guess what?" Pike asked through a stuffed-up but empty nose.

"What, guy, I'm busy?"

"You're going to be an uncle," Pike said with a stentorian voice.

"You serious?"

"I just found out like 12 hours ago. We'll see what happens."

"With your girlfriend Mary I take it? You're going to have a brown baby. Wow. You serious, how's that even possible?" Dale knew his brother was serious—Pike had lost voice and gained sound.

"Well, when the majority of your sex is cumming through blackouts, these things happen."

Pike was white and from Oregon. Mary, a first generation Mexican American, born in Pennsylvania, who did her post-grad work in Oregon. Her parents split up when she was eight years old. Her mother returned to Mexico shortly after the divorce, while her father stayed and obtained citizenship.

Before the news of the offspring, Mary had been offered jobs in her hometown, Penkal, Pennsylvania, also Austin, Texas, and Portland, Oregon. She had just completed her residency and was looking, at age 29, to transfer hospitals and become a young medical doctor in her own right.

After a nap, Pike was on his way to Mary's apartment in Florence. When she opened the door, Pike gave her what he wanted her to feel was a reassuring hug, that everything was going to be OK, and that he was there for her.

But no such reassurance was needed. She loved Pike, had a great career lined up, and felt confident she could raise/love/nurture the child with or without him.

"So what do you think you want to do, like buy a house around here, or what?" Pike asked Mary after he used a lighter and leverage to open a Portland micro-brew from the fridge.

She always stocks $10-minimum six packs. Even the striated cardboard costs extra.

"Around here? I was going to tell you over dinner that I got job offers from three great hospitals. So, here's what I'm thinking about, and I know you're from here, and your brother and parents still live in Oregon, and I know it's your baby, too—"

"You're sure about that, right, that it is my baby? And it sounds like you want to keep it? It wouldn't matter either way, I would support any action you took."

"I'm not aborting my baby if that's what you're asking. And yes, jerk, it's yours. Anyway, I have an offer to work at the cancer center in Penkal, and I feel like I need to be back home, with my father around for support."

"Wait, so you and my baby are moving 2,000 miles away? That's fucking great."

"Darling, don't worry, I want you to come with me. It'll be fine."

It was actually quite fine with Pike. After college, he had worked entry level "shit" jobs, and was unable to land consistent writing work.

I'll just go trophy husband style. Be a stay at home dad. She'll make enough money for the family, I'm sick of Oregon

*anyway, and I'll just write books and raise the kids and be a
tennis dad that actually knows how to play the game.*

Two weeks later, he was done carrying brick and block
for a mason, and was on his way east, with all of his belongings
lining the back window of his '93 Ford Taurus.

Although the hospital wasn't exactly excited about Mary
going on maternity leave six months into her start, they still
accepted the transfer and hired her. Mary's father, Mauricio,
set up a house buy and Mary was all over the dotted line a day
after she landed at the airport.

Pike smoked a pack between rest stops and
complimented those with a green kind of another, and by the
time he got to Penkal, he had a house to live in, a girl that
would become his future and stability.

It was time for a life change, Pike thought. For starters,
quitting smoking. Which was easy after Mary would leave the
room or not kiss him or give him dirty looks after he came back
in from extra inhales.

*She used to smoke, but with a baby in the belly, there are
a lot of "used-tos."*

Mom is the breadwinner, I just need a hobby.

They had been in Penkal for two months, and Mary was
showing well for her first pregnancy and all of her somatic
functions were great.

*What the hell does "showing well" mean? It's like a nice
way of saying how are you?*

Then there was a miscarriage. The future first born,
dead. Pike drank for a month, and finally told himself enough
times that it was just a fetus and was ready to move on.

It hardly hit Mary. She was sad, but embraced the reality
pretty quickly, and used an excess amount of hospital work to
train her mind off of the issue.

They stayed in Penkal, and it was endless "pointless"
career paths for Pike. He had a creative writing certificate from
Florence Rock University, along with a B.A. in English. Upon
graduation, it wasn't so much that Pike wanted to write for a
living, but that he wanted a writer's life.

Insanity as an excuse for everything. Too complex and deep and artistic for the "normals" to understand. A license to be a wastoid.

But even in that contrived idea of depravity, even if one should turn out to be the worst writer the printed word has ever had to endure, one still must write. And that is what always escaped Pike.

I have a great new story idea. Better call and tell all my friends back out west that I'm starting a new project and they might not be able to hang out or contact me for awhile.

And after a solid day, or week, or a complete month of a writing binge, the project would die, and a new entry-level, low-salary salvage job would be had by Pike. Mary paid the mortgage and the bills. Bought the food. Pike basically just worked for spending money and birthday presents.

As you could imagine, just over a year after the miscarriage, Mary's infatuation that turned into love soon reverted to infatuation and eventually annoyance, contempt and bitterness.

"I don't want a boyfriend that smokes and drinks," Mary said in one of their last desperate appeals to one anther. Mary to end it; Pike to say it was a matter of circumstance, and circumstantial evidence never convicts.

Post break-up Pike moved into a fully furnished apartment owned by Mary's father. All pride was easily swallowed for $225 a month in rent.

I will not move back west. I will not move back west. Only two people know me, and not even they really do anymore. A fresh start and ghosting through another half decade.

4.

"You will have to get used to living without results and without hope. You will work for a while, you will be caught, you will confess, and then you will die." G. Orwell, *NEF*.

Life is finally ready for me, Pike thought, at age 32, after being in the new eastern city of Penkal for six years, five of it alone and filled with vexation.

In the middle of February of '12, Pike emailed the editor of a newspaper in Winherst, 35 minutes north of where he lived, after he saw an ad in the Penkal newspaper that was always sitting on the break room table of his furniture delivery job.

"Neat Opportunity in Winherst" was the subject of the email Pike sent to the editor.

The accompanying resume was full of lies about a consistent writing career and other sinecures.

Employers simply don't do good enough background checks because the humans' default is always set to lazy. It's how we survive famines.

Almost three weeks after sending that email, Pike received a response email from Theresa, editor of the Winherst News-Times.

The subject of the email hadn't changed (other than the addition of RE:), and Theresa's response was one line: "Pike, if you would still like to interview for the Winherst position, please call me, 555-6805."

Before the excitement and possibility of this news could even change the facial expression on Pike's face, self-manufactured insecurity entered.

Winherst? That's too far of a drive. Like 45 minutes from here. They're not going to hire me; I'm a fake creative writer. Sally in third grade is a creative writer. Journalists have gone to school and have degree accreditation to their craft. Screw it, I'll give her a call.

"Winherst News-Times, how can I help you?" asked the secretary. Pike could tell the voice was young, but it was a bit of a perplexing paradox, as young voices are not usually so coated in a monotone frequency of defeat, he thought.

"Yes, hello, this is Pike, Logan Pike. Is Theresa Yonmill available, please?"

"One moment," the secretary responded with even less enthusiasm.

She must have started working there right out of high school and has, like, a young voice for someone in her 40s.

In the four seconds on hold, Pike straightened his posture, flexed his smile back and forth and was ready to be completely humiliated. But with no choice, Pike had to totally sell out for this job and leave himself wide open for any sinuous truth to seep in concerning not actually having the qualifications to call himself a "writer." Or, again, this was his mental progression.

"This is Theresa, can I help you?"

"Hello Theresa, this is Pike, Logan Pike. We've been emailing back and forth and you told me to give you a call if I still wanted to apply for the job. *Stop there, good opening.* And I'm still very interested in this *neat* opportunity in Winherst."

"OK, when can you come in?"

"My schedule is pretty open, I can do it anytime, I mean, tomorrow's fine."

"Are you working now?"

"Yes, I have a job right now."

"Because I don't want to interfere with that."

"It wouldn't, I kind of have a weird schedule with them."

"So do you want to come in for an interview tomorrow?" Theresa asked.

"Sure, that'd be perfect," Pike said.

"What time?" editor Theresa asked.

"What time? Umm, whenever is fine. What time is best for you?"

"I'll be here all day," Theresa said.

"Umm, is 10 a.m. OK?" Pike asked.

"Do you know where our office is?" the editor asked.

"Umm, I know where Winherst is," Pike offered while trying not to act confused.

"We are at 105 Main Street in downtown Winherst across from the courthouse. You know where that is?"

"Yeah, that shouldn't be a problem. I see it on Bing Maps now. Everything is good on my end, anything else from your end?"

"Nope, thaaat's it," Theresa said in a northern Pennsylvania accent, not really hard on the vowels, but apathetic towards suffixes.

"OK, see you tomorrow, and thanks again."

"Bye."

All right, an interview! Which pretty much means a new job. I know, I know, everything I've ever applied for has been so remedial, an inebriated chipmunk probably coulda got the job, but either way, I'm always offered the post. It's all about research, being a rat, conman, that is so desperate for the job anything goes. Anything.

5.

"You see, control can never be a means to any practical end...It can never be a means to anything but more control...like junk." W.S. Burroughs, *NL.*

Pike always had to endure three self-inflicted pains every time he jumped/transferred jobs.
1. Quitting the job.
2. Searching for a new one.
3. Getting hired.

Although those seem like logical steps anyone would have to complete, it was always Pike's sodden anal intricacies that made it such an endeavor.

Starting with number one (quitting the job): *I hate quitting a job. The employer is all mad and sad and takes it personally, and you must leave on good terms, even if you hate them.*

Pike called his boss at the furniture company, said he was moving out of town, and that it was a crevasse-fall-tragedy that he couldn't continue working for the company.

The boss "understood," invited him back if anything should change, and a two-week timeline was established.

Even if the interview should fail and he not get hired, Pike felt it was time to move on from the art of making giant reclineable couches fit through a seemingly always narrowing doorframe.

Most employment position failures had no follow up. What proceeded was the abhorrent cycle of job hunting. But since Pike had an interview before he quit, on to the third step—getting hired.

Why has Pike always been offered a job after every single interview he has ever endured? Two reasons:

1. 90%, the most glaring/obvious/easiest suggestion is that pretty much every position for which he has ever applied was, more or less, an entry-level no-responsibility job. Tier one construction, server, cook, merchandise sales, delivery.

2. 10%, he can understand any expectation of any menial job and convey his want to execute that demand while making the person doing the hiring not only feel good about themselves, but actually want to work with this applicant in the future.

So in between sofa assembly and delivery, Pike finally, after a week of daydreaming about getting the job, sent the email to the editor of the Winherst Gazette with the subject "Opportunity in Winherst," and the response, return call, and an interview were all arranged.

That seemed difficult. Didn't seem like she wanted to set up the interview. What the hell is going on over there?
Pike had two days before the pre-employment screening game and didn't need to prep at all. His suit was clean and in his closet. And it was a nice brown trendy expensive suit he received as a wedding gift after being in the wedding party of an old college friend who saw his soon-to-be-wife *fitting* the bill via her corporate CEO father.

In terms of the interview process itself, Pike felt prepared.
I am well versed on how to answer all the cliché, big company, "tell me a time in your life when you went above and beyond the call of duty to overcome an obstacle," "tell me a time when you had a conflict with a co-worker and how you resolved it," and "what are your greatest strengths and weaknesses."

In his early 20s, and just after graduating from Florence Rock University, Pike helped his friend Kat move down the coast to Los Angeles and land a big corporate radio job in sales. She received an offer for a position in Oregon, but her heart was set on America's second biggest city.

During the Pacific coast cruise south, Kat read out loud thousands of different interview questions that they took turns answering. She got the job, and Pike learned the art of the interview.

Get a writing job. I mean, that's what I should be doing *anyway. The furniture world is nice, and you get to help tons of* *people, but it's like, no matter how many couches you deliver a* *day, there will still be as many more tomorrow,* Pike told himself while sitting in the living room, ankle deep in needed-to-be-folded laundry.

My mother was a social worker, so I have a soft spot *there. But that whole system is a failure. "I had a son with DD,* *but I don't want to pay for his care that I don't want to do myself,* *so I'm going to get money from the state, so he can be put in a* *home, and then I'm going to pay the person in the home that is* *actually taking care of my kid, fuck-all. Nothing." Social work is* *the lowest paying profession. The lowest.*

Everyone bitches about social services. Oh, the welfare *queens, lazy people on unemployment, it's the drug addicts fault* *anyway, blah, blah, blah. They don't want to deal with it, and* *they don't want to pay for it. But they will stand in silent* *acceptance of a billion-dollar-a-day war in the Middle East.* *Maybe if we built one less tank...*

I'm just done with the idea of social service, all these *jobs of zero value that I make myself get involved with. I mean, I* *gotta get famous.*

Due to the solicitous situation of wanting to be hired, Pike showed up in the town of Winherst a good 40 minutes early for the interview after a 35-minute drive.

He sat in his car, listened to sports-talk radio, and waited until 10:20 a.m. to head into the office.

10:20 shows that I'm early, but not too early. Like, you *can expect me 10 minutes early every day all day. But not really.*

The office had main-street frontage and a nice brick building built by Amish 60 years before, with an oak-fence-supported sign that read "Winherst News-Times."

Pike entered through the revolving wind-blocking double doors and in his daydreaming almost ran his thighs into the secretary's desk, even though the visage of the lobby was quite spacious. There was no overhead background music in the waiting area and Pike felt an overall quiet chill about the black bodies and their energy.

The secretary and Pike met corneas. He smiled as her face remained unmoved when Pike said, "Hello, I'm Pike, Logan Pike. I have a 10:30 with Theresa Yonmill."

Usually Pike's smiles are returned, but instead the secretary just half-pivoted her chair back to its 9 to 5 resting position and said, "OK, have a seat."

Where Pike sat down, between the glass face that was the front of the office and the secretary's desk, there were two middle-school-sized lunchroom chairs, but allowed for the legroom of first class. For about nine minutes he sat there, very still, as he could hear the beams in the ceiling sponge, expand and contract.

Finally, at exactly 10:30 a.m. by the flicker of the faded cell phone, an extremely tall lady (even by WNBA standards) came down the hallway that led into the front lobby with a sedulous approach.

"Hi, are you Pike? I'm Teresa Yonmill. Do you want to follow me upstairs?" she asked with the "uncompleted A" sound you get in northern Pennsylvania.

Pike and Theresa ascended the brown-tiled steps to the second floor that opened into the newsroom. Cubicles everywhere, and a lot of motion from the humans working the area. Theresa led Pike into a comfortable office towards the back of the press floor. They sat on opposite sides of a lopsided and massive desk.

"You live in Penkal, is that right?" Theresa opened.

"Yes, that's right, but we are looking to buy a house in the area right now. (lie) My wife (lie) is a lawyer (lie) in Penkal, but we want to move up north, we're not the biggest fans of Penkal right now," Pike responded.

"That's good. It would be hard to be a reporter for an area if you lived 40 minutes away."

"Yes, you're right. That's why, when I saw the ad, I thought this opportunity could be really great," Pike said.

"What have you been doing for work recently?"

"I've been doing writing work since I graduated college. My degree is in English with a creative writing certificate, and that's what I've always loved doing. I did freelance writing when I was in Oregon. I have done editing, but it hasn't always been that financially rewarding. So I've been involved in investment furniture to make money. But that's all set up now, so I want to focus full-time on writing again."

"Now you know this is journalism, not creative writing?"

"Yes, I took journalism courses in college as part of my writing certificate."

"I see. I read some of your clips, you used to write a blog or something for the Seattle Seahawks?"

"Right, Seahawksmix.com, I wrote bi-weekly stories about all team affairs."

Bullshit blogger site, but will she know?

"Yes I read the one about keeping all Rams fans in a pen before the game. Interesting," Theresa said.

The interview continued in a bit of an awkward fashion. Because the publisher of the paper had to leave suddenly, it was Theresa who was conducting the interview, something she felt confident in doing but in the end wasn't that competent in executing—bad transitions into new questions and a general sense of no emotion.

After about 11 more minutes of the "get to know you" portion, Theresa grabbed four, 12-page-thick newspapers from the chair in which she usually sits for interviews beside the publisher's desk and placed the periodicals down.

She slid the stack open across the desk poker-dealer style and said, "Well, here are four examples of our paper. I want you to take them home, read over them and let me know if you would still be interested in writing for The Winherst News-Times."

"I want to report for Winherst for sure. I've read stories from the Winherst paper online and feel I'd be a great fit for the paper," Pike responded with haste.

"OK, so take them home, talk with your wife about it, and if you are still interested, I will give you a sample story to cover. Then, if the story is good, you will talk to the publisher and see if he wants to hire you. It's a three-month trial at first."

Maybe I shouldn't have lied about having a wife; this could turn into a viscous situation. I just think a "family man" always gets hired first. Or maybe they want single people who wouldn't have distractions? What have I done?

Before Pike responded, he was being too sentient and believed he had the job. Instantly, and in a lot of ways, stupidly, he began to abjure the interview in his typical aberrant behavior. Even as she was going over the details, he thought, *This axe wound is awesomely tall. And what about that freakin' foothill accent? Can I deal with that? Hell, yeah, I can. Get a writing job, and then take over the world. Don't smile, don't you start smiling for no reason as she's talking. Don't go mushroom style.*

A decade earlier, during college, Pike took a lot of psychedelic drugs that would vitiate his brain. He and his friend Yogos were emerged in mind-expanding literature and practices. They followed the LSD parties of the '60s and '70s, read about the Merry Pranksters, the acid tests, the drug influence on the Grateful Dead and the Beatles, about Ken Kesey's ideas of drug graduation. They recited Huxley and tried to recreate the academic way one could record and study mind expansion. Psilocybin, lysergic acid, certain cacti that could melt a man's face in front of a mirror. And with the intake of those drugs, Pike always had a hard time at the store.

Over the course of an eight-to-10 hour "trip," it wasn't uncommon for Pike to require refreshment from the Middle-Eastern run convenience shop by his college apartment or to happen to find himself attempting to buy something to snack on. Steps before the register, Pike would start to smile.

Dumbass, don't start smiling. They will all know instantly. Get up there, keep your eyes down and don't start laughing.

But then another voice would enter Pike's brain, to the tune of something like, *Hey, man, bet you do it. It's gonna be real funny when you get up to that counter. Come on, you know you will laugh your ass off in about five seconds.*

Voice 1*: Don't be an idiot. Get up there and don't start laughing. This is serious, do you want to get arrested?*

Voice 2: *As soon as you hold out your money you're going to lose it and it's going to be a hilarious experience.*

Pike arrived at the counter, put a squeeze bottle of lemon-lime Gatorade down, and before he could hand out the money, a giant grin ripped through his face. Pike instantly turned away from the counter, but couldn't stop laughing. There was no safety in turning around either, because his snicker smacked the next patron in line.

It eventually got to the point where it didn't matter if Pike was on drugs or not, he would constantly hear the two sides of the "don't chuckle in the strangers face for no reason" argument and proceed to always laugh. Twice in one day it was giggle mode at a baptism in the morning and then a funeral in the afternoon.

After six years in Penkal, however, the joke died.

But now, in the middle of an interview that could get him out of "investment furniture" and on to "tricking his friends that he was still special and could still one day be famous," Pike was thinking the bad thoughts and trying not to laugh.

After a long pause sans response, Theresa asked, "Does everything make sense?"

"Yep."

"Go talk to your wife and let me know in the next couple of days what you want to do."

"I can tell you right now I want the job. We've talked about it (They hadn't because she's not real.). What about that sample story I need to write? What do you want me to do?" Pike asked.

"I'm not sure yet. I'll email you something, an easy story to get you started. And you still have to talk to the publisher to see if he likes what you have written."

Pike jogged out to his car as soon as the airlock freed him.

To Pike, it was the start of a monumental day and life change. To the rest of civilized man, he was doing what he should be doing—something that he liked.

In the early evening, Pike usually had an abstemious desire for dinner, but he grabbed a 12-pack of Coors Light on the way home and cracked one five minutes before the driveway.

The open container law is so dumb. I'm not drunk, and I sure as hell couldn't get drunk on one beer. But it's illegal to drink one beer and drive? Pigs. But I can drink a pop. Sure I can be like all the other taste-driven Americans that drink diet pop all day, but not a beer. How powerful is caffeine? It's in every beverage. That's why I don't follow that stupid law.

The next day, at 9:47 a.m., Pike received a new message in his "outdated and not very trendy" Hotmail inbox.

The subject was "Assignment."

"Pike, there was a blood drive at the high school, where they broke the record for the amount collected. Do a write-up on this, who was involved, how much blood was donated, what was last year's results, where is the blood going, how does it compare to other schools and counties. Here is the number of the person from the Red Cross who organized the event, her name is Shelly. 555-5712. Theresa."

Pike's email reply was, "Hello Theresa, I got the info and will get working on the story. How long should it be? When is the deadline? Thanks, Pike."

"Make it as long as you want and there is no deadline," was Teresa's response.

"Hi Theresa, OK I will start working on it soon. Today's Wednesday, do you need the story by tomorrow or by the end of the week? I just don't want it to be late."

"No deadline, just send it in whenever," was Theresa's final email of the day.

Pike was quick with a riposte:

Why can't she just give me a goddamn deadline? Is this a test? Like if I turn it in on Friday, will she be like, dude, it took you two days to write a story about a blood drive? Ya, I think it's a test. Better start working.

> *Got my first assignment, which is good. But I gotta cover a boring blood drive, which is lame. Write a great story about a boring subject, that's all you can do.*

Pike wrote out a legal-pad page of questions for the blood drive director. He was scared. And was worried about bothering people for questions concerning the story.

> *What if they're like, dude, nice interview. First day as a reporter? Why did you ask me that stupid question? I'm offended by that question. What paper? This is your first story, ha ha hah?*

Pike took his notebook, legal pad, pen and phone to his bedroom.

Although solo, he quietly shut the English pine door.

6.

"What I have wished to evince is, that the charge brought against the proposed constitution, of violating a sacred maxim of free government, is warranted neither by the real meaning annexed to that maxim by its author; nor by the sense in which it has hitherto been understood in America." Publius aka J. Madison, *TFNFS.*

It was choppy but successful. Pike found the facts, wrote up a story, and sent it to Theresa by 6 p.m. that day.

Email: "Theresa, here's the story. I just went ahead and did it since I wasn't sure about the deadline. Let me know if you have any questions. Thanks, Pike."

The next day, Thursday, Pike hadn't heard anything in the morning. Close to noon Pike got an odd area code on his phone.

"Hello, this is Pike."

"This is Rob McCoy, News-Times publisher."

"Hey, yes, Theresa said you would probably be calling me."

"Yep. So I had to leave the other day or I would have done the interview. Theresa said it was good though. So do you want to work for us?"

"Yes, I definitely want the job because—"

"I read some of your samples and your clips for the Seahawks. They were funny. There is a sports reporter in the office who is a big Rams fan, so you guys will have a good time together."

"That will give me a chance to teach him something about football."

"Haha, yes. So talk with Theresa about when you want to start."

"Great, I will—"

"Did Theresa talk to you about pay? You're looking at taking home $350 a week, it will work out to around 19 thousand a year."

"She said it to be a starting salary—"

"Yes, it comes out to about 19."

"OK, well, I think—"

"OK, goodbye."

The publisher must be a sports fan. That's why I'm getting the job. He likes my dumb sports stories. Bet the editor doesn't. Whatever. I got the job, time to call all my friends and brag. Maybe send a group email.

Before the "look at me" email, Pike called Theresa with a lot of confidence.

"Hi, Theresa, just talked to Rob. He wanted you to set up a start time for me at the paper."

"You did talk to him? And he did say that? Well, OK. I got your story. Needs some work. I will send it back to you with some things I want added. When do you want to start working?"

Isn't that usually decided by the employer?

"It doesn't matter to me, I can start whenever," Pike said.

"Aren't you currently working?"

"Yes, but they know I've been looking for another job because we are planning to move around the Winherst area (lie)."

"Because you should give a two-weeks notice, that's what I would expect from anyone leaving here," Theresa said.

"Oh, yes, no, for sure, they know I only could work a little bit more."

"OK, then, when do you want to start?"

"Like I said, whenever you need me, I'm ready."

"OK." (Pause)

"Should I come in next week?" Pike wondered as a bit of frustration entered his thoughts.

"Sure. Come in next week. What day?" Theresa asked.

I'm losing my mind here lady, I don't know!

"How about Wednesday?"

"Wednesday is no good. That's one of our biggest days trying to get the papers to the press."

"OK, how about Thursday?"

"Thursday is fine," Theresa concluded.

"Should I come in at 8 a.m.?"

"Reporters on your beat don't come in at 8." She said.

"Well I don't really know—"

"Come in at 9 a.m. That's a better time." Theresa said.

"Great, I'll see you in a week. Next Thursday at 9 a.m. And one more thing," Pike began, "I have two (*salacious*) weddings I have to attend. One in July, and one in September. Will just need a Thursday and a Friday off both weekends."

"OK, that's fine. Re-work the story I'm resending you. See you next week."

Re-work the story? Who in the hell cares about some blood-drive bullshit? Whatever, I'll do it by Thursday since she didn't give me a deadline.

Theresa sent the email without a salutation per usual.

"How much blood did the winning team give? What were some of the teams' names? Was there a prize for the winner? Are there any salubrious or harmful effects from giving blood?"

I can't call that place back. Like, they'll know I didn't do it right the first time. They'll know I'm a novice. This sucks. But I have to call.

And he had the hire.

Pike delivered furniture with no affinity but with great alacrity Friday, Saturday, Sunday and Monday morning. Then it was all over. He was actually on the handwritten-in-pencil schedule for Tuesday, but he caught a case of apathy and fake flu and called off. He didn't want to do the goodbye with the co-workers that he had formed a nice, albeit contemptuous, relationship with over the last two years. Pike always hated seeing the emotions and reactions that he knew were coming, and he never could allay their thoughts and curiosity. "Oh, I'm going to miss you. What are you going to do? Where are you going?" The faces that don't try and hide the sagging eyes and the ends of the mouths that gravity had overtaken.

7.

"'I'm going up the mountain to look for the beast—now.' Then the supreme sting, the casual, bitter word. 'Coming?'" W. Golding, *LOTF*

On Tuesday, Pike decided he needed to go on a "wastoid binge" before work started Thursday.

Gonna get wasted the next two days. My whole life, job and existence are going to amalgamate for great change Thursday morning at 9 a.m. But don't get too drunk now, I mean, your life is just starting. The world's greatest journalist is about to break out onto the scene. These are my last two days of freedom before existence begins.

Pike has some justifiable reservations manifested through six years of self-described ineptitude.

Day one of the two-day "wastoid binge" was actually pretty light, which meant slow drinking some watered-down cheap domestic beer, beginning around 5 p.m.

Crack a beer, start thinking about dinner. Pike's a vegetarian. He looks in the fridge.

Must go through the perishables first. Can't let food go to waste. Wasting food is the piggiest thing Americans do. What a luxury while others starve.

Fresh broccoli florets and milk were pulled from the cooler enclosure.

I can have a banana for my fruit. Now just need a meat alternative for my protein, a grain and we got the five food groups, muthafuckas. How about a frozen fake chicken patty? Sounds good.

Pike finished off beer five by bedtime. Then to the routine, brush teeth, wash face and pee. Waiting on hot water in the bathroom where the method was executed took awhile, so often Pike's buzzed impatience cost himself a good face, which 20 years ago cost him many a woman, confidence and popularity.

Day two was a much better binge by Pike's standards. The first day allowed for tolerance build-up for a real good liquoring down Wednesday evening. Also, there was a bit of a New Year's Eve vibe in Pike's head.

Last night of freedom before serious life begins. Gotta go out like a champ. Gonna get all wasted and smoked up, then start real life tomorrow. Do what you want to do tonight. But be ready for tomorrow. I'll be fine. I don't need to prepare. It's a writing job, and I know how to write. Sure, but you don't want to be hung over. A hangover? Please. That's for people who write for crappy hometown newspapers. I'll be fine. Not even gonna drink that much.

Pike did drink that much. And forced himself, around 2 a.m., to go into the smoke closet for another unnecessary joint.

When the cell-phone alarm went off at 7 a.m., on May 3, 2012, Pike's state of mind hadn't changed at all. Neurons were still being blocked by THC leftover residue, and whatever was left that was actually getting to the brain, the brain could do nothing with. The liver had failed to prevent all the toxins from going into Pike's head.

In retrospect, it would be easy for Pike to ask, why would you do that before your first day?

Don't try and repine; you did it to yourself. A first day that was on a Thursday, so all you had to do was make it through two days until you could get wasted all weekend.

But oftentimes, when one is dealing with the artist, degenerate or reprobate (Pike believed and used as an excuse), the smoke and the alcohol decide when they will be ingested by the human, not the other way around.

No clothes or outfits had been ironed or laid out the night before, so Pike, after really never opening his eyes in the shower, got dressed with all that he could.

A nice wrinkle-free orphan-blue dress shirt his father gave him and non-holey jeans made the cut. There were probably 10 total collared shirts in Pike's possession, but without a dry cleaner or serious ironing skills, none of them were viable options. It was the same for the one pair of suit pants and khakis Pike owned.

He skipped his usual bowl of cereal for breakfast because of his body's daily timeline. After a good bout of drinking, where Pike would consume fried snacks and calories from beer late into the night and early into the morning, he wouldn't have an appetite until a good hour or two after he got up. The body needed to de-comatose, start to metabolize and Pike would have to do his daily morning bowel movement.

Around 7:50 a.m. Thursday morning, Pike got into his eight-year-old Ford Taurus (the second he had owned in his life) for the first of hundreds of 35-minute one-way-trips to work. The winter weather had died and spring now asserted its dominance.

The first commute to work was a moment for Pike. Within four minutes of the drive, Pike's breathing and heart rate slowed and he didn't move his entire body for 10-minute segments of the ride. Although it was a 35-minute-travel-time trip, the route was three roads that all ran together northbound from Pike's corner apartment development, making navigation to and fro thoughtless.

Pike used downers and despised uppers, so he never had the kick of coffee in the morning to cheat the results of the previous night.

For 20 minutes, Pike sat in the parking lot outside of work until five minutes to nine.

I'm not going in early. Sure, the nonsense first impression would be nice, but it's also a trick. They think or they'll expect you to be in early every day. Not to mention the fact that they will probably hoe you one day, so screw 'em in advance. Go in early, give them free time, for what? Nothing. I can't think right now. I'm actually conscious of how stupid my mind is. Oh, well, first day, I won't be doing anything today anyway.

Pike entered the front door of the office, through the same twirling air lock, as the company sat on the town's main street.

Wonder if secretary lady is going to be in the same mundane mode?

Wanting to set the tone, Pike smiled first at Terri the secretary, and offered a hello, feeling ambivalent.

Once Terri saw it was Pike and not a customer or someone that she was required to pay attention to, with all the pain and effort in the world, Terri somehow manipulated her lower face muscles into something resembling a smile and beneath her breath said, "Hi," and in turn she turned back to her double-computered desk.

Well, at least I'll never have to see this disgusting creature ever again. There's got to be a back door to this place. We all know your life sucks and you never want to ameliorate it, but everyone's life sucks, and even if it doesn't, we don't want to hear about it either way. Kinda a cute face though. If she dropped 30 pounds, totally changed her outlook on life and existence, I would take her to a wine tasting, where the sipping would slowly ease and trick her into getting drunk, and then back to her place, where she would feel so absolutely safe with me she would think that it was actually her idea to have aggressive sex. But alas, she is gross and I'm gameless.

From the square receptionist area and through the lobby, Pike went upstairs and looked for Theresa. All the employees were working quietly, and every chair adjustment, keystroke shortcut that was hit with excess vigor, and cough, fought for top sound as all the others mashed together.

The newsfloor itself was quite roomy, a long 65' by 35' rectangle.

Luckily, without anyone noticing or caring about Pike, he stood staring for a bit. Editor Theresa came in with her lanky height-induced wobbly approach from the back hallway by the publisher's office and spied Pike across the floor.

"Oh, hi, Pike, how's it going?"

"I'm doing well, thanks," Pike said with great difficulty. A conditioned response that usually followed a simple greeting was hard, as there was obviously a break in the synapses.

"That is your computer over there," Theresa instructed.

She is dressed in "tall casual." Not jeans and a t-shirt, but not really dress clothes, either. Certain types of humans were allowed to wear free flowing pants and slacks with weird blouse tops and long sleeves because no one really cared what they were wearing.

My computer? For the day?

"All right, my computer. What would you like me to get started on?" Pike wondered.

"Just relax a second. Let me sit down and see what's going on."

Pike sat in a waterlogged-wood overly-used office chair without armrests and stared at a blue desktop background that had yet to go to screensaver mode.

A loud crackle shot into Pike's ear. The radio scanner had picked up some white noise and when it broke through the level of loud in the office, Pike's heart physically burned a bit. He could feel the repercussions of the startle.

Am I dying? All the smoking is killing my heart and holing my lungs.

"Pike, I'm going to have you train with Carly, she's going to show you about uploading content to the web. Carly?"

A round black-haired-head slowly turned around from its wall-facing desk and asked, "Yes, Theresa?"

"Can you show Pike here how to do the web stuff?" Theresa asked, knowing Carly heard all of the previous conversations. Her cubicle was close enough to Pike's.

"The web stuff?" Carly asked as if confused, but knowing exactly what Theresa meant and wanted.

"Yes, Carly, the web stuff. Downloading things to the website and everything."

"Yes, Theresa, I can show him 'downloading.'"

Carly spun her chair and made eye contact with Pike for the first time. Pike's eyes showed friendliness and mutual respect. Carly sought dominance and was widely viewed as a redoubtable journalist.

"Pike, why don't you bring your chair over and we can cover everything," Carly said without a handshake, introduction or smile.

Pike grabbed a legal pad that was lying on his vacated desk, and rolled his refulgent chair five feet across the thin carpet to Carly's cubicle. Insecurities about dress crept into Pike's thoughts.

So the other two cubicle guys that I can see are wearing collared shirts tucked into dress pants. I got a short-sleeved collared shirt on, not tucked into half-faded Levis. Is that a problem? No one told me how to dress.

"Are you familiar with Typepress at all?" Carly asked.

"Uhhh, no."

"No? OK, Typepress is the program we use to run and maintain our website. Have you done much work with website maintenance before?"

"Uhh, no." Pike responded. *I gotta learn website stuff today? No way, oh, my God, my brain can't think.*

"No? Well, maintaining our website isn't an arduous task at all. It is very basic in its set up and logarithms; the company is too cheap to upgrade the software and most of the employees wouldn't be able to handle the change anyway—"

"Carly, please," Theresa gave a quick "stay on task and don't talk bad about the company" reminder.

"Here's the web address. You might want to write that down. Then it opens to a log-in page. The password is Winherst and the username is your first name. Is that set up for Pike yet, Theresa?"

"Is what set up, Carly?"

"The access point log-in characters for Pike here?"

"Oh, I don't know, ask Rob."

Before Carly could respond, the publisher Rob was passing from the back hallway.

"Yes, it is all set up for him. Did you try it?" Rob asked in frustration.

"We've had so much change over here I wasn't sure. OK, yes, it worked. So Pike, that's how you log in. Do you understand all of that so far?" Carly wondered in indifference.

"Uhh, yes," Pike said.

"On the left panel after you've logged in, there is an option for "posts." Click on "posts" and then select "new posts." Now are you familiar at all with widget paste for line breaks?" Carly asked Pike.

"Umm, no, not really." Pike answered.

"Not really? So you have some familiarity with widgets? What do you know about it?"

"Umm, I don't really know too much about it," Pike answered reluctantly.

"Are you familiar at all with the key stroke shortcuts?"

"Umm, I don't think so."

At this point Carly believed that the company had somehow hired a complete brain-dead moron. Although the brain of Pike was quite dead, it was more circumstantial than actual, he would always argue.

"You don't think so? OK, if you hold down the apple button and press C, that will copy. If you hold down the apple button and hit V, that will paste. If you—"

"Yes, I can do that. I had a computer one time that had a broken 'S.' So every time I wanted to type I had to find an S, copy it, then hit apple V as I was typing. I got copy and paste down pat."

Carly found the story to be indicative of Pike's shortcomings and didn't respond at all to it, but kept going through all 50 keystroke shortcuts that she had memorized.

Notes were taken on the first eight, but soon Pike was fake writing and brain wandering, as his mental health undulated.

"Now, over on the right hand side of the setup menu, there are different news story categories. Now you understand the different stories in terms of sports, local, current, things of that nature?" Carly asked, and although in the long run it would be more work for Carly, she actually wanted Pike to be as clueless as possible in the news world. It would give Carly instructional power over Pike.

"I know the difference between a news story and a sports story."

"Great, just checking," Carly said behind a backpedaling chuckle.

"What you're going to want to do," Carly continued, "is copy and paste the story from the shared editorial drive, and, because of the line breaks, use this widget so it formulates nicely online. Then you select where it will appear, local news, current and things like that. You want to keep in mind a couple of things, how we do our bylines and if there is art attached to the story.

"We want people to buy our papers. If they don't buy our papers, we don't have jobs." Carly continued, "The content uploaded for online viewing is more of a taste test than anything else. If we put all the great and late-breaking stories online as soon as they happen, people wouldn't be buying our papers. The readers aren't very smart, so you have to guide them in the direction—"

"Carly, please," Theresa chimed in from yet another wall-facing desktop.

"I'm just saying, I'm sure it's something Pike will learn very soon anyway. Alas, please let me continue," Carly responded. "Every couple of days, after the papers come up, we upload the web content, and just make sure it's good, but you want to leave something for the reader in print. I get calls all the time asking, 'Carly, I loved that story, is it available online?' Or, 'Carly, I'd really be interested in seeing that interview you did with so and so.' You know what I tell them? Go buy a paper. It's a dollar, don't be so cheap."

"Ya, they should just, like, buy a paper," Pike said.

"Once you've picked the content, you paste it in the box, select the category for the story, and add your byline. Our in-house style is lowercase 'by' and only capitalize the first letter of your first and last name. In the papers, we put bylines in the beginning of the story under the headline. Online, we put bylines at the end of the story. We do that for a couple of reasons. One, if the online content is that important the readers should be buying papers not reading online. And secondly, it doesn't look that good on a web page where anywhere from five to 15 stories can be crunched onto one page, so you want headlines and eye-grabbers not your name written a hundred times," Carly said.

"Makes sense," Pike replied.

I'm officially going to remember none of this. I need an anodyne like morphine to get through this.

"Let's move on to whether or not your story has feature art to go with it. If your story has good art that you want to compliment the story online, then you select the "story with pic" option under the categories," Carly said.

Pike kept twitching as Carly kept explaining. He felt very trapped, although in a spacious office, with low neuron function, and a short, skinny little woman going over a million things that he would have to know at some point, and feeling very confused about his job description.

"Now, are you familiar at all with Photoshop or another photo editing program?" Carly asked.

"Umm, yes I know what Photoshop is."

"A lot of people know what Photoshop is, but can you use it to edit pictures?"

"I'm sure it wouldn't be that hard to figure out," Pike replied defensively.

"No, it's not that hard, but there are some things you will need to know about the program's operation. But we'll get to that another day," Carly said.

Oh, what joy!

"The photos that we use for the papers are different sizes. But for online, the pictures need to be set at 495 x 278 at a 72 dpi. Does that make sense?" she said.

Time to start some bullshit. Going to have to will this day out. I messed up. Shouldn't have gone brain-dead style before I came in today. But we're here. Step it up or you're going to get fired and this girl is just going to slowly humiliate you concerning your lack of newspaper knowledge.

"That makes perfect sense, I'm familiar with picture sizes," Pike said.

"Terrific," Carly said.

The web tutorial continued for another hour, and eventually Pike wheeled himself back to his desk.

"Play around online, try to do what Carly told you, and we'll talk after lunch," Theresa instructed Pike.

No way I'm doing anything after what I just had to endure. What the hell is this place? There's a hallway on one side that leads to the publisher's office in the back. What else is back there? And all these horseshoe cubicles. The skinny tall blond guy that hasn't even turned around to acknowledge, if nothing else, that things are changing around him, our areas are right next to each other. At least I can look out onto the floor. Why are they facing the wall? Why do I have the best seat? How long will I be in this office? This website shit is crazy. One guy, me, to manage a whole website? No, but we prob have to upload our own stuff and stuff. And I was just instructed to basically do a shitty job at that so people buy more papers. Does a journalist actually write?

8.

"If any book in verse, they chance to spy, / Away profane, they presently do cry: / But though this kind of writing some dispraise, / Sith men so captious are in these our days, / Yet I dare say, how e'er the scruple rose, / Verse hath express'd as secret things as prose." E.S. Bradford, *TTRIVOTB.*

At lunch, Pike walked around town looking for a place to eat. Due to his vegetarian diet choice, a complete meal was always hard to find in the small Pennsylvania towns where Pike lived and worked. But Winherst had Chinese and Mexican and a Juice Bar with veggie options, so he had a chance.

After eating, it was mentally siesta time. Full belly of Mexican veggie burritos mixed with the lack of sleep and alcohol oozing all of the way out.

Theresa slowly rotated her chair off the wall with every blood-carrying vein in her thighs, got up and walked the 14 diagonal feet over to Pike's desk where he was staring at the Winherst paper's homepage.

"Let's go over some stories to work on for the week," Theresa began.

"Sounds good."

"Monday, I have a meeting with the school superintendent. I would like you to go, watch how I interview him, and meet him. His name is Coy Franks. They are in the works of trying to get another levy on the ballot in November."

"It won't pass, Winherst will never build another school," chimed in Finn, the tall skinny blond reporter sitting next to Pike in the cubicle.

So he can talk and listen.

"Anyway, the middle school has been around for over 150 years, but yes, they have never been able to pass a levy," Theresa said. "We are to meet him at 10 o'clock in the morning on Monday, but be there by 9:45. I'm never late to an appointment. It's one of my pet peeves. If you're going to interview someone, be on time or it kills your credibility. To be early is to be on time as the old apothegm goes," Theresa continued.

Before the last couple of words were spoken by Theresa, Pike let out a huge yawn that matched his low-sunken eyes.

"Am I keeping you up?" Theresa asked in frustration.

"Oh no, sorry about the yawn. I'm listening to everything and I'm excited about the meeting Monday."

Day one finally concluded. Pike was never given an actual nine to five timeline, and even though most employment places don't count the half hour lunch break as work time, at one minute till five, Pike was standing up getting his jacket on.

I'll just start walking towards the door, and if they say something to me I'll stop.

The Ford Taurus was reached without interruption (The publisher, who hadn't spoken to Pike all day, told him to go out the back door as he was leaving.), and Pike began his two-lane highway 35-minute commute back home.

That's my plan all along, start off like a dumbass and slowly grow into awesome. If I started like the world's best employee right away, then they would expect me to always perform in that manner. Some people just do a good job all the time. Oh, I'm going to be doing a good job, I already set up a meeting with the school superintendent Monday. That's what I'm talking about, baby.

Although Pike went to bed early without drinking, he still got up later than he wanted to, which lead again to raiment consisting of jeans and a slightly wrinkled, untucked shirt.

He took the easy driving linear route to work again, parked out front, circled around and met the publisher as they were both entering the back door at three minutes till nine.

"Where'd you park?" publisher Rob asked Pike.

"On Main Street." Pike said.

"No," said Rob.

"No? Where should I park, I wasn't told?"

"Haha, that figures. I'll get you a parking sticker. You can park in either of these two lots behind me. Have you met the ad department yet?"

"No, I haven't—"

"(Sigh) Come on, I'll introduce you."

Through the rear door, the long beige brick building opened up to a receiving workstation that was connected via hallway to the ad department that was connected to the employee lounge and kitchen.

"Hey, I want you to meet Pike, he's one of the new Winherst journalists," Rob announced to the room.

The 45-year-old dirty-blond male sitting closest to the door jumped up quickly with a hand extension.

"Hi, what was it—Pine? Nice to meet you. I do a lot of the ads for our paper here in Winherst so we'll be talking a lot. I'm Joe," he said.

"No, not Pine, Pike, P-i-k-e. Got it?" Rob seemingly unnecessarily confrontationally said to Joe.

"Hi, I'm Cindy. Nice to meet you," Cindy said from the other side of the room, not looking up from her computer. The three other ad department people were out following leads.

"It's nice to meet you both," Pike began as Rob left the room. Unsure, Pike began to slowly back out of the room as well. Joe followed.

"Did you know about Power Motors this weekend?" he asked Pike.

"Umm, no," he responded as they walked down the hallway, then up the back stairwell to the second floor newsroom.

"Yes, yes, yes, big news at the dealership. They are donating 11 dollars to cancer research every time someone test drives a car," Joe said.

Nothing like using cancer to sell cars.

"I was not aware of this event," Pike said.

"Yes, yes, yes, so you should go down and cover it and write a story," Joe said as he abruptly stopped before entering the newsroom, as if there were an Iranian border fence.

"I'll check it out. As a fabulous raconteur I can spin it, so we'll see, thanks," Pike said, as he sat down at his full-floor view of the news team of Winherst.

Theresa was already at her desk and quickly got up and went to Pike's.

"You won't be checking into that story. The ad people will try to sell ads and say a news story will be attached to it," Theresa said softly.

Carly added in a similarly soft tone, returning from the restroom, "It's not only against everything a good journalist should be involved in, it's borderline illegal and unethical."

"Yep, that makes sense, I won't get story ideas from him," Pike said.

"It's like this with every new reporter, he tries to get them to make him more ad money," Carly said.

Day two ended up being just like the first day, save that Pike's brain was a little higher functioning. And it was Friday. But mostly the day was filled with "condescending Carly" going over .jpeg quality, editing pictures, resolution and the set up of the shared network of Mac computers.

Around 4 p.m., after the ad department had been gone for hours, the publisher and secretary left, both of whom spoke a total of two sentences to Pike over the two days, the editor left, followed by Carly, the sports reporters, beat reporters and a few other stragglers.

It was just another reporter, Finn, and Pike, for the final 45 minutes of their vapid work day (a fresh shift would be on soon) on the south side of the news floor. Something was being faxed beside Rob's office, but there was no radio or background noise.

Dude has made no effort to acknowledge my existence for two days, not even a forced introduction, so I'm not going to break the ice.

Finally, Finn spoke.

"We usually can get out a little early on Fridays," Finn said.

"That's cool, would like that for sure," Pike responded in a reserved, "please like me" tone.

"Once the publisher leaves, it's a domino effect."

"I see, once someone's superior leaves, they leave?" Pike questioned.

"You got it."

"I was curious about the dress code. Are jeans OK, I've been wearing jeans the last two days, am I the only one?" Pike wondered.

"Jeans are fine, we wear them all the time," Finn lied. He wanted a more casually dressed office, and felt like Pike could continue to perpetuate that if he didn't know any better.

9.

"I hated them terribly, though perhaps I was worse than any of them. They repaid me in kind, and did not conceal their aversion for me. But by then I did not want them to like me; on the contrary, I continually longed for them to humiliate me." F. Dostoevsky, *NFU*.

The Friday drive home felt to Pike like he had just completed his last final before Spring Break.

What a good week. Did my two days. Not sure what the hell is going on at that place, but now it's time to reward myself this weekend. I can get as high and as drunk as I want 'cus I've arrived. Made it. Can't touch a pro writer now can you?

Pike pulled off the state route, through the variegated traffic lights downtown, and into the development and his short and heavily slanted driveway. A package was waiting for him on the front steps.

It was from his father. "My son, good job on the new hire. But you won't go far if you look like shit."

There were four new expensive dress shirts from Ralph Lauren in the box.

Pike laughed, and walked in through the established front door.

Get some pizza. Do I have money for delivery? Yes. Could start drinking now, too. That way I will be half sober when the weirdo delivery guy arrives. What do I have in the fridge? Oh, yeah, all those Fosters still from the other night. Nice. OK, eat around seven, then see. Tomorrow, get up at eight, go for a jog or maybe sleep on the couch. Maybe I go wake n' bake, see the sports lineup for the day. Start drinking around three on Saturday. Sounds like a good plan.

Monday was fine because of a no-drink Sunday. Outdoor soccer had started for Pike on "a very competitive co-ed league."

Pike was more of a binge-on-a-random-day drunk than the natural, perpetual alcoholics. He usually would not drink during the week, feeling as though he had earned the future spots on his liver by the weekend.

First day of the work week and it was 12 minutes to interview time and Pike was trying to find the entrance to the massive Rover school building that housed grades four through eight. Built in the 1850s, the structure had been Lego-assembled with additions and technology over the past century and a half.

There's Theresa's car I think. Nice, will park beside her.

They both met where the brick ended and the doors began. Theresa hit the intercom button as Pike looked up at the glass-encased camera.

"Hello," offered the voice from within the school.

"Theresa Yonmill from the Winherst News-Times."

A buzzing sound was followed by Theresa pulling open the door.

"It's kind of a maze inside here. I always get lost on the way to Coy's office," Theresa told the 6'1" Pike, who thumb-tucked his shirt under his belt buckle and 34-waist jeans.

Uneven floors, walking down to go up another flight of steps, the lifelessness of dented lockers and cum-white walls.

Theresa and Pike arrived at the super's office that sat in the middle of the Rover school building.

Wait, this is fourth through eighth? What the hell kind of middle school is that? Poor fourth graders getting bullied all day by tough guy eighth graders.

The secretary alerted the super to the reporters' presence, and after 45 seconds of sitting, they were called back to superintendent Coy Frank's office behind a closed door.

"Theresa, good to see you again," Franks started.

"Hello, this is Pike, he's a new Winherst reporter," Theresa said without emotion.

"Hello, Pike, Coy Franks, superintendent, good to meet you."

"Hi," Pike said, wanting to keep as reserved as possible.

Don't say too much. If he thinks you're some hack journalist that can't interview, you'll be humiliated. Then he'll tell everyone else. Wait a minute, what is that poster on his back wall? A muthafuckin' World Cup '06 picture of Italy holding up the trophy? Nice, so there's the possibility that we can talk soccer and get along that way. But an Italy fan? No way. Worst style of soccer on the planet. Yes, I'm a bit jealous, but their pure style of soccer has changed. Now it's all get a goal via some questionable foul and then sit back and play rat ball for the next 70 minutes. Does he root for the Italian team over Team USA? Just like that dick in Rochester. I'm waiting in line for a beer at a semi-pro soccer game and that dick is talking about how well Spain looked in the Confederations Cup. I talked about how they looked bad compared to USA. He laughed, then told me about how Spain has so much soccer history and will always be better than the U.S.; that's just how it is. Jizz how it is. I asked him if he was an American, and he said his whole family was from Spain, well actually, he clarified and said Barcelona, they are their own country you know, but that, yes, he was an American. An American that roots for Spain? What a pathetic need to belong. Look, I'm all the awesome things that I want to be from Spain, but ya know, an American. You don't get both. If you're an immigrant, whether you hopped a fence, fetus or plane to get into this country, this is your home now. Welcome. You don't get to fly a Spanish flag or a Russian flag outside your home. It's not that there should be a law against it, it just doesn't make sense. If Spain and Russia were so awesome, why'd you leave? We're 120 years removed from the start of Ellis Island. There's no Polish-American, Asian-American, just American. Of course, remember your roots, bloodline, certain traditions, but realize that you don't live in that country anymore. By choice. Even second generation immigrants, feel free to leave anytime. It ain't hard to get into France or Mexico, believe me. Hard to leave though. I'm just so tired of the super-hero heritage talk. Dude you don't want to mess with me, I got a temper, I'm Sicilian. Really? 'Cus you know the majority of people from Sicily are just as big of pussies as everyone else on this planet? Scorsese makes a few movies and then all of the sudden, all Sicilians are mad mob men. I'm Irish, so being a drunk is in my blood. True, you may have a predisposition, you may be more susceptible to addiction, but come on, did you grow up in cold, food-less Ireland, where after a 14-hour-day taking a nip of whiskey helped coat the muscles

with calm? No, you grew up in a well-off east-coast
neighborhood that had a cliché Irish pub around the corner and
it was always easy to chalk up a huge tab on your attorney
mother's extra miles credit card. Should I ask him about the
poster? No, just keep cool so you don't expose yourself.

"Well, go ahead and have a seat and we'll get started.
I'd offer you a coffee, but the pot's broken," Franks said.

Theresa wasted no time in beginning the interview.
She believed there was no place in reporting for fluff. You
weren't there to make friends, to have a group like you or offer
you backstage passes. Ask questions that lead to truth and fact,
devoid of what's on the other end.

"Coy, it is my understanding that you will be trying to
get a new levy on November's ballot. What can you tell me
about that?" Theresa began.

"Well, as you know, and as you've seen, this building
does not facilitate learning. From the heating and cooling,
leaking ceilings and outdated classroom technologies, we owe
it to our kids and our community to upgrade this facility,"
Franks said.

The interview concluded 20 minutes later. Pike didn't
say anything else except thanks for the time. He took notes
alongside Theresa, but started faking it halfway through. He
wasn't going to write the article.

Theresa was the editor, but 28 years ago, got her start
as a reporter in Winherst. So anytime a big event happened, or
there was an interview to be had with someone important, she
would always cover and write the story until she felt as though
the other reporters could handle it.

When Pike got into his silver Taurus in the school
parking lot, there was a dead-skin-on-leather feeling on his
elbow. He twisted his neck downward to discover a three-inch
tear in his new green and cream-striped Polo dress shirt from
his father.

What the heck? I had this hole in my shirt the whole
time? That's just great. All I wanted was a fresh start. Sure, on a
long enough timeline, they'll see I'm just a grind-it-out, do-just-
enough-to-get-by conman, but not right off the rip. Oh, puns.

Man, it was set up so perfectly. A new expensive shirt from my dad, the bottom half of my expensive California wedding suit, a million bucks I was. Then the homeless tear. What did the editor think? And the superintendent? How could you show up to an interview with a Tijuana whore giant-pussy-gash for a shirt? Whatever, just roll up the sleeves and head to the office.

When Pike arrived, he was relieved to see that both Finn and Carly were gone, even though the newsroom itself was quite busy.

"I want to go over some story leads with you," Theresa said standing beside Pike as his desk, still in the morning on Monday.

"That's fine. Good interview with super Franks today, I'm glad I got to touch face with him, so to speak," Pike said.

"You don't have to thank him for speaking with us. That's part of his job. The schools want to be really nice so you print favorable things about them."

"Well, at least it's a school and not a corporation—"

"Doesn't matter. We are here to report the facts without bias," Carly interrupted as she manifested from the back hallway.

"Oh, ya, no, for sure," Pike tried to say assuredly.

"Couple of school events I want you to cover this week," Theresa said as she gave Pike three little squares of paper composed with editor font.

"The first is Southwood Elementary's field day. All the kids go to the park at the end of the school year for a fun day," Theresa said. "You need to meet with the principal and see if there are any kids on the 'don't photo' list," Theresa said.

Great, I'm going to end up taking a picture of some abused kid or witness protection nonsense and get fired.

"Are you aware of the 'no photo' list?" Theresa asked.

"Umm, it's a list of kids that can't have their photo taken?"

"Yes, that's right, so you need to be aware of that for field day tomorrow."

"Field day, I know all about it. I looked forward to field day every year when I was a kid. It was like the only non-boring event we did at my public pre-pubic school."

"OK. (long pause) The other event is the high school talent show, but that's not until Friday. Field day is tomorrow," Theresa said. "Here is a camera you can use for tomorrow, get some good photo art," Theresa concluded.

10.

"He sometimes talked in a way that astonished her at first and brought the crimson into her face; in a way that pleased her at last, appealing to the animalism that stirred impatiently within her." K. Chopin, *TA*.

The next day, Tuesday, due to rain, Pike was indoors at the Winherst Community Fieldhouse at 10:02 a.m. Same suit pants, and the second of dad's three gifted shirts (that was triple checked for holes). Dark dress shoes. No jacket needed as the weather was warm outside and Pike could "out run rain."

Perfect, field day. Totally in your wheelhouse. What the hell does that mean, in your wheel-house? I always think it's hamster related, like, the wheel in his cage. Anyway, you know all about field day. Some of your best young memories. How about the end of seventh grade? Big time. I went to field day and my best friend and I were talking to this eighth grade girl. She had developed great C-cup breasts and even though she had quite a fun and cool personality, boobs were all that mattered.

So my best friend Jay just kept talking to her all day about her breasts. He would tell her he just wanted to see them after school, that it wouldn't be a big deal. I just stood beside him and listened. And daydreamed. And let the blood fill up where it would.

After we got back from field day and school let out, she agreed to show us behind the Dairy Mart woods minutes away from the public middle school. Oh man, what a chance. So we went behind dairy mart, and screened ourselves beside an old foundation near the store, and she took off her cherry blouse exposing a very basic pale bra, but it was a Victoria's Secret fashion show to us. Jay instantly went to grab her right tit.

"Hey, you can't do that." "Come on, you already have your shirt off, just let us feel them," Jay begged. "I read in Cosmo that it's really fun for the girl, but what does the guy get out of it?" she asked. "We just want to see what it's like, just let us feel them," Jay persisted.

She never actually said "Yes" or "OK," but Jay made a move and he had a firm hold of her left knocker. I followed suit on the other cone, not wanting to miss out and so horny for this girl. "Can we go under the bra?" Jay asked. "No way, I'm not that type of girl." "We want to see what it's like," Jay said. "Cosmo said the nipple is very sensitive, but what would you get out of it?" she asked again.

Jay, having two older sisters, knew a bit about the setup of a bra, and again without her acquiescing, slid the shoulder strap down, de-flapped the bra, exposing the most perfect, pink panther hue, slightly unsymmetrical nipple that a seventh grader soon to be eighth could ever have seen. "Ouch, you can't pinch it!" she told Jay. I went to work on the other tit, and after two or three minutes of fondling, Jay wanted more.

"Let us touch your bush," Jay asked/told. "No way, I'm not that type of girl." "Just the hair, we just want to touch the hair," Jay said. "No way." "We just want to see it, we'll never have a chance again," Jay argued. "No way. I'll show you it, but you can't touch. OK?" "Yes, OK, we just want to see," Jay said.

She unbuttoned the top of the navy pants, pulled the elastic of the panties out, and curly dark pubes lacerated our eyes. Jay threw his hand down towards the prize. "No, I said no," she stated as she pulled his hand back. I followed suit and just as my fingers touched that thin top hair layer, her hand vice-gripped my arms. I'll never forget that feeling of knowing I had crossed the line, and trying to rationalize the action to medicate the gross gut feeling that had befallen me.

The fieldhouse in Winherst was very clean. No chipped paint on the railings, well-maintained dead-leaf-brown track and non-faded equipment. The city cared about its youth sports teams and the facilities on which they played.

Crossing the freshly lined parking lot diagonally, Pike found a spot close to the back to park.

Don't want the kids or teachers to see what car I drive. Not like it's a piece of crap, but it will be good to stay as ghostly as I can in this town, for fear of them learning all my evil truths and illegal addictions and my mean personality.

OK, got the camera, my little spiral-bound reporter's notebook, my dress is not alternative but quite regular and *dressy, hair is probably two weeks away from looking weird and needing cut—I'm ready. First and foremost, find a teacher. Don't talk to any kids other than to ask where a teacher is. Don't be too nice to any female students as they might think you are flirting. If one person suspected you to be a pervert, it'd all be over. You're not anyway, so don't trip.*

Between the tennis courts and shot put one, a tall light-haired adult was walking across the gym.

"Hi, excuse me. I'm Pike. I write for the Winherst News-Times, I'm—"

"Hello, thanks for coming. I wasn't sure if anyone was going to show up, I never heard back from the editor," she responded.

"Yep, I'm here for the whole total coverage thing of field day in the field house."

"Well, great. You may know me, but I should introduce myself anyway. Principal Dion, nice to meet you," Dion said as she extended a hand weighed down by the huge charm bracelet on her wrist.

In that brief moment, Pike tried to look at the extended hand for signs of a wedding/engagement ring.

Wait, oh no, what hand is it on again?

"Great, I wanted to talk to you first," Pike said trying to hide his excitement and not wanting to make it seem odd that a fairly attractive woman was the principal.

"Basically, I'd just like to observe some events, take some photos, and then write up a story about the day," Pike said.

"Let me introduce you to Ms. Kearny. She organized this whole event," Dion said.

I'm a real reporter, lady, so I can't go make love to you behind the pole vault mats. Yes, I know we could do some student-teacher fantasy, and even though you are mildly cute, I have to stay professional. So we'll just have to copulate up here in my head. What is wrong with you, dude?

"And I'll have you meet the Phys. Ed. teacher as well, Mrs. Trateman. Come on," Dion said.

Dion was attractive by the American standard. And in shape. And in a Winherst town of 30,000, a six or a seven can be Cleopatra by comparison. She walked with a purposeful pace towards a group of first graders standing by the hurdles, as Pike was trailing.

This is the exact moment of will we talked about. Sure, you could glance/stare/gawk at her butt, but you will go to hell for sure. This is a grade school fun day, and you want to get caught looking at the principal's ass because your mind is so fuck-driven, infantile and boring? But you could go spy-style, act like you're going to tie your shoe, check it out. Check what out? It's a female human backside in jeans, dude, come on. If you're out in the world and a nice rear passes in front of you, you glance and go about your business. It's like a neat moment when two dragonflies are stuck together and hovering in front of you over an extra-green-algae pond. You check it out and continue with other fluid thoughts.

It turned out to be a successful no-look campaign for Pike, and he was introduced to teachers, organizers and kids throughout the next couple of hours.

With every new group, Pike would ask about kids being on the "no photo" list. The majority of the instructors were oblivious a list even existed, but wanted to play professional and gave Pike the green light.

When Pike thought that there was nothing more to add to the story, he began to head to his car when superintendent Franks showed up in a dry-silk Italian suit and non-matching shoes.

"Hello, it's nice that the superintendent came to get some exercise," Pike said trying to humorously start a conversation.

"You kidding me, with the energy these kids have, I wouldn't even try to keep up," Franks said.

They exchanged pleasantries, with the super wanting to keep the press close and the press wanting the super even closer.

The men separated through the photons and as Pike was about to dive past his car door, he hesitated momentarily and eye-followed Franks to the side of the pole vault mats, where Principal Dion was standing, leaning against the blue support pads.

That little rat, he stole my idea.

The principal and superintendent seemed to be old friends and lovers the way laughs, shoulder slaps and hand motions seemed to criss-cross in a very welcoming motion.

Jokes aside, I wonder what they're really talking about? You can't trust these people. Teachers are always caught embezzling, fornicating with a student or giving them drugs, can't trust a one of them. Really they are the true cradle of our society and without them we've have nothing. Secret little pole vault talks—I'm on to you both. Ya, you thought I left and I'm a new journalist that don't know shit. Well, guess what, I'm watching you (and that butt) right now. Not really the ass, never looked. I mean, thongs look good, but "ass addicts?"

"How was field day?" Theresa asked back at the office.

"It was nice. I told them how much field day meant to me when I was a kid. Talked to the superintendent, thought there could've been a secret meeting between Franks and the principal behind the pole vault mats as I was leaving," Pike said.

"What do you mean a secret meeting?" asked "ears always on" Carly from across the south office.

"Nothing really. Just saw them talking away from everyone, thought it was weird. No big deal, really," Pike said.

"No big deal? You have a school principal and superintendent acting shady in a secret meeting and you don't think that's a big deal? Theresa, you might want to look into this if Pike is unable to," Carly suggested.

"Wait, what were they doing?" Theresa took the bait from Carly and was now more interested.

"They weren't doing anything, just talking. It looked weird, so I made a joke. Sorry, nevermind," Pike said pusillanimously.

"We don't joke about news in the newsroom," Carly said.

"Is that like 'No fighting in the war room?'" Pike asked.

"Pike, go ahead and write up your story and upload your pictures for the rest of the day," Theresa said.

"I'm not sure about where to upload the pictures," Pike painfully said, knowing that instruction would soon follow.

"Have Carly show you," Theresa said while turning around to stare at her computer.

A good couple of minutes passed before Pike said, "Carly?"

"Yes, Pike?"

"Pictures?"

"What do you mean when you say pictures?" Carly slowly asked.

"I thought you heard Theresa talk about uploading pictures."

"I did."

"Well, all right, when you—"

"I'm ready to teach you now. Go ahead and slide your chair over here," Carly insisted.

It's not a need for this job, you don't need this job, I can make this salary in eight months with tips delivering furniture, but you want this job. So shut up, slide your chair over and get taught.

"On my way," Pike said.

After the tutorial, Theresa explained more about the business model to Pike. The Winherst News-Times was owned by Veritas Media, LLC, which owned 40 publications in the state. For Winherst, there were eight reporters, a couple of part-timers, a couple of freelancers, the sports guys, the content editors and layout. And the paper is printed at a press off site, unlike the "old days."

Pike: i c. how many stories do you think i should be writing a week? (iChat)

Theresa: Shoot for six or seven, probably end up using four or five depending on content and art.

Write stories for nothing? No way lady, you'll be printing them all, just watch.

Pike: ok cool thanks.

What did I get myself into? An-hour-and-20-minute roundtrip commute to work every day? Can my butthole handle that? Will the hemorrhoid poke out so far and squishy that I can no longer drink, have sex or sit ever again? Well, tell you one thing, it's been a solid four days so far. Not the best job, that freakin' Carly is such a dick. For what? Why make an office atmosphere of cocksuckerness? But my hole is holding up. Literally? No. Oh, well, just like my brother said, grind it out a while and if nothing else, just think of this as a three-month paid internship for journalism.

Wednesday was like every other day—ad ladies running back and forth, "Can you fit a 2-by-4 on page seven? No? How bout a 4-by-4 on 13?" The editor and content editor smashing page layout after page layout, the publisher pacing back and forth and looking over everyone's shoulder. Non-stop work and stress until the pages were sent over to the press.

When Pike arrived on Wednesday, he was feeling pretty good. Had some beers Saturday, but took off Sunday because of soccer and he usually didn't drink during the week. Sure, he'd catch a buzz in the closet and watch sports high, but what a difference a week makes. Last Wednesday Pike was ingesting everything he could in the "last night of freedom."

Nonsense excuse to get wasted. Always an excuse. For the normals, it usually took a wedding, graduation, concert or other big event to get the average person who actually drank wasted. But for the binge alcoholic, at least once every couple of weeks it was wedding wastoid. But recently, outside of last Wednesday night, I've kept things low key and was pretty fresh for the morning.

Even though it was only work-day five, Pike had established a parking routine in the lot, after consciously thinking about where was really the best parking spot at 8:55 a.m.

Through the big rust-proof brown, conquered-steel back door that was double-secured by two deadbolts at night, Pike entered the quiescent office feeling content about his life and mind.

Before he could set his backpack beside his computer, Theresa was on him.

"Pike, come over here please. (small pause that didn't allow enough time for him to cruise across the floor) I've already been here two hours working on layout. You see, (noticing that he hadn't arrived yet) Pike, please come over here," Theresa demanded.

"I'm coming," Pike said, and left his light, spring, black Adidas jacket on and posted up beside the editor.

"So by our daily deadline, hopefully but never actually, I should have all the content for the paper," Theresa began, "Once all the content is in I can start looking over the pagination and doing final edits. Some pages are really easy, like the cooking page, where the outlines and framework are the same and I simply add the newly submitted story. Others, like the sports pages, are done new every day or week, depending on the lead, art and length of the stories. It takes time, but I usually don't even deal with sports."

"OK," Pike said.

"Just watch me for a couple of hours while I do it all."

Oh, the ardor of futility.

The overwhelming workload discouraged Pike, and after about 13 minutes of keystrokes and shortcuts and never ending pagination, Pike just daydreamed and said, "Yes, I understand," after every question.

I'm not going to be laying out these pages ever so it doesn't matter. What did someone tell me, that Theresa has been here 28 years, so I'm not exactly looking forward to working 20 years to become editor of some small-town, small-time, shithole newspaper. And how is the world's greatest journalist, Carly, working here? With her skill and never-ending news knowledge, how did USA Today not scoop her up yet?

Theresa was gone for the day by 1:30 p.m.

After two hours, Pike was bored. He didn't really want to do any work, but he felt like if he didn't at least inquire it could come back to haunt him. Pike sent an iChat to the secretary.

Pike: hey, do you know when theresa is getting back from lunch? thanks.

Terri: No.

Pike: ok thanks

Terri: She took her purse.

Pike: im not sure what that means

Terri: It means she won't be coming back in today.

Pike: i c. thanks

A new iChat was then sent to Finn, even though they were sitting seven feet from each other.

Pike: so i guess theresa isn't coming back the rest of the day? what do you usually do when she's gone and your stories are done?

Finn: She's probably not coming back the rest of the day. She gets here a little early and then tells Rob that she's been working here since 4 a.m., then goes home.

Pike: that's a good idea, i should try that

Finn: I did once, and Rob went out to the parking lot and felt my hood. It was warm and wintertime. Almost lost my job.

Pike: damn.

Finn: Yeah, and I really need this job right now.

Pike: how long you been working here? (Pike was trying to propitiate.)

Finn: Well over a year. I started out at your desk working the beat in Winherst. Then they fired a sports guy, so I took his desk, job and other assignments.

Pike: i don't understand why you would all want to stare at a wall all day.

Finn: I come in here, go do my work, come back and go home. The less people I have to talk to the better.

11.

"WOMAN—a pleasing but a short-lived flower, / Too soft for business and too weak for power: / A wife in bondage, or neglected maid; / Despised if ugly; if she's fair—betrayed." M. Leapor, *AEOW*.

When Pike arrived at his desk Thursday morning, already waiting for him was the new edition of the Winherst News-Times.

The backpack wasn't taken off and Pike remained standing and he quickly scanned the paper for his name. And there it was, on C3, the blood drive story, by Pike, Logan.

What's up now? Told you all, I can be a journalist, no problem. Got my first assignment. Gotta save this paper. Gotta save every paper ever. OK, so the story itself sucks, but whatever, already wrote the field day story. Can't stop now, can't mess up. Bite your lip, don't play around, take all the stuff that the editor and Carly throw at you. What does the publisher even do? Why does he never speak to me? Doesn't matter, just don't foul it up. You're 32, dude, you can't start another career now. This is it, last chance. How did they even hire me? Sports writing, I guess. Maybe I should try to flirt with the editor and maybe our relationship will improve? Could I bang her? No way. And that secretary, what happened to her? Before the Chinatown double chin set in, there were sex-instigating eyes and a hot face. Nice tits to match. But the tits are fat tits now. Reminder bags of excess, not sex. And that personality. Why is she so beaten down? How long has she worked here? Is this it, all she really cares about, working here and watching TV between bites?

"Pike, this morning I want you to upload the content to the web, OK?"

"Yes, I will do that. Carly showed me it all perfectly last week, so I feel like I can do it."

"It's not hard," Carly added.

OK, tough guy, just trying to be nice. Is it hard to be a jerk?

There were a couple of untoward snags in the uploading process, but Pike's ego couldn't ask Carly or Theresa for help. So he iChatted Finn, who was very reluctant to help, but did.

For lunch, Pike found the juice bar and restaurant around the square. It was empty. The girl at the register was called cute in high school, 22 years ago.

No dreads, no dirt under her fingernails.

"Hello, I'm new to this area and have never been here before, what would you recommend?" Pike opened once their bodies were facing each other at the counter.

"Super, an out-of-towner. We get a lot of people from everywhere because of the Amish tourism. What would I recommend, hmmm, well, what do you like?" she asked.

"Something warm and hearty, I wanna feel like I got all my nutrients and protein today. I'm so tired of the salad lunch. Not like I really ever eat a salad, but unless you're at a good veggie restaurant, it's basically a salad," Pike said, aware that he was flirting a bit.

It wasn't that Pike wanted some physical involvement with the worker, he just wanted to be liked. He felt, "This lady is old enough that she would feel honored to have me flirting with her." And then when she actually did flirt a little back, Pike felt accomplished. It was the same with homosexuals. Pike doesn't want to have sex with a man, but if a guy is going to be attracted to other guys, why not Pike?

Not being liked is not being liked. Doesn't matter who's on the other side.

"You should try our veggie chili, it's one of our two best dishes," the worker said.

"I'll try that then," Pike said.

"Something to drink?" she asked.

"I'll just have a water, thanks."

"Tap or bottled?"

"Tap is fine," Pike said.

"Well, since you're from out of town, I should tell you that the tap water isn't very good around here."

"Not very good, how could a cultivators-of-the-earth farm town like Winherst have bad water?"

"Not sure, it's always been bad," she said.

"Well, I'm going to take my chances," Pike said.

Halfway through the meal, the lady came by Pike's table to ask, (unnecessarily with the take-out format of the establishment) if everything tasted good.

"Water's the best part," Pike joked. She laughed.

The chili is disgusting.

Pike took about a 45-minute lunch break. On his first day he tried to ask about lunch breaks but Theresa said, "Take as long as you need."

So naturally...

When he got re-seated at his desk, he heard the office silence break with the semi-swivel of Theresa's chair.

"Pike, do you remember that you're covering the high school talent show Friday, right? Quick write-up with some art, who performed, some quotes... So finish up whatever you need to do before that."

Umm, I got nothing to do. You must know that, right? You've assigned me one story so far all week. It's done, a bunch of little kids played at the field house, wow, what news.

"OK, I'll work on a couple of things," Pike responded.

12.

"The coloured people may be said to be roughly divided into three classes, not so much in respect to themselves as in respect to their relations with the whites." J.W. Johnson, *TAOAECM*.

Friday afternoon, around 1 p.m., Pike was outside the Winherst High School sitting in his Taurus, parked in a fire lane, trying to decide the next course of action.

Let's see, I got like 15 minutes to kill. What if there is a group of hot girls that make fun of my clothes? They're like, look at that old guy, nice pleated pants. Girls, give me a break, all two of my real dress pants are dirty. I worked all week and never did laundry. But I got high. Disgusting, my priorities. Can't do the simplest of things to better my life, but will sit and complain about them endlessly. What if there is some frat-boy in training that is going to talk smack to me? I can't hit a high school kid, but he can humiliate me and that's not a crime? Talent show, ain't no talent in this town of 30,000.

With minutes till the event started, Pike made his way to the office. The secretary and principal were gone, and a student aide came from around the corner. Her yellow skirt was short enough that fellow male students thought they might be able to see her underwear while she was just standing in front of them.

Nice skirt you fool. What's the point? You're in high school, dude.

I've never had a hard time when it came to attraction and young ladies. Before I even entered the school, the sex-drive was turned off. No matter the cleavage, shortness of the skirt, or prettiness of the face, if I even got the smallest inkling that the girl was under 21, I wanted absolutely nothing to do with it. Never tried to flirt or have a single bad thought come into my mind.

I know too many young girls to have any sexually sick thoughts about them. Can't and won't.

The aide directed Pike to the auditorium where Pike was convinced every school basketball gym was exactly the same everywhere you went.

There were four entrances/exits to the rectangular court, and as soon as Pike went through a passageway, he immediately sought a teacher.

Who's got a tie on? Come on, I can't talk to any students, then they'll think I'm trying to hook it up with someone, or sell them drugs, and my reporting reputation will be destroyed forever. And the kids will make fun of me.

Pike walked along the back wall, under the hoop, and spied a thick-mustached man in a long-sleeved navy dress shirt and a coral tie.

Gotta be a teacher. Can students have facial hair? Not when I was in school. And, although I could never grow any, I was always like, "Stupid teachers just abusing their puissant position and making us shave," but now I'm like, "Good idea, separates students from outsiders and teachers." I'm a sellout.

"Hi, I'm Pike. I write for the Winherst News-Times," he told the lean man that equaled his height.

He put forth his hand and smiled, "Don Parker."

"Hey, Don, I'm covering this event today for the paper," Pike replied with a bit of nervousness.

What if he knows you're a new journalist and doesn't think I'm good enough?

"I see that," Don replied.

That was all that was said, and Pike stood beside Don until the marching band began promptly at 1:15 p.m.

The students were punctilious and the talent show started typically—couple of singers, a band and a dance routine. Then things got odd.

What is this girl doing?

A sophomore girl had signed up to do a solo interpretative modern dance to Chariots of Fire.

This dancer is doing awkward body twists, dry-humping the floor, moving her body in a very un-succinct and whack fashion throughout this interpretive experience.

But the giggles, yells, bully argots and taunts from the crowd never came. When the performance was over, the crowd cheered very loudly. The same thing occurred when a boy tried to unsuccessfully ride a unicycle and balance blocks on his knees. The kid's face got red, and after three or four failed attempts over four or five minutes, he gave up, and again, no one poked fun or jeered, but cheered, like a drunken World Cup mob.

Pike stopped taking news notes and wrote this poem:

Something different here,
punks without passport
checking border guards-
a step away from the
clicks and clacks of
condensation, dripping
down the arms of
outstretched supporting
hands called classmates.
The worst time of public
life, now, friends with
the same zit smear mirror,
behind the same fucking
hope of future.

On the southbound road by 2:36 p.m. To be fair to the employer, Pike should have returned to the office.

There is just never a scenario where I can voluntarily waste my time, even getting paid.

First full week of new job complete. Earned sex, but no one around to accept the voucher.

Down towards the cul-de-sac towards the apartment, the thoughts of his attractive ex-girlfriend driving blood to the shaft.

I choose this woman to be my wife for life. That statement of matrimony speaks a lot about the needy nature of people's personas. I mean, can any true introvert be in love? Sure, sure, sure, they can be in love, but it won't be the "you complete me" nonsense. How can a truly independent person need someone else? "I'm nothing without you, honey. Without you, the world could end and I wouldn't care." I know that that's a cliché example, but the point remains, what does that say about you when you are so dependent in order to reach nirvana? Maybe it's not true as you get older, but I always thought that young love was totally based in weakness. You have to be with your boyfriend/girlfriend all the time? You always have to be touching, talking, thinking with them? It's not that it's a bad pleasure, but your greatness is always contingent on them. Perpetual first lady.

But I knew that going in. I wanted the self-sell-out. My being and greatness was at a level. And I was and am an extrovert, anyway. So I chose to bind that level with another. Super-greatness. (But only achieved together.) And I was fine with that. She liked sex. She knew I liked sex. That may sound typical, but why, before you get married, would you not sit down with your wife and talk about the frequency, duration and general feel of your sex life? This does not apply to pre-marital virgins and other weirdos. Why wouldn't you have that conversation? You talk about everything else before you get married, right? Financial expectations, if not directly said, implied, offspring, living locations, the way you poop, everything. Talk about whatever you like and need. For one person it is sex, for another, something different. Maybe it's getting dressed up in camo like a wanna-be navy seal and shooting earth creatures? Maybe it's pet cats. Whatever you like, if they don't 100% support that, why are you marrying them?

So I told my ex sex is my love language. A wife that doesn't want to do the married man is called a stripper or a maid. She's like, "OK, cool, here are my demands." I said, "OK, cool, no prob."

But as it turns out you can't negotiate love and I was wrong.

When Pike opened his unnumbered apartment door, he did it slowly.

Always could be a human with a forehead close to the door.

He doesn't want it to open it slowly. He wants to explode into the area, to get excited about the weekend, future life, the night.

I've learned to be calm when I come home, learned from experience, the more excited I am, the more likely it is for failure. I wrote a poem one time in college about expectations after the true story of skinny dipping with a Native American who would later land the anchor job on Weekend Update on Saturday Night Live. Anyway, bunch of us were in our college 20s, on the barren beaches of Savannah after midnight high tide broke, and I was staring out into the ocean. Yes, into the ocean and not her vagina (that I did picture later to be quite bushy—probably not accurate and stemming from an imbedded savage/racial stereotype). About 60 yards out into the polished-coal ocean bleak there was a sandbar. I swam out and I watched my friends wait for the waves, try to time their jumps and leaps and fun, with the slightly inconsistent movement of the liquid body. We returned home, a poem was scribbled and the last line read, "Waves are for people with expectations. Sandbars."

Monday, Pike was able to go into the office around noon because he had to cover city council that night. Starting the second full week of work. Although it was only a two-lane highway to his place of business, Pike was already driving back roads and other routes to try to find a faster way and to kill the monotony. Scanning through AM and FM frequencies to find new music or talk radio that existed in the Pennsylvanian north.

Parking lot same spot, brushing the fast food breakfast from his teeth and spitting paste on blacktop. Same two or three steps inside the back room before the door closes. Same echoes up the steps to the second floor. Same dim at first light growing stride stronger, same computer awaiting its function. Same gross feeling of passing Carly on the way to his desk. Waiting for the editor to say, "Good morning," in her soft jaw accent.

"I want you to watch the last couple of high school softball games to get a feel for that, but don't write it up," Theresa told Pike as he did his morning routine of checking email, looking at the website and generally wasting time.

"And I want to go over city council tonight. What to cover, what to look for, things like that," she said.

Later that day, at 4 p.m., Pike was in downtown Winherst, sitting at a heavily initial-carved table, inside the dining area of a bar n' grill. He needed to get dinner, and be across the street for council by 5 p.m.

I can have one beer, with my dinner, and I'll be fine and won't smell.

The waitress, who had outgrown the hippie revolution but still had long straight hair and a Harley shirt, came over for Pike's order.

"Do you have any beer recommendations, like a local or micro brew? I always drink boring beer and want to switch it up," Pike said.

"Umm, we got Budweiser on tap for 2 bucks, and we just got in a whole bunch of Great Lakes, a beer from Cleveland."

"All right, I'll try one of those Great Lakes please, and I need a menu. Thanks."

The waitress brought over a Great Lakes "Lake Erie Monster," which had almost double the alcohol content of a normal beer.

Pike finished it before he ordered his food.

Well, no stupid veggie options here, I should have known better. I'll just get a couple of appetizers, like onions rings and mozzarella sticks, and eat when I get home. And I'll slow sip another beer; it's only 4:15.

Since Pike was seated next to the kitchen door, the cook, who was running in and out, noticed what Pike was drinking.

"Yo, my man, sic beer, for sure, I love Great Lakes. I've been to their brewery," the cook said with dilated pupils.

"First time I've ever had one, pretty bitter and bite-y, but good. Definitely can feel it," Pike said, noticing the unconventional body movements of the cook, whose apron was covered in smears and grease and chicken-gut skid marks.

"It's a good beer. Never seen you in here before," the cook said, looking around the bar slowly.

"First time here as well. I saw your Deady bear tattoo, my old friend Yogos used to always try to get me to listen to the Grateful Dead, but that Phish type of music at one point was the enemy of rock, or so I was taught."

"My little bear forearm tattoo, that's nothing," the cook said as he proceeded to lift up the back of his restaurant-pale t-shirt, exposing a full back piece that consisted of three bears dancing in a line, with arms interlocked. "I used to go to festivals all the time."

"Music just isn't music without drugs," Pike joked.

"Dude, you cool?" the cook asked with asperity, suddenly becoming suspicious.

"Yes, I'm cool, what's up?"

The cook leaned closer to Pike, "I'm trippin' balls right now. You want some doses?"

Pike was not sure what doses meant, even with his background, but he thought it was "boomers" or "shrooms" or "magic mushrooms" that contained psilocybin. The cook meant lysergic acid diethylamide, or LSD.

"Nah, I'm good man, thanks, I gotta leave soon."

The flatscreen at the bar was showing the 4:30 p.m. local news that was just getting underway. The sound was off, but the closed captioning was running and Pike was reading.

"Good evening, everyone. We start tonight with our top story—a Penkal woman was found strangled to death in South Carolina today. Authorities have identified the body of Courtney Brean, a 31-year-old mother of three. The main person of interest in the case is Brean's ex-husband, who was with her on vacation. For more on the story, we now go live to South Carolina..."

What the hell? No way, I know that girl. I used to have a huge crush on her when I first moved to town. Which is insane 'cus her family was friends with Mary's. She was gorgeous, what the fuck? What the fuck! Someone killed her? She's got kids!

Pike finished his fourth Great Lakes and left the grille, a little after 5 p.m., feeling the effects of alcohol hard on his thoughts, walking pace and speech. He arrived at council minutes later and sat close to the back. Every 20 minutes, Pike became more inebriated, as his stomach kept processing the liquid libations. After an hour and a half of council, they adjourned, and Pike ran back across the street to the locale. He ordered a Coors Light while sitting at the bar itself, on a barstool, and waited for the cook. Pike's beer can was shallow when the cook appeared, who after Pike said hello, did not remember him.

"Remember, like an hour ago, I was sitting over there, we were talking about doses?"

"Now I do. Give me a minute."

Three minutes later, Pike followed the cook out of the back door that emptied into an alley. The man was searching through his pockets when a waitress opened the back door and said, "Hey, our orders are backed up, you can't go on break now." She made eye contact with Pike, and slowly retreated behind the screen.

"Don't worry about her, she's a bitch," the chef said, pulling a jar from his bottom right cargo pant pocket.

"Hey! What are you doing?" The owner of the establishment was a basketball-hoop-length behind them both, finishing a cigarette. Pike and the cook had not seen him. "We're overloaded in there, you can't take a smoke break now."

The cook, without motioning, quietly said, "Wait here for five minutes," and sauntered back into the bar. The owner followed him in and walked past Pike with very suspicious and confused eyes. Pike quickly ambled down the alleyway, found his car and got a notepad. He wrote this poem:

Courtney Brean
I followed you close (looks like dose)
Gave a drunken tear,

Almost bought boomers to honor you.
But got scared.
"You want a little dessert?" he asked.
"I'm trippin' balls," he said.

Pike slowly accelerated out of town, and just past the city limits he found himself behind a car traveling 44 mph on the 55 mph state highway. Pike let the car get a good bit in front of him, hit the pedal, and at 60 mph, turned his signal on, entered the other lane and passed the vehicle very smoothly. He drove another 22 seconds before he saw blue and red lights taking over his rear window.

No way. I'm dead. What an idiot I am. I lost it all. I lost my job, my driving rights, my name is going to be smeared; Mary's father will kick me out of his shitbox apartment. Don't try to deny it, don't play games, don't blow, and take your punishment. I would not pass a breathalyzer. I wasn't speeding though.

There were two Tuscarron County Sheriff patrol cars behind Pike when he quickly pulled over. With no air conditioning and it being summer-hot in late spring, all the windows were down in Pike's car. A bald and very fore-arm-fit deputy exited his vehicle with great pace and was beside Pike's driver-side door in less than two seconds.

"What the hell were you doing, didn't you see it was a double yellow line back there?"

"I'm a reporter for the Winherst Gazette (wrong name of the paper), and I was just on my way home and I guess I just got ahead of myself," Pike replied, miraculously not slurring, and making eye contact.

"Did you think you could just pass like that with two sheriff's cars behind you, and nothing would happen? If we don't pull you over, how do you think that makes us look?" the deputy said, very frustrated and in a loud stern tone. When Pike didn't respond, he said, "Give me your license, right now!"

Thought it was rhetorical, Jesus!

Pike's wallet was resting gently on his two testicles after never properly placing it when he jumped into his car, and he quickly reached down and pulled out his ID and handed it over. The officer from the other car positioned himself beside the back passenger-side bumper, with his palm resting on the butt of his 9mm-law-enforcer.

The first deputy went back to his car, ran a check and came back within the time it took Pike to hold his breath in two forty-second intervals.

He hasn't smelled any alcohol on you. Just be cool, be as calm and as cool as you have ever been. Take the ticket for the illegal pass, which, I don't even know how that was a double yellow, it was flat as shit, but don't argue! Be nice, say how stupid and sorry you are, and pray to God he doesn't get suspicious.

"We are on our way to a call," the officer said to Pike, "I would love to give you a ticket right now, and maybe try to talk some sense into your stupid ass, but we have to leave right now, so you are extremely lucky. But if I ever catch this car, or you, doing something that stupid, you're getting more than a ticket." The ID was then thrown back into the car, narrowly missing the end of Pike's nose and landing on the passenger's seat floor. The officers returned to the vehicles, and with lights still pulsating, exited and even overwhelmed the highway.

Yes! What a lucky little bitch I am. And how stupid. Never again. That was so dumb to do, I am never, ever, drinking and driving again. I can drive my car no problem, but I would blow over and go straight to jail.

Pike drank four more beers when he got home.

13.

"I couldn't understand why they had taken them away when they didn't hurt anybody. Later on I realized that that too was part of the punishment. But by then I had gotten used to not smoking and it wasn't a punishment anymore." A. Camus, *TS*.

The next day, Pike barely made it through the first phase of his Tuesday routine when the editor was very curious about last night's council meeting.

"So how did last night go?" Theresa asked.

"It was good. Didn't have any problems," Pike assured her.

"I meant what happened?"

"Oh, it was pretty routine I think. The different assiduous departments had their committee meetings an hour before council began, umm, last night it was the public works committee and finance. And then the police committee met after council," Pike said.

"Anything interesting happen during council?" Theresa pressed.

"I'll write it all up, but it was just like financial reports, reports from the committees, reading of ordinances. They didn't vote to change anything, and there was no real new business."

"What about the police committee meeting?"

"Well, that was kinda funny because one of the councilmen was complaining to the chief of police that cops were like hanging around downtown too long or something, which that's what I thought small town cops did?"

There was a moment of silence.

"Wait, what? What councilman?" Theresa excitedly asked.

"The tall bald dude, acted very aggressively the whole meeting." Pike said.

"Must have been Johnson, he's an ex-cop himself and he is very aggressive. So what did he say again?" Theresa wanted specifics.

"Well, it actually happened after the committee meeting, the two of them were talking casually, they didn't know I was listening and I'm pretty sure it was all off the record," Pike said trying to prevaricate.

"There is no 'off the record,' ever," Carly was quick to chime in returning from her routine 9:15 a.m. bathroom visit. "If you say it, then we can print it, bottom line."

"That's fine, but I was there to cover council, not eavesdrop for something that's not even a story," Pike said.

"A councilman and chief of police arguing about police behavior downtown is definitely a story, and I decide what is or isn't a story," Theresa said with power.

It was no use. The front page headline was, "Cop Problems Highlight City Council."

Pike's byline hadn't been omitted, even after he pleaded with Theresa concerning the story, stating that this will ruin his relationship with both the police and council, and implored her to wait until there is actually something going on before we rake them over the coals.

Tractable Theresa couldn't see and didn't care.

Later in the week, Pike was heading out to the softball diamond to "cover" the regular season finale of the high school team. Earlier at the office, the sports editor had given Pike a color photo of the roster.

There was a dark-haired gorgeous Egyptian girl that is burning bad thoughts into my brain the whole ride to the park. Which is odd, considering I never have had any thoughts of high school girls.

High school girl, dude, so don't even think about it. I'm not, bro, she is just pretty, that's all. I hope she grows up and doesn't suck a bunch of dick at college and finds a husband that isn't exceptional at anything but makes money working for NASA as a chemical engineer and she'll have all of the islands in the Caribbean mapped out from their frequent jaunts there. But she is hot. But not in a sexual way. Little high school girls don't know how to have intercourse. How could they? It comes from years and years of listening to individual pubic hairs from each girl until you finally realize that every female is different, and thus, every technique must be tweaked and form fitted for each vagina. Basically, anyone over 23 that messes around with a teen is basically a molester. You crawl up on them, and they lay there motionless, with their eyes opening and closing in terror, while you whisper to reassure them in a very pedophilliatic way. Gross. No sexuality in that, just power and perversion. I'm simply acknowledging that this softball girl is very pretty, that's all. And she's a senior, which means she's close to 18, which is not a 'pound me' indicator, but simply means she is older than others in high school. Last name Rampart, what a catch. Bet her dad is a prick.

Next week, Theresa confronted Pike about his writing style.

"You really need to work on your A.P. style. It's "a.m." not AM, state abbreviations don't follow the postal style, and here, I made you a list." Theresa handed Pike the list.

"Also, this is a small town paper. Although you didn't need to write up those softball stories, I'm glad you did, so I could remind you that even the sports stories should reflect the small town. You can't write, 'It was a pitching death matchup between a coward and a lion.' You understand?"

Pike was only thinking about the Rampart girl when sports got brought up.

A day later on Thursday, Theresa told Pike that she had learned that the Winherst superintendent was resigning, but he didn't have to worry about that, she'd cover it.

After calling in "sick" on Friday, Pike was invited by female friend Joan from his apartment complex, who worked from home, to take a day trip to Erie to do some birthday shopping for her father. They arrived in downtown Erie during the gap between breakfast and lunch.

"Look, they built a new casino, we should check it out," Pike said.

"You trying to buy my dad a slot machine for his birthday?"

"Haha, no, but it's still pretty early, let's just check it out, stay for like 10 minutes. We're already here and we got all day."

"Fine, let's check it out for a minute," Joan said, remembering her youthful trips to Vegas and Niagara Falls.

Joan had a very young face, and her dark black pigmentation held her wrinkles well, and so she was ID'd at the door as Pike walked on through. Everywhere they looked their eyes were caught, and reeled in by signs of easy wealth, fun, shiny slots and mirrored-ceilings.

They took the escalator to the second floor and Pike spotted a bar.

"Let's get martinis, I've only had gin martinis before, and I want a vodka one, like Bond. I finally made it through all of them last week, did I tell you that?" Pike asked.

"Finally, now will you stop trying to do that horrible Connery accent?"

"I will, but let's get drinks. Just one, and we will walk around looking all cool with our martinis."

After the drinks were ordered, Pike was upset that they were put in plastic cups and not martini glasses. He also held off ordering the drink in any kind of shaken, not stirred, manner.

"Let's get some money out and gamble," Pike suggested.

"Get some money out and gamble then," Joan said.

The direct deposit hadn't hit yet, I need you to get money out of your account.

"How about this, I'll buy the drinks if you get the gambling money?"

"What? I thought we were only having one? Fine, I'll get 60 bucks out for you."

"Nice."

They found a 10-dollar-a-hand blackjack table, and Pike played for 25 minutes before getting up, down $20.

"That table was no good. I was getting pushed on 20, and the dealer kept turning over blackjack. We were smart to leave."

The gambling stopped and Pike and Joan posted up at the fake-leather-padded bar and continued to ingest.

"I'm starving, let's get something to eat," Joan offered.

"But not in here, it's too expensive and I don't trust this place. Probably a secret Indian casino with altered decks and shit."

As soon as they left the building and were on the downtown Erie sidewalk, Joan, with inebriation backing her decisions, tried to jokingly push her male friend. But she stumbled before they made contact and all of her athletic African-American body weight smashed into Pike, sending them both to the concrete.

The downtown business people and walkers stopped and looked and felt concerned, as Pike and Joan both continued to lie on the ground, laughing. They finally got up and kept walking, Joan with a new hole in her jeans and a bloody knee.

"How about we go into this Kilt Restaurant?" Pike said, eyeing the low-cut plaid-skirt-wearing waitresses he could see through the glass.

"That would be fun for me, watch you stare at a bunch of girls. How could you even suggest that?"

"'Cus I'm a scumbag and I'm drunk, sorry."

Agreeing on a restaurant was difficult, and finally, after 30 minutes of walking, they were back to where they started.

"I'm hot, let's just go into any place," Joan said.

"Any place, like the Kilt?"

"Fine, whatever, let's go there."

As soon as Joan had given them permission to go to the Kilt, Pike lost all interest.

"I don't want to go there anymore. It's awesome that you would go though, I mean, pretty sweet. But let's walk for just some more minutes."

They took a dilapidated one-way, and rounding a corner, Pike heard "My Girlfriend's Boyfriend" by Her Space Holiday, splashing sound over a patio grill.

"I know this song, Kat used to play it all the time. She's an old friend from Oregon. I helped her move to LA, to get this job. Well, she would play this song over and over again. Or maybe I did, anyway, let's eat here."

They ate. There were many vegetarian options for Pike. They returned to the casino, where after four spins of the roulette wheel, they had lost all of the $60. Then home without shopping. Joan fell asleep in the car and Pike raced an orange Hummer down the highway, eventually calling it quits and conceding defeat at 95 mph.

May had closed and Pike had put in a couple of solid tax-return-months at the paper. And as June began, so did the high school graduation season for journalists.

This means I'll be covering the valedictorians, graduation ceremony, senior picnic and all the great "successes" of teenage kids.

"Graduation is in a week," Theresa said Monday morning, "so you'll have to work all next Sunday, OK? It's mandatory."

"That's fine," Pike lied.

Who cares about high school graduation? I gotta miss my soccer game to go stand in what I'm sure will be a hot-as-shit gym and watch a bunch of grandparents constantly cry with pride? I'll make you pay, I'll make you all pay for this.

"We do a whole graduation section in the paper, so I need you to go to the high school, find out who the valedictorian and salutatorian are and interview them for the special issue. Take your camera," Theresa instructed.

Pike stood outside the faded brick built-in-the-'70s high school and buzzed the secretary. Once inside the office, he explained his mission to a student aide, who told someone else, who finally got an adult to address Pike.

It was the gym teacher, err it should be said, Physical Education teacher, that told me I would have to go to the guidance office for further assistance. The male gym teacher openly flirted with the short-skirted office aide, too, I saw it. She liked it. His face was not proportionate and if not for the power dynamic of teacher/student, she would have called the cops months ago.

The guidance office pulled the salutatorian from class for the interview. The valedictorian was off campus taking college classes at the bigger and next-county-over's local community college.

It was painstaking to hear the goals and aspirations of an 18-year-old that couldn't possibly know what they wanted in life, Pike thought.

"I'm going to Albany and I want to be a nurse. My two older brothers go there and I've visited the school and I love it. I also want to travel. I think it would be neat to backpack around both the cities and sylvan Europe. My major is going to be nursing and business, and I'd like to have a minor in German. I really want to go to Germany. But I'm really going to miss Winherst, this will always be my home, and I'll always come back to visit," she said.

The other interview will be exactly the same.

The senior picnic, however, was not typical.

It was held at the local rec park, and although the rain had let up before Pike arrived, the ground was soaked in May mud that hadn't dried out yet in June. Pike spent his usual two to three minutes in his car before he entered the high school event.

Senior picnic. These dudes are all going to be way too cool for me. I mean, basically, when you're a senior, you think you're on top of the world. Everyone thinks that they've really done something, achieved at great milestone in their lives. That's all lies. Graduating high school? Everyone graduates high school because it's not hard. Until your 18, your parents send you to a free babysitter that they call school. No parent is going to sit around for eight hours and teach their kid long division, direct object pronouns and all that shit. No way. How are they going to work if that were the case? So they just gratefully send them off to school, and when you're finally done, it's not, "Great job, how did you manage to graduate high school?" it's, "OK, you are to the point in your life where it actually starts to begin." Sure there are nice high school memories, but if everything you do after high school isn't better, then you have failed.

The kids were under the pavilion, wet, fistful of chips and pop lips, laughing, hugging, posing for pictures while saying, "I can't believe we did it."

Pike got some quotes, took some feature art, and was about to call it "another boring story" when a senior pulled a big foam sword from underneath the picnic table.

This could be interesting.

Half-body shields, more swords and more troops gathered outside the open-air shelter in the swampy grass.

Pike trailed the last soldier and asked what was going on.

"Going to do a little *Dagorhir*," the student said.

"Sorry for my ignorance, but what's Dragonhir?"

"*Dagorhir* is live-action fighting. It's the real deal. There are tournaments and real battles and if you get hit, you must act like you really got hurt there, have to hop on one leg and things like that," the student clarified with proud probity.

Seven students circled each other, whapped each other with foam bats, hopped around on one leg, fought with one arm, rolled around in earth's sweat; it was a very entertaining scene to Pike.

But what of the other seniors? They have to be laughing their asses off at this dork army, right?

Pike turned back to the pavilion. The seniors were disinterested.

No one is yelling "role-play pussies" and whispering insults. They don't care. These kids had some way-beyond-their-time understanding of letting people do whatever the hell they wanted to do. But high school kids are supposed to be brutal. Is this a class of 250 students that are all friends? Where are the cliques? Are the different groups of students only different to the outside world and completely harmonious with each other? Weird. This could have never happened at my school. Thin girls with light eye makeup and nice faces would tell other attractive people how weird and stupid those roll players were and then covertly attack them. But not here. Winherst students seem very fine with themselves. And people who are fine with themselves are never mean.

Pike covered graduation on Sunday, and was still upset on Monday that he missed his soccer game and had to compromise his weekend.

They want me to go cover some Tuscarron County Beauty Awards tonight, so I'll act like I'm going, read about it online because I know an Erie daily paper will be there, and instead, get my Sunday back.

For the rest of the week, Pike interviewed a retired police officer, wrote a story on a 200-year-old home that was set to be destroyed after a millionaire bought the property to make a semi-truck entrance to his plastics factory, and the last assignment of the week was to interview a pastor at a church.

I'm doing high school shit and God shit. This will win a Pulitzer. Why can't I pick my stories?

The church was outside of the city limits, surrounded by farmed fields, weather-worn-white in paint, with basic small budget church construction used from the time of the puritans.

Pike pulled into the gravel parking lot, and before he could do his pre-interview meditation, a little beagle was barking at his door.

Ya cute dog, but I've seen beagles bite people, so I'm not getting out of my car until this dog is under control. Stop barking.

"Roger, get back here," a voice commanded from the cracked front door of the church.

Pike thought he was well dressed and was happy when he caught his window reflection from the car. He had the cleaners press his dress shirts, now up to nine over 15 years, and made a trip to Goodwill for three new pairs of dress pants.

Goodwill is like a freakin' department store now. How can donated goods cost this much? Because someone realized charity can be very lucrative.

Once inside, the interview began in its fashion...

"It worked so good I did it again. Instead of worship, we cleaned and repainted the whole inside. There was once an old library, which was turned into a storage closet, and we turned it back into a library," Pastor Pete said.

Pike noticed that all the books were Christian in nature.

That's not a library, it's a propaganda room.

"The Sunday after that we planted trees, landscaped and put in a garden out back. Now close to 50 people attend worship on Sundays," Pete said proudly.

"This is just like Sister Act," Pike tried to joke.

"What do you mean?" Pat asked.

"Nothing, it's a movie where Whoppi Goldberg turns a dying church around, just like what you're doing," Pike said.

"Whoppi Goldberg?"

"Never mind."

14.
"Age is always out of fashion." A.C. Mowatt, *F.*

It was the middle of June and the workload increased daily, as Pike was to cover any and all events in the town— retirements, overflow sports, city council, school board, as well as take and edit pictures and feature art. He was overwhelmed and felt like the Winherst News-Times hired desperate need-a-job reporters and writers that were willing to do extra work all week because they had no other good options and really wanted the experience.

"I really need this job right now," Finn said one late Monday afternoon after most everyone had cleared out of their section of the office.

"You've said that before," Pike responded, "it's cool to have a professional paying writing job, but this place sucks half the time. The publisher never talks to me, the editor says as little as possible and Carly is a complete jerk, some of the other people are nice, and the ads people are fine, but it's tough," Pike said.

"It's true, but I came from selling cars. Used ones," Finn said.

"Wait, you were a used car salesman? Man I don't think I could do that."

"It was dumb but I didn't have a job and needed one after the divorce."

"Wait, I never heard about a divorce. If it's a sore subject..."

"No, it's fine I brought it up," Finn said. "She's a bitch and if there is one person I would kill or punch, it would be her."

"Whoa-there, guy, let's not talk about beating up ladies, makes you look weak," Pike said.

"She's not a lady, she's a bitch. You have no idea what she did or put me through," Finn said.

I suppose that's true, I have no idea.

The whole feminism thing still calls for equality. The old adage, "You never hit a woman, under any circumstance," is still circumstantial. I can remember in fourth grade and seventh grade hitting a girl. The first, in fourth, was this girl who would never leave me alone. She'd walk by and pull my hair, scratch my face with long nails, and I would always just yell at her, but it never stopped.

So during one the school's basketball games, the always-tan Mexican-American nemesis of mine walked by and smashed gum in my hair. So I, with speed and rage, punched her in the stomach and moved to a different section of the seats. 16 minutes later a friend of mine came over and asked, "Hey, what did you do to Lupita, she went crying to the bathroom?" I felt guilty, but she stopped harassing me.

In eighth grade, it was a girl named Chelsea, who at the time actually liked me, and I her, but we were both oblivious to the attraction.

We were playing a ridiculous pass-out game at my friend Jay's house, the same friend that I went behind the Dairy Mart a year earlier at the end of seventh grade with, where we shared our first tit-touch, whose sister, coincidently, was the stomach punch.

"You have to take like tons of deep breaths over and over again," Chelsea instructed me as the friends watched in their lower-class not-a-lot-of-yard backyard.

"Then, after like 30 seconds, hold your breath, cross your arms over your chest, and you'll pass out for a second," she said.

"You can't pass out from that," I assured her.

A series of deep breaths, I held my breath, and boom, I was on the ground with no memory.

"I'm sorry, I forgot to catch you," she said. My friend Jay was just laughing. He's dead now and I miss him.

Weeks later we three were in the backyard again. I was at my best friend's house a lot and she was the skinny little, cute blond, raised-through-white-trash girl that had perfect pointy tits that beat everyone else out in terms of their raised mound structure.

"Have you ever played the nickel game?" she asked through the confidence of being a freshman over an eighth grader.

"No, what's that?" I wondered.

"You throw a nickel on a person and then, wherever it lands, you have to go get it," Chelsea said.

"That's not how you play it," my friend Jay said, even though he had never heard of the game, he was quick to improve it. "Where ever it lands, you have to get it with your mouth."

I remember the warm sensation of positive blood flow.

"I'll go get a nickel," I offered and ran into the house. My friend's dad was sitting on the floor in his usual torpor, with his back resting on the couch, smoking and watching HBO. They could barely afford anything outside of hotdogs for dinner, but two packs of cowboy killers and HBO always found funding.

He didn't have a nickel, nor did he care what we were doing. We made it to middle school, and almost to high school, so his job was more or less done.

There was old Taco Bell on the coffee table. I quickly grabbed a "mild sauce" packet.

"Best I could find," I said as I showed Chelsea and my friend the orange package once used as a dumb joke, placing them under car tires in the parking lot.

"You couldn't find a nickel, or a quarter, or a penny? You're dumb," my friend Jay said.

"This will work," I said.

"Ya, that will work," she said.

She was on board. Possibilities.

The first couple of attempts were failures. It was wet-sucker-sticky hot in the pre-evening middle Oregon summer, so everyone was in the square pattern style of the early '90s, with full denim jean shorts and baggy t-shirts.

My friend started things off, wasting no time or trying to "pussy-foot" into the game, as he instantly got close and threw the container down the small V-neck gap in her shirt. Chelsea half screamed in excitement and fear, and just as my friend was going for a hand lunge into and beyond the bra, she smartly untucked, and the salsa fell to the ground.

He still tried to get one-on-one with the breast support system, but she denied him.

"Rules are rules. It's on the ground, so you have to get it with your mouth," she said.

My friend bent down, acted like he was going to bite it, and at the last second, used his hand.

"My turn," I suggested. I didn't have the confidence of Jay, but I definitely had the young insatiable quest and desire to explore the female body. I was very attracted to girls, and it is just that simple for the gay community.

How to beat the system was the question. If I tried the shirt trick I'd be licking the ground.

"Let's sit down and play round two though," I suggested.

She bit. The packet went down and stayed down. I moved in, she backed out.

"This game is stupid, I'm not playing anymore," she said. So close. But just the idea and attempts made it worth it.

I'm getting off track. Anyway, during that summer, if I said something dumb, or if I made fun of her, she would kick me in the shins, and one time, while in this magical backyard of young teen exploration, she spit in my eye, so I pulled her hair so hard that tears tsunami-filled her face. Again, I have a vivid memory of feeling really bad for her, and I felt that I wanted to take care of her, to comfort her and love her. The opportunity finally presented itself on a blanket-warm summer night while I was sleeping over at my friend Jay's house.

A face appeared through the living room window. It was her; she was motioning me outside. My buddy and I proceeded out back, past the cloud of smoke made by the lazy, fired, ex-probation-officer dad, and Chelsea and her pal were outside. It was close to 11 o'clock, and her classmate leaned over and whispered to me, "Chelsea wants to make out with you."

Her friend wanted to make out with my companion, but my cohort Jay wanted nothing to do with the bigger less attractive under-developed neighbor.

We went behind an old boat that hadn't moved from the backyard since they lived there, and she wasted no time moving into my mouth. Her tongue was on coke, thrashing around the inside of my gums at full speed, doing circles around my lapper with hers, tapping the top of the inner jaw. She was completely

out of French-kissing control and I was about to call it quits,
when I remembered her boobs. I slowly started to untuck her
Guess short-sleeved, and after two or three seconds of no
resistance, my hand was on the stomach and found the belly
button. Nowhere to go but up from here. I was a bit too quick
and smashed into her left bra and breast causing her to break
the trapeze tricks in my mouth for a split second. The whole
over-bra under-bra take-it-off, move it, undo it from the back, I
didn't have a clue even with the Dairy-Mart-rub-fest a year
earlier. The pressure was too much, it was dark, so I just rubbed
her left breast with my hand over the basic, skin-colored (if
you're a WASP; I think Band Aids are racist, too) bra. Perky. Nice.
Why can't I get my tongue into hers, she's like a cavity hog?

"I suppose every situation is different, but it always
comes off bad talking about hitting a woman," Pike told Finn.

"I'd hit your mom, if you know what I mean?" Finn said.

"A 'your momma' joke, that's awesome, I was just
reminiscing about the '90s," Pike said.

"What are you covering this week?" Finn asked.

"A teacher just retired, they hired a new
superintendent, and I guess they are going to build a bridge so
we don't have to wait for those goddamn trains every five
minutes downtown."

"They won't pass that, they've tried to for like 15 years,
but there is one powerful South American family in town that
keeps it from happening. They live right where all the changes
would be made," Finn said.

"Nothing like screwing over a whole town for your own
personal betterment," Pike replied. "But it's going on the ballot.
The Pennsylvania Department of Transportation is covering
the cost."

"Guarantee it won't happen."

The following day Pike was heading to the Rover Middle
School building to interview a teacher that was retiring.
Several months in, Pike was dressed for success with the new
shirts, Good Will dress pants, and confidence from having a

time under his belt and business cards for validation. Footwear was an issue, as he only owned one pair of black dress shoes, so when it was a brown and khaki day, he thought no one would notice. In less than a month, while in New York City, Pike would learn matching shoes and belts were no longer a style "must do."

She looks like a school teacher—bun hair, glasses dangling from the neck, moderately thin, a warm smile and a general look of both optimism and defeat.

They covered her whole teaching life story.

"Oh, the years," she went on, "almost every time I go out in the community, a kid that's all grown up tells me thanks. Thanks a lot."

When Pike left, Mrs. Bess forgot to say 'bye, but just stared at a spot on the wall where a poster once hung for over four decades.

The end of June was nearing and the start of the summer festivals and fairs in northern Pennsylvania were beginning.

"Pike, I need you to cover the Penn Irish Games at the Tuscarron County fairgrounds in Winherst this weekend," Theresa told Pike a week after he had interviewed the teacher.

"What's the Penn Irish Games?" Pike asked.

"It's really neat. You can go back to last year's paper in the archives and see what it's all about. People dressed in kilts and Irish garb, bagpipes and drinking."

After work and lounging in Joan's apartment, after a re-heated cream sauce spaghetti dinner, this news broke:

"I was at my dad's today and saw an ad in the paper," Joan said.

"What ad?" Pike asked.

"It was in the Penkal paper, they're looking for a reporter," she said.

"Realllllllyyyyyy, looking for a reporter, eh?" Pike said.

"Might be something neat, closer to home anyway. I know you said that you'd never write for—"

"Don't worry about all that. It's a solid "daily." You see, I gotta keep climbing. I work for a nice publication and all, but if I put in for the Penkal job, it will save me like 35 to 40 minutes each way, plus I could negotiate for more pay, or that's what they say anyway," Pike said.

"Then you should do it." Joan encouraged without an ulterior motive. She enjoyed Pike's company, but he was not her preferred race for the mating ritual.

"Yes, maybe I should," Pike said.

Pike left dinner rather quickly after that and drove six minutes to buy a $12 bottle of pinot noir to celebrate the possibility of a new job and betterment.

Consumption passed and Pike sat in his back closet smoke room with the doors drawn and daydreamt about sending an email to his friends about his progression, next-level achievement and assured himself that he had the job, in between inhaling.

At the end of the week, before Theresa left the office on Friday, she reminded Pike of the Irish Games the next day.

"So you're good to cover the games tomorrow, right?" she wanted assurance.

"Yep, I'm ready. Should be fun, my first real event." Pike said.

"And you said when you started you have to go to two weddings, is that correct, in July and September?"

"Yes, that's right, First weekend in July and last in September. Going to New York in July and Santa Fe in September," Pike said.

But don't you worry about that, I won't be working for this lame paper anymore. Sure, you took a chance on me and I probably should repay you with more than three months of work. But this paper's style is too small town. I need to evolve, get famous, so I can lay around all day and get high and bet on sports and have sex and raise kids and occasionally think about my financial future. Occasionally.

"Cover the games and I'll talk to you on Monday," was Theresa's Friday parting.

Like usual, it was just Finn and Pike left in the south corner of the office, with the sports guys wrapping up the day in the north end, both counting the minutes until it was clear for everyone to leave early as well.

"Didn't you say you had a wedding out west earlier in the year?" Finn asked, piggybacking on Theresa and Pike's conversation from minutes earlier. It wasn't eavesdropping, but more distracting, as in that forced proximity, every conversational swallow in between breaths echoes.

"I went to my old college roommates wedding in San Diego back in January. It was fun but also a huge stress fest 'cus I was best man and felt this obligation to be perfect and do all this shit all the time," Pike said.

"I've been to San Diego tons of times, my sister lives out there," Finn responded.

"Oh, what part?"

"She lives in El Cajon, you know where that is?" Finn asked.

"What, is your sister Mexican? I think that's a Mexican-dominated area."

"Ha-ha, no, she's as English looking as me," Finn said.

"You don't look English, dude, you look like the failed master race experiment, all tall and blond but with weird facial features pointing to the miscalculations of the scientists," Pike said.

"Your mom," Finn said.

"Well I'm glad you were able to fit your weekly 'your mom' joke in, I mean, you almost ran out of time, it's Friday, brah."

"Friday night, do you think your mom wants to go out to dinner?" Finn asked followed by a grin.

15.

"On the eve of the Civil War the County was no longer the wilderness into which the Colonel had come full of impractical hopes. The forests had vanished and the Town sat surrounded by fertile, cultivated fields. Some of the Colonel's democratic hopes were already withered or dead, but the Town still had none of the ugliness nor the corruption of a city." L. Bromfield, *TF*.

San Diego Wedding Flashback, five months earlier:

Pike was still working at the furniture store and had saved about $400 (after airfare) for a Thursday to Sunday trip out west.

I drove two hours south to a buddy's house in Pittsburgh, arriving around 10 p.m., Wednesday night.

Pike's friend, Randy, was also excited about the trip and as soon as he got home from the electrician jobsite, he started drinking. Randy's love of food equaled that of drink, and the buzz was slightly slowed from cheese enchiladas. Pike and Randy had similar family structures (nonexistent: single with no kids) that contributed to their sustained success as friends, some 6 years after they worked together when Pike first moved to Pennsylvania and took a temp job doing manual labor with Randy north of Pittsburg. Randy had gotten settled down with his profession at a young age and become more responsible (during daylight hours anyway) than Pike, working a solid and consistent construction job. And Pike always envied and wanted that stability.

Steady good paying job, own a house, get a girl someday, then everything is taken care of. No desires or wants except the road. And we are about to hit that pavement once again.

Randy's house was on the north end of the University of Pittsburgh's urban campus. Randy never attended the college, but that's where all his younger friends and the scene and the music and the party around the Pittsburgh area went after high school. The U of Pitt was the state school of choice for most graduates that had no concern in terms of what major or field of study they wished to pursue.

Just last year, after a decade in that area, he bought a house in a rather tranquil but definitely not suburban area of Pittsburgh, and kept the love life tank full.

When Pike went through the back door (it was still very nice to go to a place and feel no obligation to knock, it really speaks to being welcome, Pike thought), he was still in prepare to travel mode—up tight, half-serious, no patience, efficiency-only mentality. The five-beer head start of Randy and his excitement for not only seeing his friend but for another indication that job and routine were to be, not so much forgotten, but slid aside so debauchery and hedonism could reign.

"Bubber bubber bubber!" Randy yelled and went for the high-five-hug-punch hello.

"Whoa, guy, take it easy," Pike responded without smiling.

"Bubber, so nice to see you, you ready, you want a beer? Let's get it going!" Randy encouraged.

"Just relax a second, bud. You already drunk? Great." Pike said sounding un-relaxed.

"Oh, boy. George! Hey, George, Pike's in dick mode already, I'm not going with him, I can't go to your wedding, sorry," Randy yelled from the back door kitchen area through the living room.

"Oh, boy. This is great, I'm finally in a good mood and everyone around me is acting like an baby," Randy said.

"Buddy, I'm sorry. Just drove down here, and need to relax a bit, my fault," Pike said.

"Go out to the garage and take your medicine you stupid doper."

"That sounds like a plan, I just might do that. Beers out in the garage fridge?"

"Yes, bubber, they are. I got a case of Yuengling, we need to have 'em all down the old gullet before we get on that plane," Randy said.

"Dude, like I would ever get on a plane with drunk Randy. Did you forget Las Vegas?" Pike rhetorically asked.

Two and a half years earlier, Randy and Pike's brother were not allowed to board a Southwest airlines flight due to their high intoxication levels. While waiting for the plane to board, Randy and brother tried to sit on the lap of two girls in jest while waiting at the terminal. The only problem was that they were too drunk to realize that those two girls were not in the mood for the insulting behavior. So a Southwest employee was called over to investigate and Pike pulled Randy away from the waiting area in hopes of dissolving the situation, but a lady from the counter bird-dogged them and watched as Randy tried to high five strangers as he strolled through the terminal. The lady finally reached Pike and Randy.

"Excuse me, hi, can I see your boarding pass, please?" she asked of Pike.

Pike knew better, and even though he had some drinks, was far from the drunken state of Randy and his brother.

"Thank you, but I know where I'm going, thanks," Pike tried to sly his way out.

"Can I see your boarding pass, please?" she persisted, not actually knowing the particular flight they were on.

"I don't understand, why do you want to see our boarding passes?" Pike asked.

"Because you and your friend are too drunk for travel."

"Too drunk? I'm not drunk at all. You've seen a drunk person in your life before, right? My speech is fine, and I'm walking fine," Pike said.

"Well, two girls just came up to my counter and said that you and your friend tried to sit on their laps," she said.

"I didn't do that. And you can't say I did because it would be an impossibility that you saw me do that, because I didn't do that. I actually walked over after they were already talking to you." Pike said.

"Someone is not flying, and if not you, then your friend, who does seem pretty drunk and has been high-fiving people, I was behind you watching," she said.

"I know you were behind us, I saw you leave the counter," Pike said.

There was real fear in Pike now. It wasn't anything deep, like the fear of failure instilled by his perfectionist teachers, or the way that the court and police system had beat so much disobeying will out of him from countless community service hours picking up cigarette butts and cleaning out cop cars. No, it was simply about work. He had used up too many sick days and call-offs, if he didn't show Monday, he was gone. And not that Pike believed the job to be the greatest, but he hated looking for a job more than anything else.

"I'm fine to fly," Pike almost begged.

"What about your friend?" she asked. Pike turned to Randy, waiting for him to defend himself, but there's no way of knowing if he even knew what they were talking about. Pike froze up, acting like a coward who was willing to sacrifice his friend for a timecard.

"Let me see your boarding pass," she instructed Randy.

"OK, lady," he said, jibing. Pike again said nothing. It was quite deplorable for Pike, and he watched his friend pull out bar receipts and credit card customer copies showing non-stop ingestion, until he finally located his boarding pass.

"Here," Randy said as he gave her a piece of paper.

"That's not your boarding pass," she responded with more conviction and power.

Randy still was unaware of what it would mean when he finally handed the pass over. Eventually, there was an exchange of power and tickets. The group went back to the counter, where Pike's lone brother was engaged in a similar "I'm not too drunk to fly" argument with someone that had already made up their minds. Even though the airline was not libel, the brother proceeded to tell the Southwest employees that he and Pike had flown internationally on mushrooms and that alcohol was no big deal, as Pike backed away with pace. And those comments, mixed with the state of Randy, and the ticket agents were already printing out tickets for tomorrow.

"There is a flight to Pittsburgh at 8:10 tomorrow morning, that's the best we can do for you boys."

Pike joined the pack that was heading into the plane.

And as for Randy and the brother, they stormed back into Vegas, couldn't afford a room, snorted Styrofoam they thought was coke to stay up all night, and Randy ended up puking in the cab on the return ride to the airport at 6 a.m.

They were out of money, and when the alcohol began to withdraw with every foot of elevation climbed, the real leaving of their trip began.

"No, bubber, I haven't forgotten Las Vegas. Best and worst trip I've ever taken," Randy said.

"That's why I refuse to fly Southwest to this day, no matter how cheap the travel is," Pike said.

"That plane ride home was so bad, especially with the hangover coming on and we were too broke to buy the expensive drinks. It was like Shakes on a Plane."

"Hahah, that's good, bud, now let's see what all that garage talk is about," Pike said, needing to address his desires.

Hours later Randy was passed out and Pike couldn't get to sleep. Not enough beers to really forget. Also, too excited, and a short couch so he couldn't fully extended his over six-foot-frame. Just a mental decision to fight sleep.

He checked his phone every 45 minutes to make sure they wouldn't miss their 6:45 a.m. flight. They didn't. But Pike got super high before the cab "departures" drop-off the next morning, and even though the boarding passes had been printed off and there were no bags to check, Pike envisioned getting stopped and harassed by security, and thus, being late and ruining the wedding.

The captain turned off the "pointless" seatbelt light (the illusion of safety, Tyler Durden says) and both Pike and Randy could hear the beverage cart rolling closer.

"What you think, bubber, get some liquor going, maybe a Bloody Mary?" Randy was thinking out loud.

"Not sure if they have Bloody Marys, buddy. And I don't want to start with liquor. Or really beer. Why do you want to start drinking this early?"

"Bubber, we're stuck on a plane, we're on vacation without our jobs, so ya, I'm going to have a flippin' drink. You do whatever you want," Randy said.

"Relax guy, OK? I'll get a drink."

"I don't really care what you do, bubber, just stop crying."

"I guess I could afford to pay the avarice-driven beer price since fantasy football paid for my flight."

"You play that dumb shit? I don't even know what it is but I know it's stupid."

"My first year was last year, bunch of old weed heads from The Rock started a league, so I joined. And won. I totally got lucky 'cus it was a return yards league and no one realized it except me at first. And when the check got mailed to me, the league commissioner said, 'Here's 350 bucks, hope it changes your life.' He was being sarcastic, but it got me here."

Seven hours of total travel time and seven dollars a beer, they were both drunk when the plane was making its approach into San Diego.

"Damn, I can't believe this bar bill, and I'm paying with a credit card that has usurious rates," Pike said.

"Airplane bars suck," Randy said.

"Used to be free."

"What used to be free?"

"Drinks. Beers 'n' shite."

"When were there ever free drinks on planes, bubber?" Randy asked.

"International flights used to have free drinks—"

"International flights maybe, but not—"

"No, not maybe, for real. You never heard about me and Yogos soaring to Belgium and getting all smashed on the flight across the pond?" Pike was distrait and asked not realizing that both of their voices had continued to increase in volume. Most of the passengers had boarded in Dallas/Ft. Worth around 9:47 a.m., and were indifferent yet curious about the early morning drunkards.

"Maybe you told me about it, I dunno," Randy tried to remember, but not really.

"When we were moving to Belgium, drinking Scotch on the rocks the whole way."

"I thought you hated Scotch?" Randy wondered.

"Yes, I kinda do anymore, but that's just 'cus Daniel got me hooked on bourbon, and then I couldn't go back. Anyway, so we're all wasted on the plane, and the stewardess was like, 'That's probably enough drinks for your two.' So Yogos had this great idea. He had long hair at the time, so he took off his sweatshirt, tucked his hair up under his hat, and walked back to the rear of the plane to ask for more drinks. The muscular male flight attendant said, "You and you're friend are really drunk, here's the last two bottles, don't come back here again."

He didn't fool anyone be we got further saturated. And we smoked smokes back then, so the plane lands on the runway, eventually stops, and we walk down the steps." Pike said.

"Down what steps?" Randy asked.

"At the airport in Brussels in '02, I don't know if all of the planes did this, but we walked down steps and right on to the runway. So we instantly light up our smokes. And seconds later we hear, "No smoking!" Some bag handler guy was yelling at us for our transgression—inhaling on the runway. Whatever."

"Haha."

"And what was so odd or whatever, was that once you got inside the terminal, you were allowed to smoke. For real, at baggage claim, people were smoking next to pregnant ladies and kids being put in strollers," Pike said.

"Man, you think we're going to make it tonight?" Randy asked.

"Sure buddy, big bachelor party tonight, better get ready," Pike advised.

16.

"Nietzsche was the last of the great philosophers to attempt a tragic justification of life. His central and famous dogma—'Life is good *because* it is painful.'" J.W. Krutch, *TMT*.

The groom George and his brother Lou picked up Randy and Pike at the San Diego airport. The tourists, as soon as they exited the free-standing glass-enclosed rat-race air of the arrivals area, were renewed with the scent of the saltwater sea. Total brightness even in cloud cover. They noticed the influx of brown and tan girls wearing furry faux boots and four-inch shorts. No, the fur wasn't fake—it was the girls getting off the plane with magazine picture assimilation as their style process.

After hugs and luggage were thrown into a '12 Chevy four-door, Pike wasted no time.

"My good friends, it is sooooo good to see you. Big bachelor party tonight. But we will need supplies, where can we get some weed?"

"I knew you would ask that first thing," George said.

"Bud, we're on vacation, trying to get a little goated, what's wrong with that?" was Pike's defensive reply.

"Hue will have some for you, I already set it up," George said.

"My honkey!" Pike was relieved.

From the airport, going the back way down Harbor Drive, the foursome arrived in the seaside community of Ocean Beach within 12 minutes.

George was a biologist, and was the only human in his group that landed a good job out of college, stuck with it, and owned a condo with his soon-to-be-as-long-as-the-bachelor-party-doesn't-ruin-the-wedding bride. The black eye almost did.

Two bedroom, two bath condo, five blocks from the Pacific Ocean, with back stoop ocean-gander-ability and a front ledge serenaded by the moon's furious pull of the waves sounding on the shore. "Let me go, Earth!" one can hear the moon often cry.

The bride was gone with her sisters and mother, and the four boys poured some screwdrivers and leaned against the wall on the back stoop.

"So you going to call Hue, could use a smoke, brah?" Pike persistently asked in his best "So Cal Lo-Cal" voice.

"I already called him," George said.

Hue showed up. They got smoked up. Except George, who didn't prefer the high.

The drinks continued until around 3 p.m., with extra hot sauce burritos from a food truck in between. The dimming-day crew was groom George and his younger brother Lou, Randy and Pike, and a local "O-beachian" mad scientist Rohan, who volunteered to get yet another friend, T, from the airport that was due to arrive.

Lots of named humans to be in OB for the nuptials.

"Hey, I'll go get T from the airport, but I need a couple of bucks for gas," Rohan said. Everyone threw in, and Rohan ended up with 10 bucks for a first-four-songs-of-Use-Your-Illusions-II ride. Randy volunteered to tag along. Pike was in no shape to move. He was 3 a.m. drunk at 3 p.m. It was pounding water and food for the next two hours if Pike was going to make the bachelor party of which he was in charge.

When Randy and Rohan returned from the airport with T, Randy pulled Pike aside.

"What's up with your boy Rohan?"

"Rohan is awesome, ex-Marine man, met him through George when he moved down here from Oregon—wastoid, infected, genius—our kind of human," Pike replied.

"That's fine, but after T got in the car, he asked him for a couple of bucks for picking him up," Randy said glad to divest himself from Rohan.

"What a scumbag, dude, what'd you say?"

"I didn't say anything, they're your friends," Randy said, alluding to meeting George through Pike five years ago.

"Whatever, dude, they're your friends, too. What a dick. George said he's lost it anyway. Just gets drunk all the time, big decline from when I used to know and hang out with him. But that was the path I was on in Oregon. If it wasn't for the whole sobering pregnancy turned miscarriage that lead me across the country away from my drunk friends thing, I'd still be in the same place," Pike said.

"Right, 'cus you're not drunk now," Randy said.

"Shut up."

Three NBA quarters later, everyone left George with instruction to wait for his bachelor party to begin. All the pre-planning emails had been done without George's knowledge in order to maximize the wow factor of the event.

The biggest quandary for Pike in the early stages was deciding what exactly to do. He tried to rent a replica pirate ship, but it was way too expensive. He thought about a trip to Tijuana but feared and knew that half of the wedding party wouldn't make it back across the border. Eventually, Pike decided on a two-part bachelor party event. First, they would do a "Top Gun" bar hop around San Diego.

The '80s Tom Cruise pop classic movie was filmed in San Diego and many of the bars and locales were easily accessible by train. Ideally, the group, that ended up being 17 humans strong, would go from site to site, blasting "Danger Zone" in every jukebox, until they were good and sauced and ready for stage two.

The second step was speed dating. Pike had signed George up for a speed dating event at a restaurant around the Little Italy port area. Friends had added to and improved upon the plan as well.

Here is an email from groom George's friend, Three, months before during the planning process:

"Before we do the bar hop, we should send George a wrestle-gram. We all put on luchador masks, and when he answers the door, we storm in, wrestle him, and kidnap him to the bars."

Groom George was back at his condo, and the friends he had worked to acquire showed up to the designated corner by his house. Pike had pre-ordered luchador masks and had them delivered to Rohan's place. The box was carved opened, and the colorful Mexican wrestling masks were passed out. A thick-upper-armed firefighter did not require one; he owned his own.

"Let's call two cabs, go in and kidnap him and get it all started," Pike advised.

But there was dissention in the air and ranks.

No one wants to follow any one plan, but continually complicate the situation with extra ideas.

"I say we take a bus." "Let's just go to bars around here." "Cabs are too expensive." "Let's just do the cab thing but start at Old Town instead of that Top Gun thing."

The cabs were ordered while George, who was supposed to be waiting in his house, took the dog for a walk with his fiancé. The wrestle-gram had to continue as four or five of his "friends" descended on him instantly. The dog tacitly approved and hid behind her master, as they punched and pulled and carried George back to the meeting point. The transportation had failed to arrive on time. With every second of waiting, the mutiny grew.

"Let's just take a bus." "These cab drivers are pricks anyway." It continued until there was an actual break in the group, as half of the luchadors started walking toward the bus stop. Pike finally relinquished control, realizing it was George's night, and everyone else's as well.

The posse, totaling 14 (3 members would be coming later from Los Angeles), arrived at the stop where still more were waiting. There was a watering hole next door. The luchadors lurched in. Pike was very concerned with getting on the bus. Lot of planning went into this night, and even if a good time was to be had at a local drink spot, Pike believed George deserved a night out of his town, even if it was in his city. The bus arrived. Pike was about to scream when the mass of masks dropped their drinks and ran toward the machine.

The driver was not particularly happy to see that swarm of invidious no-face faces charging towards him, but on they entered and rode. The masks never came up, and in the minutes to Old Town, confused passengers boarded and left. Randy fell asleep/passed out. Pike had stopped drinking around 3 p.m. and was still drunk.

Off at Old Town San Diego, the historical little village that attempted to re-create and capture the days of the 1800s and before. Top Gun had been abandoned for dinner and tequila at a Mexican restaurant within the replicated area. Again, even though dinner and drinking and smoking were harder, the masks stayed down and the prating and stares up.

After dinner, the itinerant humans hopped on the trolley towards Little Italy to get closer to speed dating and the hotel. Pike had reserved three rooms. Two for sleeping, one for entertainment.

There was a seedy place in Little Italy that had a spacious backroom that looked to be able to handle various impacts, and that's where the contingent hung out. It was devil-dim, without good music or bar games, but the company was feeling wild, and each human wanted to show their worth and jokes to the group. Eventually the establishment sent a separate bartender back to accommodate everyone's needs. Shots. Yelling. Consuming excess. Eventually it became obvious that speed dating was never going to happen.

The dinner of chimichangas and extra salsa couldn't slow the flood of poison into everyone's throat. A blurry mass wanted to buy George extra shots so that he would be well on his way to walking the line of alcohol poisoning.

The last three arrived: Yogos, Tar and old Kat from LA. Many wives and girlfriends were upset that only one female was allowed to attend. It was Pike's exception. She was an endurance friend of George's, a tom-boy from adolescence, and she knew none of the bride's friends and didn't really want to go to the bachelorette party. Pike would learn later that she in fact did go to the bachelorette party. And as randomness rewards, played a negative role in corrupting his entertainment.

Oh, yes, the entertainment. Pike sent out this email in the months prior to the bachelor party list of humans:

"Gentle jerks, couple of things regarding a show for George's bachelor party. There is going to be a female. But it needs to be special and original.

"Listen, I don't want to hear a bunch of feminist this, or my girlfriend that; it's a right of passage. The last time you can ever be around another girl in that aspect. I don't really believe that, but I'm trying to sell here. I understand married men go to strip clubs, I don't. I understand you can't cheat on your wife just 'cus it's a bachelor party. I don't want to go to a strip club, but rather, I say we get a joke-themed stripper to come to us. Like she's dressed up like a werewolf or something funny. It must be funny. Sure, tits and all that too, but I want it to be a joke, not a serious thing where we all sit in a small hotel room in silence like a bunch of fucking creeps while she steals all our money."

Within the bachelor party group, there was a notorious strip-club-frequenter and resident pervert named Ian. He responded with this email:

"Yes, we need strippers for sure. I can handle it, no problem. Get us a good deal and everything. And not some skanks, but really nice and pretty girls."

Pike's response:

"But it must be a joke. There has to be a werewolf or other costume involved. Can't just have a normal boring stripper event. That would kill the whole idea."

His response:

"No problem, jokes. I got it. I'll take care of it all."

The group was set to meet the werewolf at 11 p.m. at their hotel in Little Italy. Pike wanted to confirm one last time, as it was 9:30 p.m., that everything was set.

"Ian, so everything good with the werewolf?" Pike asked.

"What the hell you talking about?" Ian asked confused.

"The fucking werewolf stripper, you got it under control?" Pike asked annoyed.

"The stripper is good to go. But wait, you weren't serious about that whole werewolf Halloween shit were you? This girl is classy dude, she wouldn't go for any of that nonsense," Ian said, feeling that he had untenable points.

Pike wanted to dot the bone under Ian's eye with his supreme middle knuckle. But like everything else, it was futile; the plan had faded and he had to do what he hated most, relinquish control, again.

And then the countdown began, every quarter of an hour, from 9:30 p.m. on, someone would come up to Pike with an evil and happy grin and say, "Almost 11 o'clock, dude, and you know what that means."

Pike's temperament was changing towards the pouty and grumpy. He'd tried to start drinking again, but that was a hard buzz to re-achieve. Everyone else was having a splendid debauchery-based time, except maybe Randy, who was in the same boat, sitting in a chair quietly and by choice not conversing.

"Dude, it's like after 10, dude, might be time to start heading towards the hotel," Three offered, excited.

"I think we still got some time," Pike said.

"Gonna be awesome, werewolf stripper dude, gonna be hilarious."

"Well, according to dumb Ian, the stripper is too classy to wear a werewolf outfit."

"What, dude, that was the whole point!"

"I know, never should have let Ian take over the operation. But at the same time, I didn't want to do it, that way I could be dissolved of all wrongdoings by his future wife and my fake moral code."

A little past 10:30 p.m., the dam could no longer hold the semen river in everyone's pants, and the group again, in unison, got up and started walking towards the hotel. George was in the worst shape out of everyone. When you see a drinker stumbling, you know he's good and drunk.

Everyone piled into one location with a queen-sized bed. This was not the show room. They needed to get that ready. Ian was in charge of that, of course. He went down to the lobby after the place was prepped and met his "classy chick." Then they returned to the second floor and he texted Pike that it was time to bring everyone over to the "amazement facility."

Although the hostel-ish hotel room from which they all came was exactly the same in design as the one they were about to enter, no one would have known. Ian did do some thorough "mood setting" work in terms of leaning the bed against the gasoline yellow walls, lowering the lights, lighting candles, spraying some kind of perfume/incense—just as he envisioned and wanted. Everyone filed and filled in and lined the walls of the 70-buck-a-night-rate-for-one-person chamber. There stood a lone chair at the far end of the small area, and she was beside it.

And she is in charge. You have to be at one of these events. The only way to control a drunken lot is through the threat of missing out.

"Gentlemen, I'm Jersey, who's ready for a bachelor party!?"

The response was weak.

"Come on, that was such a pussy response. I said, who's ready for a bachelor party!?"

Huge yells, whistles and claps followed.

"Now, that's more like it. Couple of ground rules so that this doesn't end before it's supposed to, 'cus I want as much time with you men as possible, and I don't want it to end early," Jersey said with a fake sad face.

"Rule one, touch only if I say to touch. But for the right price, you can touch anywhere. Rule two, no crying like little bitches (Disorganized yells from the group). Rule three, don't be cheap. It's your friend's bachelor party and you have to show him the night of his life; it's his last night as a single man!"

More sound waves lurching out of their vocal holding pattern. Jersey went to hit play on her little portable soft silver CD player that served as her talisman, and she noticed Kat. The two females locked eyes. Jersey didn't care; she'd been involved with freaky couples events before, but this was slightly different. There was no joy or giddy immature anticipation in the formation of Kat's face. It was a look of disrespect and disappointment for what Kat believed the stripper was doing to the female gender. And that mood and infectious behavior soon ruined the whole event for Pike, and the other two guys that were sitting on either side of Kat. Certain realizations had begun to seep in through osmosis.

"Bring the bachelor up here," Jersey commanded.

George stumbled up to the seat, with a big grin on his face as if he was looking at a new fire truck at Christmas. Not sure if he had even noticed the stripper, but his stomach noticed gravity when it was forced to thrash-throw the massive volume of liquid from one side of the bulging lining to the other.

The house music of a techno blend was clicked into max volume, adding Cobain-like distortion and making talking and jokes very hard. But the men could yell and smack their slick palms together in celebration at different points.

Jersey started with the slow strip focused on the bachelor himself. She was already close to the ceiling without the six-inch heels, so it was a relief for her to do some chair work.

First she removed a faded peach fishnet shirt that was covering the hot-pink bra.

Easily C to D cups, but implants. The huge gap between the tits is the gross surgical giveaway.

Jersey straddled George, smashed the bra into his face, and his hands instinctively or wastoid-ingly went on her hips.

"Sit on your hands," she instructed him.

The strip was very basic. Straddle front, then turn around, straddle back with butt grinding on the crotch of the pants, then back to front, breasts into face, the rubbing of the head. Not that erotic or original, but George was close to blackout oblivion and there were plenty of encouraging shouts from the crowd.

She was down to just her mid-spine dyed blond hair, eyelash extensions, pink bra, matching fuchsia thong, habit-black high heels, and southern California tan.

"Now I need you guys to throw in some money for a little game we're going to play. It's called, can, sorry what's his name?" Jersey asked.

"Cocksucker." "Dickhead." "George." Were some of the ebullient responses.

"The game is, George has 20 seconds to remove my bra, with only his teeth. Come on guys, throw in 20 bucks for your friend," Jersey was selling hard.

Money magically moved itself instantly into the center of the hotel room, road-rash-worn floor.

At first, George tried to attack the back of the bra with his inebriated mouth muscles, but could not unlatch it. He had failed to accomplish the same task with his hands many times before throughout his life with little avail.

The men were full on screaming and counting, and at around the 12 second mark, he tried to just use brute force, attacking the straps and eventually with two seconds to go, buried his mouth in the cups and wonder of her plastic importance. He failed, but the game a success. George passed out moments later.

She was soon naked after 50 more bucks had been thrown in, and Pike and a few others were growing impatient with the hustle and the fact that they couldn't even fakely be interested with Kat so close. She would report back to the women, since she is one of them, they thought.

After a flat palm roll as Jersey was leading another business venture, the last thing Pike, Yogos and Tar heard before they cut out early to go smoke marijuana in the parking lot, was the upside down shot.

"Now, for a 100 bucks, someone can do a shot out of my vagina," Jersey said.

Pike rebooted to someone sleeping perpendicularly across his thighs in the bed. Instantly he knew he was going to be fine, hangover wise. It had been a long night of sobering up. He lifted his head and saw he was the outside part of a three-man sandwich, with a pickle sprawled across all of their legs.

The other mattress only had two people in it. Randy entered the room via key card.

"Get up! I've already been down to the port; it's awesome. What you gonna do, sleep all vacation? George is getting married, you might want to realize that," Randy said.

"Buddy, get this piece of shit off my legs," Pike requested.

"Why you guys sleeping like this? There was an unused bed next door," Randy said.

"I went to the parking lot, got goated, then after the capitalist stripper who was in fact, not a freakin' werewolf, left, I crashed out. Probably around midnight. Lame bachelor party," Pike said.

"Your boys kept getting one on one with that girl, going into the third hotel room for like an hour for like 500 bucks," Randy said.

Pike ushered the body off his legs and stood up. No great blood rush or stability check. He felt good. Well rested.

"It was more like five minutes for a hundred bucks," said a voice from the sandwich.

Luckily, as humans began to disperse and not make eye contact with each other out of shame, Randy and Pike were able to catch a ride with the posse from LA back to Ocean Beach to grab luggage, as the next two days were all wedding and all in La Jolla, a San Dieagan sub-city north of downtown.

The groom had taken a cab home earlier and met the group of five outside of his door.

"I put all your stuff in the garage, we were just about to leave," George said.

"Damn dude, your eye," Randy said.

There was a nice army-green-turning-black smear of periorbital hematoma under George's right eye.

"My soon to be wife isn't too happy about our effete and degenerate behavior," George said.

After Pike and Randy were long since passed-out, George's San Diego friends, a good handful being ex-military, sat him on the edge of the bed while another ran at him and smashed him into the various parts of the hotel. A black eye was getting off rather unscathed.

17.

"With mortals, gold outweighs a thousand arguments."
Euripides, *M.*

Up (the) I-5 to La Jolla, mission architecture, colors of
ocean reflection. A rich community with a fair share of artists,
surfers and venture capitalists.

The hotel was a five-story two-block-walk from the
beach, with a balcony overlooking the sea (as long as you
requested the correct room). The wedding party had the whole
fourth floor, and you could easily jet your head around the
railing and wall and see a row of soon to be loud and wasted
individuals. Men and women of the future had come from
Europe and some 20 states for the union of George.

Friday was a pretty usual and a normal rehearsal day.
Once everyone got checked and settled in, it was showers and
off to walk the block and a half to both the wedding reception
and coast, where the ceremony was to take place. Everyone
presented joy. Single women of the wedding party looked for
rings on fingers while single men stared at breasts. Who was
going to be paired up with whom?

Please don't let me get paired up with a mud duck. I
understand, it's George's day, but come on, I'm the best man, and
I should be paired up with the best woman, not so much in
loyalty or friendship to the bride, but in terms of beauty. I got
plenty of scars on my face, in my lower 30s, a slight beer drinking
gut, but still cute and I got the thing that girls love most, besides
money, humor. Let's see who I get.

The wedding party posse had assembled near a cliff
overlooking one of the seal-dominated beaches of La Jolla.
They were eight strong, not including mothers, fathers and the
bride and groom themselves. The wedding planner, who
gripped her clean and flowery binder Gollum-like to her chest,
began.

"Everyone, first, let's start with me. I'm Michelle, the
wedding planner. If you should need anything, and I mean,
anything, you need to call me. If Denise wants to change her
shoes last minute, you call me. If Denise wants a bottle of

champagne at three in the morning, you call me. If George wants to back out, you call me (She waited for the laugh line, but it didn't come.). Right now, take out your cell phones and put my number in it. We are already in crisis mode. Who is the best man?" Michelle asked.

"That would be me," Pike almost whispered, not vaunting, fearing a lecture.

"We have the best make-up artist in La Jolla coming down here shortly to see what we can do about George's eye. We'll see, but what exactly happened last night? You all were supposed to take care of him," Michelle said with frustration.

"He kept punching himself in the face, what could we do? Sure, maybe not give him so much mescaline, but he's a drug head, what can you do (There was laughter.)? No, but seriously, I'm sorry Denise, I don't know how that happened," Pike said to the bride.

Denise did not respond but smiled at the wedding planner to continue.

"So my number is 555-0767. Call me. You have no idea what I can do to save a wedding. Now, this is the venue IF IT DOESN'T RAIN! I know, it never rains in San Diego, unless there's a wedding going on at the beach. If it rains, we will have the ceremony at the reception site. Now are there any questions?" Michelle asked.

"Does anyone have a flask, I'm fighting a hangover?" said Tom, wedding party friend of the groom.

Ignoring the question, Michelle continued to instruct, "Now, we will be walking down these stairs to my right. Correction, the girls will be walking down the stairs, no wait, that's right, you both will be walking down the stairs, then down the aisle, and the boys will stand next to the groom, in the order that you come down, and the women will be standing next to Denise. Any questions? (Michelle didn't wait for another nonsense question.) First, it's Tom and Martha.

Who is that little lady? Well, not little, but tall and attractive. She has a big mouth, too. That's not a sexual thing, just a nice wide joker grin. And cute. Who is that? I swear I'm not a scumbag. It's just, who wants to walk down the isle with a

*swamp donkey? Makes everyone look bad. I don't buy into that
whole, "I'll look better 'cus my partner looks bad." No way, I'm
trying to go for super hotness, like David and Posh Spice. But not
too hot. I don't want some girl that guys have worshipped her
whole life and she's used to being spoiled and having guys be so
nice to her 'cus she's gorgeous and they think impossibly down
the road that they can bang her. 'Cus they won't. But she'd take
the attention all the same. And they hang on to her every word,
even though she is extremely un-read and devoid of deduction
concerning logic. But old joker face here, she might be the perfect
homogeneous blend of nice, cute, and most importantly, no
maintenance.*

"And finally, Pike and Alice and Victoria will be going
last," Michelle said.

"What? Listen, I'm not complaining and don't want to
interdict, just confirming, I get two girls?" Pike asked the
audience.

"Since Fred bailed at the last minute—" George began.

"Wait, Fred is seriously not coming, what a dick?" Tom
said.

"I told him that the spot in my wedding party was for
him, and no one else, so if he didn't come, then I wasn't going to
fill it," George explained.

A little back-story—when George moved to San Diego
after college at Florence Rock, he and Fred became really good
friends. And as a great coincidence, both the girlfriends of Fred
and George were also friends. So there were endless foursome
group hangouts and activities. Then Fred's girl cheated on him,
gave him an STD and eventually convinced most of their
mutual friends to turn on him. And she was still invited to the
wedding, so Fred said he wasn't showing up. Very messy and
an internecine situation.

"Either way, I'll take one for the team and walk with two
pretty ladies," Pike said with a wink, as he desired the
occurrence.

The rehearsal dinner was next, followed by bar hopping,
but the mode and mood was light and so was the drinking as
everyone prepared for wedding Saturday.

Then it came. The groomsmen all got ready in one hotel room with tie adjustments and tequila shots. It was announced around 11 a.m. that the wedding would be moved indoor, due to the chance of rain. The wedding was in two hours, slated for 1 p.m., but Tom refused to accept the change in venue.

"What's up, George? You want to do this indoor?"

"No, I don't, but I don't think we have much of a choice," George said.

"Bullshit, George, let's run down there and see how it looks. My phone says it's not going to rain, look at this lack of dumb-dar, err, I mean radar," Tom insisted.

"Well it's not just the rain, it rained last night, and the wedding planner said it's a sloppy mess down by the beach; you don't want people with a bunch of nice clothes getting all muddy," George said.

"Let's go check it out. We got like two hours, brahhhhh. Come on, it's two blocks away," Tom said.

The group agreed. The ground was not, in fact a muddy mess, but had dried out quite nicely once the sun burnt off the cloud cover surrounding the shoreline.

"Call that bitch, right now, George, and tell her you want your wedding down here at the ocean," Tom said.

"You can't call my future wife a bitch," George joked.

"Haha, seriously, wait, I got her number, I'm going to call her. (Phone came out, touch screen dialed, and the wedding planner Michelle answered.) Hi, this is George's wedding party, we think we should have the wedding down at the beach like the original plan. (Pause) No, this isn't George, he's right beside me. (Pause) Please do, thanks. (Phone was slid back into his front suit pocket.) She's coming down here to see for herself, but she doesn't think it's possible, everything has already been moved to the reception place. Dang. We'll see," Tom said.

"It's your wedding, dude," Tar said.

Michelle came down and was surprised how well the ground looked; it would only have a tangential bearing on the proceedings.

"Well, it actually isn't that soft. But look boys, it's 11:30, we have less than an hour before guests will start to arrive. The chair company has already moved it all and won't do it again. So unless you want to run chairs back and forth over two blocks for the next hour, it's not going to happen," Michelle said with a degree of insouciance.

Tom had already taken off his tux coat with effrontery and laid in on the retaining wall near the cliff edge, with his mind made up.

"George, where do you want your wedding? Where does Denise want her wedding?" Tom asked.

"Here," George said.

"Then we fucking do it here. Boys, let's go, we got some work to do," Tom said.

The male wedding party got to work and felt fresh. All except Pike. He cheated the night before and drank whiskey on the rocks at the bar. He was trying to make up for the bachelor party night where, even though he was inebriated throughout the day, he wasn't able to enjoy an inhibition-less night. He was fighting to maintain.

The chairs were stacked five high, placed on backs like a rich person's gear on a sherpa, and the groomsmen marched mindlessly, like the North Koreans on Dictator Day, until the job was completed. It was a cool afternoon, a light 72 degrees with perpetual ocean wind, but the boys were drenched in sweat by the end.

When they finally said 'I do,' seven shades of ocean matched the eight eyes of the wedding party, as they looked on in happy love devoid of doubt.

"Double rum, Bacardi if you have it, and coke please," Pike ordered from the bartender once the reception was underway. He was again trying to play catch up, as he sobered up sometime during the ceremony and was attempting the near impossible "drunk twice in one day game." Sure he could have kept it rolling, poured strong drink into the veins, but he had a best man speech, and the two-day drunkard is a gross sight.

Take Friday night, for example, at the rehearsal dinner. Tar had continued his buzz from the bachelor party and was good and brain-dead drunk as he was talking to wedding participants.

"Soooo, how do you know George?" Tar asked a man.

"I'm George's uncle, his dad's brother," the man replied.

"Sooo, are you on the groom's side or the brides?" Tar asked. The man thought Tar was joking at first, but then politely excused himself.

The best man speech had haunted Pike. He wanted to do a good job for the obvious reason of wanting to show a great friend that he was indeed, just that. But also, and quite possibly more of a tortuous driving point for Pike, was the humiliation factor.

What if my speech sucks and everyone is like, that's him, that's Pike, Logan? He isn't special. He isn't elite. What if I'm not? That's fine. But they can't know it. Will the con finally end? I have to have a great speech, I have to have a great speech.

Pike's self-motivational redundancy would have worked if his mission was sports related. But it wasn't. You actually needed to prepare something to say. Winging it might leave the crowd without laughs and friend without thanks.

The bartender did not want to honor Pike's request.

"We're actually not serving doubles this early sir," the bartender said.

"It's for the groom, I'm the best man. Hi, I'm Pike, but I'll go tell him that—"

"No, please, let me get that drink for you. Anything else?"

"That's it, thanks. Where's your tip jar?" Pike asked.

"We can't accept tips, it's already been included sir," he said.

"We'll work something out later," Pike said. But he didn't mean it. Pike always tried to tip the wedding bartender early so they would be cool and he could get good drinks all night. But really, it was an action done out of insecurity. Pike always feared that a wedding bartender would cut him off, embarrass him in front of everyone, so he always wanted to ensure that didn't happen.

Pike took the already cracked dirty-windshield-white cup that was never for George and approached the seat assignment table in the outside lobby area, housing names corresponding to tables. He couldn't find his so he walked through the hallway that opened up into a nice hardwood-floored hall.

Two girls, wives of Pike's friends from college, were smiling and laughing at him.

"Don't know where to sit, Pike?"

"Not sure, I know there's not a wedding party table, so I dunno," Pike said.

"You're at table 13, we took your card, hahahah," they said after their inchoate plan actually worked.

"Funny."

Every reception is different, even if you could argue they are all the same. What kind of table settings—types of flowers, in what vases, plates and matching napkins, seat covers, take home gifts, lighting, music, inside, outside, on a roller coaster.

Pike hardly moved from the seat at table 13, thinking about the speech. Making little notes, fast sipping his drink.

Stupid crushed ice. I hate eating and chewing ice, so I have to make a stupid dam with my lips to let a little drink seep through so my mouth isn't full of ice. OK, got the where'd we meet story, a funny story, a serious story, a story about Denise, raise my glass, and I'm through. Perfect.

Up first, oh, ya, she has two maids of honor. Her sister will be going first.

A hand calloused by construction slapped Pike's back.

"You ready, bubber? Big speech coming up," Randy said, somehow seemingly already drunk and the reception was only an hour old.

"I'm ready, guy," Pike said.

Another slap on the back.

"Big speech, is it going to be funny? I want to laugh, bubber. But I want to cry as well, so make it happen," Randy said.

Pike had scooted three feet back from the table and had his hands slicing through the sides of his hair, with his elbows on his knees. He did not respond to Randy's inquiries.

"Bubber, what are you going to talk about? Bubber, what's wrong, bubber?" Randy asked with tautology.

"Hey, bubber, go fuck yourself," Pike said.

"Wow, bubber, just trying to get you pumped up. Only you could be a dick at your best friend's wedding."

"Sorry man, I'm like really trying to focus here. I can't mess this speech up. And I'm the best man, that doesn't mean that—"

"I'll leave you alone, bubber, but try and not be a dick during your speech," Randy said.

The sister gave a true and from-her-heart-speech. The problem was the inability to control the emotions produced by talking about those real and true events. And so she cried. And Denise cried. And their mom cried. And soon no one had any idea what was said, but they knew it mattered and it was felt by everyone.

One down, not bad. Sure the bride loved it, that shouldn't be axiomatic, but my speech is more for the crowd. I know, sounds horrible, but if the audience is not entertained by the best man speech than the talk is a failure to the groom anyway. The hot joker mouth up next. She better not just be all, "Hey, I'm like cute and shit, George is a weirdo but Denise is fun and hot, cheers, everyone!" And everyone cries and laughs and frowns when my name is called next.

The speech of the second maid of honor was a very clean, comical, memory-emotional trip of joy bordering orgasm.

That Druid. I'm done for now. How many freakin' note cards does she have? You can't use a projector in a speech. No visual aids! I'm screwed. Stick to the plan. Why is everyone laughing, that story wasn't that funny? Of course, George is going to puke somewhere inconvenient and embarrassing and stupid.

Why don't you tell the time he was in love and got dumped and started crushing wood boxes in the middle of a downtown Florence Rock street on New Year's Eve? He told me, "She was the one." Tell that story. No? I'm not going up there, nope. Why can't I just go to a wedding and not have some obligation and job?

The indolent DJ, who hadn't quite mastered voice inflection, said, "Allll right, ladies and gentlemen, up next we have, Logan, errr, Pike, Logan, to give the best man speech. Let's make some noise for him..."

The after-wedding Sunday morning never begins with a hangover. Well, for continuous drinkers anyway. The human first realizes that they are in a hotel room, and then they instantly try to chase brain synapses back to how they got there. Pike did anyway. The immediate fear caused by years of guilt and "miscalculations" only revealed the next morning.

How'd I get to bed? How'd I pass out? How drunk did I get? What kind of bacchanalian nonsense transpired? Not that drunk. Couldn't do the two in one day. Couple more drinks at the reception, but that was it. Mostly just smoking weed outside of the reception hall. Man that Cali chronic. Snoop Dog/Lion really was right in those songs. But how the hell do you write a song that high? The wedding planner. She had an attitude the whole night after "chair-gate." You might actually have to do some work? Well, she was dealing with a lot of drunken inconsiderate jerks, but isn't that the wedding formula? It's like New Year's Eve, the normal casual drinker gets to, for one night, live like us, the bingers. It's the same at weddings. That's why cousin Joey or Uncle Marlow is saying inappropriate things to young girls and sister-in-laws he never cared for. It's tolerable, anything goes, it's New Year's, or your nieces once in a lifetime (even though she will actually get married four times) special nuptials. But for us, once a week, it's drink until pass out. But I kept it cool. Wedding planner was all, "You guys, you cannot smoke pot out front here. This is actually an affluent neighborhood and they will call the cops on you." I bet she wanted to hit it. No ring on her finger, a little dope might help loosen the clenched fist that existed

between her fibulas. But the make-up person she found really did
a great job, couldn't tell the sins painted by God under George's
eye. Remember that part in Kevin Costner's Robin Hood, yes I
know he was the only person that didn't have an English accent,
when a little girl asked the Moorish Morgan Freeman, "Did God
paint you?" to which Freeman replied with an understanding
grin, "Yes." Everything with intent.

Did a guy jump in a fountain last night? Yes. Was what's
her face and dude fighting all night, beside everyone else, making
it uncomfortable at the post-reception bar? Yes. And a proposal.
And confirmation about another wedding.

Daniel told me his July wedding in New York was
definitely on. Man, New York. Can I still endure the greatness of
that city, or will it crush me? And the proposal. T's girlfriend and
future wife, Margaret, proposed to him last night. Weird
scenario. Did he want to marry her? Did he just give in? She was
tired of waiting. Guess it's love or it isn't. T's brother, nicknamed
Saint, was skeptical, "I'm not calling mom yet and getting her
hopes up like you've done before. I'm going to wait and see."
Margaret was quick to reassure, "It's happening, I proposed and
he said yes. That's how it works, right?" "Well, that's kinda of
how it works," Saint said.

I'm supporting it. Let's do another wedding. Marry it up
boys. I wonder how many people really are in love or just want to
follow the current trend? Come on, no one is trending into a
marriage. Who the hell is yelling in the hallway?

Randy's voice could be heard through four hotel rooms
on the floor. Pike poked his head out of the door with a fake
frown and said, "Hey, guy, wanna shut up, there are nice
humans sleeping everywhere."

"Bubber, can't believe you woke up with something
negative to say. It's 10 fucking 30, check out is in like 20
minutes, so, time to get up little guy," Randy said.

"Checkout is at 10:50? I don't believe you."

"Whatever, keep sleeping. Me and Tall's wife already
been drinking all morning," Randy said loudly.

"Tall? You seriously don't know his name? And you
were drinking with his wife?"

"Tall was too busy cleaning up the room so the maid didn't have to do any work or something I guess, while we sat and watched the dumb ocean and looked over the balcony and down some gullies, if you know what I mean. I hate the ocean. Let's move here, I'm telling my future roommate wife that we're moving here."

The 10:30 a.m. realization sent Pike into efficiency mode, turning the emollient vacation switch off. He couldn't count on Randy for any kind of travel or logistical planning, and he didn't want to spend any more time in San Diego. Plane ride, home, routine, life, relax, safety and no expectations. That's the order and driving force for the flight.

The best Pike could arrange was a ride 25 minutes south back to Ocean Beach in the back of a small bed Ford pickup, lying over luggage with Randy sleeping. Rohan had called his girlfriend that he fought with all weekend for a ride back to Ocean Beach, where they shared an apartment.

Originally, T, Margaret, Rohan, Randy and Pike were going to split a cab, but Rohan tried to haggle the expensive price, and the cabbie dangerously accelerated away.

"You got any weed at your house, Rohan?" Pike asked after the ride was arranged.

"I got like half a joint that you can have if you buy me a drink down there," Rohan said.

"Deal. It's a long day of travel, especially with raging rhino drunk Randy," Pike said.

When they got to Rohan's small one bedroom apartment, Pike smoked what he believed to be a tenuous amount. There were still a couple of hours to kill before Randy and Pike needed to catch a cab to make their 3:10 p.m. flight home, against the time zone and with the jet stream.

They holed-up in a little hole in the wall bar, the Tilted Stick, and ordered Bloody Mary's and Cajun french fries. Pike didn't like the horseradish in his bloody and could barley finish it, with Randy, T and Margaret loving theirs.

"Dude, let's change our flight and go home tomorrow," Randy offered against red gums and tar-stained teeth.

"No way," Pike said.

"Dude, come on, we can stay at George's, change our flight for like only a hundred bucks or something, it will be awesome. No more of these three-day-trips bud, what's the point of getting a plane ticket, coming all this way, and only staying three days?" Randy asked.

"Four days. Four long days, guy. I hear what you're saying, really, but I'm ready to go home. What are you talking about staying at George's, dude? He just got married. After the wedding, no one is to see anyone ever again for like at least a month. And only a hundred bucks to change flights? Man, they lining electrical lines with gold these days? I always wondered, when plumbers are on one of your electrician job sites, and someone is bent over, do they just call it a crack?"

"Hahaha, that's funny. First joke you've made all day. And I have to travel with this grumpy jerk the rest of the time. What fun. Come on, we can stay at Rohan's," Randy said.

"You can do what you want, but I'm the fuck gone from this place."

A quiet terminal stay, quiet connecting flights. Everyone seemed to be fine with talking low and minding their business and completing the homeward jaunt that makes up most of Sunday air travel. Back home.

Back to the grind and intricacies of the sofa fold-out.

And back to the present.

18.

"Unhappy youth! Haste to your certain doom." J. Racine, *P.*

The Saturday of the Irish Games. Pike was excited. Friday night he finally sent his resume, writing samples and cover letter to the editor of the Penkal daily paper. In his mind, it was just a matter of time before the interview and job change. That confidence allowed him to approach the Irish Games in a way he believed true reporting and journalism should be done. Half maniac, half Gonzo and half true.

Sometimes it is better if you write the real truth, even if it necessarily didn't happen.

Since the Games were at the Tuscarron County fairgrounds in Winherst, the drive remained only 35 minutes. But the route was the same. Same country road cut-throughs with bad uneven railroad tracks, Amish hand painted signs selling windows and baskets, old farms with steel and material and plastic toys all over the yard, new homes with unpaved drives, double wides turned into legitimate houses, garden goods for roadside sale. Rural northern Pennsylvania two line highway with just AM and FM for entertainment. And Pike sold out music for talk radio.

"Time for the crazy morning news," said the radio man's voice.

"A man is being arrested for rape in Wyoming. According to Wyoming law, if you are having sex, and the person says stop, you have five seconds to get off them or it's rape," the radio girl's voice said.

"Five seconds? What! You can't get off a girl in five seconds, no way. It's takes like five seconds to even hear what she said," the man's voice said.

Another station.

"You have to understand what it means to be a championship team. It takes everyone, front office, owner, coach, players, everyone must work together. And I just don't see it here. These players aren't playing for their coach; all they've done is enervate the team. That's the problem with the

NFL mindset, they all already got paid and they don't care. They don't get mad after a loss, they go buy a PlayStation," the analyst said.

Another station.

"I'm not too proud to mow my grass. And I have money. And my kids aren't too proud to mow the grass either. They may complain, sure, but they will get out there and mow. I don't pay immigrants to do these kind of jobs. I hear it all the time. That's a brown job. Housekeeping, mowing, things that we pay others to do now. You want to stop immigration? Want to stop giving succor to the enemies of our economy? Try attacking the pocket books. No green card, no work. It's that simple. But people hire undocumented aliens, pay them under the table to do jobs they should be doing themselves."

The small town of Winherst was blessed with a huge country facility. Due to its farming and agriculture history, the fairgrounds exploded in the 1930s and '40s, and the land stayed and the event bubble finally blister-popped and the dead skin fell back to the surface.

Pike pulled in and asked a young lady waving an orange flag, directing parking, if there were any special places for the press.

"What press?' she asked.

"The press, like newspapers, I write for this whole county," Pike said.

"I'm from Pittsburgh, they make us volunteer up here. Just like drive over there. Just like everyone else," she said followed by a huge yawn.

Dear God, woman, find your purpose. Guess you're looking for one with that shirt. The tightest, see-through, thrift-store Ghostbusters shirt of maybe a 10-thread-count. Be like the Buddha, be fat on knowledge and make a man worship your mind.

Pike placed his vehicle, and did a supplies check.

Got my awesome huge official reporter's camera, got a press pass that I attached to rope so everyone would always know, a pen behind my ear, two spares in my right front jeans

*pocket, and a spiral bound-at-the-top notebook. I can't be
anymore legit. Let's go meet some people and write the best
story this town has ever seen.*

Pike sauntered around the fairgrounds for the first
hour, taking shots of kilts and traditional garb, bagpipers,
bands and people eating fair food. He was trying to figure out
an angle for the feature beyond the simplistic and obvious idea
that Irish heritage was being celebrated at a fairground.

*Tons of Americans acting Irish. Are they Irish? That's it.
The story will be about that transition. Irish immigrants come
here, have kids and raise them. But they're in America. And the
kids, American. Raised with Irish traditions in the home but
American outside. And the kids grow up, and they can come to
these festivals, put on a little costume, but for how long? Third
generation Irish-Americans will have less of the Emerald Isle in
them, and their kids less still. When's it time to call it quits?
When do you realize, there is nothing really connecting me to
that country? I'm an American, and part of that is understanding
mutts don't have a pedigree chart to follow.*

Pike saw an alcohol tent. It was 11 a.m.

*If I'm going to do this story without fear, as a means to
convey truth about something, I must be a part of that truth. I
love Tom Wolfe and the like, but just for the writings. They
documented and followed, but never seemed to be actually
involved in the great cultural event they were covering. Which
may or may not matter, but I don't want to be exposed as some
phony bitch. So I'll get a drink.*

"So what's the deal with beer? I gotta get tickets or
something or what?" Pike asked the red-bearded, big-bellied,
kilt-wearing man manning the beverage tent.

"You give me four dollars, and I give you a pull young
man," he said with an inviting look.

"Deal. What are my choices?"

"We've got some average domestics, but really, for the
same price, you should get a Twisted Kilt. Nice red ale—"

"Lemme get one of those, please."

*I got a five, perfect. Dollar tip, good rapport, this could
work.*

After the transaction of green for red, Pike sat down at a splintery picnic table in the shade. The heat was growing. End of June mid-western summer heat increasing by each second of earth's 1,000-mile-an-hour rotation.

He noticed a boney blond girl in an exceptionally short kilt by a man in matching gear.

Confidence wasn't flowing hard enough for Pike to just start interviewing strangers, so he finished off the traditionally ephemeral first pint and went back for more. Half way through round two, he approached the duo.

"Hi, I'm Pike, I write for the Winherst News-Times, I was wondering if I could talk to you for a second about this event?" He asked the man.

"Sure. I'm Bob and this is my daughter Sally."

Don't look at Sally, you had a feeling that she was young and you don't play that game. Furthermore, you are here to work, so just ignore her, talk to dad and move on.

"Great, basically, I'm trying to figure out how families and people carry on Irish traditions, living in America. Does that make sense? Like, how do second and third generation Americans keep an Irish and an American history?" Pike asked.

"Wow, I thought you were just going to ask me how I liked the fried food," Bob joked. "That's interesting. Well, first and foremost, you raise them to be Americans. I'm ex-U.S. military, so everyone understands, at least in my family, who we are now. But our blood comes from somewhere, so it's good to know where that blood comes from."

"Good answer, really good. But after, let's say, three or 400 years, all there will be will be an American tradition and bloodline. Won't the kilts get lost for apple pies?"

"What do you think, Sally, will you lose your kilt?" Bob asked his daughter.

No, no, no, don't get her involved. I'm not going to be nice, I'm not going to look at her. I'm sure she's great, and I don't want to be a huge dick, but she is wearing less than what most plaid skirt strippers wear. And she had to have a bleached shirt tied in the front, exposing the not-exposed-to-too-much-sunlight skin surrounding the umbilical cord scar? And it's not even buttoned

*up for shit. This is a father/daughter whore game, that's what
this is.*

"I'm never giving up my kilt, I love wearing it," Sally
said.

"Well there you have it, some things never die. When I
was in Haiti for the Air Force during carnival, crazy time to be
stationed there, it was a mix of everything. The island culture
of old voodoo and blacks, with the conquered influences of the
Spanish and French. Everyone was dancing in the streets, and
the outfits were native for some, and more modern for others.
You know they sent me into that shit storm with just my
pistol?"

"Why weren't you in a plane?" Pike asked in jest.

After acquiring his third Twisted Kilt, Pike moved from
the shade and into the action. Even though he had to set his
drink down to write interview notes, strangers didn't seem to
care what state he was in. They either wanted their names in
print or they didn't, a consistent theme throughout this story
and journalism.

Through combing the grounds and sundry shops, Pike
located another alcohol area across the quad.

*Nice, now I can get a buzz at one tent, then go to the
other tent, and they will never know how much I'm consuming,
thus keeping undercover, professional and without the worry of
getting cut off and embarrassed by everyone in the beer line.*

A man in a coal long-sleeved shirt with a more yellow
than gold coat of arms on the chest and matching soot-colored-
kilt stood, leaning against a black walnut, beside tent two. Pike
approached the man who was finishing an amber lager.

"Hey, I'm reporter and I was wondering if I could ask
you a very serious question?"

"OK, ask away," the man said.

"How exactly, or perhaps I should ask, what is the
proper way to urinate in a kilt?"

"Haha, what kind of a story are you writing? I don't care,
I'll tell you," the man said pointing to a supine pool on the

backside of the tree. "You stand here, spread your legs a little bit, lean forward and piss," the man said.

"Wow, awesome, so you just pee right where you're standing? So you're not wearing underwear then, right? Not trying to get too personal, but I need all the facts," Pike said suppliantly.

"That's why you lean forward, so you don't get yellow on your kilt."

The pavilion bounce left Pike drunk around 3 p.m. There started to be a compromise in professionalism, as words got slurred and there was a risk of someone reporting to the paper that the reporter was drunk.

On the way out of the parking lot, windows down, dust pouring in, sweating forehead, Pike was looking for the Ghostbusters shirt girl for some visual candy to suck on for the ride home.

19.

"Since according to you, men judge of the reality of things by their senses, how can a man be mistaken in thinking the moon a plain lucid surface, about a foot in diameter; or a square tower, seen at a distance, round; or an oar, with one end in water, crooked?" G. Berkeley, *TDBHAP*.

"How did the Irish Games go?" Theresa asked in her usual loquacious Monday morning mode.

Mondays seem to be her brightest and nicest days.

"Really well, covered it completely. Going to write the story up now. Going to be long I think, lot went on. Going to be the truth."

Over the next three hours Pike composed the story in a raw and "I'm out of here anyway style," rich with descriptive words, the "enemy of journalism."

Via iChat Pike wrote:

Pike: irish games story is ready to edit. hope you like it.

26 minutes later Theresa responded.

Theresa: Pike, a lot of your story is not suitable for a small town paper. So I cut it down and made it usable.

Pike: cut it down, what do you mean?

Theresa: You can't talk about a guy pissing on a tree through his kilt, that doesn't fit our paper's style.

Pike: ok, i guess i understand, but that's what happened.

Theresa: Bagpipes, the types of food, the dress, that's what happened. War stories and a guy talking about how he lost a finger trying to pet a wild hawk aren't the types of stories our readers want. Nothing else needs to be said.

I can't wait to give you my two weeks notice, and say, "I'm off to write for a bigger paper, so have fun in shitty small-town news world."

Later in the day, Finn read a newspaper article from one of the bigger dailies out of Erie.

"You see this rape story in Oklahoma?" he asked Pike.

"What rape story in Oklahoma?" Carly asked indifferently, while standing up and stretching her arms upwards. The veins were quite visible.

"A guy caught some Guatemalan farmhand raping his daughter so he killed him."

"Good," Pike said.

"No, not good," Carly said.

"Not good? It's a complete case. He raped his daughter, he killed him, it's all over now," Pike said.

"It's all over, except for undermining the fundamental principles of due process, on which this country was based."

"Due process, he saw a guy raping his daughter and then killed him. I mean, the police have to investigate. If that, in fact, happened, if it did, why would you care if some rapist got killed?"

"I don't know, possibly because we have a justice system, and when you eliminate due process and the courts we find ourselves in a savage society based on opinion and not law," Carly said.

"The medical examiner said that the girl was raped," Finn chimed in.

"That's fine, there still needs to be a trial," Carly insisted.

"What's the whole story? Is the dad being charged?" Pike asked.

"No, based on OK law, you can reasonably protect your family with deadly force," Finn said.

"I really want Oklahoma law to be the primary example of how to lead a nation," Carly said sarcastically.

"But what did the dad do, go get his gun and shoot the rape guy?" Pike asked Finn for further clarification.

At this point, Carly crept through the cubicle hallway and joined Pike and Finn in their area.

"According to the story, I guess he tried to call 911. It says the father heard screams from the backside of the barn, and when he went to investigate, found this guy on his daughter, who is eight-years-old, by the way. Then it says he got the guy off him, punched him a bunch, and then called 911. The Guatemalan died later in the hospital from the punches I guess. That's what it says. I tried to tell you all about letting Central Americans work for you," Finn said, trying to offensively joke his way out of the conversation.

"So let me rehash, a dude walks around a barn, sees a guy raping his daughter, gets him off her with punches that lead to this guy dying, and you have a problem with due process somehow?" Pike asked Carly confrontationally.

"You don't just beat a man to death, no matter what he's done. The courts decide punishment," Carly retorted.

"You're crazy, dude, when you pull a rapist off your daughter, you have to get that rabid disgusting animal under control. You don't use logic or words; you're not dealing with a logical or real human. This dude is raping your daughter, you don't know if he's got a knife or a gun, I mean Christ, he's raping someone, how can you claim equanimity—all of the sudden getting stabbed would be too far of a reach? No, you start punching that dude as hard as you can, and if there's a metal pole around, you grab that, too. When possible, sure, I want due process. We can't have hangings behind the courthouse like the old days. But this seems like a perfect scenario where a rapist can die and we don't have to deal with it further," Pike said.

"Keep supporting actions like this and you'll see how fast we'll be back in the Old West. I would have handled the situation differently, made him stand trial, and let the courts decide his fate," Carly said.

"Whatever, that's awesome that you can control your punches and set them for knockout only, but me, I'm trying to implode his face until the cops arrive," Pike said.

"Another reason I'm glad I'm not you," Carly responded.

The next day, Tuesday, Pike didn't even make it into the office before news called.

"Good morning," Pike offered.

"Pike, it's Theresa, are you on your way in?"

"Hi, Theresa, I'm probably like six point three minutes south of Winherst, what's up?"

"I need you to go to Southwood Elementary, from what I understand, the principal is resigning," Theresa said.

"It's summer, will there be anyone there?" Pike inquired.

"They are having an in-service today, go see what you can find out. It could be nothing, she could be just changing districts, but we need to know. And we need a story by tomorrow morning so we can send it to the press, OK?"

"OK. I'm on it for sure. No worries, I'll get you a story tomorrow morning," Pike assured.

I hate chasing news. I know, wrong profession, but it just seems so rat-like. Gotta harass a bunch of people, cling to them, try to squeeze out info and news even if there isn't any real story to tell. "Well, sometimes no story is the story," says Carly. Too bad about Principal Dion. Bet some parent is getting her fired. I'm not going to the school. I'm going to call the school board president. He'll let me know what's going on. Not like we're pals, but he's an old boy from Tennessee and he likes straight talk and even straighter shooting.

"Hello, this is Payton, can I help you?"

"Hi, Payton, this is Pike, I met you at the school board meeting last month, I'm the new—"

"Hey there, fellah, how you doin'?" His tone quickly changed from business to casual. The school board had an obligation to try to befriend and control the press to try to better the school, especially when it came to the public's perception around election and levy pass time.

"I'm doing real well, thank you. I just had a couple of quick questions if you had a moment?"

"Sure pal, what can I do you for?" Payton asked.

"I'll just get right to it, it is my understanding that principal Dion is leaving the district, can you comment on that?"

"Well, the first thing I'd like to say is that school board meets next week so we haven't officially accepted her resignation. But as I'm sure ya'll know, that's just a formality. But the big picture is that we are sad to see her go. Just between me and you, we thought she'd stay here longer, a year isn't very long for an administrator. We kinda took a chance on her, and now she's off to another district." Payton said.

"Ooohhhh, so she is just moving schools, that's all?"

"Yeah, we can't figure it out, I thought she was happy here, Southwood is doing real good, but I guess she wants to leave."

"Can you tell me the name of where she's going, please?"

"Yes, I can, but it might be a good idea to talk to her about all this. You have her cell number, right?" Payton asked.

"I do at the office (lie), she gave it to me in case I had any questions about Southwood (lie), but I'm out driving now, and don't have it."

Short pause. Silence.

"I suppose if she gave it to you I can too. Hold on, let me get my rolodex," Payton said.

Who the hell still uses a rolodex?

"OK, pal, you got a pen, you ready?"

Once Pike had the number, he knew a phone call probably wouldn't get him much info, even if she answered. Plus, as it stood, there wasn't much of a story. Teacher going to another district.

Pike called his father.

"Sir, are you by a computer?"

"I'm on my desktop. What do you need?"

"Can you do a reverse number search for me, I need an address? The name is Dion, and—"

"Hold on a second, what are you doing right now? You should see how nice the weather is. Do you remember the beautiful Oregon summer?"

"Father, please, I just need an address."

"OK, but this is why I keep telling you that you need a smartphone so you at least appear erudite. It's 2012, why be so reluctant? Your mom and I will pay the bill if you can't—"

"The name is Dion. The number is 555-1147. Please do a reverse look up."

"I'm doing it now. How's the job going? Are you eating right? Do you know there are toxic chemicals in rice?"

"No."

"There are. I'm going to send you some information to your email."

"Got the address yet?"

"Here it is. Broad Street, 129 Broad."

129 Broad wasn't a house, but the address to an apartment complex. Green siding, two story, borderline poor. Not where Pike thought a principal should be living.

I need to find the mailbox, find her name and rap on her door. Can I really just appear at her door? Am I crossing a scumbag line? Why are reporters such grief-seeking creatures? Well, if you want the truth, and if the public has a right and a need and should know the truth, then sometimes you have to pound on someone's entrance to get it. But you've watched the news, there is always a reporter at someone's house for some truth, and the news decides exactly what that reality is and how to convey it. I'm not doing it. I'm just going to call her, try to find out some info, like where's she going, and for how much, and why'd she leave. If she doesn't call me, then no story. I'm too cowardly for this profession. Wait a second, that's old Franks, Superintendent Coy Franks. And Dion! What the hell is going on?

Pike noticed them exit a second floor apartment, out onto the community walkway and down the steps towards the parking lot.

I better say hi, like, I was just around.

Circling the mailboxes, Pike cut through the lot and met the two head on.

"Superintendent Franks and principal Dion, how are you?" Pike acted surprised.

Without a flinch, Franks extended a hand.

"Pike, how are you, how are you finding the town?"

"I love this town so far, not being from here and everyone has accepted me with open arms. It's really a unique and caring place here," Pike said.

"Well, that's good to hear, what can I help you with?" Franks asked.

"Nothing. I'm here to interview the landlord concerning a story that I can't technically go into right now," Pike said.

"I live here, you can tell me," Dion joked.

"What are you two up to?" Pike asked in the most innocent manner he could muster.

"I'm just helping Ms Dion here tie up some loose ends," Franks said.

A few more pleasantries and Pike parted ways.

How gutless. Why didn't you ask Dion about leaving? Why didn't they tell you she was leaving? I have no story. And now what, you going to call her and be like, by the way, I've just heard you're resigning, any particular reason? Leaving for another district, OK, neat. Bullshit coward.

Pike arrived at the office close to lunch, after taking a two-hour break at a local state park, daydreaming at the woods.

Per usual, Theresa wasted no time trying to find the facts.

"So what did you come up with?" she asked Pike, who had sweat marks under his dress shirt from the humidity.

"She's leaving for another district, pretty typical move actually, wants a change, so that's it. Got another job. Talked to the school board president and everything. I'll start getting to work on this now though, although, I think you'll find there's not much to it."

"Did Payton tell you with whom they were looking to replace her?" Theresa asked.

"No, we didn't go into that, but I'm sure it will be a process."

"Don't assume that," Carly invited herself into the conversation when she arrived onto the newsroom floor. "You don't know if they've already hired someone, if they are going with an interim principal. Bad way to write a story, with your assumptions."

"Like I said, I'll figure it all out and have the story ready to go for tomorrow," Pike said.

"If you want, Theresa, I can look into it and see what I can find," Carly offered.

That's a polite way to steal a story.

"Seriously, I have it under control," Pike said hiding frustration and rage for the imbroglio. "I actually have to go talk to superintendent Franks this afternoon concerning everything."

"Why would you talk to him?" Carly asked.

Shortly after the conversation had ended, the search engine on Pike's computer lead him to the Yahoo movie listings. He really wanted to see the new Batman, and its box office stay was running out.

Fuck Carly and this job. "I can look into it." What a dick. Why don't you worry about your own shitty assignments, and leave real news in a real city to me, the real Winherst reporter? I can't even think that last line with a straight face. OK, show times, I can catch the 1:25 showing in Aglon if I hurry. Damn, that's another 20 minutes north. I'm not staying here any longer, and they can't catch me.

The previews, opening credits and opening scene had all passed when Pike walked into the theater. He loved seeing movies by himself, and furthermore, he loved being in a place where no one knew where he was. It was an extra bonus to be getting paid to hideout as well.

Salary job is something else. I never knew about it. But what a concept. Miss work, get paid. Call in sick, get paid. Have full benefits if one were so inclined.

Halfway through the movie, in 5K-pace-intervals, someone would come in, walk to the front of the theater, look around and leave.

What is going on? Oh man, I forgot about the movie theater out west that got shot up during a Batman film. Is this a copy cat assassin? Or copy bat? Trying to figure out the weakest group of moviegoers? Where are my exits? The way I came in and at the front. I'm dead. No way I can get away. Either door the gunman would enter, guess it could be a gunwoman too, I'm right in the middle. Easiest target. Why did I have to try to get a good seat?

What Pike didn't know, was that one rural county away, in another theater, a man was apprehended trying to bring in a bunch of knives into a showing of Batman. He said he wanted to protect himself against a shooter, but the police weren't buying it. As a result, all area theaters were alerted, and employees walked in every so often to the Batman showings to check on things. It ruined the whole movie for Pike, who was lost in paranoia.

He never returned to the office, but went straight home.

Sleeping was hard that night. It was an every-40-minute-check of his phone.

I don't have a story. I went and saw shitty Batman instead of getting a story. For what? The look-how-cool-I-am punk nonsense is really getting old. You want to get fired? Write the freakin' story. You were going to make some lady that you'll never see again upset by asking her public information? She's a public employee!

Getting up an hour early, Pike realized he hadn't even grazed REM sleep. He could feel the stress ulcer tighten up right below his esophagus. No aggravating red sauce could be consumed that day.

Small bowl of plain Cheerios, and then, at 8:01 a.m., he called Dion.

She answered.

"Hello?"

"Hi, Principal Dion, this is Pike from the News-Times, is this too early to be calling?"

"Hello, Pike, no, it's not, I have a good idea why you're calling."

"Terrific," Pike began, using a Carly vocab term and acting as a supplicant, "it is my understanding that, to many people's chagrin, you will be leaving the district, is that correct?"

"Yes, Pike, that is correct. I really will miss the great people of this town."

"It really is a great town. Where are you going to be going, to a new district?" Pike asked.

"I'm moving up north to the Centerworth district."

"Centerworth? Isn't that smaller than here?" Pike asked confused.

"Yes, it is a bit smaller actually, but a really great area," Dion said.

"That's understandable, a smaller district really doesn't mean anything if the situation is better, both geographically and financially," Pike said.

"What do you mean?" she asked.

"Well, I don't mean to cross any lines, but public employees' salaries are public knowledge, so I assume you will be making a little more money?"

"No, actually I won't be."

"I see, my fault. Wow, so I guess then, let me ask, why are you leaving the district?"

"Personal reasons, and that's all I can say."

I bet a local witch gave her a hermetic imprecation and she has no choice but to flee.

After the morning interview, Pike left his underdeveloped development and drove to the office, and even though he was fear-driven into productivity, his mind still looked at the same things during the cruise. The same old campground near the half-way point, the way the certain signs were hung along the road; it was as if the mind repeated the road's consistency concerning the daily drive.

At the paper, it took less than a half hour to finish the story, and around 9:35 a.m. Pike iChatted the editor.

Pike: principal story is ready to edit.

Theresa: OK. Also, we need to talk about next week. You are going to be leaving, is that right?

Pike: yes i have that wedding in new york the weekend after the fourth of july.

Theresa: But you'll be here for all the 4th of July activities, right? There is a parade next Wednesday.

Pike: yes i'll cover all that. only miss thursday and friday. be back on monday.

Theresa: School board will also be a big deal Thursday night. They are going to be unveiling the final levy plan to replace the Rover school building. It will probably fail like it always does. Everyone always says, 'It was fine when I went to school there.' Too bad that was in the '50s.

Further into that week, in a special session, the school board accepted Dion's resignation, had punch and cookies. They talked about the levy. It was a slow start to the campaign.

The next day, Friday, was the last of June. Summer would come engulf even the night in heat. But the news office in Winherst would not be affected.

Due to the multi-turtle-neck layers surrounding the body of the editor, the air conditioner set at 67 worked like a pyramid builder, relentlessly and with a whip always close to the back. The dramatic temperature change from outside to in is causing serious headaches for me.

That Friday, as brain matter seemed to pulsate against the skull, Theresa told Pike about something that had just come across the "wire." Really she just read another paper's website.

I'm not checking another news source. So I can rob some stories that will be old news by the time it goes to press? Why don't we try to make our own stories? Instead of chasing fires, let's get into the humanity of structure and society.

Although Pike had noble thoughts concerning copyright, all news is for all news outlets. A reporter can break the event and get the credit, but once it's out there, all the media sources descend on the issue, evaluate, manipulate, process and "report" the happening. There is no trademark attached to a city councilman embezzlement scandal.

At 2:20 p.m., Pike began getting ready to leave the floor for an interview. It was just the editor and Pike on their side of the newsroom.

Theresa swiveled her chair around and looked at the side of Pike's face for a minute. She sighed. Stood up.

"So Pike, how are you getting along?"

Pike was putting story notes, yellow legal pads (he hates the white ones) and five manila folders (labeled sports, current, format, schools and city council) in his black LL Bean oversized-for-the-office backpacking backpack.

"Yes, I think I'm fitting in rather nicely. Umm, what do you think?" Pike asked with a bit of reservation.

"It's good. I think I'm just bored here. Rob doesn't say a word to me, I just come in every day, edit, format, stare at my computer."

"But you're the editor. You can do whatever you want."

"Ha. I wish that were true. There are other editors and the publisher and Veritas Media."

"Spice it up. What do you want to change? Let's change it. It doesn't have to be an execrable beat. I've thought there were plenty of things we could do to liven up the Winherst paper. Let's give the readers something to read, let's go crazy style, what do you think?"

"No. This isn't the National Enquirer. It is a very old and conservative reader base. I was just thinking about my job as a whole."

"Oh." Pike wasn't sure what to say. On one hand, he felt like she had been a very emotionless banal boss that never seemed to care at all about Pike personally, and now she wants to talk about her feelings, no way. But Pike was not a stranger to torment, so he empathized, and realized, that an unhappy co-worker, who was also a boss, never worked out well for anyone.

"So what do you think is the main problem? The one thing that makes you bored or whatever, what do you think that is, and how do you see yourself trying to change it?" Pike asked.

"I don't know. I'll be fine. Don't be late for your interview."

Pike didn't push the issue.

OK, do you want to talk or what? Worse than a sitcom husband that can't open up and talk about what's really going on. I was down, was going to get to the root of it and help you change. But you're on your own. Like your life is so bad anyway, you're the editor of the paper. You've made it. You've got the career, the power, the skilled job training. You don't have to do anything except continue success.

Pike shut down his computer, but regretted doing so, thinking that Theresa might realize he had no intention in coming back to the office. But it never seemed like she cared. Although Pike had nothing to compare and contrast Theresa's personality to over the last year, or five or 10, he still felt like something was happening to her.

The screen went to sleep, Pike grabbed his BPH-free water bottle, made sure he had a two pens in his pocket, and said, "I'll see you Monday morning."

"You have council Monday night, so you can come in late."

"I forgot, that's what I'll do then."

"You also have to cover the 4th of July parade and Tuesday night the library board meets, so we should probably have something on that as well. I know it seems like a lot, but you will be gone Thursday and Friday so we will need some back up stories for the following week."

Back up stories? No way, lady. I'm going on vacation. You expect me to do a week's worth of work in three days? Damn salary job got me for the first time. I guess I can't be like, well if I'm going to be doing all the work for Thursday and Friday then I want to get paid for those two days. But I will get paid for those two days. Still not fair. Little baby is sad about real world work? Go get you a fucking time clock job, bud, wear a cute little blue vest and be a door greeter at some giant chain that kills the local economy. But can you blame the mega store? People won't shop at the local shoe store downtown because the lower quality shoes at the chain are cheaper, and you can get tampons, shoes, oil and light bulbs all in the same trip. But they're killing themselves. The lady that owns the local shoe store shops at the chain. She likes cheap convenience, too.

Tightening a shoulder strap on his backpack, Pike turned towards the rear hallway. He passed the publishers office with a cheap name plaque on his desk, then down the steps and Pike was gone from the office for the weekend, and he felt that everything was fine. On a Friday, when the obligations and expectations and life-fulfillments are completed for the week, Pike felt free. And sure, he is among millions that feel the same way, but his voice changed, the hunger for consuming increased, and he wanted to yell at strangers, get punched and laugh about it, taste gross things that look like blood. No one could hurt him on a Friday.

The 12-second walk from the back exit to his auto was usually an obstacle course, where liberal bikers and high-water-pant-wearers were traveling with great speed towards their progressive futures.

There was a brief moment of confusion, however, when Pike was unable to unlock his '04 Taurus. He stood beside the driver's side door and kept pressing the open padlock icon on the key fob.

I'm locked out. My key fob battery is dead and I can't get into my car now. How can they have an invention like this? Who's watching me? I bet someone is laughing at me not being able to get in. Ya, is it funny to laugh at someone in a vulnerable moment? No, no it's not. Stupid car keys.

Wait, I have a car key. I'm a moron. Now they can laugh at me, it's deserved. How long has it been since I've locked or unlocked a car manually, using a key? Man, the dependency I've chosen to adhere to and create for myself. So sad.

Down the alley and out onto Main Street.

The chains haven't gotten this town yet. The grand and grandiloquent city council won't allow it. Local shops selling chocolate covered grasshoppers, bikes, antiques. There's even a free garden that volunteers cultivate, and anyone can pick from it at anytime, no questions asked. And there are at least some humans of color. It gets so boring seeing variations of pallid European blood. But Winherst, sure, nice and old-fashioned and a farm community. But they ain't open to new ideas. That's the way it was when I was growing up. Yawn. My only sense of self is to belong to the past.

The people do care here, though, they that strive for real equality. Most don't. You lost your leg, OK, do you need me to do something for you? 'Cus if you don't need me to physically do something for you that you can't physically do yourself, then why are talking about or concerned about your leg? Again, I know how it sounds, but no one cares about your unfortunate luck, what they care about is your happiness. It's like, and I know I shouldn't compare sports with real life, but fans only care about whether you won or lost. You have a new coach, you have injuries, you don't have a big payroll, you're in a small market, blah blah blah. No one cares. Win a game. Or if you lose, don't tell us about how injured your team is, we don't care. Going blind could be the worst thing in the world, but let's keep living. Let's hang out, have fun, talk about golf, but don't expect me to be uber nice or give you a special pass. What I will give you is the most honest and real hangout I can provide, without ever really even thinking about your problems. Look at my face, wait, bad wording, but it's covered in life's tattoos. What I would like is for no one to ever mention them. It may seem forced and game-like, but the worst thing in the world is to hang out with someone in a wheel chair and listen to them say self-pity lines like, "That bar looks neat, wait, never mind, it's a dance club. Guess I won't be going there." Some depressed person just blew their head off out in Erie. Personally, I'd take the wheelchair over blood brains.

The radio on the ride home: "Just learn from a pro. Nothing worse than getting advice on how to golf from your friends or dad. Doesn't matter how good they are, it's a matter of how good of a teacher they are. And they will tell you things that work for them, but that might not work for you. Then you get involved in bad habits, and it takes just as much time to unlearn those bad habits as it does to learn them in the first place. Listen to my syllogism. Pay the extra money and get taught by someone who devotes their whole life to golf, not just as a hobby."

When Pike finally made it home around 3:45 p.m., he was excited, and tried to have a serious conversation with himself about the upcoming New York wedding and drinking.

Skipping every other step as he ascended to the entrance of the complex, Pike rounded the top of the stairs and went down the half-torn-off-in-remodel-stucco tunnel to his apartment.

The thick wood of the front door seemed skinnier to Pike when it was open and sideways.

"Can you believe that you will be in New York a week from now?" Pike said aloud between deep, stair-stealing breaths.

New York in seven days. But it's going to be hard, I have to train for it. Dude, if you think you're going to change your body type in that amount of time, you're crazy. I know this is coming from someone who steps on the scale and yells, "I lost two pounds last night," never taking into account water fluctuation. Don't get all doctor-y on me with your agua talk. And my weight can change over night for two reasons—One, my metabolism is like no other the world has ever seen, so I can actually lose many pounds while I sleep. And two, I'm not talking about changing my body weight. If anything, I'm going to be adding to it. I have to start drink training. Oh, this sounds healthy. You know how many raging maniac drinkers are going to be at this wedding?

If you don't drink 'til you puke they will think you're, like, totally, like, not cool anymore. But mostly, I will be trying to drink with all these idiots either way, so I need some tolerance built up, or I won't survive the first night. Seriously though, I'm getting real tired of the whole bachelor party thing. So don't go then. I wish it were that easy, I wish I could tell them, "Hey, I'm tired of acting like a teenage cum-bucket, so I'm not going to the bachelor party." You see how easy that was? But I'm in the wedding party, which is only three people deep. So if I don't show, everyone will know. And it's not even the bachelor party, it's the bachelor party activities. You really ran for your life as soon as the stripper arrived at George's bachelor party, the one you were in charge of, right?

Yes, it's true, but as I've explained, and as Kat could verify, I did not enjoy the show, left early with Yogos and Tar and it wasn't supposed to be a normal stripper. I guess the real issue is that I just want to go to a wedding as a bystander. I love Daniel, sure, and I was super honored to be chosen to be in his wedding

*party, I mean, what that does for my ego you have no idea, but, I
just would like to go a wedding and not have to participate in
anything. Maybe someday other people's weddings will be more
about you, asshole. Until then...*

Six Bud heavies glided into Pike's stomach that night,
followed by an 11:30 p.m. fake-chicken-and-rice-casserole-
mashed-potato, wine-hunger-maximized feast. The food killed
the desire to continue to imbibe, and Pike was asleep before
midnight.

At 2:11 a.m., he sat up in bed to the grousing of his body.

*Ouch, acid reflex. Pain. Man, all over stomach pain. Worst
acid reflux I've ever had. Wait, am I? Am I? Am I going to puke?
No, not on six beers. I'm going to puke.*

To the toilet, head hovering. One knee on the white tile,
one knee up. Both hands on the recently raised seat. Three or
four seconds until hell...

Some kind of flu had hold of Pike. Pure liquid bowel
movements, three or four bouts of dry heaving after the yellow
stomach acid had coated-up and burned the esophagus. No will
to watch or experience life. The bed was painful to simply lie
in, standing even worse. Complete dehydration, the insides of
the cheeks suffocation-dry.

After the reaction and subsequent vomiting urge had
ceased around 4:30 a.m., Pike went to the bathroom and
turned on the cold water. He did this every 20 minutes. He
would bend over, grab the top of the faucet with one hand,
encase the other end with his mouth, and flood the inside. Like
the shipwrecked sailor out at sea, no mater how thirsty you
are, you can't drink the water. And Pike wouldn't, knowing it
would just come up again. But he would daydream about the
thousands of gallons of Gatorade he was going to consume the
next day. And that all this suffering would be worth all that.

*The flu isn't as bad as a really bad hangover, because of
the guilt.*

It was a 24-hour bug, and by Sunday afternoon the
halcyon feelings returned and Pike was eating Mexican and
pounding water, which may have not been the wisest choice

considering his intestinal track thought it still needed to clear the virus.

So the attempt at a week-long "alcohol tolerance" was a failure.

Building up addiction can be tricky, ironically.

20.

"It is absurd to demand of such a man, when the sums come in from the utility network which the projects of others have in part determined, that he should just step aside from his own project and decision and acknowledge the decision which utilitarian calculations requires." B. Williams, *AU*.

Because of city council, Pike was able to stay up late Sunday since he could go to work in the afternoon the next day. With control being the main issue, Pike laid out his clothes the night before, something he hadn't done since growing up through grade school. Pike got a desk in his room when he was in third grade for completing homework, and every time he got up, he would push his chair in. Even when he knew, knew he was just going to the bathroom or to get a different pencil, he would push that seat back in. The rocker and the drawers and the alignment had to be perfect every time. The garments laid out the night prior on the ground in functional order, top to bottom, as if dressing a murder scene chalk line.

Nice, got my outfit all laid out, I set two alarms, because I can't trust this stupid old 1G phone, and what else? We should be good to go. How's my car look? Not washed. Why can't you wash it? Do you think people want to be interviewed by a degenerate that can't wash his vehicle? It's not that old, it's not that bad, if I just rinsed it now and again. Tell ya what I'd rather do, trade it in for a new Taurus. If I had credit, could get a good rate and put down a good down payment. How much to lease a Ferrari?

An uncomfortable tingling on the backside of Pike's thighs. It was the first time he noticed it. He dismissed the feeling and figured it was his legs falling asleep after the 35-minute commute to his place of employment. It was close to 1 p.m.

Boss lady says come in around noon, so I'd say this is around noon. If she don't like it, she can tell me. But she won't. No one says anything. 'Cus I could've been working on a development. And I always have at least three nonsense stories that I could say I'm working on. They're really not even fake. I'm

not really working on them, but if I had to get out of a mo'fo jam,
I could make it into a piece. Like the tumors. Didn't know, buddy?
Know that I've actually being doing a little rat journalism work
myself? 'Cus that's what you have to do to make news, any news
worth reading anyway, and if you're picking the topic and the
lead to follow, maybe you're trying to find good news, ya know,
like corruption or like a toxic waste cover up or babies getting
mistreated at a hospital or what, didn't this lady get what she
should have? So you gotta be a rat if you want the story. Sheep
do the weather and write obits.

Move the mouse, the screen pops, begin the routine. Check
email.
Seven muthafuckin' messages! Hell, ya, who's the most
popular news guy in Tuscarron County? What the? The first five
are Facebook nonsense. Kirk Thomas, you have three
notifications. Guess what, Kirk doesn't work here anymore and I
don't check or mess with the News-Times Facebook page because
it's mentally stultifying. I probably should, I get that, I mean it's
2012, as the sore-neck generation says. It's just that I don't have
an account and I don't really want to learn or ask Theresa 'cus
she will tell Carly to teach me. I think I'm in a good mood today, I
can tell 'cus I'm cussing a lot. It was that city council routine
breakup. I hate the routine.

Pike put his headphones on and began typing. Today, it
was The Black Heart Procession's "Blue Tears." Other days,
he'd like to listen and compose to The Beatles' "Tomorrow
Never Knows," Buena Vista Social Club's "Chan Chan," Fear's
"More Beer," Fifteen's "Predisposition," Tom Wait's
"Singapore," Modest Mouses' "Edit the Sad Parts," or Mozart's
"Symphony No. 25."

The music of the iPod was interrupted.
"Hello, Pike, how's it going?" Theresa asked loudly.
"Not as good as Gordon-Levitt, I'll tell you that much,"
Carly felicitously said. Finn snickered, and Theresa stayed
silent. "That was an inside joke from earlier," Carly added.
"Neat," Pike said. "I'm good, Theresa, any big news?"
"You tell me."

"I got nothing, city council tonight, though. We'll see what that's about. Do you know if the council clerk sent the agenda over?"

"Is it in your email?" she asked.

"Haven't checked all my mail yet—"

"You do know that you can check your email from home over the weekend?" Carly asked.

Yes, you little Roman, I do know that, but I don't work on the weekends unless I'm working. All you care about is your little news world, oh, can't miss a story, can't miss an email. Can't—

"It might be advisable to check it at home in case some really big story breaks," Carly added.

She just interrupted my mind.

"Anyway," Theresa said, as she tightened her calves, swung the three-legged desk chair around and used the momentum to stand and walk towards Pike.

"Are you working on anything today, right now?" she asked him in close quarters.

"I've always got stuff to do, why?" Pike asked trying to conceal his concern.

"The library board changed their meeting schedule and ended up meeting this morning, so if you can, I'd like you to go talk to the library director, Gabele Richie. Just give her a call and see if she can make some time for you today, before council tonight. Then if you can get me the library story, the village council write-up after tonight, and the 4th of July activities, you know, the parade and everything, with art, we should be good for you to leave on your trip."

"I can handle that, I think."

"If I had a kid," Carly said, "I would never let them go to a parade until they were at least, at least eight years old. It's dangerous and crazy how they entice kids into the street with candy. Do you know how many kid accidents are caused by parades each year? Think about how many holidays have parades, everyone!"

"What are you talking about?" Finn asked. "The parade floats are moving two miles an hour. If your kid gets hit by something that slow, you can't gainsay that the kid is probably doomed anyway."

"Typical response devoid of empathy by the perpetual cynic, who in this case couldn't care, because he does not have the ability, as he has yet been able to produce offspring," Carly said.

"There is actually an ordinance in Aglon that prohibits the throwing of anything, candy or otherwise, along parade routes and by parade floats. And I'm quite proud to say I had a hand in passing that ordinance," Carly gloated, moving across the floor and back to her desk.

"Awesome, girl, you ruined parades for kids in a whole town. You're right, I don't have kids, but I used to be one, and that's the dumbest thing I've ever heard," Finn said.

The library director was more than happy to meet with Pike concerning the monthly board meeting. Much like the school district, the library wanted to befriend the press for similar reasons. One, to let the public know about the opportunities and offerings of the library. No patrons, no book building. And secondly, public opinion of the library itself mattered. Library levies for improvements and funds go before the voters in November just like constructing a new school.

The Edith/Allen Smith Memorial library in Winherst passed a bond three years ago, so as far as funding, they were doing fine. But no sense in letting the public view not be reminded of all the good work they were doing, or so library director Richie thought.

All brick, symmetrical and next to the downtown square, the library was well kept and added civility, history and aesthetics to the area. But the parking lot was small, so without seeing a spot, Pike parked around the block.

Got my two pens, notepad, camera in case I see any art, got a copy of the library's agenda. Let's be nice. A library is a state institution whose whole purpose is to help educate, right? Right. But be on the lookout. Who knows, could be an embezzler right under my nose. Don't sign anything in there, could be a set-up. They got microfilm in there. I want to go look at old microfilm like I'm trying to get to the bottom of some crazy scandal. Then on the back page on the 1941 News-Times I see the picture of the man who is the missing link to the whole case! Or something like that.

Crossing through a grassy area from his parking spot, Pike entered the double doors and quickly went to shut down his cell-phone. But it relieved him of that burden by turning off by itself in his pocket.

It just seems smart in here. I want a huge library like that Beast had. They should just make a library-scented cologne.

He introduced himself to the indifferent lady at the counter, and was subsequently ushered back to the director's office.

"Hi, you must be Pike from the paper, please come in and have a seat," director Richie offered.

"Hello, yes, I am, nice to meet you. Thanks for meeting with me on such short notice. I'm going to be out of town later this week and we really want to cover the happenings at the library, so it kind of had to be now or never, so thanks again," Pike said as he sat down across from the director's desk.

Her office was small and representative of the lack of need for excess required in state buildings. All of the walls had been converted to bookshelves from toe to ceiling, and there was even overflow stacked high on the little space remaining on the floor.

Smells like rotten books in here, that vituperative smell is appalling, Pike thought shortly after the door closed.

"You had your director's meeting, or board of directors I should say, so let's just start at the beginning in terms of major talking points from that meeting," Pike opened.

"I went ahead and typed a summary for you and printed it out. Hope that's fine," Richie said.

"For sure, I support any action that makes my life and job easier. But seriously, that's great, that way everything is laid out and there won't be any confusion," Pike said.

That old book smell. How does she work in this office?

"You can read over it and let me know what questions you have, but the main focus of the meeting was trying to meet the expectations and demands of the downloadable world."

"What do you mean by that, the downloadable world?" Pike wondered.

"Here, let me show you our circulation numbers from this spring compared to last," Richie said as she printed out a graph and handed it to Pike.

This lady has it together, I like that. For some reason I thought the library director wouldn't be such a business-y person. More like an ex-hippie, with glasses, salt-n-pepper hair, well-read but always having trouble with technology. Although I assumed the age to be right around 50, she's a dark red-head with no glasses and a business suit and seemingly great knowledge on how to manipulate Microsoft Office.

"Hmmm, this is interesting," Pike said without really knowing what he was looking at.

"The graph shows how many patrons came into the library last spring, and how much material was checked out. Then you can compare that to this spring, and the third chart shows materials checked out here on site versus materials checked out online."

"I see."

"The numbers continue to drop. Fewer people coming to the library and fewer materials being checked out. However, the number keeps increasing with materials checked out online. It's becoming obvious that we must meet the online need. It's a Netflix world; no one wants to go to the movie store anymore. We have movies too; you might want to put that in your article," she said in a garrulous manner.

"I'm going to consider everything (lie)," Pike said.

"If we are to face that reality, we must change the way the library operates. Right now, you can go to our website, and download a book, movie, or game, right to your desktop, laptop, tablet, or Kindle-like device. For books, you have a two-week timer, and when the time's up, the book goes back into our database for the next user.

"Now, there are a couple of problems. One, you can extend your check-out time, so often times popular titles can be out for a week or two extra. Now, we do have multiple copies, but there's always a waiting list for popular selections, especially in the media of film and music," Richie said.

"Wow, I had no idea that things were switching that fast. I thought not a lot of people actually like reading via a Kindle, I heard it hurts their eyes and nothing beats a soft cover book, especially when you're traveling," Pike said.

"People can take 10 books on a single device while they travel, and if they read them all, they can download new ones. I haven't heard any studies about tablet readers having damaged eyes."

"I dunno, maybe not. Guess your numbers here on this chart don't lie."

That putrid smell. Maybe I should say something about getting the musty books out of here. There was probably some kind of leak/flood in the basement, and due to space, some of the books were transported up here to dry out. Only they never fully dried out, and mold came a' calling. And then the smell increased slowly yet daily, so she never noticed.

"Another big issue from the meeting is that we are going to be doing a late fee forgiveness event here at the Edith/Allen Smith Memorial Library. It will be a week-long deal next month."

"Really? Now that sounds intriguing, please tell me more about this. I also should maybe get a library card and start checking things out, since, ya know, there won't be an late fees," Pike joked.

"You don't have a library card?" Richie asked seriously.

Wow, relax director, I got a card. Reminds me of the time in Florence, Oregon—what a great coastal town I used to live in—and I applied for a job at a members-only natural food co-op. 'Bout half-way through the interview, the acting manager asked me how I like shopping at their location. I told her I loved it, and that there were like tons of great groceries and products at the store. Then the manager tried to find my membership information that didn't exist. So in that same light, it's not a good idea to interview a library director without having a library card yourself.

"I have a library card, in fact, oh, wait, it's in my car or I would show you how beaten up it is from over-use, but I frequent the Penkal library all the time. That's where I live, down in Penkal, and have only been up here a couple of months."

"Great to hear, welcome to Winherst. The program will be a no-questions-asked return program. You bring back the materials, and we will wipe the slate clean. If you have lost the materials, come in and tell us that so we can change the info in the files, and all will be forgotten. Other libraries have called in collection agencies and things like that, but I don't want to go there. We are a library, not a corporation, but we have to do something, or else, as sad as it is to say, people would just check out and never return anything."

"And perhaps even sadder to say, is that someday, people will never check out anything here, it will be all online, and the library itself may never return," Pike said.

Jumping in his car after the interview, Pike thought he had about an hour and an half to kill before city council met.

Wait a minute, I still smell like old rotten books. How could this be? That scent stuck to me and followed me all the way to my vehicle? I'm never going back in that fecal-smelling office every again. No way that's books. What is that stench? My runners. I stepped in dog shit! I can see it all over my fetid shoe. The grass cut-through before I got into the library. What was the director thinking that whole interview? How much I smelled like ass!

Fortunately, the burnt-bread-brown mush was only on one. And it was a pair of cross trainers, not his dress shoes. Pike had no tolerance for dog manure, and by tolerance it is meant that he instantly threw the damaged footwear away, refusing to clean each feces-filled tread valley.

With only one runner and two brown socks, Pike strolled into the city council committee meetings that happen just prior to the official city council meeting.

Budget reports. Projections. How did this little project go? Do we need to paint a building? What would this or that cost? Government by actually not doing anything at all. Then the council meeting itself. Second and third readings of ordinances concerning payroll and pensions. Approve the hire of a foreman for public works. Hear from the crowd. No one had addressed council in the two months I've covered it. New business. Adjourn. Then whatever committee meetings couldn't be fit in before were had. In this case, police committee meeting.

Some officers will be getting training in this, should they hire a new part-time officer, is everything safe and ready for the 4th of July parade? New business. Old business. Adjourn.

Usually, Pike was first to explode through the council chamber doors, and down the steps that lead out of city hall. But he wanted to be last, so as to not draw extra attention to his pair-less shoe situation. The police chief Troy Knox and councilman Cody Johnson were talking and thought they were last ones in the room.

"We have a huge cocaine problem right now, Cody,' chief Knox said. "We can patrol all day and all night, but our manpower is what it is, and next to that stygian drug, we ain't got a chance. The addiction is causing all these break-ins and petty theft. The scrap yards have never seen so much business, and the pawn shops. I'll tell you one thing—"

The door closed and decapitated the conversation.

That sounds like a story. And why didn't they talk about it during the committee meeting? Finally, we might have a cover-up! Let's follow them.

An uneven and slow walk by Pike had him inching out of the door, and then shuffle-sprinting down the staircase when he didn't see either of the two men. Outside, he was confused.

Where the hell did they go? The chief ain't that mobile. He's gotta be 275, easy.

The town hall elevator opened at the bottom level, and out walked the chief and councilman Johnson. They shook hands and once they cleared the glass doors and were out in the open, went different ways to their cars.

I missed it, trying to be all James freakin' Bond, and I let them tell all their secrets and I missed it. But hold the press, I think I got a nice front page story once I dig a little deeper. Tell me Chief Knox, if that is your real Christian name, why are you covering up the cocaine problem in Winherst? Do you do drugs? Don't lie to me, I'm a reporter, all we do is lie. No, it's not you, is it? It's your son. How many times have the boys brought in Junior, all syrup-glazed-eyed and slobbering, fresh off jamming a needle between his toes. He did always try to hide it from you, ya know, Chief? He always cared. But you created the monster, didn't you, Chief? Too much control. Always meddling in your son's affairs, always the pressure to be perfect, and when he messed up, he got the belt, the hand, the switch and verbal torment. Eventually, he just accepted that he could never harden into the form you wanted while he was in the kiln of his youth; his sides would melt and his top would bend. So he took to the hard-line way out—drugs, drugs and more drugs.

Wait, I remember now that the Chief doesn't have any kids. All part of the story. All part of the investigative process. Ya see, Theresa, this is what I'm talking about, this is what you burn the bridge for, when you can take down council and the police department all in one story. Then I sail to New York, and when I come back, I've already accepted the job at a new daily in Penkal. Clean up the mess, Theresa, and send Carly to interview the Chief next time around.

12 hours later, after fatigue helped add to self-doubt and laziness, Pike had given up on the story. The whole 35-minute drive was Pike vacillating back and forth dialogue about how he couldn't just show up at the police station, tell the chief what he had heard, get quotes from the councilman and research the drug statistics for the town; it was too much work at such a high exposure level.

At the office, when Pike was asked about the council meeting exactly four minutes after he sat down at his desk, he didn't mention anything concerning the police committee meeting or drugs.

I'm going to write an awesome story about cocaine in this town, but I gotta take my time, do it right. It could take weeks or months if I want a great story on this issue.

The intercom buzzed and secretary Terri told Theresa that someone from Winherst was calling about the superintendent.

"I didn't know they got a new one, or that the old one was leaving, did you know anything about that?" Theresa asked Pike before she picked up the receiver.

"No, I mean, that would be a pretty quick hire if they did. I didn't even hear about any possible candidates or current problems. I can call school board president, Payton, if you want."

Without a response, Theresa picked up the phone.

"Hi, this is the editor, how can I help you? (Pause) OK. (Pause) Really, no I didn't hear anything about it. (Pause) Well thanks for calling, we'll get right on it. (Pause) Yes, you too."

She hung up.

"According to that lady, Mrs. Rhineocofor or something, the board is going to approve an interim superintendent in a special session next Monday. Call Payton and find out what you can. Need that story before you leave as well, OK?"

"Sure," Pike said.

"Are you sure? That didn't sound convincing."

"Sorry, just thinking about where I put Payton's number. Now I remember. Yes, I'm quite sure, no problem."

More work. It's like I'm not even taking those days off. I mean, technically, but not mathematically, 'cus I'll still be putting my 40 hours in.

"Hello?" Payton answered his cell phone from a downtown bakery.

Umm, why does he sound so unsure? Was he confused about how to answer the phone, thinking maybe "hello" wasn't the right word?

"Payton, hi, how ya doing? (Pike was trying to "Southernize" his dialect to gain an advantage.) It's Pike, with the News-Times, how's it going?"

"You must really be concerned about me if you asked how I was doing twice," Payton joked.

"I was wondering if you had a minute to talk?"

"Sure, I'm down here at Stella's Bakery, on Main, you ever been down here before? Great bread, best bread in the county. I'm on lunch break, my shop is right next door, you should stop in some time."

Along with being school board president, Payton owned a shirt and embroidery shop downtown. As coincidence would have it, whenever any school group, fundraiser, camp, or graduation event needed shirts made-to-order, they always called Payton.

"I've seen your store before, sure, I'll have to do a little two for one, get some of that bread and stop in and see you."

"Yes, sir, that's what you should do all right, young man, now what's on yer mind?"

"Well, I don't know what you can and can't say, but it is my understanding that you have decided to hire an interim superintendent, is that correct? And that Franks is suddenly leaving? What can you tell me?"

"Well friend, the Franks move has been in play for awhile now, we just didn't announce it. Can't say why or how, but he's moving on. We are going to approve the one-year interim contract of Pierce Elber. Once approved, he will be compensated at 104,000 dollars a year. I can give ya his cell number, too, but don't tell him I gave it to you, wink, wink, if you know what I mean."

"Sure, wink, wink, I know what you mean," Pike said, causing Carly to stop her walk-by of Pike's cubicle.

The heavy receiver with a built in neck guard to talk and write at the same time was set back in its resting area, and Carly jumped in.

"What was the wink, wink, talk? You know you can get in serious trouble if—"

"Carly, please, you don't have any idea what we were talking about. (To Theresa) So the new super is Pierce Elber, ever heard of him?" Pike asked.

"Ever heard of him? No, why would we have heard of the superintendent for the Erie School District?" Carly said sarcastically.

"If it's the same guy, which I'm sure it is, then yes, it's the superintendent from Erie. He retired last month, but is actually from the Winherst area I believe," Theresa said.

"How is he allowed to do that? He's going to collect his retirement and pension from the Erie School District while getting paid, you probably didn't ask Payton how much he is going to get paid—" Carly said.

"Umm, 104 grand, ma'am."

"So he's getting retirement from one district and salary from another. That's double dipping to me, shouldn't be allowed to happen. If he wants to still work for the schools, fine, but don't expect a check from the tax payers for your retirement in the mail," Carly said.

"I usually disagree with Carly's fulminations, but ya, I kinda agree on this one," Pike said, seriously.

"Teachers are scumbags, especially administrators, and even more especially, the fancy superintendents in their bedizen suits, so I'm not surprised," added Finn. He had taken a momentary break in iChatting with the secretary Terri to join the conversation.

Finn thought secretary Terri to be his "work wife." He was always iChatting with her, a floor away, flirting when no one was around when he came in through the front, and attempting to be subtle, smiling and acting as if they were great old friends moments away from damp sweaty basement sex if left alone in the building. And it worked both ways.

Terri married her high school lust interest by age 20. And four years later, Terri and her husband Chuck were devoid of passion and desire, but were both fine with that. Having sex with the same person over and over again is going to lead to some kind of boredom, they thought. Married couples, that's how they get, it ain't a honeymoon all the time. Hell, it keeps getting duller every day after the honeymoon, and that's OK, that's how it really goes when you're married, just ask our parents, they thought.

So when a freshly divorced Finn came into the office a year and a half ago, the enzymes in Terri's vagina that had lain dormant for so many years, awoke, when the tall blond Finn came a' flirting.

"You know, Pike," Carly began, "You don't have to be so nice to teachers and other public servants like the police. They *have* to tell us information. Not only is it illegal in most cases for them to withhold said information, but also in most cases, highly unethical. If the school board is going to hire someone, then the name, rate, all that information is a matter of public record. Are you familiar at all with the Sunshine Laws?"

"A little bit from mock trial in high school," Pike said.

"A little bit doesn't cut it in this business. Gosh, you really need to know this stuff, but hey, why should I care about the Winherst News-Times? Because I work for them."

Before Pike could respond to that question, Carly continued, "I'll print it out for you to read over. Might be good to know before you call the new superintendent."

With great haste Pike picked up the phone to call the new super's number he had gotten from Payton. He wanted to make sure he was talking to him before the "helpful" printouts arrived at his desk.

Need to make a good impression. This dude was the head of a huge district, so he has talked to all the daily papers up there I'm sure. I'm sure he knows all the super-educated, super-experienced, resume-exploding journalists from the Erie Telegraph. Can't let him know the truth.

Three or four rings, all right, I'll just leave a message and if I can't get ahold of the guy before I leave, then—

"Hello, this is Pierce Elber."

Is he answering or is that his voice message?

"Hello?"

"Yes, hello, who's calling please?"

"Sorry, sir. (*Sir? Don't kowtow to this guy straight out the gate.*) This is Pike, I write for the Winherst News-Times—"

"Pike?"

"Yes?"

"What's your number there?" Pierce Elber asked in a deep and soft, but stern voice.

"The office number?"

(Pause)

"Pike?"

"Yes?"

"I'll have to call you back. I'm in the middle of a meeting," said the low voice, forcing Pike to press the top of the receiver hard against his ear.

"OK, let me give you my cell number," Pike suggested. Even though his phone would randomly turn off, Pike preferred to give out his cell number so he didn't have to do interviews in the office, where Carly could appear and be ready to critique his every question. "It's 814-555-9987."

"814, you an Erie resident?"

"No, Penkal, actually. It's weird, but for some reason Penkal and Erie have the same area code. Lublock and Smithville do as well."

"I knew about Lublock. (Pause) Pike?"

"Yes?"

"I'm going to have to call you later."

"OK," Pike said beyond confused and frustrated with the man's phone behavior.

Putting down his soup spoon later that day while eating lunch, Pike was also baffled as to why he was back consuming chili that he knew did not appeal to any part of his mouth.

Am I eating in this shitty lawnmower-grass juice-bar nonsense place just so some 50-year-old lady can help my poor ego get through another day? Yep. Which is OK, but she ain't even here. Then I got stuck in a line and panicked when it was my time to order not wanting to hold up things and wanting everyone to know that I've been here before, knew what to order, that I belonged. So I got the gross chili again.

His phone rang.

"It's an 8-1-4 number, wonder if it's my boy?" Pike said out loud to himself as he answered his phone.

"Hi, this is Pike, Logan Pike."

(Pause)

"Hello?" Pike asked.

"Pike?"

"Yes?"

"I thought that was your voicemail," superintendent Elber said. "How are you?"

"I'm doing great, I'm full on lunch, or had my fill, I should say. Thanks for calling me back. I wanted to know if you had some time, I know it's short notice, but possibly today, to get together and talk about your new appointment as interim superintendent of Winherst? Just sit down for 10 or 15 minutes and get a pic to be subsumed with the article."

"Pike?"

"Yes?"

"We might be able to do that. I'm actually driving home from Erie right now, and I live out in Core Township, about 10 minutes east of Winherst, do you know where that is?"

"I've never actually been, but yes, I can just take 104 from downtown."

"Pike?"

"Yes?" *I'm going to kill this guy when I meet him.*

"Let me give you the address to my house, I live on 104, so it won't be hard to find."

Really up against it now. Let's see, it's a quarter till one. Parade at 2:30ish I think. Gotta get art there, that's for sure. But gotta have this interview.

Jogging back from lunch, Pike manipulated his body through the double doors at the front of the office, ran up the steps, entered the newsroom, grabbed his backpack and camera and fast-walked down the back hallway and eventually into the full daylight of early July.

21.

"In the decades before Darwin, French medical anatomists developed three categories: missing parts (*monstres par defaut*), extra parts (*monstres par exces*), and normal parts in the wrong places." S.J. Gould, *HTAHT*.

Several attempts at knocking had failed, and Pike returned to his car parked outside of the address he was given in Core Township.

Maybe I beat him home? Not sure, he said anytime after one would be fine. Less than an hour till the parade. Going to be close!

Jumping slightly, Pike was startled by a big Caucasian male knocking on the side of his car.

"Pike?"

"Yes?"

"I'm superintendent Pierce Elber, please come on to my house."

"Thanks, I tried knocking but—"

"You should have used the door bell."

Leaving the windows down, Pike walked up the driveway with Elber as he led them onto the front porch.

"Let's have a seat right here," Pierce said.

What? That swing? That's a love swing. Our hips will be touching!

"OK," Pike said.

They sat on the swing. Elber stared at Pike and answered every question demanding eye contact. Pike was very uncomfortable. After about eight minutes of "what are your goals and aspirations for the district," Pike concluded that this man was in fact guilty of double dipping, and cut the interview short.

"Well, I'm sure this is the start of many meetings to come, but unfortunately, I have to get to the 4th of July parade."

The parade route melted down Main Street where the majority of the homes were restored historic works of the 1800s. This allowed for nice lawn lots, complemented by wide grass areas between the sidewalk and the road. The parents and their offspring set up with blankets and foldable mesh lawn chairs in that area, and waited for the parade to begin.

Positioned south of downtown, thinking he could get good shots of the floats with the city as a backdrop, Pike waited for the entertainment to begin.

My goodness me, I sure hope this town doesn't totally endanger their children by throwing candy into the streets and thus guaranteeing thousands of torn up and destroyed bodies.

The parade lasted less than 15 minutes. Couple of cop cars, couple of fire trucks, the mayor, couple of local businesses, kids walking, the high school band, boy scouts. No real floats or anything really representing the Independence Day holiday. Candy was thrown from a couple of groups, teeth-melting suckers and Tootsie Rolls.

This is the lamest parade I've ever seen. I understand, they all can't be Mardi Gras floats, but what a waste of time. I can see the boredom and disappointment on every child's face.

The next day, Wednesday, was New York trip deadline day for Pike, as he had to finishing writing, editing photos and getting everything together before he left for New York. He was driving through downtown Winherst, on his way to the office, when he saw the police station on the corner of the square, and made a decision.

Once his car was parked, he opted not to cut through any grassy areas to arrive at the front of the police station.

Be assertive, don't let the chief intimidate you and don't take any crap from the dispatchers. I swear, the dispatchers are bigger dicks than the police can be at times. They think they actually are law enforcement, and they feel a bit invincible because they know all the cops by name. And most of the radio controllers become a work wife/husband for some officer. You ever call 911? You can almost guarantee that the person on the other end is going to be a jerk. And if you call the station directly, you have to sell the dispatcher if you actually want to speak with a deputy.

I knew a dispatcher once. A half-friend of my father's in Oregon. She got cancer. Then the whole town had a fundraiser for her. Raised thousands of dollars, and the police department was all behind her. When they presented her with the check from all the money they raised, her hair was gone. But someone noticed that her hair was buzzed, and not smooth and bald. I guess Chemo patients can't grow hair at all while they are undergoing treatment, so if you're trying to lie to a whole town, might want to take the straight razor to your scalp and not the quarter inch clippers. She went to jail. Dispatchers.

The police station wasn't a new building. In the '70s, the department moved from an actually designed-for-policing structure, to a bigger place that was centrally located, and adapted it to fit their needs. The windows were bricked up, holding areas and cells added, first floor exits eliminated. With the internal modifications done to the downtown building, the frontage was left quite bare. A flat sign that said "Winherst Police Department" was put above the single-door entrance. There was no off-street parking. No lobby. Pike opened the tinted glass door, took one step forward, and his nose was already close to the bulletproof divider separating "half-cop dispatchers" and the public. To his right, there was a key-pad-secured door.

I can never tell how loud I'm supposed to speak at this thick glass.

Before Pike began, a young chestnut-haired woman with large-mouth-bass eyes and a very straight face pushed herself away from the computer screen and monitors showing the guts of the building.

"Hello, what can I help you with?" she asked.

Why is she being nice? Her face belies her position. And why is she young and attractive? Is she an actor? Bet she is researching a dispatch roll. Bet it's some new TV series where the dispatcher solves the case but the bumbling detective gets all the credit. Kinda like an Inspector Gadget/Penny relationship. Or this is a reality TV show where they are either fulfilling her lifelong dream of becoming a controller or it's some kind of career/life swap thing.

"Hi, how are you?" Pike asked very suspiciously.

"Fine, what can I help you with?" she asked.

"I'm Pike from the News-Times, is Chief Knox available, please?"

"Umm, hold on, let me check. You said your name was Pike, from the News-Times?"

"That's right."

She clicked off the two-way microphone and picked up the house phone and hit the top right button. Pike couldn't hear her talking, but watched her head nod in silence. The mic was clicked back on.

"Chief Knox is not available at the moment, let me take your information and he'll give you a call."

"Let me give you my card—that has both my cell and office number on it. And if you could please, tell him that we are on deadline and I just have to ask him a question before we go to press at, umm, in a couple hours from now (lie). Around 10:30 (lie). Here's my card. And thanks again."

"Have a good day," she said smiling. The low electron noise of electrical humming ceased as the mic was once again turned off.

At the office, Pike was back to work. Feverishly.

Got the city council write up done and it's ready to edit. I uploaded my parade pics, no Pulitzer's, that's for sure. I'll wait to edit them last minute, and if there's no time, there's no time. Wrote the library story last night, she's editing that now. Gotta type up that new super hire. What the hell was wrong with that guy? Whatever, don't write a mean article 'cus of your personal opinions on double dipping.

The new super was finished and placed and Pike walked towards the bathroom that was off of the hallway in the back. Pike was always afraid to have a bowel movement at work because from his low-walled cubicle, he could hear the toilet flush, and figured he was one loud flatulent sound away from humiliation. He also hated going to the restroom because he had to walk by Carly's office space. They wouldn't usually interact on the pass-by, but Pike hated even having to share atom space, even if for just an instant, with the woman he had grown to hate. His fingers were barely dry from the hand sanitizer when he got back to his desk and a call came in.

"Pike, Chief Knox is on line one for you," Terri said through the intercom.

"OK. I mean, OK, thanks, I've been trying to work on saying thank you after you tell me I have a call (*since no one else in the office does*)."

"You don't have to do that," Terri said, not being nice, but sincere. She really was vein-filled with apathy and was not wistful concerning any part of her life.

Here you go, big boy, the chief of police is right behind that red blinking light of line one. Maybe I should make him wait? No, don't piss him off. Let's just do this, you stopped in at the station, you couldn't let your hearsay go from council the other night, so it's time to man up. I always hated that "man up" mantra. Being a man means tough not smart? Let's do this!

With confidence, Pike picked up the turn-of-the-century phone receiver, straightened out the cord and pressed line one.

"Hello, this is Pike."

"This is Chief Knox returning your call."

Umm, I never actually called you Captain Details.

"Hi, Chief Knox, thanks for taking the time and giving me a call. If you have a second, I'd like to ask you a few questions." *Of course he has a few seconds, he just called you, guy. Wake up, let's go, you know Carly has just tuned in when she heard the intercom.*

"What do you need?" the chief asked.

"Well, I'm just going to get right into it. It's only early July, but already, according to the Tuscarron County Sheriff's Office, there have been a record number of drug-related deaths in the county, mostly from overdoses. I know Winherst is affected by this as well, what can you tell me about the drug problem in Winherst?"

(Pause) "Well, Pike, we have a big cocaine problem right now."

"Really, and when you say a big problem, what do you mean?"

"I mean that there has never been this much cocaine seized, or deaths related to it and similar drugs in our community."

"I was unaware of overdose deaths in Winherst, can you be more specific?"

"I can, but I'm not sure how far into detail I'm going to go as the sheriff's office is still investigating and the case is ongoing."

"How many people have died?"

"This year, we believe two residents have died from drug-related causes. But the second one is still ongoing, we have not received the coroner's report."

"Do you know when the first drug zealot died and who it was?"

"It happened during the Tirlway fire. It is believed that the individual was on drugs at work, and when the fire started, was either asleep or couldn't get out in time. But we think asleep. According to the report, drugs were in the individual's system, but they died of smoke inhalation and the body was not burned. So that usually points to being passed out when the fire started, and they failed to wake up as the smoke entered the room."

Probably not a coke-head then; they never sleep or shut up.

"I see. Yes, I remember the person who died, well, I read about that fire. It happened before I started working here. And you said 'drugs seized,' what can you tell me about that?"

At this point, both the editor, Finn, and Carly stopped what they were doing to listen.

"Someone was selling drugs out of a downtown business. An insurance company. You'll need to find the report if you want the name of the business, but they sold bath salts in vials right there on Crescent Street."

"So what is being done to stop this drug influx?"

"The truth is, we need help. Residents need to start locking their garages and reporting any suspicious behavior to us immediately because the crimes and the drugs are related. They can't afford the drugs, so they have to steal. A common way is to strip abandoned houses, or ones on the market that sit empty, of copper and metal for scrap, robbing leaf blowers, chainsaws and power tools from sheds and pawning them. Anything that they can easily get their hands on they will nab," Chief Knox said.

"Wow, well I'm really glad you called me because I can let everyone know the severity of the situation." *You should also know that when I get home, I'm going to find some way to do drugs. Well, probably something that's less harmful than alcohol, but on another note, I do like some of your money strategies.*

"If it's late, and you see someone walking around backyards, call us. No one is doing a tree survey at midnight."

"Chief, thanks again, and if there is anything you may want to add after we get off here, please feel free to call me back."

"Goodbye."

"'Bye."

After slowly and gently setting down the phone while smiling, Pike stood up and looked at Theresa, who along with everyone else, was staring at Pike.

"Theresa, got a big story for you. Going to need you to clear out that giant American flag art you were going to run under the header, and make room for a real front page story about drugs, theft and addicts burning alive."

"What, what did Knox say exactly? How did you hear about this, why were you talking to him? Tell everything from the start," Theresa demanded.

"I think you should just wait and read the story like everyone else," Pike joked after his confidence got the better of his judgment. Theresa did not respond. "Just kidding, umm, where to start? So I know my workload has been pretty heavy lately, especially with me leaving tomorrow, but I still have side stories I try to grind out, ya know, at home, when the world is asleep." Pike was laying it on really thickly, but he was just so proud of his story. "So in talking with the sheriff's office, I started realizing what a crazy drug problem this county seems to have this year."

"The Erie Telegraph ran a story about the drug problem two weeks ago, you sure you didn't just read that story?" Carly asked.

"I don't steal, err, I should say, I don't use the dailies as my source for good story leads, Carly, as some people in this office do. Anyway (looking back to Theresa), I wanted to localize the issue. That's what you and Carly are always telling me to do, take an A.P story, and localize it. Take a state story, and localize it. So, through my research, I knew there had to be a problem in Winherst as well. And I read the police reports, all that petty theft sounded like junkie behavior to me. So I stopped at the police station this morning to chat with the Chief about the issue. I was really planning on doing this story for next week, ya know, with me being gone two days, I wanted to plan ahead. He wouldn't see me this morning, but called me, and spilled the beans that there is a serious drug problem in Winherst," Pike said as he could feel the condescending nature of his *speak* seep from his chipped but repaired front teeth.

"He said there's a big problem, what are they doing about it?" Theresa asked.

"Wants the people to police for him. If we see any drug heads or thefts, to give him a call."

"And what were you talking about, deaths in Winherst?" she asked.

"You know that factory fire, the person that died, according to Knox, but kinda not officially 'cus it couldn't be proven, but he thinks some junkie shot up at work, fell asleep, and then died of smoke inhalation. No burns on the body I guess."

"What!? Oh, my gosh. OK, Rob," Theresa yelled towards the back. She hit his page button on her phone. Within moments the publisher was on the floor. "Rob, call the press, tell them we will be sending Winherst late today, and it might not come till 4:59. We have to run with this cocaine story."

Yes! Although it wasn't verbatim, she didn't actually yell, "Stop the press!" but I'll take it. I created a story and stopped the press. Well, I delayed them anyway. It still counts.

That moment was the last of the joy of the day Pike saw. It was running around calling coroners, other officers, looking up old police reports. And every hour Pike would send across, via the office-shared drive, what he thought was the completed story. Only to have Theresa send it back with questions written in huge fonts and in all caps. WHAT WAS THE GIRL'S NAME? WHAT WAS THE ADDRESS OF THE INSURANCE OFFICE? HOW MANY WEEKS? WHAT DID THE VIALS LOOK LIKE?

Close to 4 p.m., and without lunch, Pike finally couldn't do it anymore. He sent a draft over to Theresa, and told her via iChat that that's all he could do, that he was burned out and if that story wasn't good enough now, it probably was never going to be. There was some back and forth, but Pike was southbound by 4:44 p.m., excited and ready for a trip to America's biggest city.

22.

"He stood six inches above the floor. Women panted. Suddenly he collapsed in a heap. There were exclamations of disbelief followed by prolonged applause. His assistants helped him to a chair. Houdini asked for a glass of wine to restore his strength. He held the wine up in the spotlight. It turned colorless. He drank it. The wineglass disappeared from his hand." E. L. Doctorow, *R.*

It was 5 a.m., and outside his apartment door, in the breezeway, Pike could hear Randy's voice that had been growing in anticipation from the drive up from Pittsburgh.

"Bubber, let's go, New York ain't gonna wait for honkies like us. Let's go!"

It was going to be the second wedding of the year for Pike and Randy, but with an additional pal, Timmy, who they both met working construction a half-decade ago and a friendship was forged.

A rented, clean, cream, '12 Ford conversion van with satellite radio, air conditioning and a lot of room for humans and their cargo.

"I got shotgun," Timmy said. He was always decorated in faded bleak. Ash converse with wine shoestrings, tight skinny dark felt-colored jeans, some kind of rock or metal band or dead idol shirt, or a funny thrift store one. Or maybe a Star Wars one. Long thick sideburns glued to a skinny face and slicked-back Ponyboy hair.

Groom Daniel, originally from Oregon but now in New York, would visit Pike in Pennsylvania and they'd all make a "whimsical" night or two of it in Pittsburgh, and Timmy was added to Groom Daniel's friend and eventually wedding list.

"Shotgun? You don't even know who's driving," Pike said as he exited the front door of the complex, descended the concrete steps and stood beside the un-dented van on the blacktop.

"Nice to see you buddy. Funny, when you come to Pitt, you only call Randy, and never me," Timmy said as he moved in for a bro-hug of Pike.

"Well, you never leave your house, now that you are a homeowner, so what's the point? I heard you even play cribbage with the old couple across the street," Pike said.

"They live next door, actually, and I'm awesome at cribbage. But we play hearts if you must know. I thought journalists knew the facts, wait, that's way off."

Turning to the side, "Randy, go fuck yourself, let me guess, you're already five beers deep?" Pike said.

"Now, Timmy, I tried to warn you, Pike might get fun in New York, but the whole drive will suck with him," Randy countered.

The luggage was loaded. Suits hung nicely in the back back.

"I'm driving the first part," Randy said.

"And I'm in shotgun," Timmy said.

It was hard for Pike to relinquish front seat control. He loved driving on road trips, loved being in charge of a pragmatic navigational route, too. But, after 11 minutes, he relaxed and accepted that others would do just as well.

The six-cylinder was a bit of a gas-guzzler, but it had pick-up, so every time Randy accelerated to compensate for the lack of cruise control, the back passenger felt the liquid in his stomach bifurcate.

The rear speakers were right beside Pike's ears.

"Can you turn the music down a little bit? Or just put the speakers more to the front?" Pike yelled up to the nose of the van.

"Aww, little guy have sensitive ears?" Randy asked.

"I have normal ears."

"I forgot to tell you about the crazy dream I had last night," Randy told the vehicle.

Pike had not remembered a dream in 9 years. The lifestyle inhibited the dream cycle and made sleep thoughts susceptible to the void.

It took an hour of southeast driving before the group hit I-80, the road that would take them the length of Pennsylvania, through Dubois, Danville, south of Scranton, past Stroudsburg,

Parsippany, through northern New Jersey and into and onto the island of Manhattan.

The speakers were not switched to the front, but turned down a bit, providing little relief for the rear ears.

"We should be there in like eight or nine hours," said Timmy as he looked at the map, one foot on the dash, silver bracelets making noise as he scanned the page with an extended pointer finger.

"Eight hours, you out of your mind, guy? Be there in five, tops," Pike said.

"Five hours, ya right, New York is way further away," Randy said.

"Well, according to best man Earl, we will be there in five hours. He's lives in New York, and drives all over the states all the time. So I think I'm going to believe him over Bill and Ted's Excellent Navigating Adventure in the front seat there," Pike said.

"Earl? He doesn't drive all over the states. And Earl might be the best man, but the groom, Daniel, told me specifically not to listen to Earl if it has anything to do with New York. He's always telling Daniel, 'Don't worry, we can walk there,' and it's too far away. 'I'm sure they're open,' and they're closed." Randy said.

"Well, let's make a little wager," Pike suggested.

"I'll bet whatever you want that it takes longer than some five hours to get to New York City, 'cus if that was the case, I'd have already gone their like every other weekend, bubber," Randy said.

"Let's bet a dollar. Pride bet. You say eight, I say five, however long it takes, who's ever closer wins, OK?"

"OK, bubber. Did you know it only takes three hours to drive to Florida, just ask Earl," Randy said.

"We'll see, tough guy," Pike said.

"If you big penises are done, I'm hungry, let's get some breakfast," Timmy said.

They followed the ramp off the highway. They had been traveling for an hour an 45 minutes. Not wanting a sit-down, it was fast food or nothing for the van.

"There's a Dunkin Donuts. Let's go there, I heard it's good," Randy suggested.

With Pike always being behind and missing his bowl of cereal on his way to work, the McDonald's egg and cheese biscuit had been a daily staple.

"Let's go to McDonald's. It will be good, everyone knows what to get, it will just be easy," Pike said.

"I have to piss, so let's go in either way, plus we can't have six different orders in the drive through," Timmy said.

"Why do you want to go to shitty McDonald's, that you always eat? We're on vacation, dude, you might want to try something new." Randy said.

"Last time you told me that, we went to White Castle, and they gave me some mini fucking penny sandwich that tasted like shit. I just want a good base to start the trip," Pike pleaded.

Reluctantly, Randy gave in. After breakfast, they were back on I-80, and Pike wasn't too happy with his meal.

"My sandwich tastes like crap," Pike said. No one responded. "Sorry, everyone. My need to control made everyone support one of the worst chains in the world. Did you know there were federal indictments handed down to McDonald's for their cruelty to chickens? They had an extra-brutal way of sawing off the beak so they could pack them in tighter to transport them across the country. But all is not lost, I have a couple of pre-rolled joints that will save the day."

"Great, the doper is about to start. Well, Timmy, guess we don't have to worry about the back seat getting too loud," Randy said.

"I have a feeling that there's not going to be any talking back there in five minutes," Timmy said.

"Tim, we must have hit a skunk. Do you guys smell a skunk back there?" Randy asked.

"Smells like a dead skunk to me. Wow, dudes, it looks like the sky is made of diamonds, and like, Lucy is up there, too," Timmy said.

"What, I'm too high to understand you?" Pike bantered back.

"I know that's right," Randy said.

The rest of the ride was countryside. The slopes of the Appalachian range fell behind the wheels as the group made their way to the far eastern end of Pennsylvania. They stopped to use the restroom again and Randy refused to let Pike drive. Timmy left shotgun, and traded places with Pike, who couldn't wait to get out of the loud back seat. Pike was in a big pout fit about not being able to steer, but his easy chemical escape cured his petulance, and again the van became cloudy.

"Damn, did someone hit a skunk?" Randy said.

"Dude, that joke's even better the second time, can't wait for the third," Pike said.

"Smells like a dead skunk to me," Timmy added.

The horizon was blurred with buildings when the van approached Newark, New Jersey.

"There she is boys! New York City!" Randy said.

"That's not New York, guy; you can see a beginning and an end to that skyline. New York's never ends. Some say, like a rainbow, it's impossible to find the beginning," Pike said.

"I think you got that rainbow thing backwards," Timmy said.

"Either way, I don't know what city that is, but no way in hell is that New York. Bet you five bucks," Pike said.

"Bubber, five bucks. Tim, don't worry about the hotel room, bubber is going to be paying for it all with these stupid bets," Randy said.

The van circled around Newark and started making its approach to the Holland Tunnel.

Look at all this steel. It's everywhere. Giant pieces of support all over New Jersey. Garden state? They can grow steel? These bridges have massive metal beams, like it seems that the arch technology never made it to New Jersey. A support beam to support a support beam, and it never ceases. Where does the New York soccer team play? Didn't they just build a new stadium in New Jersey? You could take a subway, err, an underground, just like in Europe and go to a game. And the subway car, err, tube, would be filled with drunk home fans all singing the team's song. Wow. Probably not how it goes though. Although, this is

New York, 90% of the population just landed on the shores. So maybe. I wonder if New Jersey gets jealous of New York? They probably don't care. I guess I'm not jealous of New York, and I'm sure Hoboken or Newark are all a million times better than Penkal.

Right before the entrance to the Holland Tunnel, Randy pulled over.

"Fine, little baby, you can drive now," he said while looking through the rear-view mirror.

"I can drive now, can I? No, you got it, bud."

"I'm not driving in New York City. I've only been here once, and that was when I was like 10 with my parents."

"Bud, you'll be fine."

"Nope, I'll kill us all," Randy said, and he exited the driver's side door. Pike's ego did allow for him to believe that he was best suited for the transport, but that same ego didn't want to satisfy what he believed was the selfish way Randy divvied-up the drive times.

The van paid the toll and had no chance of turning back as the two lanes behind it filled up quickly; it and everyone was in a hurry into the city.

I love being under this much water. No fear at all 'cus you're totally fucked if something happens, so no point in worrying. It's like turbulence, either the plane is going to crash or it won't, might as well enjoy the feeling of the stomach falling out. Now, bungee jumping and shit like that, that's different, because you're not trying to travel to the bottom of the gorge via bungee. Life risk for thrills not function scares the shit out of me. But just feel it. And I can feel it. I'm beginning to feel it, as soon as you can see all that man-made defiance of gravity and convention and need, endless rows of buildings lasagna-layered on each other, and everyone is fine with it. And I feed off of that. I eat that energy of 9 million humans running around the same small area. I steal and consume their energy, and borrow some from the lack of space between buildings, and from the buildings themselves, housing drugs and murder and love and marshmallow cereals. 80 billion different kinds of chairs in New York. And for every one that is not currently sat in, I steal its energy. All black bodies give off energy. All light is waves that rip through the epidermal layer of the skin and pass through most without affecting them. But I'm too aware. I'm not from here, I don't have a taste for the coffee of New York, so the caffeine makes me jittery and jumpy and wide-eyed and ready to be stabbed, 'cus I will eat the knife, too. And the human wielding it. And I can feel the positive pressure from the water above. And I'm cumming and smoking and drinking and fighting, all in the same feeling, all under the same tunnel.

The daydreaming and weltering stopped suddenly as Pike's eyes adjusted to polluted sun rays when the Holland Tunnel popped the van from its intestinal track without care or mercy, letting New York deal with them.

Start. Stop. Begin to start again, but stop. It took them an hour to cover the short distance to the Manhattan bridge, as bikes and humans on foot blew by effortlessly. Pike was stressed out, worried about wrecking and trying to focus on driving while being immersed in Chinatown and Little Italy.

Every other shop on the corner selling the classic "I love New York" slogan via bumper sticker, cheap t-shirt and coffee mug. Thousands of different faces showing thousands of years of single-continent-only breeding, now all thrown together on an island, to mix the color pool. The different texture and hues of hair colors, styles, tucked under hats, and shaved off. Light summer dress, men with muscle shirts, no shirts, offensive shirts, shirts in other languages. Every girl being so distinctly different, and the tourist and even 10-year New York vet begging their eyes to stay on task, to not stare and awe and daydream about what color their insides really look like.

No one in the van had ever been to Brooklyn before, where the wedding was to be held, where groom Daniel and best man Earl lived, where the hotel was. Pike saw one of many bridges that would take him out of Manhattan, and he was relieved. But still consuming the energy, even as it distracted his driving.

Once on the Manhattan Bridge (Pike chose the low road over the high), there was some debate on whether the transport was suspended over the East River on the Brooklyn

Bridge or the Manhattan. Pike was incorrect even though he passed the sign telling him on what he was driving. Then they landed in Brooklyn and Pike was confused.

This is Brooklyn? This looks like every other urban area I've ever seen. Look, there's a Walgreens. Where is Jay-Z and the Huxtables and kids playing in fire hydrants and cops running after bad guys? Where are the big buildings? This looks just like the area around the University of Pitt. I want my money back.

At a stop light, Pike glanced down the road behind him via the passenger door mirror. There was an automobile speeding in their direction, attempting to squeeze between them and a car parked by the curb to the right.

They won't make that, no way, they are going to crash into the side of my van!

Without much of an option, Pike accelerated into the next lane that was also stopped and found three feet of room in between his bumper and the front and back of two cars in the other lane. Horns blew as the car flew by the van, nicking the mirror, and on through the red traffic light and into real Brooklyn.

"That guy almost smashed into us!" Randy exclaimed from his front row back seat.

I will not let Brooklyn eat me. I do the eating of cities. I do.

The wheels found their three-day resting place at the hotel. The check-in to the double queen. Pike always tried to get a corner room for noise (both that which he may cause and any from the neighbors) and distance from the elevator (which was also a sound wave issue). Also, he incorrectly believed exterior outside cameras had a hard time capturing corner rooms, due to their location.

The collective decided to walk around Park Slope, the community of Brooklyn in which they were staying, until they found someplace to eat.

The second pizzeria was good enough, and the all-glass frontage invited them in. There was an 80-year-old Italian guy sitting at a checkered table smoking a thin Sorel cigar, but other than him, the place was vacant. Cautiously, they approached the counter, as many do in the overwhelming city of New York. The group was greeted by a man in a flannel shirt under a clean white apron.

"Hey, how you guys doing? What can I do you for?" he asked with a smile offering blandishment.

"Well, what's the best deal?" Timmy asked, constantly cautious of price.

"However yous want to do it, guy. We got pies by the slice, or I can do a couple of pies for the lot of yous."

"Probably be cheaper to get two pizzas as opposed to by the slice?" Timmy wanted to confirm.

"Ya, as opposed to. Just tell me what you want on the pies, grab a seat, I'll bring right out to yous. I make pepperoni and sausage for ya?

Is he making a statement or asking a question?

There was debate, as Pike was a vegetarian, but they decided on a mushroom and onion pizza and a sausage. Pike hated mushrooms, but the three-minute conversation as the cook looked on wore on him, so he conceded.

Sitting down, Randy was curious about drinks.

"They got beer in this place?"

"Doesn't look like it." Timmy said.

"You don't need to start drinking at noon, Randy," Pike said.

"I'm on vacation, honey, and I can have one drink at lunch."

"You don't know what one beer is," Pike said.

"So big bachelor party tonight guys, what's the plan?" Timmy asked.

"Wouldn't you like to know? But sorry, it's top secret guy stuff," Pike said.

"Top secret? We're going to get drunk, watch some gross stripper and spend all day tomorrow trying to get laid," Timmy said.

"Wait, are you really getting a stripper?" Randy asked.

"Hold on, I'm not getting a stripper. I don't know what Earl has planned, but we're going to get wasted with the big groom Daniel, and that's it," Pike said.

"And if there's a stripper I'm sure you'll look the other way," Timmy said.

"I'll try not to fall in love, I mean, nothing," Pike said.

The food came. One sausage pizza, and one half-bacon and mushroom, half pineapple.

Glaring at the pizza in bewilderment, Randy knew the pizza wasn't right. But the lone cook, who had already accepted their payment upon ordering, had gone to the back. Well into the cooling process, he still hadn't resurfaced, so they ate what they could of the 16 inch, flat, thin, New York style greasy goodness. Pike only had one piece due to the meat and mushrooms.

"But really, what are we doing tonight?" Timmy asked about the party.

"It's not real clear, but I think we're going into the city, gonna bar hop and Earl has a hotel room somewhere. And we wear our outfits. That's pretty much all I know," Pike said.

He did, however, know a bit more.

In the weeks leading up to the wedding, Earl compiled a list of humans and sent them email updates about the party he was in charge of planning. Earl loved being in charge of not only the party, but the fact that no one could argue or change the plans that he wanted. One of the groom's friends, who lived in New York, suggested a "Requiem for a Dream" bachelor party.

"Requiem for a Dream" was a cult movie about the horrors of serious drug use. At one point, the female lead, who is desperate for drug money, goes to an expensive hotel suite where she gets naked with another girl. They then proceed to get on their hands and knees with their butts facing each other and have dildo sex as businessmen in ties circle them up, yell and drink and throw money at the women performing the act. The scene was intended to be repulsive, but oddly for some, like rape scenes in horror films, it is erotic.

Although the plan was suggested mostly in jest, by the end of the night, certain realities of the theme would come to fruition, causing some men to be scarred and others aroused.

The real "official" theme of the night was Andrew W. K., a rocker paying homage to the '80s hair bands of old. Everyone was to wear white pants, a white t-shirt and look dirty. It was to be the living re-creation of one of the rocker's album covers. Pike forgot his trailer-park-snow-colored pants and texted Earl, who said he would pick an extra pair up and give them to him when they met in Manhattan later that night.

"So when does it all start?" Timmy asked.

"I think we're supposed to meet Earl in, like, Grinch Village around seven tonight," Pike said.

"Umm, you mean Greenwich Village?" Randy asked.

"So we got some time to kill, what should we do?" Timmy asked.

Randy pulled out a subway map that he swiped from the hotel lobby. He recklessly unfolded it out on the table, sliding the pizza pan away, and everyone crowded around.

"Dudes, Coney Island, that's where we should go, that's the Warrior's home. Come on, let's go to Coney Island," Pike begged. No one answered immediately, and with that group, if there's not another suggestion the first one wins.

"Looks like we might be able to walk down there from here," Randy said.

"What? You ever read a map before? You already owe me six, want to make it seven and bet we can't walk to Coney Island from Park Slope?" Pike asked.

The cook emerged from the back, sweating.

"How'd yous like the pies, good, right?"

No one wanted to complain about the mix up.

"They were awesome. Hey, can you walk to Coney Island from here?" Randy asked the man.

"Yous sure can. It would take you a couple of days, but yous can do it, ahahah," he said.

With subway directions given by the pizza cook, the half half-dozen departed and went down into the underground.

The smell of hot shards of aligning alloys and power. The hot oxygen-less wind that sprints by the platform with the ride. Neat and new ways to travel.

The train did not stay underground long, as it would pop out above ground as it glided south, passing massive cemeteries, neo-gothic churches and 70-story apartment buildings next to vacant lots.

How would you ever get off this island if there was an emergency? Everyone in New York dies in the apocalypse. Food for 200 in a populated area of two million per barrio. You'd have to stash a boat somewhere. Like a little blow up one to get to the mainland. And no one could see you walking with it, or they'd gut you and take it. No trees or woods to hide in or behind, total exposure as everyone kills each other and eats the liver. But if the end doesn't come, they get to spend their lives around art and music and progression and thought and any kind of food you want at any corner.

Almost to Coney Island, Randy noticed a tear in the crotch of Pike's cut off dark hue Dickie shorts.

"Nice dick, dude," Randy said.

"What?" Pike said.

"Nice hole in your pants, guy."

"That's been there for a while. These are my travel shorts, I meant to change at the hotel, but I got distracted."

The train stopped in Coney Island and everyone got off except the three.

"Are we supposed to debark?" Timmy wondered.

"No, it says Coney Island is the next stop on the map," Randy said.

"Why did everyone just get off then?" Timmy wondered.

"Ya, and no one is getting on," Pike added.

"Let's just get off, I can see a roller coaster," Randy said.

As they descended the stairs from the elevated train platform, people in swimsuits and towels walked passed them.

New York has a beach community? Wow. And it is filled with color. All boring and uni-race in Oregon. Look at that black lady, those tits are pouring out of that suit. And the man beside her is ripped; better not get caught looking. Those people look like they're 11 years old and they appear drunk. What is this place?

They didn't make it to the boardwalk before encountering the Cyclone, the historic wooden roller coaster of Coney Island.

"Let's go on this, come on, we have to," Pike urged. Timmy was in. Randy was reluctant.

"We two will just go, and we'll meet you on the boardwalk over there," Pike said.

Almost to the top of the first hill, Timmy confessed to everyone in line that this was the first roller coaster he'd ever been on. Pike had been on many before, but for some reason, forgot the old rule about not riding in the last car on old coasters. Moments into the thrill ride, Pike and Timmy were troll-tossed around and jerked and pulled so much that they both had tears in their eyes by the end of the ride. And Pike's bowels had not at all reacted well, finally processing the McDonald's breakfast from earlier.

On the boardwalk, the team reunited, and Timmy was quite proud of what he had accomplished and the great travail he had endured.

"I'm sure Everest is hard, and I'm sure base jumping might have it's challenges, but I just rode the Cyclone; looks like my bucket list is complete."

"That roller coaster isn't even a fair ride," Randy said.

"A fair ride you wouldn't go on."

"I don't like roller coasters, bubber, so why would I ride one?"

Nice wide dark wooded boardwalk, shops and snacks on one side, views of ocean and humanity on the other. But where's the bathroom, I gotta shit? Oh, I see one.

"I need to hit the head, so I'll catch up," Pike said.

It was July 5, and Coney Island had not even begun to dig itself out of the trash heap caused from the holiday celebration the day before.

All of New York went to Coney Island yesterday, to drink and eat and piss and dump and light fireworks and scream and throw things into the sea.

When Pike approached the permanent bathroom structure, water was running out from under the door.

My shoes are going to get soaked just walking in there. I don't have beach gear. Got no choice.

The floor was saturated in multi-shades of coffee and powdered wigs. His shoes got wet and soaked through. Pike was able to find one stall that was not completely destroyed, and accomplished his goal.

"Where are you" phone calls were made, and Pike found Timmy and Randy in the back of a giant eatery that had a series of industrial fans running to keep the high Fahrenheit air moving.

They both had Coronas.

"Get yourself a beer, bubber," Randy suggested when Pike sat down.

"No way, too early. Made that mistake at George's wedding in San Diego. I'm not doing that here," Pike said.

"That's a first, you not trying to out drink everyone else," Timmy said.

"Well, it's a day of firsts, isn't it Cyclone boy? I am hungry, though, might get a snack," Pike said.

"Hungry, we just ate tons of pizza," Randy said.

The fries Pike ordered were soggy, and even a nice ketchup glaze couldn't help the taste or texture. Pike noticed an older man on the boardwalk with a sign hung over him that read, "Free Hugs."

What is wrong with that guy? Who wants to touch him? He's not out here spreading free love and human acceptance; he's a pervert. Can tell.

On their way back to the train, they passed the spot where the hot dog eating championships were held every year.

I don't know how I feel about that. Hot dogs are disgusting, in terms of fuel and what's in them, and we celebrate and honor a bunch of gluttony and waste as the world starves? Easy high horse, the world's going to starve with or without a hot dog competition.

The 40-minute train ride back to Park Slope was quiet. Randy's Shooter Jennings shirt was graffiti-ed with pizza sauce. Timmy just zoned out at the floor. Everyone just wanted to get home to the three-day nest of the Best Western.

George and new wife Denise flew in from San Diego and got to the hotel around 6 p.m.

Timmy, Randy and George were dressed in chalk. Pike had a notebook-paper-colored shirt on, but was waiting to meet up with Earl for his pants.

23.

"The organisms which cause the various treponematoses have different names—*Treponema pallidum, Treponema pertenue, Treponema carateum*—but they cannot be differentiated under a microscope." A. W. Crosby, Jr., *TCE*.

They took the train from Brooklyn to the Lower East Side of Manhattan, not "Greenwich Village." Everyone was to meet at the Dolphin Bar around 8 p.m., and in rolled the dirty-shoelace white-outfitted posse. They totaled 14 in mass, and the bar was doing a happy hour till 9:59, so the drinks were downed at a great pace, even at six dollars a beer. At 10:00 p.m., those same beers would be $12.

Earl showed up late, but had the groom Daniel with him. Everyone started chanting "wife" when they arrived. Pike changed in the bathroom. Only one person wasn't wearing the bland ensemble, and it was Sam, the human whose idea it was to go Andrew W. K. in the first place.

"I didn't think anyone would actually do it," Sam said while opening a $14 pack of Camel Lights.

A little after 11 p.m., the group walked a couple of blocks to another bar. There was a man with a large pizza eating by himself when they walked in.

"Man, thanks again for the pants, waist fits perfectly. So what's the deal with everyone eating pizza in a bar, I don't get it?" Pike asked Earl.

"No problem on the pants. It's quite common for people to be drinking at a bar in New York, then leave, go get a pizza, bring it into the bar, and start eating it. It's just what you do," Earl said.

Someone from the group, another local New Yorker, did just that 20 minutes later and Pike picked off the mushrooms and ate a slice.

I needed a base or I'd be puking tonight for sure.

At a quarter till the compass needle was pointing due north, Earl made the announcement that it was time to head to the hotel for more entertainment. Groom Daniel pulled Pike aside.

"What's going on tonight? Earl is being all secretive, is he getting a stripper, 'cus I'm not down? Peggy is not down either. I'm not even staying out tonight. Probably leave shortly."

"I don't know much about it. There might be, I kept hearing about some fucking 'Requiem for a Dream' recreation," Pike said.

"What? We're all going to be doing a bunch of heroin? Now that sounds cool," Daniel joked.

"No, I'm talking about the double-sided dildo."

"I know. This is dumb, I should just not go to the hotel room."

"I feel you, but Earl has gone to a lot trouble. Just go and stay for a bit and then leave if you want. Let me buy you a shot in the meantime," Pike offered.

Someone else got involved and they ended up doing back-to-back shots of Maker's Mark at $15 a tip back.

Cabs were easily hailed from the curb after Pike lit a joint and passed it to the humans that had similar interests.

"We're going to 31st and 7th, the Affinia. Go there now," Earl told everyone before a head first dive into the back seat of the cab.

Night had taken over the city, and cabs and sidewalks were filled.

Timmy, George, Randy and Pike got in one cab, with Pike in the front seat.

"Hey guys, where you guys headin'?" The skin tag-covered cab driver with an American accent asked.

"Umm, hold on, I put it in my phone, corner of 31st and 7th," George said.

"You guys aren't from around here, huh?" the driver asked.

After about 20 minutes, Randy saw that the driver had taken three left turns.

"What's up with the three left turns driver? I don't know New York, but I know that's a circle," Randy said noticeably drunk, having not stopped consuming alcohol since Coney Island.

"Whoa, guy, there's construction all over this city. I'm taking you the fastest way. Ya know, the police in this town don't put up with drunks the way they used to. Just last week, I had some problems, and I pulled over next to an officer, and they ripped two guys right out of my fuckin' cab, and took their asses right to jail."

"How much longer do you think?" Pike asked, trying to dissolve an escalating situation.

"As long as it takes, guy, I'm driving over here."

There was silence until the cab arrived out front of the Affinia hotel next to Madison Square Garden.

Pike paid and gave him an eight-dollar tip.

"Why the hell did you tip that guy, he was such a piece of shit?" Randy asked on the sidewalk, with the towering towers around them.

"I dunno, man, I was stoned and scared of the police, I guess."

They walked through the spacious and velvet-laced lobby and took the elevator to the 23rd floor.

Earl welcomed them into the suite. Full bar on the left, living room one, then hallways to the right and left that lead to smaller living rooms and two bedrooms.

"This place is so clutch," Pike said.

"Clutch? Nice word, douche," Earl said.

"My neighbor hates when I use that, too. Prob should stop. Where's everyone else?"

"Not here yet."

"Looks like they got screwed harder on the cab ride than we did."

Earl's iPhone vibrated.

"Shit, they're here, and downstairs," Earl said looking at the screen.

"They? How can you even afford this place? I know we all threw in 50 bucks, but come on," Randy said.

"One of Daniel's buddies is on the chamber of commerce for this area, so he booked it under their name. Got a deal, little under a thousand for the night. Does someone want to go down with me and get the entertainment and try to find everyone else?" Earl asked.

Pike was left alone to mind the room. He took the left hallway and sat at the desk in front of a window in the back bedroom and rolled a joint. Then he moved the desk and tried to open the window.

Freakin' pane won't budge past the first foot. Must be some safety thing so someone doesn't jump or throw a chair out.

The gap was big enough for Pike to poke his head out, and when he did, the downtown breeze blasted him in the face and the loud street sounds carried up 23 floors like he was on ground level.

Look at this city. Look at its flow. What flow. All those tiny yellow cabs down there, and the people, and the structures, all this moving together in perfect energy. What a nice breath. What vision I have from up here. Hey, there's Madison Square Garden. The roof anyway. I should smoke a joint to honor this moment of the complete visual understanding of this city.

The joint was smoked, but the warm air was rushing into the cooler room so even with his head outside, all the smoke was ushered back in by the atmospheric pressure.

Moments later the group arrived. Everyone was in awe at the magnitude of the place. Earl walked through the door with two Latina girls and A Man as well, who Pike would grow to hate.

Their entrance was accompanied by ear piercing applause, yells and whistles. A Man said they needed a place to get ready, and Earl directed them to the back left bedroom. But halfway down the hallway, A Man stopped and said, "You got a non-smoke-filled room we can get ready in?" Earl was confused, but backed them up and sent them down hallway number two. Sam had just had a massive bowel movement in the bathroom of bedroom two, and the whole room was consumed by the odor. It would have to do.

For the next half hour, the boys drank in the main living room, force-feeding groom Daniel and themselves shots. A few wondered what had happened to the entertainment, but they were still getting ready.

And their preparation was snorting crank/speed/meth in a smelly suite bathroom. When the girls and A Man finally appeared from the hallway, the girls had runny noses and amped up minds.

There are like 4 million girls in New York, and we gotta deal with these nasties? Both have little pouch bellies like they're five months pregnant, not cute faces and tits that sag like Snuffleupagus's nose. Probably better that way.

Daniel had already passed out sideways on a loveseat in the living room, and everyone hopped on the two couches and remaining floor spots.

Pike and George posted up at the bar; they had a clear sight line to the action, but were separated by the wood structure itself.

A half-gallon jug of brandy was handed to the first girl, who straddled an onlooker and proceeded to pour it down his throat while everyone counted the gulps. He got to four.

The girls didn't try to kid themselves with an actual striptease, but got naked almost instantly, even their footwear, something strippers usually always keep on. After about 20 minutes of working the room, collecting tips, and not being able to hear over the shouting and music, the girls took a break. Almost another half hour of snorting and mind bending in the back bedroom and bathroom.

80 percent of the drunken men had forgotten about them completely, but when they came out again, the switch was flipped and it was back to yelling and clapping and slurpy smiles. Eventually, there was a meeting of the minds.

"I just talked to the stripper's guy. For 200 bucks, they will have strap on sex in front of us," one person said.

"No way, that's too expensive," said another.

"No way, that's cheap. Let's start a collection," another man argued.

"Strap on sex, with Daniel, they are going to pound Daniel in the ass while he's passed out?"

"No, with each other."

"I want back-to-back, two-sided dildo action, or nothing, we gotta stick to the theme."

"That theme was a joke."

Before everyone could drink one beer, 200 American dollars had been collected. Pike thought he might want to tip at some point during the night, so he asked A Man if he had singles.

"You got 20 singles for a 20?"

"It's all good bro, just throw the 20 at them, that will get them going."

"Umm, nah, you got like 20 singles for me, though?"

"Nah, bro, I ain't got 20 singles for you."

"Bud, I've seen you put about a 1,000 singles that you've picked up from the floor into that little Crown Royal bag."

"I know what you're trying to do bro, and it ain't going to happen."

"What?! Whatever dude, fine I just won't tip 'em."

"Bro, I've been doing this a long time, it ain't going to happen, nice try," A Man said as he padded Pike on the arm.

Don't touch me you half-cunt. What game you think I'm trying to do here? How 'bout I split your fucking face open. Bet he's got a knife. He should have a knife. I would. He's probably got a gun; it's New York. Just get away from him and don't cause a scene and ruin it for everyone else.

There was a third and final break before "the show." Pike was unable to let the conversation with the A Man go. He was drunk, felt disrespected and wanted to leave. Taking a piss in bathroom one, Pike felt the "one-shot-too-many flick" hit his stomach. Projectile vomit into the bathtub. Maroon colors from pizza. Wanting to clean up after himself out of embarrassment purposes not moral ones, he turned the shower on and was on his hands and knees hand squeegee-ing the bile towards the drain.

"What are you doing, bubber, taking a shower?" Randy asked when he arrived at the scene. In three minutes, Randy would be passed out for the night on one of the couches.

The show began with one girl lying on her back. The second secured the purple dildo strap on around her waist, and brought it to the mouth of the first. A "Requiem" chant was started by the boys. Then the sex toy was moved back down and penetration began, and one guy took money and shoved it deep into the mouth of the girl who was getting poked on her back. It was the last straw for some, as the group was cut in half and the show ended minutes later. The girls were already packed, and made a quick exit.

Not knowing how to cope with what they just witnessed, there seemed to be a general understanding that the next best thing was to flip over couches, puncture the walls with lamps and wake up Daniel and team up on him. He was thrown to the ground, and then mattresses and box springs were pilled on top of him. His laughter and inebriation kept him from having the will and power to get up, and out of nowhere, but with good cause, he started puking as he laid there, smashed down on his stomach.

"Let's storm to Times Square, we are too awesome not to let the city of New York have more of us!" Someone yelled as he took a "puke 'n rally" shot of Jim Beam green label.

The Clockwork Orange white mass made it to street level, without Daniel, and started walking towards Times Square from The Garden. But fatigue won out. Pike wanted to be back in his hotel room and with his security. He was done with the party, done with ever seeing or being involved with any stripper ever again; he felt the reality of his participation set in, and stopped at a falafel truck.

"Extra Mediterranean sauce," he ordered. As the group continued forward, Pike, George and Timmy ate. Pike sat on a step and drunkenly destroyed his Middle Eastern cuisine. When he was finished, there was a creamy pool between his feet.

The train ride home was hard, and Timmy slept most of the way. Due to certain trains not running at 3 a.m., the trio ended up with an hour walk through Brooklyn, a usually inadvisable jaunt for rural tourists with different physiognomy.

Five hours later, at 10 a.m., Pike could feel his hip bone digging into the thin carpet, and his phone vibrating.

"What's up?" Pike answered.

"Idiot, you were supposed to be here an hour ago," groom Daniel said.

"What? What time is it?"

"What time do you think it is if you're an hour late?"

"I don't know, man, I think I'm still drunk."

"No shit, everyone is. Peggy is super pissed at me. I said I was coming home last night, but obviously I didn't since I woke up at 6 under a whole bunch of mattresses and covered in my own vomit. Well, I assume it was my own."

"Hahah, I remember that."

"I pretty much don't remember anything past leaving the bar, then it's all blackout from there."

"Man, Daniel, this could be a rough day for me."

"I don't care, get over here, you need to help me get ready, and Peggy is super mad that we haven't done a thing and none of my quote friends are here to help."

"I'm on my way," Pike said, hitting "end" on his phone.

24.

"Dear Cumberland, / I have been very near the Gates of Death & have returned very weak & an Old Man feeble & tottering, but not in Spirit & Life not in The Real Man The Imagination which Liveth for Ever. In that I am stronger & stronger as this Foolish Body decays." A letter from W. Blake to G. Cumberland, April 12, 1827.

Daniel lived two blocks from the hotel and Pike blazed a small joint out on the way. Daniel's apartment was the bottom of a four story, with a nice big backyard. Pike walked through the community hallway from the road and knocked on the freshly-painted-for-the-festivities door and was told to come in. Bride Peggy's brother, along with groom Daniel and his parents, were in the kitchen. Hugs, introductions and handshakes were all passed around.

The rehearsal dinner slash cookout was being held in the backyard at 3:30 p.m. Which was just about the right amount of time to set up chairs, hang bows, add flowers and blow up balloons before guests started to arrive. The wedding would also be held there Saturday at noon.

"Why doesn't your backyard have any grass?" Pike asked.

"Because no backyards in Brooklyn have grass," Daniel said.

"Well, they might want to change the name then, maybe drop the whole 'yard' part."

"Prison yards don't have grass, not all of them."

Peggy forgave Daniel and Pike as the day progressed and everyone was in an agreeable mood for the cookout. It was 93 degrees, sans shade. Both Daniel and Pike continued to drink, downing whiskey and waters throughout the day. Then they were both drunk for the rehearsal, which put them back on Peggy's negative side. And Pike broke one of his rules about staying drunk all the way through day two.

Wedding Saturday. Pike woke up in a similar state, still buzzed from the past 48 hours of drinking, but on a bed.

"What time is it?" Pike asked in a panic.

"After nine," Timmy said, rolling over and exposing his butt through baggy boxers.

"I gotta get ready, the wedding is in like an hour."

"You have at least two hours, relax."

Pike was there 30 minutes before the ceremony was set to begin and had to go wait in the basement with the two other groomsmen, Sam and Earl, along with the groom.

"I'm starting to feel sick," Pike said.

"Me too, I don't know how I feel about all this," Daniel said.

Piquant whiskey was brought down in coffee cups to sip on and medicate the alcohol withdraw and nervous anticipation.

"My suit doesn't match your guys'," Pike said. "It's too dark of a gray. I'm going to look stupid. My belt is the wrong shade, too, it doesn't match my shoes."

"No one cares about your suit, I'm going to get married. Crap, this is big, too big," Daniel said.

"In New York, no one matches their shoes and belt anymore. That's an '80s thing, man," Earl said.

The ceremony was under way. A very fashionable, hipster-based crowd of people in their young 30s filled the yard. Daniel and Peggy really were quite in love, and it spilled over into the audience. Before the vows, the rings were passed around to everyone in attendance. A female judge, acting as a justice of the peace, was doing the ceremony. She did not speak loud enough and habitually shook her hands and legs throughout the nuptials. The bridesmaids were sweating profusely, even with airy caramel short dresses. The men in suits looked like a bucket of slow moving, salty water had been thrown in their faces about every five minutes, keeping the run-off fresh and consistent.

One of Daniel's local friends owned a bistro in Brooklyn that hosted the reception. It was very chic and classy. Shiny nice hardwood, expensive tables and silverware, in a part of Park Slope that was lined with well-maintained houses and mature trees planted in the sidewalks decades ago.

The wedding party, after pictures, made their entrance, and soon Pike found himself in an inhibition-less conversation with a younger girl, AnaBeth, he had met through Daniel years ago.

Tattoos and the way you purposely didn't let your tank top straps completely cover your neon green bra.

"You look so gorgeous, AnaBeth," Pike told her. "Seriously, those high heels, your thin legs on display from them, the short dress, the way you define garment strategy!"

Two hours into the reception, and with liquor as the impetus, the woman found Pike to be quite attractive as well. So much so, that as they were talking, as the world was louder through inebriation but quieter around them, AnaBeth slapped him across the face and asked, "What are you going to do about it?"

Blood avalanche-slid into Pike's penis, as he sexily smiled back and gave her an aggressive kiss. She slapped him again.

While the weird foreplay was going on, Randy was talking to some English friends of the bride, and attempted to do an English accent, only it came out completely like a New York accent.

"Hey, look at me, I'm from England, hey, I'm walkin' oh-va heeeere." They were not amused.

Back at AnaBeth and Pike's table, she grabbed Pike's suit pants and pulled him close saying, "Let's go, I want you to teach me a lesson."

"Sure."

They got up, and walked toward the door. Before they left, Daniel's brother asked where they were going. AnaBeth rested her open palm on his chest and said, "I'm going to fuck this freak."

Not wanting to miss the speeches and too much of the reception, Pike loaded up the lady piggyback style and jogged down the sidewalk towards the hotel. Without going into the motive, Pike leaned back and sat his inebriated prize on the concrete while he ducked into the convenience store on the corner. After only seeing condoms, he asked the older man with dark hairy arms behind the counter, "Do you have any lube?" The clerk pointed to the condoms. "No, lube, not condoms, lube?" The clerk pointed to a bottle of cooking oil. Pike entertained the idea, but left with nothing.

What Pike enjoyed most about the intercourse was how much she demanded and forced and pulled their ribs together.

The great hug intercourse.

An hour later they were back at the reception. When they walked in, half the place cheered, half looked disappointed.

"Where were you, guy?" Daniel asked of his groomsmen.

"I'm sorry, man, I got this problem, and that AnaBeth girl is gorgeous, which doesn't help my dilapidating dilemma."

"You missed all the speeches. All three groomsmen were supposed to speak, not just the best man. And so everyone was looking for you, then my brother was like, 'He left to go have sex.' Nice, dude, nice."

"I apologize, I'm an idiot."

"I don't really care, you were probably going to just say something stupid anyway, but Peggy is mad and so is my mom."

"Wow, this sucks, I'm sorry."

At six o'clock, the reception ended, but the free drinks would not. Daniel had reserved a three-hour open bar slot at a locale that he frequented when he moved to the area five years prior from Oregon. The owners had given him a good deal, and Daniel wanted the party to be able to continue after the reception if people were so inclined. Of the 70 guests, about 30 made the 25-minute walk north to the new location. Both Pike and his new love interest compromised filling their bellies at the reception for sex and drink, and were well on their way to dangerous drunk grounds.

The bar was narrow and rectangular, but had a basement open-air patio. Most of the guests settled down there, and after the three-hour block ended, the bar let the public enter.

A very muscular, tall, coral-collared shirt-wearing man and his girlfriend entered the bar around 11 p.m. and made their way to the patio. The man was very intrigued by both Pike and his newfound lust, but mostly her, and bought them drinks and eventually ran out and gave them a pizza per the custom of the area.

The slice of pizza saved both from imminent vomiting, but the drunkenness was there to stay. Eventually, the man brought up the four of them leaving, and possibly going back to his apartment down the road. Pike wanted nothing to do with it, but the tattooed queen seemed opened to hang out.

At this point, Pike didn't know what the woman that he had touched naked hours ago was thinking, wasn't sure if she wanted something to do with this man, something possibly sexual, but on day three of drinking, all rationality, logic and reality were gone. Pike didn't say anything to anyone, but walked up the steps and out of the bar, heading towards his hotel.

You go do that guy. I don't care, hope you burn in hell. What a fool I was to believe in love and spending the rest of my life with that whore. Foursome, ya right, you and that dude will just hump each other's brains out all night while me and his girl, who I'd be getting the short end of that stick, watch. I hope he kills you in his apartment after you've had the night of your life. Bitch! What a bitch! I should go buy a knife and stab that cocksucker for trying to screw my future wife. We made a commitment, something the moral-less disgusting piece of shit city of New York knows nothing about. Here I am, mighty Brooklyn, here I am. Look, it's some dumb poor cracker, drunk, walking alone in tough-guy Brooklyn. Come get some cunts. 'Cus I cut eyes. I dig out sockets, you see. I don't punch, but I take the end of my thumb and drive it into the corner of your cornea by the nose, dig it down real good, then come across and out pops your eye like a cube from the ice tray. Pussies. This whole wedding sucked. I'm never going to another stupid wedding ever again. And I'm sure as fuck not being "in the wedding." I'm not buying or renting a suit, not going to some bachelor party where a bunch of dudes can't admit that they really want to poke each other, so they have to abuse a drug addict whore. Never again.

Back at the hotel, Pike rolled a joint, and tried to smoke it out of the window because the bathroom didn't have a fan. But the window would again, only open a foot and the smoke just bellowed back in.

The phone buzzed in his pocket.

"Hello, what do you want?"

"Hey, where are you, what are you doing?" AnaBeth asked. They exchanged numbers shortly after intercourse that day.

"Who the hell are you doing?"

"What are you talking about, I'm still down here at the patio? I went up to look for you, but couldn't find you."

"Oh. (slight change in voice) I'm actually outside, I'm coming down now."

Pike hung up and drunk-ran back to the bar. Out of breath, he was shocked to see her still talking with the panther-shirt man and his girlfriend.

"Hey, there you are, you were gone forever," beauty said.

"I want to leave, right now," Pike said.

"OK, fine, let's go."

They started to leave and Valentine man caught them at the bottom of the steps as they were about to ascend.

"Aww, you're leaving, too bad. He leaned in and gave the woman a hug, which left Pike standing in insecure pain. Before he could react, the man squared up with Pike and planted a big closed mouth kiss on his lips. "Next time," he said.

They walked back in silence, as Pike refused to answer or talk to the girl who was "out of his league" based on age, looks and intercourse-ability.

Not being able to trust his memory when he woke up close to 11 a.m. the next day, Pike got up slowly out of bed and used the bathroom. He was in her hotel room at the Western. He had a clear memory of the previous night, but his memories were made through an inebriated haze, so his conclusions may have been forged through insecurities, fear, jealously and a general un-reality.

"Are you still mad at me? I don't know what I did, either. You were being a huge dick last night for no reason," she said, when the noise from the hotel flush had subsided.

"If we never talk about last night as long as we live that will be fine with me," Pike said, not wanting to know or admit the truth, and if the truth was what he thought it may have been, his fragile ego could never understand, process or deal with it.

"Whatever, I thought we were having a good night until you wouldn't talk to me the whole walk home."

"I dunno, like I said, if you never want to speak of last night again I sure as shit don't."

"Don't get all cuss-y with me, though. You still should be sorry for treating me like that, you jerk."

"Sorry."

She would never return a call, text, email, or a salutation passed through a friend back to Pike for the rest of the summer.

From a physical standpoint, Pike's body needed a beer to ease the pain of withdraw. But he wouldn't drink one. Timmy and Randy had already gotten Bloody Marys in the morning, were showered and had the van packed when Pike was trying to wake up and accept himself in a room that wasn't his.

They were on the route and across the Manhattan Bridge by high noon. Pun intended.

There was little to no traffic in the city that Sunday compared to what was seen on Thursday, which was good because Pike refused to drive. No one pushed the issue either, they could tell the torn up nature of Pike's head and heart. But there was no sympathy towards those that self-inflict.

Around the west end of Chinatown, Pike yelled for the van to be pulled over. There wasn't time so he vomited in a chain-store plastic grocery bag. It was mostly orange juice and stomach bile. The bag was tossed in a trash can, and another one made ready, for he would need it three more times before they got back home to Penkal.

25.

"Many individuals have more sense than their male relatives; and, as nothing preponderates where there is a constant struggle for an equilibrium, without it has naturally more gravity, some women govern their husbands without degrading themselves, because intellect will always govern." M. Wollstonecraft, *AVOTROW*.

The Monday, or any day after a trip, like most, was very hard for Pike. Physically, his body had not yet recovered from sleep deprivation, excess poison that the liver tried to filter and the general wear and tear travel had on the body. But mentally, it was even worse. Guilt and self-hate for consuming so much and not trusting his life, feeling that everyone in New York was living such cooler and more meaningful paths than anything he could hope to do in Penkal. To cope, Pike's mind usually slowed close to a shut down.

Not thinking and barely breathing in the shower at 7:30 a.m., one eye squinted open, the other held shut from a lack of will to break through the crust seal in the corner of the socket. The drive to work, barely steering, gawking at the road until his eyes would water and he would be forced to blink. He was told once that binge alcoholics suffer serious yet small bouts of depression once they got back to the function and efficiency-driven aspects of their lives. If there was no point to getting all destroyed on substance for three days straight, then there certainly was no point to the other side as well—going to work sober and facing the very thing that perhaps he was trying to drink away in the first place.

It was a packed office Monday morning, and when Pike arrive 20 minutes past 9 a.m., the employees could feel the apathy and pain in him, and even Theresa, who was chomping at the bit to give him a new story and ask about his trip, laid off until after lunch. The color in Pike's face wasn't faded, but looked like a bad blush job, the lightened vibrancy of pale makeup saturation of the ballerina right before a show. And there weren't huge black semi-circles under his eyes either. What really happened was the skin around his eyes sagged, making it appear that the lower brow had jettisoned the skull, and the eyes themselves had fallen further back as a result. The first hour of the morning Pike opened his email account and just daydreamed at the screen. Pike did not care if there was a point to anything. He didn't really think, feel or react. Just sat, and looked, and at one point, puddled his keyboard from his leaking, watery corneas. A front pocket full of single dollar bills representing his usual state of penury.

Styrofoam drawing with his fingernail on the take-out box of Pad Thai, instead of eating. Pike maybe had six or seven bites off of the rough edges of the plastic fork, then placed the container on the stained bottom of the work fridge. Back to the desk. Looking at the computer, slowly blinking.

Theresa herself was returning from eating, and used the entrance eye contact to begin a conversation.

"Pike, how was New York?"

"New York? Best city of all time, but I couldn't handle it. It devoured me."

"Interesting. Well, there's been a lot happening since you've been gone."

"I missed two days."

"But they've hired a new principal at Southwood, some guy is suing the police department and the new school levy will be officially on the November ballot, so we'll need write-ups on those two and, well, really all of it."

"What's the deal with someone suing the police department?"

"Speaking of the department, have you been typing up the police reports, staying on top of that? I haven't seen any in awhile."

"Why do we do those, I mean, I know why we do them, 'cus gossip sells newspapers, but why do we do them?"

"It's not gossip," Carly said, standing behind Theresa making her own emergence from the lunch cycle. "They are police reports. And if you commit a crime, the media reports it. That's reporting 101."

"Right, Carly, right. Let's just forget the whole 'innocent until proven guilty' thing. In a small town, it doesn't matter whether you're actually guilty of the crime or not, if your name goes in the paper under 'police blotter' or 'logs' or 'arrests' you are guilty as far as the town is concerned," Pike said.

"I have no sympathy nor do I care how a town views criminals," Carly said.

"I'm not sure I can deal with this human today, Theresa, not today. Let's go over the stories I need to cover and I'll go out and cover them."

"That's typical from you," Carly said.

"Carly, it's just that sometimes you are so boring. So absolutely boring. Isn't another thing from journalism 101 to cover a story completely? Why don't we ever report residents that are found not guilty? Why don't we ever have a "court decision" section in the paper? A man gets arrested for drugs, we print his name beside the charge, and what's the whole town going to think? Well, he goes to court, and it turns out that the cops got the wrong man, that he's never done a drug in his life. Where's our story about that? We never run it because we don't care, because police blotter is shite journalism," Pike said.

"OK, let's keep moving on people," Theresa said.

"Did you know the three special education teachers are being let go from the district?" Pike continued. "So I could go police blotter style, and write that up, because that's what happened. It's the truth. But instead, a good journalist will talk to the super, administrators, the director of the program to make sure he has all the details. And guess what, they are dropping three people, but that's because they are re-working the whole set-up, they are going with inclusion in the classrooms, and will actually be bringing in five more-accredited Special Ed teachers," Pike said, with his voice raised.

"You are more than welcome to camp out down at the courthouse, and follow all these cases, and report what happens, I did it for years," Carly said.

"Or, we could just not run this nonsense gossip column. I mean, do you even think we get all the police reports sent to us? They send the traffic offenders, and minor drug arrests, and DUIs, so that it looks like they are cleaning up the streets and to make everyone conform and feel good. Why didn't we get anything about the cocaine theft issues? Because the police department doesn't want everyone to know certain truths about what a junkie-filled island Winherst has become."

"I want the rest of the police reports done by the end of the day, and printed and placed on my desk. I'm pulling you off the story about the department being sued. Tomorrow you can start working on the new school levy and meeting and interviewing the new principal, OK?" Theresa told.

(Pause) "Sure," Pike said.

"Sure?" Theresa asked.

"Yes, I sure will," he said.

We coulda had a nice relationship. I coulda been your little slave around here, covering all your little bullshit stories, but you had to push me. I'm so buried. The Penkal daily never called me. Why would they not want to hire a local boy who's been in the town six years and actually knows how to write? Experience? That's such a corporate excuse. Read my writings. The proof is in the word pudding. I mean, what the hell? Oh ya, this guy can write, he has covered all the shit that you need to cover in a town, but I'm worried his lack of experience might make him forget how to write. That's possible. Really, I bet it's just jealousy. And how people want others to suffer the same way they did. This person has to suffer through years and years of waiting for a promotion like I did. If it was good enough for me, it's good enough for them. Like everyone over 21 doesn't think the drinking age should be lowered, 'cus they already made it. I had to wait so you should, too. Why do you want people to suffer, just 'cus you had to? That's right, weak personalities love company. The breadline in my poor war-torn city is three hours long. The next day, you go outside and see that it's only two hours long. What's the human's first thought? That's not right, that's not fair, the line should be three hours, 'cus that's how long I had to wait for bread yesterday. Why don't you think, "Hey, awesome, shorter breadline, more people can get fed quicker." But you don't, you want everyone to be as disgusting a person as you are, and you want to slowly break them down over years and years of a three-hour wait.

You don't think I'll quit this job? Pull me from a story, ya wouldn't want the truth to come too far out. What happened to the editor that was ready to burn my relationship with the department as soon as I started here? What's that? The chief goes to your church? Isn't that nice. What a fat fucking whore you've become. Work here for 28 years? Are you kidding me? A complete waste of life. Would be nice, though, to run the news for the town. The people would not even be able to handle the facts that got printed if I ran this place.

"Theresa, if you would like, I could cover that police story," Carly said.

"Does nothing happen in the areas you are supposed to cover, or do you just have a hard time writing a good story?" Pike asked Carly confrontationally.

Publisher Rob entered the writing area from his desk and caught the end of the conversation.

"Pike, come with me, let's go for a walk," Rob said, as he headed for the back door not awaiting a reply. Pike followed as Carly smiled when he walked past.

I will gut your ovaries some day, killing your future kids in front of you.

Choking a bit from the humidity outside and how juxtaposed it was from the constant pumping of air-conditioning inside, Pike said, "What's going on, Rob?" He wasn't frightened of what Rob was going to say because he was in a completely apathetic mindset.

"Walk with me up to the drug store, I want to get a pop."

"I can do that."

"Do you know why I hired you? Obviously, it wasn't the interview process, since I wasn't there for that."

"Umm, you hired me because you thought I could sell papers?"

"Do you think I hired you to be a Newsie? No. You have very little to do with selling papers. These old towns are dominated by older people. The fresh young minds aren't settling in Winherst to raise a family, the schools are crap, and there aren't any jobs. Our reader base is established, and there hasn't been a fluctuation in subscriptions, or prescriptions as

Terri often says, in 20 years. Even if you wrote the most amazing, ground-breaking, revolutionary story of all time, you wouldn't change paper sales. People wouldn't run to their checkbooks and start adding the News-Times all over the city. Sure, the stores might get a new influx of buyers, but it would only be for a week. Everyone would try to find the story online, and if it really had legs, the Erie Telegraph, and the Pittsburgh papers and national media would be all over it, and frankly, have the resources to cover it better and more in-depthly. So no, I didn't hire you to sell papers."

"All rrright," Pike said, as they walked down the side alley and out into the tree and building shade of Main Street after lunch.

"The real reason I hired you was to be a part of it. I've read a million stories by a million poets, journalist, philosophers, lazy assholes and highly educated geniuses, and over a long enough timeline, they all blended together. But occasionally, something will pop up, you read something and say, wow, not only is that good, really good writing, but I want to be involved. I want in. That's why I hired you. I read the writing samples, I read the blog work, the sports stories, the joke editorials, and I wanted to be involved. It was obvious you didn't know shit about A.P. style, this journalism rule or that rule; I thought that it could be a serious project to turn a strong, blurry, scratchy voice that was trying to yell over everyone else, into a clear, calm message being softly spoken through a megaphone. But like I said, that was all part of wanting in."

"I appreciate what—"

"But it's been three months now and I'm not seeing it," Rob said, stopping at a bench and sitting down with the flow of traffic at his back. "What I'm seeing is a constant 'the rules don't apply to me' mentality. I don't see you trying to be a journalist, but the mold of some super journalist without taking into account certain sentence structures, attempting to follow the 5 Ws, and this many quotes, and asking the questions that you're supposed to ask. The structure does not have to define your treatise, but you aren't willing to work for the foundations and your peregrinations haven't given you the necessary journalistic base. Once you understand that bottom layer, you don't have to compose the way it's taught. Some news writing can become a perfected machine of quick information rapidly relayed out to the public, and you get to choose if it is devoid of heart, intent or humanity. And we have soulless writers on staff. Everyone does. And you need them. Take the new Southwood principal, that interview and write up needs to be professional and light, and talk about the principal's history and future. Easy, borderline boring, but necessary. The people want to read about and know who is running the school to which they are sending their kids.

"Then there is this whole other side of journalism, where the writer creates the story, follows a lead from a lead he got while trying to follow a lead. A need and a want to dissect how the human being is operating in the town they are covering. What's really going on? Who's really doing things? Cops and crime and schools and city council and high school sports, that's all one story. I hired you to find the other stories," Rob said.

"Well, to tell you the truth, I would love more freedom to cover—"

"You have one month. One month, from today, to show me both the foundational growth and the other side. You know how many 'fresh-out-of-college journalism grads' would love your job? And we wouldn't have to train, and we wouldn't have to hear arguments about the police blotter, and they would know the style guides inside and out, and know the Sunshine Laws, and be young and hungry and do whatever we ask because they needed a start. There were five perfect candidates when I hired you. I had to justify the hire to my superiors at Veritas Media, and they wanted even a shorter leash on you. You have one month Pike, write a real fucking story or you're gone," Rob said as he got up and walked into the drug store for his diet drink.

26.

"*There* chiefly I sought thee, there only I found thee; / Her glance was the best of the rays that surround thee; / When it sparkled o'er aught that was bright in my story, / I knew it was love, and I felt it was glory." G. G. L. Byron, *SWOTRBFAP*.

The talk put a huge amount of stress on Pike. He didn't smoke or drink the rest of the week, and Friday night he found himself alone, with the one blind shut and a baseball game on the radio in the background, thinking about how to progress.

The summer Olympics were underway, but all the coverage seemed lost on his lost mind.

What can I do, what can I cover? I need to be revolutionary. I need to change the town. How? I'm going to get fired. Before that talk, I could have quit. But now I'm motivated but have no goal. So sick. My stomach is sick. The stress is disintegrating my intestines and throat and insides. What will everyone say? When will they have enough of the nonsense, the constant job switch, the lack of career? When you get older, women want a man that owns some nice clothes, has a working nice car, has a set up life, 'cus if you don't, it's just more hassle for them. No one likes to wonder about rent every month. Living the dream, city to city, couch to couch, is nice until the bills and the repetition and nightmares come.

I'll tell you how I'm going to change that town, I'm going to get a new school built for the kids. I'm going to drive through Winherst in 20 years and see my tag everywhere, a spray-painted stencil that can't be covered up, painted over or removed. I will be revolution. And then I will cut out Carly's tongue, and feed it to Theresa.

Monday morning, late July, after Pike had spent all weekend devising plans for the revolution, he arrived comfortably at his desk, and beat Theresa to the start of conversing.

"Good morning, everyone," Pike said with accompanied eye contact and head nods. "So, Theresa, I want to really get into this levy issue. You said we need to cover it, so I want to make it my special project. I want to be the expert on the levy situation, I want to know more than the schools know, and be aware of all sides and opposition. Sound OK to you?"

"That's fine, but don't spend too much time on it. You still have everything else to cover as well. Speaking of, there is a fundraiser this weekend for a longtime Winherst resident, Coral Derry, who is battling some kind of illness. Set up an interview and run a promo so we can get it out before this weekend, OK?"

"Yep, no problem."

The following day, Tuesday, Pike was calling the new superintendent's cell phone at 9:03 a.m. from his car parked outside of the aging middle school building.

"Hello, this is Pierce Elber."

"Hey, Pierce, Pike, Logan Pike here. I need total access to the Rover school building."

"Pike?"

"Yes, Pierce, it's Pike, from the News-Times. I need total access to your building."

"Pike?"

"You are trying to pass a levy in November, right?"

"Pike?"

"If the building is as bad as the state reported it is, and how bad the school board says it is, then let me get in there. The students are gone, I won't disrupt or mess with anything, just let me get in there with a camera, and show everyone the truth. It's bad, right? Well, let's prove it with photos and real reporting."

"Pike? (Pause) When were you thinking about doing this?"

"Today. But I need the green light from you for legal/liability purposes. But you don't have to be involved at all. I will contact principal Brown, since it's his building, and we'll go from there."

"Pike? (Long pause) Can I trust your intent, that you are looking out for the students' best interest?"

"Pierce? (Pause) If the building is, if I may speak candidly, a piece of shit, there will be no way everyone in this town won't know about it come tomorrow morning when the papers come out."

"You got the green light."

Rover grades 4 through 8 principal Reggie Brown was contacted first by superintendent Elber, followed by Pike. A little before the sun rested at its highest point, they both were standing outside the massive brick school building as Brown continued to force the wrong key into the door. Eventually it opened, and Pike and Brown were met by Marvin Ryland, janitor and building specialist.

"Did you hear us outside?" Brown asked Ryland, right inside of the first floor entryway.

"I figured it was you," he said.

"You could have opened the door for us."

"Didn't know who was on the other side."

"Could've been zombies," Pike added.

"Haha, yes, it could have been," Brown said remembering he was sent to cuddle and steer and manipulate and show this reporter the truth, the truth he believed in.

Up several flights of cracked yet flickering summer-polished steps to a closet looking room. On a ladder, opening an out-swinging man door, onto the roof. Rubber sheets, rectangular at 5'10", cover-cropped across every square foot.

"So this is where the wrestling team practices, uh?" Pike said when all three men had established themselves on the structure's highest platform.

"Haha, with our budget, it wouldn't surprise me," Brown said as he looked down at Pike's notebook, awaiting quotation. It didn't make the cut.

This is Winherst. I can see it all from here. Lot of green. Mature trees.

The tour continued as Pike documented faulty, rusted-out fire escapes, vacuous hallways and a leaking roof that would rain in on certain classrooms. On to exposed wiring, electrical boxes and manifolds spanning three centuries, uneven steps, mold growth in the basement, and then finally, the front page photo.

The tour was almost complete when Pike asked about any crawlspaces or passageways they haven't seen or inspected yet.

"Off the boiler room, there is access to a series of crawlspaces. But they don't ever get used and no one ever opens the doors," janitor Ryland said. Brown quickly shot him a look that said, "We want to show him everything, but not everything."

"Well, let's take a quick look and call it a tour," Pike said.

The key was pounded into the lock slot, and the rust particles broke as it was turned and the door opened. Right on the inside of the wall was a giant sign in caution orange, that read: "Warning: Asbestos." The whole floor was covered and coated in it. It had not been sealed or properly mitigated. Pike snapped a shot of the sign, and that was the front page feature art that went with next morning's headline. "I wouldn't walk through certain parts of that building, let alone send my kids there," a part of the story said.

It was the "shock jock" attempt at change through journalism. A floor-by-floor visual documentation of neglect for a building that monitored and raised hundreds of kids every day.

The paper received four letters to the editor, one typed, two via electronic mail and one hand written, concerning the story. One person wanted the facts checked. Another begged the town to pass the levy. One said that kids don't learn in crawlspaces so everything in the building was fine. And another said that the town of Winherst was fortunate to have a reporter that seemed to care about the town.

The next day, Friday, Theresa called a reporters' meeting at the office to discuss the county fair that was in two weeks. The Tuscarron County fair was one of the top five biggest in the state, due mostly to a rich rural and farm community around Winherst that never really changed in terms of population or ideas. The whole paper was involved for the weeks prior and during the county fair. Total coverage was a must, from harness racing, pig showing, food and vendors to ticket prices and the fair king and queen.

"Pretty much be the same setup as last year, list the events, prices, when what's showing where, etc. We will do a tab a week before then coverage throughout. Most of the tab will be bulletin board types of things, but I will need a feature story from each of you. I have a couple of leads if you would like," she said.

"I would like," Finn said.

"They added a new show barn, junior fair is being re-worked and they are adding another day of harness racing, so who wants what?" she asked.

"I have seniority, so I'll pick first," Carly said. "I think that the horse racing story could be quite expansive and—"

"Then I'll do the new barn," Pike tried to jump in.

"Hold on, I'm not finished," Carly said. "Horse racing would be nice, but seems too simple. I'll do the barn story."

"I got the junior fair," Finn said.

"Looks like I'm covering harness racing. Which actually could be pretty controversial. With all the drugs they pump into 'fair circuit' horses to keep them racing, the shady off-track betting, plus the whole gambling concept at a county fair…," Pike said.

"No. That's not what this tab is about. The fair tab is a positive insert that people read to get excited about a big deal in a small town. Keep it nice and simple or you'll have to re-write it, OK?" Theresa said.

The next week passed. Pike wrote a nice and clean and easy-going story about harness racing. He was also sent to cover a tipped-over canoe in the reservoir, a DMV worker that was named "Clerk of the Year," a bible school, a Relay for Life event that raised $40,000 for cancer survivors and the local U-10 girls' softball team that took home second place at state.

It was the last week of July, and with August approaching, the people of Winherst began to prepare for the influx of humans coming in for the fair, and to acknowledge they were a couple of lazy weekends away from being on the doorstep of fall.

A week later after the Thursday papers were stuffed in mailboxes and thrown on front steps, Theresa called another reporters' meeting.

"The fair starts Sunday, so plan on going Monday, Tuesday and Wednesday for stories. Then Thursday and Friday if you need to as well. In terms of content, there are a couple of things. Pike, I want you to cover the pavilion events. You can have the weekend off and be good for Monday's assignment," Theresa said.

"What's Monday's assignment?" Pike asked.

"Fair animals. Lots and lots of fair animals."

"I might look into the safety of the rides," Carly said.

"They aren't safe, because they're fair rides," Finn said.

"What about you, Finn, what will you be covering?" Theresa asked.

"I had the same idea as Carly, going to localize the fair and then for Tuesday I'm going to talk to fair officials about what has changed over the years, what's new this year and what they think will be inevitable changes or things they will have to address in the future," Finn said. "Then I'll come up with something for Wednesday as well."

"Any other fair stories before we get back to work?" Theresa asked.

"Yes, I'm glad you called this meeting so I'd have a chance to update you all on what I'm going to be covering at the fair. Now everyone's seen a 'carnie,' right? They work the games, have tattoos, tan and wrinkly skin, have smokers voices and laughs, perhaps a tooth is still waiting to be replaced, etc. But what are they really like? Who are these people? What happens at the fairgrounds when the gates close and the lights don't flicker and pop, how much do they get paid and are they really just American traveling gypsies? Those questions will all be answered when I go undercover as a 'carnie' worker for two days during the fair," Pike said.

"That sounds ridiculous, how could you even write that story?" Carly asked.

"Yes that seems too extreme. How would you even do that?" Theresa asked.

"I already have the job lined up. According to my awesome new boss, the workers need overflow help for 'school day' and 'senior slash military day.' You know, when all the schools get out to attend the fair and the day when seniors and military get in free. I guess they get overwhelmed, and have to watch all the little kids who are prone to steal and make mischief while at the fair and surrounded by friends. So they hire help for a couple of days. Local people. I applied. I got the job. And the story is going to be amazing. Supposed to be a madhouse."

"You didn't clear any of this with me. You're acting perfidiously. You can't just decide that you're going to—"

"He cleared it with me, last week when we went for a walk to the drug store. I meant to tell you, but I forgot," the publisher Rob said as he came into the work room from his office, wanting to catch the last parts of the meeting.

"Then I guess it's fine, if you say so. Seems a little risky for our audience, but you're the publisher, so I'll just sit here and wait to see what happens," Theresa said, as she daydreamed about the story being a train wreck and her telling Rob, "I told you so," after it was too late and had already gone to press.

"If that's the case, I'd like to go undercover as a donut maker at the fair," Carly said.

"How did you get this 'carnie' job?" Theresa asked.

27.

"'A ring of pikes, mingled with shot and horse, / Whose shattered limbs, being tossed as high as heaven, / Hang in the air as thick as sunny motes, / And canst thou, coward, stand in fear of death?' / ...*He cuts his arm.* / A wound is nothing..." C. Marlowe, *TTG, PII*

The day before, Pike was buying his favorite drink, a lemon-lime, squeeze-bottle of Gatorade at the gas station, when he ran into a retired janitor he did a story on two months before.

"How's it going? I hope you liked the story I wrote. Some say sometimes it's not the writer but what he has to work with," Pike joked.

"My wife and I thought it was a fine article," the older man said.

"So how's the retired life treatin' ya?"

"I didn't stay retired very long, I'm working the fair next week."

"Really, what are you doing at the fair?"

"I'll be working the skill games at the fair, you know, guess your weight, pop a balloon, things like that."

"How'd you get that position?"

"I got the job about 20 years ago. The fair was in town, I was there, playing a game, and a guy wanted to know if I'd work a couple of days because they were short. I've been a part-timer ever since. The bosses and games change, but there's always work if you don't mind a bit of hustling."

"You think there would be any way I could get a post? I'd love to work a fair game, always have."

They conversed a little more and the old janitor told Pike to meet him outside of Goner's supermarket at 3 p.m. later that day.

Pike arrived early and met the janitor, and they stood outside, sweating, but in the dim of the storefront's overhang.

"Is the boss or whatever showing up here at three?" Pike asked.

"He told me three but you never know." A few minutes later the peeling paint pay phone next to the cola vending machines rang. "That's probably him," he said, moving over and lifting the phone from the gravitational pull and the base from which it hung. "Hello. Yep. I know. All week, yep, I'm going to be real good, get a lot of yards. I was the only person last year to get four yards in a day. No way! Yes. Also, there's a guy here that needs some extra cash, wants to work. OK. That sounds about right. Tuesday and Wednesday? OK. No, I will, you don't have to keep telling me that. I know that..., hello? Guess he hung up."

"So what happened?" Pike asked.

"I think I got you a part-time job, buddy. Normally I'd ask about a finders fee, but that article you wrote was so nice we'll just call it even."

"Thanks. And about that, please don't tell anyone that I'm a reporter. It's in my contract that I can't work another job without telling them, and I know they wouldn't let me do this, and I really need the extra cash. OK?"

"Sure, I won't say anything. If I thought you were going to write a story about this I wouldn't have made the call. They hate reporters. And some pretty bad things have happened to writers that have tried to be sneaky and get a story. Usually they want to write about how the game is rigged, how no one can win, but the carnival workers are a tight-lipped group. They are their own society. When the fair lights go out, I'm telling you, it's a different world."

"Just for my own curiosity, why the payphone call, like a bad '70s spy flick?"

"Solomon, my boss, doesn't put an ad in the paper for help. He has to meet and recruit you himself or you have to know someone to get in. I know, it's harder to break into the carnie world than to get into Harvard, but like I said, they are one big family, and you just don't let anyone into your family. Solomon, he's old school. Before cell phones, there were house phones. But people move, lines and numbers change. But this payphone location and number have stayed the same forever. So when the fair gets close, I come here the Thursday before, and at 3 p.m., he calls. If I miss the call I just find him at the fairgrounds. Which is more prone to happen. Hahah. Anyway, they will be setting up Saturday, so come with me and I'll have you meet Solomon, and see if he wants to use you. Looks like it would be just two days, Tuesday and Wednesday. They get a lot of extra people and kids into the fair on those days. And they're already stocked for the weekend."

Two days later felt like a hangover Monday, instead of a celebratory Friday. He left the paper early.

Need to rest up for my big interview tomorrow anyway. Saturday.

The janitor and Pike met outside the fair's main gate a little before 1 p.m. They strolled and patrolled the grounds until they located a Fredrich's Amusement trailer.

"This should be it. It's weird, all the rides and skill games are all under 'Fredrich's Amusement,' the title, but each boss owns a different section. I don't think there is even a 'Fredrich's Amusement,' it's just written on the sides of the rides."

"I'm not sure I understand," Pike said as he looked around the grounds, remembering drinking Twisted Kilt beers during Irish Fest not very far from where he was standing.

The janitor knuckle rolled the outside screen door of the mobile trailer, as Pike tried to get serious and into character, although he hadn't exactly figured out who that was to be. But as far as outfit, Pike had on an old metal shirt from the band "Cradle of Filth" and jeans that were worn but not holey. And low sinking eyes were a nice incidental touch, as he had drank 8 domestic beers last night on an empty stomach, which had, sometime around 2:47 a.m., lead to capillaries bursting beneath his skin.

No one came to the door of the sun-faded chrome long trailer hooked up to a '78 Chevy pickup that had one wheel-well completely oxidized out. The janitor knocked again, this time wanting to be noticed.

"Heard you the fucking first time," yelled a voice from inside the trailer.

The janitor smiled at Pike, who's face looked uneasy.

The main door opened, but the darkness from within stole visual confirmation of a human doing the opening action. Then the screen door burst out, narrowly missing the janitor's nose, a move that seemed plotted from within.

Out in the light appeared Solomon, short cut-off jean shorts, a blue collared shirt with stains around the lower belly button area and "Fredrich's Amusement" printed across the left collarbone.

"What do you want?" Solomon asked with a frown.

"I want to show you how to manage a fair," the janitor said, laughing.

"Hahah, I can't believe you are still alive, let alone dumb enough to come back to work for me for another year," Solomon said. They shook hands, and as they did, Solomon extended his middle finger and pressed it hard into the underside of the wrist, making the janitor's hand go limp. "Always did have a weak handshake."

"Solomon, this is the guy I told you about on the phone, going to do some part-time stuff."

"Let's get started," Solomon said, turning and looking at Pike with a straight face. "Why don't you go over to the Tilt-a-Whirl, that's where we are going to have our meeting, and let me talk with this guy for a second in my office," Solomon said talking to the janitor while still looking at Pike.

The janitor pivoted his feet and began walking away.

"Please, come on in," Solomon said from the elevated step up of the trailer's base, as he held the screen door open with an outstretched and catamount-tattooed forearm.

Walking in and to the right, Solomon took a seat in the middle of a booth, and motioned for Pike to have a seat at the table across from him.

"What's your name?"

"Pike, Logan Pike."

"Pike? I knew a gymnast that liked to Pike, if you know what I mean?" Solomon said with a side smile.

Although not fully understanding the joke, but figuring it had something to do with sex and flexibility, Pike said, "One time I dated a limbo instructor, that was fun."

"Ha, ya, that would be one wife that was always bending over backward for you!"

Yes, that's the joke. You don't have to extrapolate. Ya see, skeletons don't have any insides, or guts, so that's why he didn't want to cross the road. Thanks for explaining. Wow, I just noticed the knife collection on the wall. And the collection of wolf prints. What are you going to do with a bunch of little swords? Can't call 'em that, they are like little daggers you'd find at the bottom of the cereal box. They don't do that anymore do they? Presents at the bottom of the cereal box. You have to go online to the website to claim your "prize."

"I'm not sure what you were told about this work, but let me tell you a little bit about it and make sure it is something that you want to commit to. And I mean commit, if you're thinking about being a quitter or half-assing this assignment, you should just get out right now."

"No, I'm here to work, could really use the money," Pike assured.

"Good. I don't usually hire part-time help, but this fair is really big, one of the bigger ones in the state, so we need to pick up help. If you were with me on the road, there wouldn't be any problems, we wouldn't even be havin' this talk. I know you'd work or you'd be on the side of the road with your thumb out."

"So what kind of work will I be doing?"

"Hold on son, not so fast. We'd have to determine what game you would be best at. I mean what game can you sell. Anyone can stand in front of a bunch of balloons and try to get someone to play. That's easy. It's all about the up-sell. Probably start you at the duck pond or ping pong toss. That requires not much thought, think you can handle that?"

"Yes."

"Good. Now we work 12-hour days, 10 to 10. Can you handle that?"

"Yes, sir."

"Don't give me any of that sir shit, I know sarcasm."

"It wasn't, but I won't, sorry."

"Over your shift, you will be responsible for three yards. If you don't make your three yards, it comes out of your pay, OK?"

"Acceptable. But what's three yards, like how much is that?"

"*Like*, a yard is a 100 bucks. You will get three yards Tuesday and three more Wednesday. That's the minimum. The guys that have been here awhile can pull five yards no problem. Now, since you live here in town, you won't be needing sleeping arrangements, I don't need to rent you out a cot, right?"

"No."

"And what about the kitchen, will you need to pay to use my kitchen?"

"I will probably just pack or eat fair food. I have a weird diet."

"If we were on the road, you would need it. Couldn't afford to eat fair food and without a kitchen, well-dried Ramen and peanut butter gets old after awhile. Well, I guess we are good to start. Follow me to the Tilt-a-whirl, and we'll go over the ground rules, have you meet who will be training you. And you don't get paid for today, so don't ask."

Monday, Pike was at the fair around 10 a.m. to work as a reporter, not a "carnie." The second day of the rural event was pretty quiet in the morning, one vendor per rolling food cart or shop or tent or table in the merchant building. Cool early August morning, the tan exposed bottom arms of the farmers and summer shirt wearers, and Pike walking around, bored, wasting an hour until the opening ceremony, where the king and queen were to be crowned. The smell of oil and batter and horse manure.

After covering the crowning, per usual, Pike killed an hour at the local state park, delayed another hour eating tofu, Szechuan-style, in downtown Winherst, and strolled into work around 2 p.m. on that Monday.

As he was uploading photos, Theresa turned around to an empty south office, except Pike.

"Looks like it's just us today. As long as you do your fair stories, don't feel like you have to come into the office this week. No one else does. Not even Rob, and he's the publisher. Everyone just assumes everyone is working and writing about the fair, even though no one ever seems to see anyone else actually at the fair."

"Interesting. But thanks. I was there all day and didn't see anyone. Figured I'd just do the fair animals write up here and call 'er a day," Pike said.

"And everything is still all set up for your undercover assignment tomorrow?"

"Yep. I'm working two back-to-back 12-hour days, Tuesday and Wednesday."

"Oh, really? Wow. That's a lot. So I guess we will just have to run your story Thursday then, no way we can have it by end of the day Wednesday if you're still researching, if that's what you could call it."

"Yeah, but that should work out better. I mean, we have two weeks, if you count the fair tab, of fair coverage. So the first week is normal prep bucolic boring fair stuff—"

"Boring?"

"Sorry, wrong term. Normal coverage, then when everyone thinks they are burnt out on the fair, the Pulitzer will emerge, and people will see the real life of the 'carnie.'"

"Just remember the audience. You may have gotten permission from Rob when I wasn't around, but I still decide what content goes in the paper as long as I'm the editor."

"It will be tasteful and all that. Going to write it like a professional news story, it will be fine."

"We'll see. Who knows? Maybe I should just print it no matter what's written. I think I'm just getting tired of this place a little bit. Everyone is out at the fair and I'm here typing all these stupid hand written letters to the editor. I really don't like coming into work, and I tell my cats every morning how much I hate every morning."

A cat lady. Why are you going jerk mode, she is obviously trying to open up to you? It's easy to attack the vulnerable. No shit, that's why they're a target. Weak mind, will and confidence. Confidence? Who you kidding? You're always running.

"So maybe you should just like, take a vacation or something?"

"I'm going to at the end of the year; I have vacation time saved up. But I think it will be the same when I get back."

"Well, it would suck for me if you left, but have you thought about finding a new editing post?" Pike asked.

"I don't know."

Don't know what? Am I talking to a 6-year-old right now, was it beyond a yes or no question?

"I'm going home. Put the animals story in my inbox before you leave, I'm going to come in early tomorrow."

"Will do," Pike said, thinking about the saying, "You can't help those that won't help themselves." "I probably won't see you until Thursday, then."

"Maybe you will, maybe you won't," Theresa said as she picked up her purse from the floor and slowly trotted out of the office.

Maybe I will and maybe I won't? What the hell kind of talk is that? I was "hear" to listen, but if that was some suicide hint, she's going to have to try harder than that to get me to act. Everyone has problems, that doesn't mean that I shouldn't try to help people. But if you're going to kill yourself, do it over someone else's actions. Like if I came home and found my future New York wife dead, and the murderer, wait, I should say killer, not murderer, 'cus I think you have to be convicted of said crime to be a murderer, 'cus I think that's a legal term. Anyway, if the killer had turned the gun on himself, and my future wife was dead, I could see killing myself. But I would never kill myself based on my own actions. Like if I messed up somehow, and my stupidity led to my parents or family dying, then I take it. I take the looks of absolute sorrow from the deads' families, and I take the abuse from the headlines, the trashing of my family name, and I sit in jail everyday in horrible misery and guilt from what I've done. I would stand up in the jail cell, and lean slightly forward with my hands behind my back until I began to fall. Then I would let my face smash with all the forward momentum into the floor, so hard and so many times that they would have to surgically remove my nose due to it constantly jamming up into my brain and being smashed so much that breathing was no longer possible. That's what you do when you fuck up. That's what you do when your brain tells your body to act, and things go bad, you own up and take the lashings. But if we're talking about some kind of crazy clinical depression where your mind is not letting you know how it's thinking, then that may be a different story on all fronts.

At 5 p.m. Pike was at home, gazing out of his kitchen window at the rows of apartment buildings that encased him.

There are like 30 birds on that power line, pretty neat. You see the white one? Whoa, yes, I see him. What is that an albino hawk or something? I don't know, probably not a hawk, but I wouldn't want to be that bird living among predators in the wild. Yes, but in the winter, when it snows, it becomes God. Risk death for nine months but then become God for 3... Hmm, not sure it would be worth it.

I'm tired of this place. I feel like I'm in a rut here in Penkal. I love the new job, I just don't know. You don't know; that's the problem. I'm tired of not knowing. I think New York messed with me a bit. There were all these cool people really living in New York, and then I look at myself and wonder what the hell I'm doing? I don't have children, so I could move to New York or anywhere, I could work at almost any shitty paper, but I don't want to feel like I'm in the middle, in the middle of one life while wanting to raise another. But it's all coming together now. I got the real good job, and once I get some experience, it's on to a bigger paper and bigger pay and some day I won't have to ever work again, it will just be me, my future wife from New York, raising kids, out in the country, living and loving the dream. Why didn't the Penkal paper ever call? I don't know what the fuck their deal is. I mean, if they read my clips, I don't know how they could not want to hire a great journalist that is familiar with everything here? Someone must hate me at the Penkal paper. Hard to see through the spotted-with-dirt kitchen window.

Tomorrow I start that "carnie" job. We'll see. Could go either way. My boss is shady as shit, has all these little knives displayed all over his camper. Weird, but to tell you the truth, I thought he would be a lot weirder, considering all the "carnie" tales I've heard throughout my lifetime.

28.

"'My sleeves are wet as when I wandered these / shores. / The Isle of the Raincoat does not fend off the / dews.'" M. Shikibu, *TTOG*.

At 9:50 a.m. that next morning, Pike was softly knocking on the boss's trailer.

"He ain't in there, he out prepping the games," a wide man with a skinny moustache told Pike.

Solomon was pounding a steel pole into a fitting when Pike came up from behind him.

"Boss, I'm ready to start."

"Where the fuck have you been? I didn't think you were going to show."

"You said I started at 10, so—"

"The games open at 10, but you have to prep them. You think the wagon doors open by themselves right at 10? You think all the plugs get plugged in and the stuffed animals get straightened by themselves right at 10? Jesus, come with me, I'll show you where you are starting."

Although aggravated, Pike didn't respond to Solomon's complaints. This was only half a real job, so Pike could allow some insults and nonsense to flow right off of his shoulders, the resting place of his ego.

The fairgrounds were encircled by freshly burnished barbed-wire fencing. On the east side of the grounds, right inside of those links, the caravan of caravans set up their week long community. All of the trucks, campers, truckcampers and RVs were situated along that back fence after the rides and skill games had been unloaded by the sidewalk and designated areas. The trucks and mini-homes on wheels formed a nice wall that outsiders couldn't see through, and set boundaries for the fairgoers on the inside as well.

At the Tuscarron County Fair, there were a total of four bosses. Two of those bosses ran all of the rides. That included hiring people to man the rides, to fix them, to collect money and place hand stamps on kids. These two bosses knew mechanics, and since they were dealing with such large pieces of equipment that were spinning and twirling and throwing humans all over the fairgrounds, they tended to be a bit more serious and less motivational with their employees.

They didn't have quotas or yards for their workers. The help was paid hourly, and fired quickly if safety became an issue. But they were still confined to a budget, and they never followed any local or state safety codes, so oftentimes, when they said something was fixed, it was really just patched until the leak sprang up again.

The other two bosses ran the skill games. Solomon was in charge of nine games, and the other boss, 20. Although it was not the case with this amusement company, often bosses would compete with one another, sabotage each other's trailers and eventually try to buy out the other person's games.

That is how boss three came to run 20 games. He worked a fair circuit with another boss 17 years ago. One week, it was a fixed bet that won him the ring-toss trailer. Another week, a boss owed him a debt that was not fair and eventually exploited, and he gained skeet ball. Even the big fairs have a cap as to how many games can exist at one event, and eventually boss three felt he had a perfect number of 20 games. But then he joined another fair circuit, that hit bigger fairs throughout the summer, and they (Fredrich's Amusement) then had room for 30 games, nine of which were already owned and run by Solomon. It worked out, however, as both boss three and Solomon got along, and Solomon never took a bet or a bribe or a loan from boss three, so things stabilized.

All of Solomon's nine games were all in a line. Shoot liquid through the clown's mouth, knock the milk jugs over, land the whiffle ball in the basket, ring toss, duck pond, dart balloon pop, guess your weight, skee ball, basketball shot and land a ping pong ball in the floating shallow dish.

Solomon lead Pike in front of the row of games, stopping at the "land a ping pong ball in the shallow dish" game. There was a heavy-set young man milling around the station. Upon seeing the boss, he started straightening the stuffed animals lining the walls.

"Germaine, you got a new guy working with you today. Show him the basics, and then you'll move over to skee ball," Solomon said.

Germaine looked at Pike, and without changing his facial expression, lifted his chin up in hello. Pike followed suit and nodded his head upward.

The boss took off in a quick pace. His metabolism and light meals, mixed with a heavy dose of fair exercise, nicotine and caffeine, had kept him slim.

Still messing with the animals, Germaine ignored Pike. After a few minutes, Pike asked, "So what do I need to know?"

"Less is more, dawg," Germaine said. He was short but thick, with softball bat biceps. From an urban area of Detroit.

"OK, I don't know what that means."

"You're a sub, we call 'em narcs, or temps, or Waves, 'cus you all always comin' and goin' 'n' shit. So as a Wave, it's usually best that you don't know too much."

"What do I need to know though, ya know, to do this game? Just collect money and give a prize, right?"

"How many yards Sol-dawg tell you you needed?"

"Ummm, let me think. Yesterday, I think he said I needed 300 bucks by the end of the day. That seems like a lot for a dollar ping pong toss."

"Three yards then. He lettin' you off easy, dawg, my first week it was four yards. Aight, let me show you some shit," Germaine said through his mole-dominated Caucasian skin.

The game was run out of a square front unfolding trailer. A large circular metal trough filled with water was in the center, and a little electrical pump kept the water flowing in a counterclockwise motion. On top of the water were eight shallow bowls that let the water carry them around the container.

"Aight, where to start? Guess we'll just go in order, dawg. First, the set-up. Marks give you money, you give them ping pong balls, and if they can toss one and have it rest in the bowl, they win."

"Did you just call the costumers marks? You a con man now?" Pike asked.

"I ain't no dishonest thief like a con man. Ain't no cheating here. Marks want to play. Plus they stole that term from us Voyagers anyway. You know that?"

"No, what'd they steal?"

"Mother-fuckin' con man, man. Back in the old days, when a Voyager would see a person at the fair with a big wallet, or that was real gullible and shit, they would take a piece of chalk and mark the back shoulder of the fool. That's where dat fuckin' term comes from, the mark. It's always been the term of the Voyager."

"Does the term 'carnie' offend you?"

"Shit, dawg, I been called a lot worse than that. So all the prizes hang on the walls around the game. You always want to be up-sellin', ya know what I'm sayin'? Look, it's like dis. You get three balls for a buck, 10 balls for two bucks, and a bucket full for five. Marks will walk around the front of your game and you gots to lure them in and shit. It's just a buck, blah blah blah. Then, tell them about the better deal 'n shit, and get them in for five. One of the bowls is the big prize, and I like to put a 10-dollar bill inside one of the bowls as well. Fuckin' kids will spend 15 bucks trying to win 10 dollars. So that's pretty much it, you got it?"

"Seems easy enough."

"Man, dawg, I hope Lil' Skin shows up this week."

"What was that?"

"Lil' Skin, that's what I call my Tuscarron County Fair regular. Ya see, dawg, if you get on a circuit, you end up goin' to all the same places, year after year. And a lot of the people go to the fairs in they towns, year after year. So you meet people, regulars, that you look forward to seeing each year. There is this hot little black lady that I call Lil' Skin, 'cus she small, dawg. And hot. And one of these years I'm gonna get in her nappy dugout, dawg."

At 10 a.m., even on the school district's fair day, there was not a lot of foot traffic along game row. But with every person that would pass, Germaine would try to reel them in. If it was a kid, he would ask or make a comment about their shirt. This would at least get their attention, start a conversation or bring them close. If it was a female, even though he was overweight, Germaine would flirt and throw out a compliment. "Dang, girl, your parents did a good job making you, those are some good genes." "I'm lonely, can you help me with that?" "My girlfriend says I can't talk to pretty ladies, so please, keep walkin'." "Oh my, I just fell in love, so I guess you get one free toss." When it came to the men, it was all ego attacks. "Come on, man, show your girl you know how to win. Win that pretty girl a big stuffed rabbit, then she might actually stay with you." "Buddy, come show me how to win, I ain't seen a real man try all day."

There are thousands of psychology grad students that wish they had access to the empirical data collected and then implemented by the carnival worker.

No one passed Germaine's station without acknowledging his presence in some way or another. Eventually, his roping tactics worked, and he started selling five-dollar buckets of balls. No one wins. The boss walks by the game and yells, "Move, move, move, let's go. I need those three yards!"

"He's yelling at us already, it's been like a half hour?" Pike said to Germaine.

"Better get used to it, Wave, he'll do it all day. And he'll check your progress too, dawg, better have a good start or you ain't gonna be takin' no lunch break."

"This is a cut-throat operation," Pike said.

"This ain't nothing, and you got no idea, Wave. I've seen dudes not make their yards, and have to sleep outside. Solomon is a cool guy, but don't fuck with his money, dawg. He rents us out bunks in his trailer. No yard, no bed."

The cloudless sky soon heated the concreted-over grass and atmosphere of the fairgrounds. There was some shade standing beside the trough inside the trailer, but hours from now, by 2 p.m., the sun's elliptical would throw beams of heat and light straight into the box on wheels. Pike was already sweating, regretting wearing jeans, and bored.

I hope to God this dude stays with me all day. I can't pull those yards. What if Solomon beats or stabs me for messin' with his money? What if he finds out I'm a reporter? Then he'll kill me for sure. I want to see what goes on here at night, when the fair lights dim and the gypsies begin.

Around noon, Solomon appeared at the game and pulled Germaine off. "How many yards you got?" Solomon asked Germaine.

"I gots half a yard already, and it's only lunchtime," he said.

Turning to Pike, "How many yards you got?"

"I don't have anything, I thought we were working together on this game and I was getting trained."

"You haven't made any money in two hours? No lunch for you until you get half a yard. Get moving, let's go, let's go!" Solomon yelled at Pike.

With hunger as a great motivator, Pike began harassing and yelling at and talking to everyone that passed. He got some customers but was weak with the up-sell. Around 2 p.m., he counted 22 bucks in his front pocket.

I'm going to die. Solomon ain't gonna be happy with me.

Another carnival worker, Oswald, was eating a steak-stuffed pita when he stopped in front of Pike's game.

"How's your day going, pal?" Oswald asked. He had thick Renaissance-riffled hair, a plain t-shirt on and tight-fitting stone-washed jeans.

"Pretty rough, I'm not sure how I'm going to make my quota. I need half a yard before I can go to lunch," Pike said.

"Pal, that's not good. I tell you what, why don't you go grab a bite real quick, I'm on my lunch right now, I'll cover for you. Then whatever I make you can have towards your quota, pal," Oswald said.

"Really? Thanks, man, I'm starving. Be right back."

"Pal, wait, before you go, I don't have any change, my apron is back at my station. Leave me some cash in case I get a big mark that needs a 50 broke."

"Right, that's a good idea. Here's like the 22 bucks I made so far. Just use that if you need. Be right back," Pike said.

Half way through ordering two slices of cheese pizza, Pike realized that he had put a lot of trust into a carnival worker he had just met. On the jog, he hurried back to his game and Oswald was gone.

Son of a bitch. That dude just stole 22 bucks from me. I'm telling Solomon, I don't care if there is some rat "carnie" code; that dude is a thief and I'm a fool.

Pike didn't have to wait long for Solomon to manifest, yelling at everyone in a cacophonous tone to work harder as he went up and down game row.

"Hey, Solomon, can I talk to you a second?" Pike asked. He proceeded to explain what happened with Oswald. Yelling down the line, Solomon played "telephone" and chain-letter to carry the message that Oswald was to come to the ping pong toss.

Directly, Oswald showed up, looking surprised to be summoned. "Boss, what's up?"

"The Wave here said you stole money from him," Solomon said.

"You better be careful of what lies you are telling to cover your own ass," Oswald said looking at Pike. He then proceeded to pull out a pocket knife and dig out the dirt from under his fingernails as he finished his canard. "I walked by this game and saw that no one was working it, so I stayed around as long as I could, trying to protect your money, boss. I don't know where my pal here went."

"You said you would watch the booth while I got something to eat," Pike in a tremulous voice, intimidated by the appearance of a knife, even if under the guise of a manicure.

"Wait, you left the game to go eat?" Solomon said, upset.

"He said he would cover for me."

"Oswald, get out of my face. If I didn't need you for the rest of the circuit, I would have fired you long ago. And for you Dike, or Kike, or whatever, don't leave your station, don't give people money and get to work. Three yards by the end of the day!"

Conniving bastards! Just wait until I expose this whole thing with my cover story. And I'm going to find a way to get that little shit Oswald back, too.

The pizza gave Pike's brain the fuel it needed to continue the day. It got hotter. And instead of boiling over, Pike really got into the role. Started roping them in like a 19-year carnival vet. He embraced the carnival workers' rules, like nothing is too offensive. No comments from a mark can hurt you. The super young and super old are easy money. Ethics do not exist when it comes to messing with Solomon's cash. Attacking a male's sense of worth works every time.

The pit of Pike's stomach started growling again, and with the influx of fair patrons from 4 p.m. to 7 p.m., Pike estimated he had two yards easy. He counted in between tosses. $249. He flagged down Solomon.

"Gonna make my yards, easily boss. So can I get a break to get some dinner?"

"How much you make so far?" Solomon asked. His skin was a dried-out light Arabian color.

"Close to 250, and if it wasn't for the nonsense earlier, I'd already have it."

"When you get to three yards you can take a break. And it looks like you'll be responsible for four yards tomorrow, since you got so much today and you took the morning off," he said, walking away, but yelling to the other workers about getting going and moving quicker.

What a jerk. I should just take the money and run. They know my name, but screw it, I live in Penkal. And they will be off to another fair in a couple of days. I'll go do what I want and—

Solomon doubled back. "Give me the two yards now," he said.

At 10 till 10 p.m., Pike was feeling good. He had 131 dollars in his pocket, 31 over his quota. His knees were grinding into the top of his shins from standing all day. The essence that he had left was from the last shot of adrenaline and testosterone his body oozed out when he realized he only had minutes more to go.

"Close 'em up boys, we're done for the day, aint' nobody here," Solomon yelled. The doors swung shut, were bolted and locked. Everyone was smoking their just-off-work cigarettes, and Pike handed Solomon the rest of his cash.

"How much you got, boy?"

"131, so that's three yards and 31 bucks over that as well."

"I can add; that's why I'm the boss. Here you go," Solomon handed Pike a wad of money. Pike counted it as Solomon was walking away with a silver-headed hammer in his hand.

"Hey, what's this, only 31 bucks? You said 8 dollars an hour."

Solomon turned, and smiled. "It's all there. You worked from noon to 9:30, so that's nine hours."

"Noon to 9:30, what are you—"

"We don't pay for training and you didn't make any money the first two hours anyway. I really should start the pay at two. So noon to nine, that's 72 bucks. Then 25 for the cot, another 10 for the kitchen, so you're looking at 37 dollars for the day. So you got 31, ok, here's another 5. Now don't give me anymore shit and be here at least a half an hour before your shift starts tomorrow, not like today, OK?" Solomon asked as he tapped the tip of the hammer on Pike's shoulder.

"I never said anything about staying here. I'm not staying here, so why would I pay for a bed?"

"Not staying here? That's what your janitor friend told me. Well, what's done is done."

"I guess if I'm paying to stay, then I'm going to stay. Where's my bed, please?" Pike said, trying to call his bluff.

"I'll show you. No wait, I'll get Germaine to show you," Solomon said as he walked away dragging the hammer against the chassis exterior of a trailer door.

Germaine caught up with Pike after Pike stood alone in front of his game for nearly 17 minutes.

"Dawg, what you crazy, you are trying to stay in this shit-hole tonight? Whatever's clever, I guess. Let me show you around."

Germaine escorted Pike to the backside of the games. He told him that there were four different groups within Fredrich's Amusement. They each had different camps, or areas, but they butted up to each other and because there was no bad blood, mingled throughout the night. In one camp you could catch a card game in a trailer, another camp was drinking and doing any drugs that were around, another area was the bosses, who really didn't hang out or socialize with the workers. Just depended on the night, what you wanted to do and what you wanted to get into.

Germaine showed Pike their trailer for crashing. Three bunk crates for six sleeping spots. No restroom or shower. Those were in Solomon's personal trailer extension, and the access was restricted until morning.

"When the gates close and lock up, our society emerges. There's no police or law, dawg, just what we decide and make. I heard old Oswald got you today. That was allowed 'cus you just a Wave, dawg, if it was one of us, there would be a discussion, kinda like a trial, and then punishment. Oswald actually had his teeth kicked in by Solomon one time for trying to steal a knife off him. You learn it aint' smart to be stealin' 'n' robbin' from us Voyagers, there are a thousand marks a day you can mess wit all that shit wit. Know what I'm sayin'?"

"I wanted to punch him in the face, but he was like cleaning out his nails with a knife, so I said screw it," Pike said.

"Just remember that you're a Wave, I'm surprised that Solomon actually let you stay with us tonight, dawg, just watch your shit, even from me. I could be lying my ass off just to get you to trust me, to get close to you, dawg."

"So when does everyone go to bed and should we run to a store and get some beer or something?"

"We make our own, homie. One of the guys that runs da Sea-Ray has a still that goes everywhere wit him. Best 'shine around. He'll probably sell you some if I introduce you, dawg."

"Well, how about I just go get some beer?"

"Gates closed dawg. No one in or out of Voyager City until dawn. But don't worry, thems can still make a body disappear, but it's a lot of work so they probably wouldn't fuck wit you, unless you really pissed everyone off, dawg. But you cool, stay with me, tonight's going to be fun, I think there's a group going out to work the town tonight, and that will be some *buns life* shite."

"Work the town?" Pike asked.

Around the real dawn of night, 13 workers, including Germaine and Pike, huddled around each other on the far side of the fairgrounds. Everyone seemed to be wearing an unofficial uniform of dark jeans and a faded bleak t-shirt.

"What's the fucking Wave doing? He's not going, he doesn't know the game," one of them said in a turgid way.

"He's wit me, dawg, and he's good," Germaine said.

Going to the same fairs year after year, the carnival workers got to know the towns in which they set up their week-long cities. They had an idea of local bars, shopping, food and most importantly, they got to know the fairgrounds themselves pretty well. The grounds were locked up tightly at night (protecting hundreds of thousands of dollars in livestock and equipment), which kept their nighttime society a secret, but also added protection. Once they learned a weak spot in the fence, or a place to jump the wall, one or two nights during the week they would go out in little groups to "work" the town, regardless of what onerous opprobrium that could result. "Working" could be something as simple as a dine and ditch, shipwreck con, lost dog con, a series of short cons or simple straight under-the-jacket theft from a 24-hour supermarket. And there were always at least 25 witnesses that swore so and so was with them all night at the fairgrounds.

"So what we going to work tonight?" a worker asked.

"I say a version of 'the wire,'" another added.

"Do we look like we have the tech to do 'the wire'?"

"Then let's do the 'lost necklace,' or 'camera.'"

"That game is so old."

"No one ever catches on, that's why the old games are still the best games. They say never try to swindle a good person, but I can tell this city is greed un-surrendered."

More discussion just lead to more arguing, and they finally decided, since there were two bars within walking distance of the grounds, that they would split up with a group doing the "left phone" game first, then see what happens when everyone reconvened at the second bar.

When the group got close to the fence in the burnt-out corner of the fairgrounds, where security lights had failed to hit, one of the men lifted up the bottom of the chain-link fence as everyone crawled underneath. No one talked, and in single file fashion, they marched from the grounds until they hit the downtown sidewalks. A few of guys went into a gas station, a couple into an all-night grocery store and the remaining four finally broke the silence before entering a local watering hole.

The place was beyond dead. Just the bartender watching Fox Sports One and sipping Gin.

At bar two, the drinkers of the town lived and the "carnies" reconvened. Someone lifted a wallet in the bathroom, where there weren't any cameras, and used a credit card to open a tab. They all drank for free on that. Then they were separated into little groups for short cons and bets.

Germaine bet someone they couldn't drink two shots before he could drink three pints. Oswald was set up for the three-card con. But there were no fish in the lake. Not a single nibble, let alone anything taking the hook.

The bar was getting ready to shut down at 1:30 a.m., and like a locust swarm, the whole mass of carnival workers got up and exited quickly, as if the new trick was "don't be last or you'll pay the fake tab." Pike had paid for drinks with his own money, and was pretty inebriated for the walk back.

"I'm not going back without some success," Oswald said. "Let's do the movie store bit."

Years ago, Oswald and Germaine had a nice two-man hustle going. Oswald would go into a movie rental store type of establishment and go to the counter to chat up the employee. If it was a girl he would try to flirt, a guy, appeal to his needs concerning conversational dominance. Eventually, Oswald would say thanks and walk out of the store. Then Germaine would approach the counter right after, notice the mobile and offer, "Hey, there's a telephone here." The nurtured-nice through suburbia, church and zero exposure worker would then say, "My gosh, he forgot his mobile," proceeded by a quick sprint out of the door to the land of heroes.

Germaine, who had been watching the cash register movements, then leans his heavily supported frame over the counter, opens the drawer, withdraws and leaves just as the worker returns.

"I ain't got it in me, dawg, I'm beat. Plus we'd have to do a gas station and they never leave they post," Germaine said.

Under the fence and back to camp. A card game was just getting started with a group of workers from the ride sector, but Pike thought only an idiot would play cards with these humans. That actually didn't stop him, but a lack of cash did. Germaine had his fill as well, and they both went back to the bunk trailer where Pike, despite his shady surroundings, fell asleep quickly.

A full bladder and erection to prove as much helped Pike wake up around 6 a.m. He could hear Germaine snoring in the cot above him.

Why did I let that fat ass sleep on the top bunk? Guess I didn't even think about it. Good one, drunk guy. Check your wallet. (Before passing out, Pike stuffed his wallet in his front pocket and decided to wear all his clothes to bed.)

There wasn't a sheet on the mattress and the summer night didn't require a blanket, so even in short sleeves Pike stayed warm.

Dawn on the fairgrounds. Although structurally everything was the same, the city had vanished. Tractors were being started in the distance, the gates were opening up and all the carnival workers were sleeping. There was still a good amount of alcohol in Pike's stomach, having had his last shot of whiskey less than five hours ago.

Time to run away. I'm not working another hour for this slit operation. I'm still drunk, which means a hangover all day, and I don't think I can do it. Where can I piss? How 'bout between the trailers? OK. What a crazy night. How do these guys not get killed more? Those cons are so played out, how does someone not stab them? (Pounding on the back window of the trailer he was in between.)

"Gumdrop dick, go piss somewhere else!"

Who the hell was that? I gotta get outta here. What if they drug me and kidnap me? What if dude follows me home? I gotta run, run now while they're still asleep. But what about paying that stealing jerk Oswald back? Plus I want to steal a knife off of boss man's wall. Are you kidding yourself right now? You want to try to beat a wild pack of "playas" at their own game? You got "hoed" dude, be glad it wasn't for more. Live and learn.

Speed walking lead Pike to the main gate that wasn't opened up yet. He tried two more and got the same result and was told by a sheriff manning the machinery entrance that he would have to find another way, no people were allowed to walk through. The stroll turned sprint, and Pike made it to the weak fence area from the night before, and although it was hard to do solo, he worm-crawled under and was free. When he finally made it to his car and sat down in front of the wheel, he locked his doors and told himself he would run over any "carnie" that would try to stop him. But they didn't. Around 10:15 a.m. Solomon concluded that Pike had left and wasn't coming back. He found the janitor that had introduced Pike to him.

"Where the fuck is your boy? If he doesn't show it's your ass," Solomon said without trepidation.

"I don't know anything about it."

"He's a fucking no show. And he's late. Where does he live? What's his number? I'm going to find him and kill him," Solomon threatened with truculence.

The janitor couldn't give out any real information, if Solomon found out Pike was a journalist it would be "his behind too." So he lied.

"He lives in Erie. I don't have his number. But the staffing agency might. That's how I met him, he came to the school as a sub janitor. That's all I know."

Solomon stormed off and took his anger out on his employees, upping their yard requirements.

"You can thank that Pike guy, it's his fault you gotta work your asses off today," Solomon said.

Pike made it back to the apartment, took one of the hottest showers that he ever thought his largest organ could tolerate and crashed out until 2:30 p.m. He woke up and immediately starting writing, in his boxers and without breakfast.

Crazy night, insane people. I'm like 35 minutes away from them, but I'm still scared. I'm serious, I'm not going to Winherst until the fair is over Saturday. Then they'll have to tear down, so Monday, I'm not going in the city limits of Winherst until Monday.

29.

"As for the epic verse, it has found its way to the mark by a process of trial." Aristotle, *P.*

On his way to work the next day, Thursday, Pike drove around Winherst completely and took the back way into the office. There was uncomfortable pain on the backside of his thighs.

Feels like someone is pulling the skin down my legs.

The majority of the work day was spent "perfecting-up" the carnival worker story, with a few added "half-truths" to conceal the fact that he left early. A short time after lunch, Pike asked Theresa, who had just stopped in for a minute, if Finn was still working the fair and she told him that he called in sick.

That's the first time dude has ever missed work. And why waste a freebie during fair time? Coulda just said you were at the festival and not have to burn a personal day.

August continued as Pike finished the carnival story in the morning, went and upgraded his cell phone before lunch (He still didn't want a smartphone, just one that didn't randomly turn off.), wrote up some police blotter after his meal and was counting the minutes (Time's ultimate joke) until the chain reaction started and he could go home. At 3:30 p.m., the publisher left. At 3:35 p.m., Theresa got up and grabbed her phone, when a call came in.

Over the intercom secretary Terri told Theresa, "A woman said she has information about a dog that was abused, she's on one."

"That's unbelievable. OK, I'll get it." Theresa sat back down but still had her purse in her left hand. "Hello, this is the editor. (Pause) What?! (Pause) And they're there now? (Pause) And what's your name? And phone number?" Theresa let go of her purse and began writing. "Thanks for calling, yep, 'bye."

"Pike and Finn, I need you to go to the Tuscarron Landfill. According to this lady that just called in, a worker found a dog tied up and tortured. I don't know. You both need to go because I need quotes from everyone involved, this could be big. I'll call the sheriff's office and see what I can find out, and hopefully the dog is still there so you can get a picture of it."

"Can't Pike just cover the story? I don't mind, really," Finn said attempting to salvage his Friday evening.

"That's fine with me," Pike said trying to be a team player, concerned with the possible vivisection and mad he didn't think of it first.

"No, you both need to go."

"You driving?" Finn asked.

"Sure," Pike said, not really wanting to carpool because the landfill was on the way home, but he didn't want to piss Finn off either.

Using two fingers, Pike turned down the sports talk radio in an ostentatious way, attempting to simultaneously look cool and initiate conversation in the car. Which it would, as Pike started one, "So you were ill yesterday, better not cough in my car," he said joking.

"I was lying. Probably shouldn't tell you because Theresa doesn't even know yet, but I had an interview with the Telegraph yesterday," Finn said.

"Wait, the Erie Telegraph? You serious?"

"Yep, and they offered me a job."

"Wow, dude. You going to take it?" Pike asked.

"Fuck, yes, I'm going to take it. Write for a huge daily, plus way better pay and they said I'd be doing mostly sports. How easy would that be?"

"Congrats man, keep climbing, for real. You put your time in here in lameville, pretty soon the Pittsburgh papers will be calling."

"Thanks. So you going to take over my beat in Winherst?" Finn asked.

"Wow, I never thought about that."

"That's what I did. When I started, I worked the shit stories, then a real Winherst reporter moved on, so I got better stories, and in a sense, I took his job," Finn said as he re-adjusted his hips while pulling out slack from his dress pants.

"Maybe I'll do that, see if I can switch," Pike thought out loud.

"You know where the recycling center is?" Finn asked. "Theresa calls it a landfill but it's not. It has that name attached to it from the days of old, but it's product waste management now. Basically just scrap metal and recyclables."

"I know where Route 12 is, and it's on that, right?"

"Yep. I'll tell you, too, it's going to be nice never having to see Carly ever again. She's a bigger dick to you because I don't care. She used to be that way to me, but once you got hired, it switched over. Plus, I'm a dick, too, so she knows the bully nonsense and intimidation doesn't hold water with me."

"I just try to placate, be nice, not start any trouble, but it's like she just wants to create this asshole atmosphere in the office for no reason. It's like she tries extra hard to be a jerk," Pike said.

"She has major problems. Listen, I'd deny telling you this and come kick your ass if you say anything, but she actually went to school to become a pastor or nun or something."

"Really?"

"Yes, you see, her dad was a Jesuit minister or whatever. So she was raised in a very religious house, and was very religious herself. Like way worse than a bible banger or a born again."

"OK."

"She goes to seminary school or the nun academy or whatever after high school, gets three years in, and this is what she told me after I'd been working in Winherst for a year and she stopped with the jerk mode, she said she finally realized the truth. She said she was too well-read, and smart and wise to believe the lie that religion was. So she transferred schools, confronted her dad without veneration, which I don't think they speak to this day, and became a reporter. Basically, my opinion is that at some point during her first try at college, her whole world melted around her. She began to believe in something else, and as a result, everything she was taught growing up, her life philosophy, her strong father figure, were all lies and nonsense to her. So it killed her, made her this grumpy, cynical person that blamed all of humanity for adding to the lie. She got out of college the second time, got a job as a Winherst journalist and hasn't done much since."

"How long has she been with the company?"

"I was told by Theresa eight years."

"If she is such a great journalist, and she knows all this shit and she is so smart, why is she still working for this weak paper?"

"Because she wants Theresa's chair. She's been here 28 or 31 years or something like that, so eventually, the editor's job will become available, and with most newspapers, they hire in-house, and Carly is definitely next in line. She has the skill set for it, I mean in terms of computers and overall knowledge, she definitely knows more than Theresa, but Theresa ain't going anywhere until she wants to."

"I hope I'm long gone before Carly takes over. I would never work for her, no matter what," Pike said.

The car arrived at the waste management facility close to 4 p.m. There were two sheriff patrol cars parked in the front parking lot and the gate that allowed loaded trucks with cargo to pass directly into the facility had been closed.

They both exited the car; Pike was daydreaming about being a detective who had just arrived at a crime scene. Finn was thinking about how awful it was going to be to talk to the workers at this plant. They entered the recently installed glass door of the front office. The Heineken-green carpet held no humans, and after two or three minutes of standing around, Finn yelled, "Hello!" There was a desk behind the counter and a hallway leading down to the back exit that would pour out into the plant's main yard.

"Well, I'm tired of waiting. Let's go around back," Finn said. He proceeded to lift up the sectional countertop and then he walked past the desk and out of site. Pike followed a good 20 paces behind him.

When they got to the rear, they both were a little blinded. The bluebird sky increased the reflections off the stacks of ore separated into giant 30-foot mounds. A man in a hard hat and safety vest was push plowing into one of the piles with a bulldozer. Finn continued walking and entered a warehouse outbuilding. There were five workers inside, one unloading recyclables onto a conveyer belt with a skid loader, three more at different stations along the belt sorting and tossing out trash and a man pulling long sheets of cardboard across the floor. Finn went up to the closest employee, who had a flattop military shaved head.

"Buddy, we're a little late, but can you direct us to where they found that dog?" Finn asked the man.

"Ya, the second sorting building," the man said pointing further into the yard, not sure of who these two men were, but not really caring, either.

In building two, they saw a sheriff's deputy speaking with someone who was standing next to a giant container of broken and multi-colored glass. The officer had finished talking, shook the man's hand and walked through the small gap of space between Pike and Finn, exiting the building.

"Excuse me sir, is this where they found the dog?" Finn asked the employee with long hair matted under a turquoise hat.

"No, I found him out in the yard, while I was running the dozer," the man said. Finn had found the source. He would later tell Pike that the old adage, "It's better to ask forgiveness than permission," was undoubtedly true in journalism. And it was true to some degree, as Pike would have still been waiting in the front office.

"Can you show me, please?" Finn asked as he motioned back outside.

"I already did to the other officers. But OK, what are you guys, like the specialist?" The man asked. He had a pinstriped gray jumpsuit on that was marked and stained and smelled of rotten pop, beer and non-rinsed-out plastic milk containers.

"We're the specialists," Finn responded as he looked at the trailing Pike with a subtle smile as they left the alloy-roofed building.

"All the mixed materials get dumped over here. Sometimes, on a day like today, the piles get so big you gotta push 'em flat with the dozer. So I was doing that, like I said, and I swore I saw something moving in the debris. Ya know, like at the end of the Ninja Turtles Movie, when Shredder's hand busts up through the trash and everyone in the theater screams," the man of 35 years said.

"I remember that, Shredder was awesome," Pike added.

"So I'm always thinking I'm going to find a human swimming around the mess. But today, it weren't no human at all, but a dog. I seen something movin', and I'm like, I better get my lazy ass off this dozer and see what it is. And it was so horrible what I saw. A dog, all taped up and bloody," he said.

"What do you mean, taped up?" Finn said, scanning the yard for police or other officials.

"Someone had wrapped duct tape, ya know, the good stuff, like five or six times around its stomach; it could barely breathe."

"Wow, that's crazy," Pike said.

"What kind of dog was it?" Finn asked, devoid of emotion.

"I dunno, coulda been a rottweiler or a poodle, hard to tell," the man said.

Pretty big difference there, guy.

"So what did you do when you found the dog?" Finn asked with his cantankerous nature increasing.

"I took him, or her, I don't really know, didn't flip him over and check, if you know what I mean, into the office. We couldn't even get the tape off. So we called the sheriff and they came down. The dog wasn't mean, but it also didn't want that tape coming off. It was a bad scene. So the sheriff called animal control, who also couldn't get that damn tape off, plus the eye seemed to be still bleeding," the man said, taking his hat off and wiping the sweat pebbles from under his hairline with his forearm. "The dog needed a vet. Vets cost money. They ain't like hospitals, they don't have to treat nutin' they don't wanna. Animal control knew of a free clinic for animals in Erie, so they called them. The free clinic, after hearing what the dog had been through, said to take it to a nearby vet and they would cover the cost. So that's what happened. The dog is at Merchant Vet clinic right now. No idea how he's doing."

"That is a crazy story, I wonder—" Pike was cut off by Finn.

"What did the police tell you in terms of an investigation or suspects?"

"I dunno, you tell me, you're supposed to know that, right?" he asked.

"We're reporters. We haven't talked to the police yet," Finn said.

"Oh, I thought—"

"Thanks for your time, Mr. –?"

"Sean Gran, G-r-a-n."

"Thank you, Mr. Gran," Pike said as Finn was already heading back towards the front.

When Pike finally caught up to him, Finn held up his index finger before Pike could speak. They entered the first office, went through the hallway and a worker had appeared at the previously empty desk.

"Did the sheriff's deputy leave?" Finn asked the man in jeans and steel-toed work boots.

"I think so, but check out front," he said as Finn walked by him, followed by Pike who gave the man at the desk a head nod, and they both exited without saying more.

They got back into Pike's car.

"Dude, roll the windows down. And why don't you have air conditioning? No matter how dilapidated the car, you got to have AC. And this isn't even that shitty of a car," Finn said.

"Rolling 'em down now, boss, can't Jedi mind trick the windows, I have to put the key in first."

Finn's Blackberry phone buzzed and he answered it as Pike pulled out of the parking lot.

"Hello. (Pause) The animal was gone. What'd they say? OK. (Pause) We're heading back now. (Pause) We can do that, yes, we know the place. 'Bye," Finn said tapping 'end' on his phone. "She wants us to go to the animal hospital place, but I'm not doing that, it's too late, plus I'm gone in two weeks so I'm not ruining my Friday night on this dog story. I'll call them and go sometime this weekend and get a photo of the dog. She also said the sheriff's office doesn't have any leads at this point and no suspects and they don't know who the owner of the dog is. It's going to be so great not having to cover bullshit stories like this anymore," Finn said as the four-door Ford began to push them back toward the office.

"Man, I can't stop thinking about it, it's so awesome your getting a bigger beat in Erie," Pike said later, nearing Finn's auto in the News-Times lot.

"Yep. Won't really matter though. Water eventually consumes everything. In this metaphorical case, water finally got the print media. There will always be reporting and news, but now you get to filter and choose and select the source of your content, and we humans protect ourselves when we self search the news; the consistency of the monopolized newspaper kept grief going. Everyday it showed up at your front door, at your coffee shop, in your office; it was the source. You had no choice but to consume its contents. Newspapers— the last of the true grief species."

"I always thought humans were the grief species," Pike said.

"Without the paper there's no grief to consume."

"What about our own corporeal daily-life-tragedy and death and sickness?"

"That's the point with papers; it is your tragedy, too. In the case of the printed newspaper, it's always happening to someone else but localized to you."

Finn was anticipating entering his air-conditioned ride, but paused when the passenger door was half ajar, and gleamed at Pike a bit and started, "You know, I got this job opportunity at the Erie Telegraph because I worked on my hands and knees in Winherst. All of the amazing writers you idolize actually wrote, and wrote hard. They studied the rhythm, prose; they manipulated sound into written word, applied mathematics to verse and conquered language landscapes with armies of alliterations and puns. I have the A.P. app on my phone—I hate A.P., but every one of my stories never needs corrected. You can't call yourself the world's greatest journalist if you haven't mastered any house style and have freaking spelling mistakes in your articles.

"Do you know," Finn continued, "that someone told me that they saw you all drunk at the Irish Games? You haven't earned a Rolling Stone press pass yet. You have it backwards—the anything goes "truth" journalism starts when you have actually mastered basement journalism first. At some point you have to realize that all of those productive "shit-together" people driven by goals and aspirations and success are also in the journalism field, too. They went to better colleges, have more accredited degrees, have waaaaaayyy more experience and believe it or not, can actually write just as well as you. When a writer from the Washington Post wants to go undercover as a 'carnie,' they can without question because they've earned news freedom."

30.

"The ego is after all only a portion of the id, a portion that has been expediently modified by the proximity of the external world with its threat of danger." S. Freud, *NILOPA*.

There was a slight change in the office air on that next and particular Monday morning, two days later, as everyone had learned of Finn's imminent departure. Captious Carly would not speak another word to Finn for the next two weeks. Theresa really didn't care; she was mentally on the way out herself. When Carly was gone, and Finn had escaped to lunch, Pike requested a five-minute meeting with publisher Rob and editor Theresa.

It was granted, and they all squeezed into Rob's office.

"I'll get right to it," Pike began from the other side of the desk. "With Finn leaving, I would like to put in for his assignments and beat."

"Not really enough experience to handle that," Rob quickly said.

"I've followed and seen what Finn has covered over the past three to four months. I read the paper, work in this town and believe my style would be more fitting."

"Longer hours for you," Theresa stated.

"Yes, but I'm pretty much here at the office all the time anyway, so I don't think it would be much different."

"Give us a week to think about it. Either way, you can have Finn's desk when he leaves, that's the natural upgrade of the office," Rob said, standing up as a signal that the meeting was over.

Why would I want Finn's desk? It stares at the wall like everyone else's does. I have full half-view of the floor.

"Thanks for the consideration. I'll let you know if I want to change desks," Pike said.

The next two weeks at the office were very slow. No one except Pike talked to Finn. No one told Pike if he was switching beats. The news was at a general lull, as the schools and their sports were on the verge, but hadn't started yet. The election was still months away. And everyday Pike finished the drive, the back of his thighs stung like an S&M clasp was latched to his veins. Pike completed his back to school issue on Finn's last day. He interviewed all the administrators about changes to their buildings, goals, problems they hoped to fix. Laid out the bus routes. Talked to the food service manager about nutrition in school lunches. But the thing that ate at Pike the most over those two weeks was not having job security.

Been well over a month since me and the publisher had our little talk about me stepping it up or I'm gone. I did the "carnie" story, that was cool, but I need something else. I did the Rover building picture walk-through which should be good, too. And I'll keep up on that, we need to get a new school passed. Screw the journalism ethical line. I believe I am reporting the truth. That building is a 150-year-old piece of shit, and I would not send my child there. That is the truth. It's just a matter of money. No one wants property taxes to go up, no one. But is all of that enough? I don't think so, I need another big one. I can't get fired before that wedding next month. I have to go to the New Mexican desert and show everyone that I'm still a journalist, a writer, and that no matter if I don't do a single awesome or neat thing, I will have that. I won't be selling carpet, cleaning ass cracks, delivering furniture. I just got done reading Harvey Pekar's "Cleveland," and he says, as a writer, you always have to keep working. 'Cus even if someone decides to publish you, which is a slim chance, they won't pay you anything for it, anyway. So at least if I'm going to have a weak job, it's a crappy writing job, and not a marketing copywriter or that kind of nonsense, but a journalist and stuff. But I have to come up with another feature. And I think I will take Finn's spot, so I can really focus and not stare out at everything.

To Pike's surprise, Finn stayed until 5 p.m. on his last day. They shook hands as everyone else acted like they were too busy to notice his final departure. Finn and Terri had flirted a series of goodbye-texts and chats over the past week. And as he was on his way out of the back door, Rob yelled, "Good luck!" and received no response.

Pike snatched up a pizza from a local joint in downtown Winherst an hour after Finn left and noticed a flyer on the bulletin board of the take-out waiting area. It read: "Firewalking: Overcome Your Fears and Face Anything. The Nature Spot, a holistic retreat center, will be hosting the annual Firewalk on Friday, Sept. 6, at 6 p.m. For more information visit NatureSpotFirewalk.com or call 555-6664."

After writing down the details, Pike called the number on his drive south towards home.

"Nature Spot, can I help you?"

"My name is Pike, Logan Pike, and I was wondering if there was someone in customer service, or media relations, or someone I can speak with regarding the Firewalk. I'm a reporter for a couple of newspapers in the county."

"I see. Can you please hold on a moment?"

"I can, thanks."

"Thank you, hold on."

The non-aggressive smooth jazz holding music of a holistic retreat center.

"This is Natalie, can I help you?"

"Hi, I'm a reporter for the News-Times. I wanted to call and try to get some information on the Firewalk event that you are putting on."

"That's great. What would you like to know?"

"Well, for starters, what exactly is firewalking?"

"It's where people come face to face with their biggest fears, and learn to overcome them. Then they walk across a bed of 1,000-degree coals."

"No one gets burned? I mean, the whole thing seems nugatory. How exactly does it work?"

"Those that believe don't get burned. And last year, of the 30 participants, none were hurt whatsoever."

"But I'm still unclear how the whole thing happens, exactly."

"We have video from last year on our website, that might be the best way for you to see it, or you are more than welcome to come in to the Nature Spot and get more information. You're welcome to join us as well, and participate in the Firewalk yourself," she suggested.

"Yes, maybe I should think about that. OK, let me look at your website, talk to my editor and get back to you next week."

"That sounds good. We only have space for 55 people, and only 10 have signed up, so you should be fine as far as getting in if that were something that you wanted to end up doing."

Pike looked at the website from his home computer and thought it was just another self-help seminar.

I guess all over the country people are firewalking as a means to motivate. They're like the new trendy corporate retreat team building seminars.

Look at this article, bunch of idiots in California got burned really badly during a seminar of high management. Wow. So what's the trick? Hmm, seems as though there is some bullshit thing where the bottom of the coals are really hot, but not the top. And you have to use the correct kind of wood. And you have to walk just at the right time. Either way, if these idiots burn me I'll sue them or kill them. But they won't, it's just some carnival trick. And I know carnival tricks.

August passed along with the weekend. On Monday morning, Finn's cubicle space was empty of his folders and backpack. Sometime Pike's unconscious had decided he wanted to move positions, so he sat down in Finn's old chair.

"This is way more comfortable," Pike said out loud to anyone and no one.

"So you are taking Finn's workspace then?" Theresa asked in response.

"I think I am. Any idea about me changing beats?

"Rob never talked to you? He doesn't want you to switch, so talk to him about it if you want."

I think I have figured out how all villages work. Believe it or not, a town or city is made up of only three parts. First, city government. That encompasses your roads, water, electric and who makes the laws and how they are interpreted. The second component is the school system. Where do the kids go to school, in what buildings, under what budget, how do they compare and compete against everyone in the state and how prepared are they for the rest of their lives? The third and final component of a town is the grown-ups and their jobs. What kind of employment opportunities are there in the town, what types or industry dominates the landscape, how much money does the pueblo make, how much do the houses cost and how big is the rich/poor gap? The reporter's job is to report on all of these three sections independently, but also to see how they fuse. The intermingling is what makes the city. You drive into some towns and there are nice roads and houses but shitty schools. Another place has factories and jobs galore, but the infrastructure is shot and the schools are good. And they all feed off one another. A thriving city government with a surplus might donate land to the school board to build a new building. Or a good public works department can maintain nice sporting facilities which breeds reliable athletic competition throughout the village which translates into bigger sports on the high school level which builds bigger field houses that put more kids on scholarships. Everything's related, so when one aspect of a town is lacking, such as the case in Winherst, the town suffers as a whole. Just look at the 150-year-old Rover school building. No matter the tax break, owners of businesses don't want to relocate or start up in Winherst because of the schools. Employees don't want to send their kids to an asbestos-laden building of learning, and companies look for home bases that have established infrastructure. Recently graduated youngsters from the high school or college level don't want to stay or move back to Winherst to raise a family when the buildings are falling apart. It is just as easy to go 30 miles in any direction for the same opportunities with better educational surroundings. And if you want to argue that a new building doesn't affect learning, just think about the technology. Smart boards, laptop carts that move classroom to classroom, internet-based curriculum, all of the changes in the way that information is passed along to the student requires facilities that can accommodate and utilize the technology changes that are happening. Look at the server room in the Rover building. They took a closet, and stuffed a bunch of servers on top of each other inside of it. Then, due to the heat the servers were putting off, they added fans to the inside to constantly blow air on them in an attempt to cool them down. When I first looked into that server closet I thought someone was actually trying to start an electrical fire.

When all three components are met, a city begins to establish its own identity. When all three are thriving, the city sees an influx of immigrants, jobs and the start of real tradition. Then after a 100 years, the idea of the city continues to grow until future generations and tourists perpetuate its identity. Like Paris, is it really still the world's Mecca of love? I think so, but even if it's not, the previous 500 years allow for it to possibly take a century off.

31.

"There were many, too, who carried on ultra-patriotic conversations at the top of their voice, in the naïve hope that their words would be overheard and reported where they would do the most good. / It was humiliating to be mistaken for one of this sort." E.S. Ginzburg, *JITW*.

What are you working on this week?" Theresa asked.

"What am I working on this week? Let me get my list out. Going to have to find a new spot at my new desk to get everything laid out and organized," Pike said. "Here it is."

"Wait, before you start, did anything else come up with that dog?" Theresa asked.

"No. They never found out who did it. Like I wrote about last week, the owners had called around looking for their pet and once the story broke online on the Erie Telegraph's website, they called the police. The police said they didn't have any reason to suspect it was the owners of the K-9, I guess they had pictures all over the house of the mutt and thought of the dog like it was their child. But the dog's fine, the police believe someone wrapped him in tape and threw him in a recyclables dumpster. They think he got the cut above his eye from rolling around inside of that thing. Police said it could be kids, could be a neighbor that didn't like the beast barking, but they have no leads. Nothing has changed since my write-up last week."

"That whole story made me sick," Theresa said.

"It was bizarre. But at least the dog is fine and home. Have to wait and see if there are any more dogs that turn up at the landfill. It's not like the Winherst P.D., obsequious to every cause, could solve a case anyway. Maybe they could, I dunno."

"What else?"

"You remember how I told you about the poker game that happens after village council meetings? You said you already knew about it, everyone did, but anyway, the game is with the president of council, some cops, the mayor, the law director and the public works superintendent. I don't know if I told you this but last month I asked about the game and was able to join. The chief of police told me, 'On or off the record, we play poker, and you can join us for a game. It's no secret. But if you're trying to write some underground gambling story, hahah, well, good luck with that.' Basically, it was an attempt to have me in the pocket of city council and the department. And if I played in the game, and then tried to 'expose' it, it would look pretty dumb. Not to mention I wouldn't be able to drive through town without getting arrested," Pike said.

"You can't hide and fear the authorities, in our line of work—" Carly began, making her southside entrance.

"Dude, no one is talking to you," Pike said looking over at Carly with lowered eyebrows. "Anyway, so I got in a game and took those fools. Not a player in the whole lot. One of the cops, who I will keep nameless, sorry Carly, lost a good bit of cash to me. On the way out of the top floor of the council building, I handed him his money back and said, 'We're all underpaid, I don't want to take a civil servant's money, this time, anyway. But seriously, here's your cash, just give me a call if there's anything crazy going on around town, ya know, help me out a little bit.' And my card was in the middle of the wad of cash. This morning, on my way into the office, my secret source called me, and said they found a giant lizard in someone's backyard. I was kinda hoping for a tip about drugs or murder, but whatever, take what I can get for under a hundred bucks."

"Holy cannoli, Theresa, I am plugging my ears! If any part of his story is true, my God, there are so many ethical and I'm sure legal ramifications to—"

"Yes! Did you hear that everyone, Carly is going to plug her ears? And speaking of God, Carly, you shouldn't be using the word "Lord," considering your lack of belief and all," Pike said, pulling from the dirt Finn had given him.

The publisher Rob left his desk and came to the writing floor. "Don't feel as if you need to tell us from where you received your information Pike, understand?"

"Yes."

"That said, good work."

"Thank you, Rob, really trying to step it up around here. So like I was saying before, I have to cover the lizard dragon story today, then Friday I'm going to walk on fire. But it costs like 30 or 40 bucks to do the Firewalk, so I'm going to need that approved so I can pull it from petty cash," Pike said.

"That's fine, you can get it from there," Rob said.

"Wait, what's going on? What Firewalk? I didn't hear anything about this!" Theresa said, not happy that she was confused and feeling left out.

"What part are you confused about, Theresa?" Pike asked.

"I guess everything. For starters, I thought I was the editor. And secondly, I need more details on whatever this Firewalk thing is," she said like an obdurate editor.

"The firewalking thing is at that hippie retreat place, the Nature Spot, or whatever. I guess people go there and walk on fire and face their fears and stuff. I don't have any fears, so it'll just be a walk in the fire park for me, te-he, te-he."

"I'm not sure the direction of the Winherst News-Times," Theresa said, looking at Rob for backing and trying to obviate the story.

"I think it will be a good story, both of them. Haven't found a new hire that I like yet," Rob said as he dipped back into his office.

New hire, what the hell does that mean?

The rest of the week Pike adjusted well to his new cubicle location. He was consumed by the grind.

I just want to come into work, get my shit done and not be bothered.

On Friday, Pike arrived at the office close to 2 p.m., as he had to attend the Firewalk event that night.

"So are you nervous," Theresa asked, "about putting your feet on burning hot coals?"

"No, not really. I mean, there is a trick to it. They want you to believe you have to focus and face your inner demons and all that, but I don't buy it. You could be wasted drunk or a meditating Shaolin monk, the physics remain the same. And I ain't going to be the first guy across the coals, if you are picking up what I'm putting down," Pike said.

"I sure wouldn't do it," Theresa said.

The Nature Spot was a 27-acre piece of land that hosted retreats, reunions, spiritual awakenings, seminars and the Firewalk. It was located 20 minutes southwest of Winherst, in a heavily unpopulated and rural, woody area of northern Pennsylvania.

From the parking lot, Pike followed a row of knee-high pines to an open air amphitheater encased in forest. There was a table at the opening where Nature Spot employees were collecting money and having everyone sign releases so they couldn't sue if they were badly burned. Pike had his camera around his shoulder and reporter's notebook sticking out of his back blue jeans pocket, so when he began filling out his form he was easily identified.

"Hi, are you from the paper? I think we may have spoken over the phone," said a thin woman in her late 70s, without much wrinkle wear on her face, no graying in the black long hair, and wearing a dress with a flower pattern. "Did you have any trouble finding the place?"

"No, it was pretty simple, actually. Nice *Spot*, though," Pike said, looking out into the football-field-sized meadow that extended from the theatre.

"Thank you, we like it. Now, are you going to be walking tonight, or just reporting?"

"I'm going to be reporting and walking. My editor said if there's not a picture of me walking on coals, then there's no story."

"Good. Finish filling out your forms, then have a seat in the gazebo pavilion here, and we should be getting started shortly. Let me know if you have any questions."

"Thank you, I do have one quick question. That man out there, that's dressed in what looks like a red rain suit, what's he doing with that smoke?"

"He's cleansing anyone that would like to be cleansed. Not sure what he is burning. If you go over to him he will cleanse your body and mind before we get started."

I think I'll just take some photos. I'm so fucking sure burning grass can do anything other than smell weird and cause a placebo effect. But I guess if the effect affects, then it works in some way.

Pike had a seat as the crowd filled up. 53 participants had paid $36 to change their lives.

Pretty cheap price for a complete transformation.

The founder and president of the Nature Spot welcomed everyone that was seated in the three rows of plastic chairs. He told his story about how last year he did the Firewalk ceremony, and his life has never been the same since. Then he called up, in front of everyone, the person who would be guiding the people through their experience, a certified man of the flame and life coach, Mr. Stewart Tallis.

After the applause had died, the tutelary Mr. Tallis briefly adjusted the giant WWE-sized microphone that made his lips evaporate.

"Hello, everyone, I'm Stewart Tallis. I am here to show you something. I'm here to show you that death is nothing once you've walked on fire. The very eyes of every demon that haunts you can be trampled by your invincible feet tonight! We face and kill what restricts your progress!"

Pike remembered seeing Tallis clutching a buck knife, whispering to it, when he first arrived.

He looks like a stick bug. Long and tall and pale green.

"Apprehension is a very personal thing," Tallis continued, "but it is so simple to conquer. I will light a fire bigger than the waves on the north shore of Hawaii, we will watch it consume itself, then we will walk over the coals and a new life for you will begin. Or you won't walk.

"Now I want everyone to break up into groups of three or four. If you came with a friend or a group, you need to split up so you are with people you don't know and are not comfortable with," Tallis said.

Everyone formed little circles and groups with strangers. Pike was in a group with a 49-year-old house wife and a 24-year-old recently-graduated-from-university ballerina.

"Now think about what you want most in life right now. The one thing, the reason you are all here. What aspect of your life do you want to change? Think about that right now," Tallis said.

I want to be a famous novelist. Or scribbler, or author or whatever. That's what I want most in my life, to create amazing books, and do readings at college campuses, and have people talk about my work, and turn my books into movies, and have all these obsessed fans wanting to hang out with me and have sex with me and admire me. That's what I want.

"Now I want everyone to think about the number one fear that is keeping you from actualizing that dream, that want, that life-fulfilling desire," Tallis said.

Hmm, I don't think it's just one there, Mr. Witch doctor. Where to start? I'm spoiled, I drink too much, I'm lazy and my other two attempts at writing a book have failed. I just gave up after so many years of not making it in the short story world after college. Started looking for a real profession. A lock for good pay and horrible days. But really, the main thing is the simple fact, that outside of journalism, I haven't been composing at all. No poems, drunken rants, short stories, nothing. So I need to smash out prose again, I need to write a tome.

"Now I want you to take turns, and tell the members in your group what you want most in life, and what is holding you back. It may be hard to start, but you are all here for metamorphosis, and it starts with this exercise," Tallis said.

I hope I don't have to go first; it will all be caustic comments driven by my defense mechanisms. Not sure that I'm here for life change, really just a story. Can't be certain that life change comes from a five-hour firewalking class. It comes from a series of choices and decisions you continually make over a long period of time. How many times I have been all drunk, or just getting back from a voyage, and decide things are going to change. But they never do. It's not what happens on the odyssey that matters, but what happens when you come back. Please don't let me go first, I will—

"I guess I will start," said the long-blond-haired ballerina.

Thank the stars and heavens and shit for that.

"My biggest problem, well, maybe I should start with what I want," she began as the lady and Pike inched closer to her within their quaint circle. "I want to be an actress. I've recently graduated from Allegheny College, where I was a ballet major. I can sing, dance, have been in millions of plays and performances, but I just can't take the next step. I look up auditions, but talk myself out of going. I work at a coffee shop, and everyday I say I'm going to quit and actually try to succeed in the world of acting, but I never do. So that's what I want and my biggest fear, or what I want to do, is stop second guessing myself and actually try even if I fail, at least I'll know."

I wish I was younger and hotter, with your self-confidence, girl, I could control and manipulate you so hard, and oh the flexible sex we would have. Real nice, idiot, this lady is pouring her soul out to you and you go to the "exploit like a human trafficker card?" What the fuck is wrong with you? It might be seriously time to talk to a therapist. I know that's a cliché, but the clock upstairs just ain't clicking right. I'm so tired of the gross thoughts. End your bachelor party mindset.

"I guess I'll go next. What I want most is for the second half of my life to have meaning. I have four kids, and the youngest one just left for college last week. I'm a stay-at-home mom, and those kids have been my purpose for existing. And now that they're gone, I have a hard time trying to understand my sense of worth. I feel so useless now. So I want a new chapter in my life, but I'm so scared because I have no idea where to start. It's the same with my husband, too. So much of our love and relationship was built around the kids, and now that they're gone, I feel like we don't have anything to talk about, to be connected with."

There was a brief stoppage in conversation.

"Well, since there are only three of us, I guess it's my turn. But I would like to say, for starters, how amazing and honest you both were. I think if I would've gone first, I might have just lied, but seriously, that's awesome. For me, I want to write a book, but am just too lazy and too big of an idiot to do it. I just need to put pen to papyrus, but I don't. Maybe I'm scared the book will suck. But most books do, so that shouldn't be that big of a deal," Pike said.

After a few more minutes, the groups separated and Tallis again addressed everyone, "Now, talking about overcoming fear is one thing, but actually physically overcoming what's holding you back is another.

"Now, I want everyone to follow me out into the meadow and make a circle around the teepee of logs out there. And bring your bad thoughts."

A circle was formed around the 55 pieces of white cedar, while Tallis and the red-suit-wearer cleanser man lit the kerosene-glazed wood.

"Now I want everyone, when they see fit, to approach the fire and think your problems into the fire. The fire will then have your deepest fear, the thing that's holding you back, the fire will inhabit those."

Slowly at first, and then glutton-like, everyone approached the flame and threw in their minds. They then returned to the seating area in the amphitheater.

"Being scared and cautious are not the same thing. Fear is an irrational response to something that won't be what you thought anyway. Children in ancient China were sent out into the woods with an arrow, and they were to put it in their necks, and lean against the tree. Those who returned became men."

The flames died down over the next two hours, and after some more workshopping, it was finally time for the main event.

"The coals are just about ready," Tallis said. "The fire looks good. Couple of things, if you are going to walk, keep a steady pace. If you try to run your foot could dig deep into the coals and cause serious burns. Do not try to turn around once you've started. There might be someone right behind you and that could cause major problems if you smash into them. Remember, fear wants you to believe things that just aren't true, like you can't walk across a bed of 1,000-degree coals. Those coals are the same temperature that they use to melt engine blocks. And the last thing you should know is that I will be walking first, that's something that the leader in California didn't do when all those people got burned. One more thing, sorry, it's the most important thing. When you walk across the coals, say only to yourself the fear that was thrown into the fire. You must do that."

All of the firewalking neophytes exited in silence, and again, formed a circle around the coals.

Wait, there is dew on the ground. I read that you don't want to walk on coals with wet feet. They said the coals can stick to the wet spots on your feet. Goddamn September dew, and it came early this year. Guess it is a cold night. But my feet are going to burn off. I want to ask the leader about this. But he said no talking, and I can't ruin everyone's transformation.

Tallis approached the coals, stopped short and seemed nonplussed. He was tall, his hair was silver, and he took off his shirt exposing an Iggy Pop-scarred belly. With rolled up workout pants, he put his two feet in the coals and yelled, "I won't fear death; I will get over my sister's suicide."

Umm, I think he forgot his own rules.

Someone followed right behind him yelling, "I will not fear my boss; I will be appreciated at my job." Then they all started walking. "I have to let my kids live their own lives." "My wife's cancer will not beat us." "I will date and love again."

I don't hear any screams from dew-related burning, better do this shit.

Pike totally committed to the first step, and felt confident in the second after he didn't feel the nerve endings being severed. He was whispering, "I will write, I will write, I will write" across the entire coal catwalk.

I did it! Wow, that was so freakin' fun right there. Shit yes. Wow, that was great. What a feeling. Darn, I just realized I didn't get a picture.

Pike also noticed, as everyone made their way back to their seats that the stay-at-home mom from his inner circle had walked, but the ballerina hadn't.

The car ride home was a very introspective journey for Pike, despite the burning sensation he felt over his sock and through his shoe.

32.

"To want is to have a weakness. It's this weakness, whatever it is, that entices me." M. Atwood, *THT*.

Monday, Pike limped down the hallway, across the space and to his new desk.

"No, way, you got burned, didn't you?" Theresa asked, noticing his gimpy approach.

"I was just kidding, I'm fine. Got a little burn on my heel, but that didn't even require a Band-Aid. No Carly today?"

"She's got interviews all morning. So you did it, you walked?"

"Yep. Pretty neat experience. Glad I did it. I'll write it up today and you can check it out. I'll up-load the photos, too, once I have a chance to sit down here."

"What else are you working on for this week? And when are you leaving for your trip to Arizona?"

"New Mexico. A week from Thursday. Will need Thursday and Friday off, and probably Monday, too. Going to be getting in late Sunday night slash Monday morning, so I won't be much good to anyone Monday, I don't think."

"Remember, you have to have stories to fill for the days you're going to be gone."

Already thought of that you conniving bi-otch. Nah, let's not do that anymore. So boring, bitch-cunt-whore talk. Why are you so lazy and not creative? If you can't find any other words, if you can't be specific, don't bother.

"Going to do a huge spread on the new school issue, trying to pass that levy. Going to be like 20 inches, easily."

"Don't make it too long, I'll just have to cut it and that makes more work for both of us."

"Right."

Later that afternoon Pike was sitting across from the school board president and the new churlish school levy chairman, at the bakery downtown that president Payton adored so much.

"Here's what we're getting," Pike opened with a brief compendium, "no one knows what is going to happen to the old structure, and the land it sits on. Your approach is too turbid. Those are the two biggest issues we hear about at the paper. People call in, and they feel like there are too many uncertainties. To a lot of people that school has been on this earth as long as they have."

"Did you try a bagel? They have the best bagels, man, they cook the dough just right so it's not too tumid, I'm tellin' you. I'm a straight shooter, the best," Payton said.

"We're still looking into some possibilities concerning the building," the school levy chairman said with a perfectly square moustache.

"Haven't you had tons of experts come in and say that it is just too old, too patched together, to be used as a nursing home or public house?" Pike asked.

"Yes, sir, we have," Payton said.

"And the money you got from the state to help with this project, included mitigating the asbestos, correct? But once they tear it out, they aren't fixing any of the walls and floors that will be destroyed, right?" Pike asked.

"That's right, sonny. They ain't fixing nutin' that they break."

"So the building is going to be torn down, it's just the truth of the matter. So have the school board take an official stance that that's what you're going to do. Then decide what you want to do with the land. It could be a giant park or soccer field for the community. You could say, 'Hey, taxpayer, thanks for the new school, and in return, here's a freakin' playground.' I mean, the new school won't be built on the same land, anyway. And there's money to repurpose the lot."

"I see what you're sayin' man, but let me think about it, talk it over with everyone. There's a lot to weigh here."

"Also," Pike started, "you should have a voter sign-up, register-to-vote type of event. How many 18-year-olds are seniors and how many kids are coming back for the summer? Every vote counts."

At the next school board meeting, there was an official motion and decision to tear the building down and give the greenspace to the town for whatever they saw as the best way to serve the community, as long as the levy passed.

And 53 new voters were signed up at the next Winherst home football game, as part of a new voter initiative.

The week existed and was exhausted by Pike, as his mind was on another wedding vacation. On Saturday night, neighbors Pike and Joan sat on her reclaimed-from-dumpster-doom sectional couch.

"There's going to be so much to do out there in New Mexico, going to be fun, you could go, ya know, be my date," Pike told Joan, while sipping on a glass of Spanish table wine in her living room with reality TV unnoticed in the background.

"Should be fun, but no thanks," Joan said, as she readjusted her feet that were mashed under her butt on the sofa.

"Does New Mexico have Rocky Mountains too? I know Colorado does, obviously, but I wonder if it will be like a mountain area or what?"

"I think where the wedding is going to be, in Santa Fe, it's high, like 6,000 feet," Joan knew.

"For real? I'm going to look it up." Pike got up from the couch and did a web search of New Mexico's highest point on Joan's load-too-slow laptop sitting on the bar behind the couch.

"Wheeler Mountain, like 13,000 feet," Pike yelled from his perch in the same room.

"Please don't yell like a redneck."

Re-entering the inside living tone, Pike said, "Wheeler Peak is the highest point in New Mexico. Over 13 grand."

"I think 'grand' is only money talk. The mountain isn't 13 grand."

"What? You can say, I drove 2 grand last week in my car, right?"

"No, that's saying, I drove 2 thousand dollars last week in my car."

"Whatever, so it's Wheeler Peak, at 13 thousand dollars high, and it's probably only like an hour from Santa Fe. You think I should hike it?"

"Friendo, where do you get these ideas? There's not going to be time I'm sure with the thousands of wedding things you have to do. At least you're not in the wedding party and there's not a stupid bachelor party."

"About that..." Pike complacently said, slowly.

"About what? What was all this change talk I've been hearing about for the last hour? 'Joan, I'm done. If someone is acting like a pussy, I'm gonna call 'em a coward, not a pussy. And I'm never going to attend another bachelor party, and I'm going to re-examine why I've hated and disrespected women for so long for no reason, and why I have such a hard time with equality, and most of all the combination of lack of judgment and logic."

Not sure I quite said allllll of that.

"Listen, I'm in the wedding party, but I think everyone is and I don't have to walk down the isle or anything, it's just a title. Like I said, I think everyone is in the wedding party. And there is a bachelor party, but I'm not going. New York ruined that event for me for the rest of my life."

"You're not going to the bachelor party?"

"Nope. Just wait and see, it's Thursday night and I won't be there. Back to Wheeler Mountain or whatever it's called, and I'm reading here and it says it's the highest point in New Mexico, and there's this thing called highpointing, where backpackers and climbers go to all the highest points of all 50 states. Isn't that awesome?"

"Sounds exhausting."

"I can do my first, out of the 50, state highpoints while I'm in New Mexico. Doesn't that sound sweet, go climb a mountain?"

"I'd rather sit at the spa. And when did you decide to be a highpointer? Least you got the first part of that covered," Joan said.

In the three days before the trip, Pike covered a ribbon cutting ceremony for a walking path around the rec park and a Winherst High School class of '40 reunion, which was a big year for the town, as the high school football team went undefeated that season. He covered a historic farmhouse tour, the ambulance district changing directors and the big news of a bomb squad being called for no reason downtown. And math league at the junior high. And writing obituaries. And clenching his jaw through the police blotter write-ups. Then Wednesday finally came, and he left the office until he would return again in six days, next Tuesday, from the New Mexico fury.

On the way home, Pike called his friend Randy, who was already in New Mexico.

"Hello, bubber, how the hell are ya?" Randy answered.

"Good, man, well really, freakin' great, just got out of work and gonna go home, pack, drink a few beers and get ready."

"Just don't drink five beers man, according to you, that's a bad number to drink."

"That's funny, guy. What's the atmosphere like out there?"

"Bubber, let me tell you, it's amazing. I got into old New Mexico on Sunday, rented a Dodge Charger and started headin' for the mountains."

"Umm, why'd you rent a Charger to go drive around the mountains?"

"I need speed man. Pretty sure I already destroyed the bottom of the car, not even sure how's she still running. But the little rental car guys wanted to play games, so I said 'Fuck it,' and paid 15 more bucks a day and got the Charger," Randy said.

"What games were they playing?" Pike asked, as he saw pumpkins poking out of the field to his left.

"Insurance charges for this type of car, extra driver fee for anyone else, can't rent a car in Santa Fe and drop it off in Albuquerque or it's more money. It was an endless list of bullshit with these guys, bubber."

"I get all that, I mean, you've rented a car before, right? But I don't understand why you didn't get a crossover or jeep or something?"

"I'm built for speed out here, that's all I can tell you. And boy oh boy, this baby flies, how great I take the mountain turns."

"You're a real Speed-Limit Cassady, that's what they used to call him."

"I know, bubber, I read too, more than you. You watch sports instead of reading."

"You're up in the mountains? You see Wheeler Peak?"

"No, but I got your email about that, bubber. You think you're going to climb up to 13,000 feet? Ya, right guy, have you seen your belly?"

"Little beer fat won't stop my soccer-conditioned legs from charging to the top of that little mountain. A thirteen-er, dude? That ain't nothing. What've you been doing since Sunday?"

"Everything, guy, I tried to tell you, I'm done with the little three-day trip. Doesn't make any sense. I already made it to Colorado. I was driving, I took some turns, next thing I know I'm at the Colorado border, dude, that Charger. I tell ya."

"Hahah. So you're just cruising around northern New Mexico with a modicum of funds and no plan. Where are you staying?"

"I got a plan, bubber, and the plan is speed. I've hit up some old cave paintings, some battlefield where a bunch of them 'injuns' got killed, saw an Old West ghost town. Staying at whatever hotel I find. There are a couple of ski areas that are kinda pricey, but other than that, dude, it's cheap and beautiful out here. Stay in a nice place for $70 a night, bubber."

"Wow, awesome. That's what I'm going to do, rent a car in Santa Fe, like Friday, drive around and see what's going on."

"Hope you like tinted windows. Every dude here has tinted windows on some beat up old Pontiac, and they drive slow as shit. I swear I lost a muffler when I was steering up this dirt road to a trailhead."

"Looking forward to it, we need trips, too, for our martial law minds. Well, see you in a couple of days."

"Might be hope for you here."

33.

"It reminds one of the ragged Republican army that Napoleon lead into Italy. It is probable that Villa doesn't know much about those things himself. But he does know that guerilla fighters cannot be driven blindly in platoons around the field in perfect step, that men fighting individually and of their own free will are braver than long volleying rows in the trenches, lashed to it by officers with the flat of their swords." J. Reed, *IM*.

The third wedding of the year and Pike was great at the packing routine for self. Within 40 minutes, everything was by the door.

Gonna take it nice and easy. 'Cus that's the plan, smoke a little and not get all drunk all weekend. Don't want to do it again, can't keep repeating the pattern. Not going to the bachelor party, not drinking all day everyday, going to climb a mountain, and have a nice vacation with myself. Moving into the land of the introverts. She should have killed me for how I acted that last night in Brooklyn. Prob why she never called back.

Pike was up at 4 a.m. Then, much like San Diego, the drive to the Pittsburgh airport. 7:05 a.m. flight to Dallas/Ft. Worth. 20 minutes to catch the connecting flight. Jogging up the tarmac, then up the escalator that leads to the tram that will take him to the next terminal. Only one of the trains was running, so he had to circle the whole airport. The car gets packed because there's only one in operation. Pike has to stand in the middle, holding on to the silver metal railings attached to the ceiling. He didn't shower earlier that morning, and the audience could smell the peppery and bitter aroma of his armpit.

"Dang, honey," one passenger said in slight disgust. Other passengers had to deal with it.

Then off the tram, fast stepping down the escalator, locating the gate number and hurrying back down a tarmac. He was the last to board the plane. Hour and 27-minute flight to Albuquerque. Time to relax, he had arrived.

"They call an airport a sunport here. Neat," Pike to_d a stranger as they exited the automatic doors and stepped out into New Mexican air.

"It's too bright here. But I do like the colors, factory blue and orangish-yellow and tons of Native American art everywhere. It's beautiful here. The desert color design of tinted acid and sand."

Pike had just missed the 11:30 a.m. shuttle north, so he got lunch at a "New Mexican Cuisine" restaurant just inside the entrance, at the top of the escalator. Pike felt rushed and barely ate his huevos rancheros (he was also confused when the waiter asked, "Red or green?" referring to the salsa type that was to be blanketed over everything), not wanting to miss the transport a second time.

Pike was quick to grab a window seat so his arms wouldn't spray the vehicle with body odor. The six-person van got on the highway, and Pike noticed the bridges and cement enclosing on the interstate were decorated in tribal designs, big triangles and geometrical patterns.

Every other billboard is for an Indian casino. No wonder this is such a poor and morose state. And T told me alcohol was more readily available than cigarettes at the gas station. Little liquor bottles like magnets around the cash register.

The drive pushed past pueblos, hut architecture and vast dry landscapes of sage plants and rocks of no definite shape. Pike was eventually dropped off at his hotel, near the art and culturally oriented downtown.

Nothing but old people, native art and gift shops downtown.

As his hotel door was shutting behind him, Pike got a text: "Dummy, come drink margaritas. We're at Sal's Place a block from the hotel." The text was from groom T's brother, who was nicknamed Saint.

I just got a text from Saint, he wants me to go drink margaritas. Hmmm. I like this hotel, glad I'm on the second floor. Usually I think non-enclosed hotels are crappy, but this is nice.

With the guidance of the front desk, Pike found Sal's Place and Saint in the open-air back patio drinking margaritas by the pitcher with his father and girlfriend.

Hugs were exchanged, and the girlfriend introduced to Pike.

"Pike and I went to school together for a year at The Rock. Great time, then I moved. Please grab a glass and fill yourself up. We were just talking about Andrew Jackson and the battle of New Orleans. We've been cranking out 'history on tape' for the whole drive here."

"Wait, you drove from New Orleans?"

"Yep, and learned a good bit about our country's rich history as well," Saint said.

"I was taught in high school that Andrew Jackson used to hang Indian scalps in the oval office," Pike said.

"He was a bad man at times."

After four pitchers, the group left Sal's and met up with T, who was also only a block away, getting a grayscale tattoo of a stallion on his arm. More hugs and hellos. When the tattoo was finished, Pike pulled T aside.

"Great to see you. Hope you're wearing many pairs of socks. It's a bad cold feet joke," Pike said.

"Everything's perfect, Logan. You're coming to the cookout tonight, right? Let's go get more drinks!"

Pike decided against continuing the bar hop and opted for a hotel shower. Without dinner and in the dim of dusk, Pike met up with some wedding "others" and they all headed to the pre-arranged cookout. 24 minutes to a friend of T's house, who was hosting a cookout for all the out-of-towners and wedding guests.

There were 47 people in attendance when they arrived.

Around 9:30 p.m. Pike excused himself from the cookout and the bachelor party that was just about to start and from the life that wouldn't perpetually end until 2 a.m. Pike told everyone that he had to climb a mountain in the morning, and that rest was essential.

The rental car agency opened at 7 a.m., and at 6:50 a.m. Pike called the front desk to arrange a cab. The cab didn't show until after 7:30 a.m.

Cowards, learn to show up!

It was a 17-minute ride, and the cabbie was full of conversation.

"Where you headin'?"

"To the rental car—"

"I know that, but where you traveling with the car?"

"Going up north more, through Espanola and Taos and I want to climb to the top of Wheeler Peak, but I'm not sure if that's doable or not."

"Be careful up in Espanola, it's the heroin capital of the U.S. You better know what you're doing up there. Ever seen the show "Breaking Bad," pretty much based off of life in Espanola?"

"I'm familiar with the show. Where you from, you got like an East Coast accent?"

"That's right, moved out here 20 years ago, and never going back."

After the rental car line, driving back, and getting packed, Pike was just on his way out of the door of the hotel at 8:46 a.m.

Don't forget the Camel Pack Yogos left for you. Good friend, that Yogos. You know, of all the genius friends I have, he has worked the hardest at his. He has really tried to experience it all. In a way, Yogos built his own genius.

The area around Santa Fe was filled with sloppy hills and massive areas of flat, but 30 minutes to the north, the lower Rocky Mountains and the Sangre de Christo range exploded into view. The road followed streams and dynamited gaps through Espanola and Taos and eventually Pike found the trailhead for Wheeler Peak.

"How long of a hike is this?" Pike asked himself out loud, stepping out of the blue two-door rental car that was beside four other vehicles in the lot.

Not that long, I don't have to go to the top, I just want to hike, and see what is what, do some exploring, ya know. How long is the trail, how many miles? I think only three or four, no big deal. Really I think it's like six or seven, but if I tell you that, those facts will militate you and we won't even get started.

The first two miles of the trail were all through covered woods. High pines and trees not affected by fall created shade and a canopy. Massive sparkle-less spackled rocks and boulders lined the trail, left when the glacier finally receded.

The route was a constant uphill ramp, and when two hikers were on their way out, they noticed how hard Pike was breathing.

"How are you doing, you're breathing pretty hard?" the middle-aged woman asked.

"I'm OK, just not used to the altitude, that's all," Pike said.

"Where you coming from, 6,000 feet? Around Santa Fe?" she asked.

"I'm actually from flat Pennsylvania, but drove up from Santa Fe this morning. How far, how much longer until the top?" Pike asked.

"From Pennsylvania?" the woman's husband asked.

"Wow, you are not acclimated for this climb at all," the woman said sounding misanthropic.

"Yes, it's true, but I'll be fine, I'm in shape," Pike said.

"You got to watch out for HAPE, high altitude pulmonary edema. It's really dangerous to ascend too quickly. Did you know that if they took a helicopter and dropped a person off at the top of Mt. Everest, the person would pass out immediately and die in under an hour? You have to acclimate. Just listen to your body. You're under 10,000 feet now, and it's still another 3,000 vertical feet to the summit. Be careful."

"Thanks, I will, I'm sure I'll be fine," Pike said.

"I'd say you have another 4 hours, and it's already afternoon. Better watch the time," the husband said.

After another half hour of hiking, and the trail spilled out into an opening that had a rock meadow and a lake.

Pike took a 19-minute break overlooking the stagnate combination of hydrogen and oxygen. An elegant female silhouette in dreadlocks was wading in the water in a sports bra. Pike decided to continue. The trail from the lake to the top was switchback after switchback of grueling climbing. He halted every 15 minutes for breaks. Pike was in shorts but a long-sleeved shirt and had a sweatshirt in his backpack. The temperature was 20 degrees cooler on the mountain than the comfort of 75 degree Santa Fe. Every 1,000 feet of elevation change is equivalent to driving 350 miles north in a car.

After two more hours of hiking, he entered the alpine area, where trees had ceased growing. It was just the bare side of the mountain. He stopped for lunch. Instead of bringing reasonable meals, Pike stopped at a Tex-Mex take out and ordered burritos that were smothered in sauce, making him have to pack in plastic silverware and Styrofoam boxes.

The air was thin, and at 12,000 feet, the non-acclimated Pennsylvanian was really suffering. The barometric pressure was 480 mm-Hg, giving him 40 percent fewer oxygen molecules per breath. Another couple was coming down from the top. It was 3 p.m.

Without a hello, Pike said, "How much longer to the top?"

The man looked at the altimeter on his wrist and said, "Only another 1,000 feet. Probably 45 minutes," he said. "But the worst part is yet to come. Gets even steeper and the air makes you feel like you're breathing through a straw."

After the couple disappeared down, Pike felt dizzy and sick.

I feel like I just need to take a nap. I'm sorry but I can't go on. You serious? Only another 1,000 feet to the top of the world. Isn't this awesome, trees can't even grow up this high? I'm done, I'm just going to take a little snooze, I'm so dizzy, and then I'll be good. Live the dream another time.

Pike continued on, making it to the summit 35 minutes later.

His physical exhaustion and light headedness caused him to let out a few tears at the top. There were four other contumacious-toward-gravity humans admiring the view, and welcomed him to the summit.

Wow, this is amazing. What a view. Wait, is that guy smoking a joint? I think that guy is smoking a joint over there. Should I go try joining him? Fuck no. I don't want to be all stoned and fall off the mountain. I know Kerouac says you can't fall off the side of a mountain, but I've seen it happen, it ain't fun or pretty. What if I have that HAPE shit that lady was talking about? Did I just make myself die alone on the side of a mountain? I gotta get back.

Pike was at the top for less than four and a half minutes. The descent was equally trying on his muscles, as the upper thighs had to work extra hard to keep his feet from sliding out from underneath him. His legs began to shake, and he knew he was minutes away from cramping and that would paralyze-weld him to the mountain. Every two-to-three minutes he had to stop and rest. Finally he got to a vantage point where he could see the treeline again.

Two hours later he had returned to the lake and it was well into early evening.

Pike smoked the rolled marijuana from his pack, which proved not to be a good idea. He was reminded of how bad his body was torn up, and the THC seemed to emphasize every ache and strain and pain. He made it to the car and was very thirsty, having ran out of water an hour earlier. Pike wanted his pack to be light, and it could have cost him.

I really wasn't prepared for that hike. I didn't have matches, a compass, enough water, change of clothes, the right food, a map, no sunglasses or sunscreen; that was really dumb. And I think I got the HAPE or something, some kind of mountain sickness. But I did it.

Look at my hands, they are so swollen. Wow, I've never seen them that big before.

Back in Santa Fe, Pike was late getting back to the "rehearsal" dinner in Santa Fe. T had rented out the local Moose Lodge chapter, and all wedding guests were invited for drinks and a buffet. When they arrived at the hall, everyone was seated having finished their meals and were on to drinks. Pike got a beer from the bar and sat down at a table with the "others," referring to people he didn't know.

Groom T approached, "So you did it, good job. I saw the picture of you from the top by the summit post on Yogos' phone."

"Some lady had an iPhone at the summit, so she took a picture of me and texted it to me and Yogos for backup. I left my phone in the car; didn't think there would be a possibility of reception," Pike said.

"What are you drinking, you should be pounding water? You just underwent some serious changes in elevation, take it easy," T advised.

"Thanks, but I think I'm good, but really tired, my legs are done for."

"No one else here climbed a mountain today."

Karaoke took over the hall and Pike again made an early exit.

34.

"We finished our packing and had intercourse, then went out and saw a movie. In the movie there were a lot of men and women having intercourse too. Nothing wrong with watching others having intercourse, after all." M. Murakami, *AWSC*.

After Pike's mountain megalomania had subsided, it was Saturday, wedding day. T and his future wife had rented out the Sage Ranch, a Wild West ghost town used in different movies and videos. The theme, besides cowboys, was that the circus was in town and it was also 1920. Dressing up was required. Originally Pike was going to go as a ringmaster, but he learned two days before departure that George and his new wife were going as ringmasters, too.

Then I have to change my whole plan. Those jerks. How can they both be going as ringmasters? You can't have two, it's like Highlander; there can only be one.

Luckily a seasonal Halloween store near Penkal was open, so Pike got a costume of the cartoon character Woody, the cowboy from the movie "Toy Story."

Two charter buses showed up outside of the hotel at 4 p.m. to transport the guests to the ranch, which was 18 minutes outside of Santa Fe. The majority of the men were cowboys, with moustaches that had been grown out over the months leading up to the event, and real leather chaps and horse-bleeding spurs. The women were cowgirls, some adorned in 1800s excess-fabric-dresses with matching hats and umbrellas, some flappers and a couple of circus freaks. There were 104 guests in total.

When the bus pulled off the paved road, it followed dust and dull down a gravity-reminding road, and finally turned a corner revealing the Old West ghost town, complete with a bank, saloon, jail, drugstore and shops. As guests exited the buses, a team of five mariachis serenaded everyone as T, Saint, Yogos, the bride Margaret and their families stood in front of the entrance.

For the first hour, everyone just milled around the settlement, stopping in the saloon for a drink, checking out the church, the stables, and late in the day, the endless view of desert dusk.

By a horse railing on the uneven sideplanks, Pike saw her.

"Hey, I didn't know you were coming to this wedding, AnaBeth," Pike said, hopeful, surprised.

"Hello, Pike. Not slurring your words, that's a nice start," AnaBeth said.

"I can't apologize enough for New York. Wait, how do you know T?" Pike asked.

"Met him for the first time at Daniel's wedding in Brooklyn, but I'm actually here as Earl's date."

"No fucking way!? You serious? Sorry, that's a bad way to react. Trying to get some shit going. You know I don't even say "bitch" anymore?" Pike offered.

"It's not your words, but your actions, and Earl and I are just friends," AnaBeth said, golden-god-gliding away.

Rows of single-hinged pearl chairs were placed in front of the bar, located in the center of town. As the female guests found their seats, all of the men met back at the jail, close to the entrance to the town. Then when the signal was given, with T in front, the posse of males standoff-walked down through the center of the town's brown, stopping right at the backs of the chairs. No one was standing at the front of the pub, and then all of the sudden, the still, swinging wooden saloon doors moved, and through them emerged a beautiful lady in her late 20s, in a slender and tight-fitting wedding dress, and she stopped on the sidewalk porch in front of the saloon. Then T yelled, "Mariachi, play!" And they did as he strolled down the aisle and met his soon-to-be-wife in front of the saloon.

A man in a top hat and vintage suit acted as the marriage official, and read from a thick book about the history of the couple, about their past and future love. They both exchanged original vows, and their bond became a legal matter.

When the ceremony was over, there was another hour until dinner. Pike began drinking beer from a 12-pack he found in the jail, and decided to see what the saloon had to offer.

This place is great. Dim, dead-tree uneven floor boards, faded looking bar, the sound my boots make when I walk, totally great. OK, let's see what they are serving. The beer is being pulled from a tap, and in little glasses. That won't work, I'll be back here every two minutes. The wine is in small glasses, too. They do have liquor. Nice. I'll take a whiskey on the rocks and see how that does me.

The bartender with a handlebar moustache eyeball-poured Pike a double, and it went down fast. Pike ingested three more and, he went to sit down for dinner, he knew he was drunk.

"This is so nice," AnaBeth said, manifesting next to Pike. She was letting the drinks "second chance" him. Tables were set up in the middle of the street, in one well-balanced line, with yet-to-be stained table clothes and native flora.

Pike was in an alcohol-related jovial mood, and didn't want to hamper his buzz with eating too much. He ended up hardly eating at all, but kept drinking whiskey with ice.

Dinner passed, and the next event was the talent show. One of the buildings was an Old West theatre, so everyone filed in and waited comfortably. One guy did stand-up comedy, one guy played the guitar. Saint did his best man speech. Yogos displayed a story with titanic sheets of poster board while his wife played the flute. The maid of honor cried the whole time she was supposed to be talking. When the show ended, it was close to 8 p.m. Pike was well inebriated and so was AnaBeth. They went on a walk behind a barn and ran into someone dressed like Marty McFly from "Back to the Future III."

"Where you guys heading?" he asked, like a mendicant.

"I'm going to smoke a joint, if you'd care to join." Pike said.

"I would sir, thank you very much."

The smoke ceased, and AnaBeth, in her liquid state, began really taking on the role of the circus person represented in her "bearded woman" costume (even though she lost the facial hair wig long ago). AnaBeth leaned over to Pike's ear, while they were standing, resting their bottoms on a post that the horses were to be tied to 100 years prior.

"I'm a dirty circus girl, just in town for one night," she said.

"I live in this here town ma'am, and we got ways of dealing with transients like you," Pike said. It was hard to make his roll-play persona believable, even intoxicated, because he was dressed up like a cartoon character.

"Well maybe you can show me around this town, but remember, I'm very, very, bad," AnaBeth said like a coquette, while meaning to lick the rim of Pike's ear but getting all hair instead.

Pike quickly stood up straight, and grabbed AnaBeth by the inside bicep. "Come with me, circus freak."

They walked through town, past the saloon and bank, and ducked into one of the low-rise barns on the outskirts, like old lovers organizing a tryst.

Four minutes later they were walking out of the barn, and saw Randy.

"Guys, how's it going, bubbers?" Randy asked.

"It's going real good, I just took this circus freak into the barn over there and beat her drawers off," Pike told him.

"Hey! Don't tell him that, he doesn't care anyway. But it is true, a cowboy just taught me a lesson in there," AnaBeth said with a slight smile.

"What's wrong with you bubbers, this is a nice mature wedding?" Randy said.

They departed and Pike started walking towards the saloon when he realized he didn't feel convivial or healthy. He changed course and made it behind the church before he threw up all the whiskey and excess from his stomach.

The bus drove everyone back to the hotel at 10 p.m. Pike was in black-out mode and just kept trying to molest and rub on and stroke AnaBeth, forgetting they had already had intercourse and about everything he preached about concerning his recent life change.

Pike and AnaBeth got back to his hotel room and started fooling around again. Pike had impotence issues from the liquor and when he finally got it going, managed to fall asleep on top of AnaBeth.

"Hey, get off me, hey!" AnaBeth said.

"What?" Pike came to.

"Get off me, you're sleeping."

"No, I'm not, let's keep going."

"No, seriously, get off me."

Pike scooted off the bed.

"This is bullshit. Whatever, typical from you," Pike said. "I'm going to the after hours party at the Sam's Place, or whatever. You coming?"

"No, let's just stay in. It's late and we're both super wasted."

"I'm not going to stay here with someone who doesn't want to have sex with me on vacation."

"What are you talking about? You fell asleep."

Pike wouldn't believe the truth, got dressed and walked two blocks to the lounge. Randy was doing karaoke, "Okie from Muskogee," and Pike ordered a green lager from the waitress. His mind was shot and his body was on complete shutdown mode after his vomiting episode. People would attempt to communicate with him, but he just stood, swaying, and not answering. 23 minutes had gone by and Pike had only taken sips of his beer. He then set it on the counter and walked back to the room. AnaBeth was already asleep. In a bed very far away from that room.

The next morning, at 10:14 a.m., Pike rolled over and looked at the clock.

Get up, we need to catch that 11 o'clock shuttle. Not sure, I remember going to that bar and being all mad. I dunno, that whiskey got on top of me, I puked at the ranch. I know you puked, the whole town could hear the heaving. Seriously, that's why I hate drinking. I was so close to change.

He caught the 11 a.m. shuttle south back to Albuquerque, and after another close call in Dallas, was back in Pennsylvania at 9:36 p.m.

"I'm so glad I don't have to go into work tomorrow," Pike said as he unlocked the car in the Pittsburgh airport parking lot.

The day of recovery soon ended but not the realization and depression. Driving to work Tuesday morning, the pain in his legs had increased to the point that after two radio songs of driving, or sitting, he would have to readjust how he was positioned, although it didn't really help.

I must have a bunch of hemorrhoids or varicose veins or something. I can't sit down anymore. I can't drive to work anymore. What can I do? I should make a doctor's appointment. But I don't want anyone to find out about it. This sucks, my legs are burning.

Pike felt had an extra day of recovery, for the first time, returning to work after a trip.

Theresa and Pike talked about the vacation, about upcoming news and stories and what everyone was working on for the week. Then minutes before Pike was going to call and get Indian curry takeout, Theresa sent him an iChat message.

Theresa: I have something to tell you.

Pike: oh ya, what's up?

Theresa: I'm leaving. And will be gone at the end of this week.

Pike: what? no way, you can't leave. oh come on, you serious?

Theresa: Yes, I really have grown to hate it here. I've been here too long and the last five years have been awful. Rob and I don't get along, he never even speaks to me anymore; I'm just tired. I hate waking up everyday.

Pike: well, if that's the case then good luck. and thanks for taking a chance on me. for real, thanks for the hire, it meant a lot.

Theresa: That was more Rob than me, but you're welcome.

Then I rescind my thank you.

Pike: so who's going to be the new editor, has rob been interviewing people?

Theresa: It's going to be Carly; she's been waiting a decade for my seat.

Pike: noooooooooo!!!! please say you're messing with me? she's so mean. she's the cozen queen. she's like the worst human of all time. why does rob want to promote her?

Theresa: She's not that bad, really. I think you two can get along fine. Rob wants to hire her because she is really good and knows everything about reporting.

Pike: except the whole writing thing. all her stories just fit this boring journalism profile.

Theresa: That's what journalism is, I wish that you would learn that.

Pike: damn. a decade of wait... hope it was worth it for her.

Theresa: Well, technically only about seven years.

Pike: what do you mean?

Theresa: Well she was a reporter here for three years and then she got hired by the Erie Telegraph.

Pike: really? i didn't know that.

Theresa: But after working for them for somewhere around a year, she was let go.

Pike: wait. the world's smartest and greatest journalist got fired from a real paper?

Theresa: This is a real paper, but yes, she was fired. I probably shouldn't say anything more.

Pike: oh come on, you already started down that road, don't leave me hanging. you're leaving anyway, so who cares?

Theresa: Well, she was covering a suicide, not sure of the details, but after talking with the coroner, I guess she got all the information wrong. So it got printed and the family of the dead person was upset, the coroner was livid because it made him look really bad, so she got fired. Then she spent the next two years in IT and tech support. Then this job came up again, and she re-applied and was hired. Been here the last five years since.

Pike: well i'll be damned. that is so good to know, you have no idea. but im not working for her, god this sucks that you are leaving.

The news was light during Theresa's final week. She did not stay until 5 p.m. on Friday, but left at 3:17 p.m. Again, no one said goodbye except Pike. After 28 years, there was no office send-off party, no cake, no handshakes. She left and Pike kept hoping the new editor, Carly, would not be as horrible as he envisioned.

Pike received a dollar raise and more responsibility. Rob said by March, Pike was expected to write more stories, take more pictures and do all the pagination and layout for his sections of the Winherst paper. The change would make Pike glued to his chair for the majority of the work week.

The changeover was official and on that first Monday morning Pike was greeted with a, "Hello, how are you this day?" from Carly. She had never said any salutation or farewell before.

"Hi," was all Pike said in response, suspicious of Carly's motives.

"Pike, as you may have guessed, we are going to be undergoing some changes in terms of operation in order to maximize output, become more proficient and efficient. In your inbox, you will find a list of the changes. There will be an office meeting tomorrow, when the new girl starts, and we will be going over everything. In the meantime, I've added a very big dry erase board to the office. All the stories that you are working on, please list them on that board. That's all I have for now, do you have any concerns or questions, is there anything I can help you with?"

Why are you being so fake nice to me? This is going to suck.

"Nope, nothing from my end. Actually, you said there was a new girl, what's her deal?"

"Her deal? Well, she is a recently graduated college student, with two degrees, one in journalism, and one in economics. Four-point student, great resume with two summer journalism internships at daily papers, so I think she will fit in nicely."

Pike was not a fan of the new hire. She was smart and young, which were fine qualities to have, Pike believed, but Pike thought that the new employee also thought she was never wrong.

Every sentence is spoken like gospel, along with the loud timbre of her voice, and any attempts at arguing just lead to an eye-roll and a "You simply couldn't understand" comment.

When she found out how long Carly had been with the company, she told Pike is was fortunate that Carly was 35, and not 25, because the print media was over.

"The business model for this place is so archaic and it won't last another six years. No one reads papers anymore, because there is this little thing called the Internet. I only took this job as a filler until I find something better. It is best to always be working. My father, who is very successful, says he would never hire a person who didn't already have a job. People without jobs will say anything to get hired and are usually lazy and worthless anyway, that's why they're not working. But this place, doomed to fail very soon. Did you know that the Erie Telegraph is going down to three days a week? And the Pittsburgh Gazette is changing their format, the paper is going to be printed like a magazine? It's more cost efficient and the trend is towards smaller more compact periodicals. Most of the classes we had in my journalism program were all about the rise of the digital media. Sure, you will always need reporters, but the time of the paper, the long paper that you put your feet up at night or in the morning and sip coffee to and leisurely read and become informed, all gone. And it should be, it's a slow dumb way to report the news," the new woman said, finishing her tirade.

"I suppose you're right. It's kinda like washing cars in 'The Karate Kid,' where—"

"What's 'The Karate Kid'? With Will Smith's kid?" the new reporter asked Pike.

"You've never seen the original 'Karate Kid'?"

"Nope, never."

"How about 'Back to the Future,' you like that movie?" Pike asked.

"Never heard of that either. I know there's a ride or something at Universal Studios, I remember seeing a picture my mom brought back, but I have now idea what that movie is."

It was crinkle fall and late October and Carly kept up the limpid act of acting nice and civil to Pike. The whole system had been overhauled, made more efficient. Bulletin boards, crosswords and large feature art took the place of stories that used to dominate the pages.

Pike kept to the grind of Winherst and the majority of his stories were voter-related. It was a presidential election year, along with Winherst trying to get a new school built. Carly and Pike got along fine under the façade, and Pike thought it might actually work out. A week before the ballots were cast, Pike compiled a special-election issue for the paper, and before it went to press, Pike and Carly were alone in their corner of the office.

"I just thought you should know your voting tab didn't cut it, it was really bad." Carly said.

"What? What was really bad, what part?"

"The whole thing seemed half-assed," Carly said, dropping the nice tone she had been using the previous weeks.

"Dude, I don't know what you're talking about, I worked hard on that," Pike said not being a toady.

"Don't call me dude, I'm your boss and it sounds like your are deriding me. Maybe we need to have a writing seminar in the office. Your stories should be written in the form of the inverse triangle, where each sentence leads to more information and creates a new story under it, does that make sense?"

"What doesn't make sense is why you are acting like this, trying to rip apart my writings when I worked hard and they're fine."

"They are not fine, that's why I'm talking to you about it. We are running a serious paper, not some 'zine or underground newsletter. All the 'carnie' stories and firewalking, you can say goodbye to that nonsense. I already talked to Rob about content, and told him, it's either you or me, and believe me, I'm not going anywhere."

"Why do you want me to write boring news? Why are you trying to kill what I've built? Do you know how many people talked about that undercover 'carnie' story?"

"You will do the stories that I approve and assign only, understand?"

"I knew this would never work if you became editor."

"You can quit anytime, and I would love to help you pack."

When the publisher came back from buying a drink at the drug store, Carly turned the voice and charm and professionalism back on.

Pike wrote a story but Carly re-wrote the lead, main body and end. She would start doing that with every one of Pike's works from then on out. Carly also assigned Pike stories that Pike hated covering. The unveiling of a plaque at the sheriff's office for a janitor who died of natural causes. A new roof at the fire station. There was a hurricane that hit the east coast, and even though there was no damage to Winherst, Carly wanted the storm localized. "Call fire marshals, police chiefs, electrical companies, find out what damage there was and talk to people about storm prep and the history of natural disasters in our area," Carly said.

The job was beginning to eat at Pike's insides. He could barely complete the car ride with the constant pain on the back of his thighs. He would sit on a pillow and constantly shift his weight the whole commute. All of his stories were re-worked. All of his assignments he hated. Whenever everyone was gone from the south end of the writing floor, Carly would flip the switch and ridicule his work. He had to stand and type every other day due to his leg problem. And the final nail in the coffin was the paper that came out right after the election.

President Obama was re-elected, and most importantly to the town and Pike himself, after 150 years, Winherst was going to replace Rover Middle School. It passed by 7 votes. Above the fold, and on the front page was Pike's story about the school levy result, with a big picture of kids going into the building. The final story was re-written by Carly after Pike had looked over the layout, and it was incorrect. In the middle of the story it said that the school levy failed, that a new building would not be built. There were 11 calls and seven emails to the Winherst News-Times about what a big and foolish error Pike had made in his reporting.

After the fourth call, Pike confronted Carly.

"What the hell was up with that story?"

"I made a mistake and I'm sorry," Carly said.

"Sorry?! It's not your name beside the story. Everyone thinks I did it, that I don't know how to cover the news. It's my name in the town I cover!"

"What do you want me to do Pike, cut my throat? I said it was my fault."

Later that day, when Carly left to do an interview, Pike sat down with the publisher Rob in his office.

"I can't do it anymore, I can't work with Carly. She changes my stories, sends me out on nonsense assignments, and that story today, she did that on purpose," Pike told Rob.

"She didn't do it on purpose, just settle down, it's fine."

"No, it's not fine, it's horrible working for her. When you're not around, she scrutinizes my work and tells me how bad all of my writing is. I just don't think I can do it anymore, I don't think I can work here anymore. I don't think—" Pike's desultory speech was interrupted.

"Just go home, get some sleep and come back tomorrow. You know, a lot of people don't like their bosses, it's a part of work."

"I don't need to sleep on this. You've been great, thanks a lot for taking a chance on me, but I can't work with Carly anymore."

"Well it sounds like you're already on your way, so no point in trying to stop you. But just so we're clear, if it's a choice for me between you and Carly, well, Carly's the editor, you understand? Just go home, talk it over with some friends and let's see what happens tomorrow."

    "I'm pretty sure it's all over."

35.

"We got ourselves organised and set about the task of smashing the movement he inspired with the upmost determination." D.Hann & S. Tilzey, *NR.*

At the apartment complex, Pike tried to explain it all to Joan. About the pain in the legs, about how it's not even his writings anymore, how the stories suck, how big of a jerk he believed Carly was to him, etc., etc. But all Joan heard was the same story. New excuses for the same routine.

He told himself he wouldn't get stressed out, that he could handle it, that something would come up and he would find a career that he liked and could maintain that full-time job for longer than six months.

But he was drifting. And when Pike went to puke behind a shack at the wedding in Santa Fe, the dock and shore were no longer visible.

The next morning, Pike printed out an official two-weeks-notice letter from the office printer and handed it to publisher Rob immediately afterwards. It was the same cold shoulder Finn and Theresa received. No one talked to Pike, nor he them. Pike reported on a food drive at the elementary school, donated tractor tools to the vocational school, a councilman was retiring and there was a big bake sale downtown. Pike was also required to write two big stories concerning Veterans Day.

"All the national holidays will be a big part of our papers now. They matter to our country and local communities," Carly told the office.

You don't care about veterans, you just use 9/11 and Veterans Day to sell papers, to localize national tragedy and ceremony.

With two days left until he was done at the paper, Pike decided to stop in to the school board president's shirt shop downtown to tie up any loose ends and to say goodbye. He was the only one in the narrow store. Payton hadn't heard him come in and was just finishing up a phone call that Pike could clearly hear.

"No, you ain't listening to me, I talked her out of it. (Pause) Yes, we're going to have to give her some of the booster money to keep her quiet. But she ain't gonna talk, I'm tellin' ya. (Pause) You don't want to have this thing blow up, not right after the voters just approved a new school, we can't throw mud in their faces. No students were hurt, it was just a bad decision between two adults on school grounds. And they're both gone. (Pause) Right sonny, right. OK, I'll talk to you later." Payton closed his flip cell phone and walked into the front of the store, freezing when he saw Pike.

"Hey there, how y'all doing? I'm glad you came in, I got some good news for ya, you received an award from the state," Payton said, trying to remain calm.

"Did you know I could hear that conversation? You talk kinda loud and the store is empty," Pike said, being a bit out of character with his direct confrontational approach, but the apathy that came with leaving guided his talk.

"How much of it?"

"All of it. But don't worry, I just want to know the truth, and if you tell me everything, I won't print a word of it," Pike offered.

"I might just be a dumb backwoods boy, but I ain't falling for that, you're a reporter."

"My last day is tomorrow. I really don't care and I really don't want to trash the school district after that levy just passed, and I believe I had a big hand in passing it."

"You're leaving, are they pushing you out? It seems like as soon as we get a good guy in there they replace them."

"It's the new editor, she's horrible. So tell me what happened."

"I want you to look me in the eye, shake my hand, and swear on the Lord that you will not print anything I say, and I will deny telling you any of it, and I will come for ya if you do."

"I swear."

"OK, well, you remember the old principal of Southwood, Principal Dion, and the old superintendent, Coy Franks, well, believe it or not, they were lovers. Which is fine, they aren't married and they're grown ups. But according to another teacher, they had sex in his office. I guess the teacher walked in on them and then threatened to tell unless they left the district. So they did."

"And now she wants hush money?"

"Yep. So we're going to give it to her."

"Where's the money coming from, I mean, are you taking money from the schools?"

"I can't comment on that."

"Wow. I always thought those two had something going, good for Coy, she was a smart woman."

Pike kept his word and kept the secret. Pike, as coincidence would have it, a week later received an award from the State of Pennsylvania Board of Education for his 'fair and balanced education reporting, and exemplary service to the community." The framed award was hung in Joan's bathroom.

On Pike's last day, a Thursday, he wrote his final story for the paper. He brought in king-sized candy bars for the ad ladies, secretary, publisher, editor, delivery people, human resources and reporters.

Thanksgiving soon passed, and the "hectic" holiday season, and before Pike realized it, he had been without a job for nearly two months. Then finally it came, the depression of unemployment.

The first eight weeks were great. Pike got feeling back in his thighs and knees. He was able to sit on a couch for longer than an hour. He spent good morning and after school and bedtime quality routine time with himself, his drugs and Joan, who was supportive. Then the holidays were over. Then every time Joan came home from her new interior design position, Pike was there. He hadn't gotten a haircut since he quit. Or shaved. Everyday the joblessness and physical appearance increased his diffidence and made not only his sense of self-worth deteriorate, but it rubbed off, silicone-like, on Joan. Pike felt ashamed, so much of his early readings and music appreciation came from a working-class voice, from humans enduring much longer hours and in much worse atmospheric conditions, humans that would be in such a state of lassitude, so physically and mentally drained when they arrived back home that they didn't really care about their own connection to pain. But poor Pike couldn't stare at a computer and sit in a car. But those were just verbal ways out.

Eventually, Pike knew he gave up too easily. Didn't give a real shot or fight to the calling or Carly.

It only got worse. Pike became increasingly more and more insecure about his job, life; it got to the point where he just started believing the idea of his own invented worthlessness. "I'll drink a 12-pack today, who cares? I'm just a piece of shit anyway with no job and can't even support my habits."

It was going on the third month of no work. Pike's savings were down to $109. He seemed too accepting of his own destruction, becoming more and more depressed via his own want to be depressed, to make himself feel as bad as possible, when really things weren't that horrible. Everyday, Pike would wake up, daydream about some new prospect or opportunity, conclude that he couldn't get a good job, that he was a "fuck-up," and proceed to hide a pint of plastic bottle whiskey and take shots in secret, increasing the volume when he felt like the complex was asleep.

By month four, Joan wanted to have a serious conversation with Pike, but it fell on a chemically imbalanced brain that had created its own failure destiny.

The truth is the truth. Your actions define you, not your thoughts or aspirations or intentions. Your actions. And I ain't got shit. Why are you doing this? You don't even have a right to be depressed? Do you want to see horror? Do you want to see pain? Go to a hospital or anywhere else outside of your mind. And if that's how you want to feel, that you're just waiting to die, that's fine. But you're too early. And you don't have the right to yet. Instead of owning your actions and choices, you've decided it's too late for any change, or any alterations in the design. And that's bullshit. Look, if you have a great mind...

The smartphone touch-acceptance of a call.

"Hello, son."

"Hello, father. Quick question, would you buy me a plane ticket to come visit you all in Oregon?"

"I think it's ridiculous that I would need to at your age, but yes—"

"Cool. Gonna crash in your basement for a bit. Gonna write a tome—"

"Absolutely not."

Front cover design and photo by: Sarah Wolters
Back cover design by: Ryan Patterson
Back cover photo by: Bill "Hijo" Perry
Edited by: Ginger Weisbarth
Logo by: Larry Betts
All content property of Adam Doc Fox 2014